LUNA

LUNA

WOLF MOON

Ian McDonald

GOLLANCZ

LONDON

First published in Great Britain in 2017 by Gollancz
an imprint of the Orion Publishing Group Ltd
Carmelite House, 50 Victoria Embankment
London EC4Y 0DZ

An Hachette UK Company

1 3 5 7 9 10 8 6 4 2

A CIP catalogue record for this book is
available from the British Library.

ISBN 978 1 473 20226 9

Typeset at The Spartan Press Ltd,
Lymington, Hants

Printed and bound by CPI Group (UK) Ltd,
Croydon, CR0 4YY

Contents

THE WOLF MOON

The Farmers' Almanac derives the names of the months from the Native Americans of what is now the north-eastern United States.

The Wolf Moon is the Moon of January, the moon when the wolves howl in hunger and want; the moon of deepest cold and darkness.

NEAR SIDE *of* THE MOON

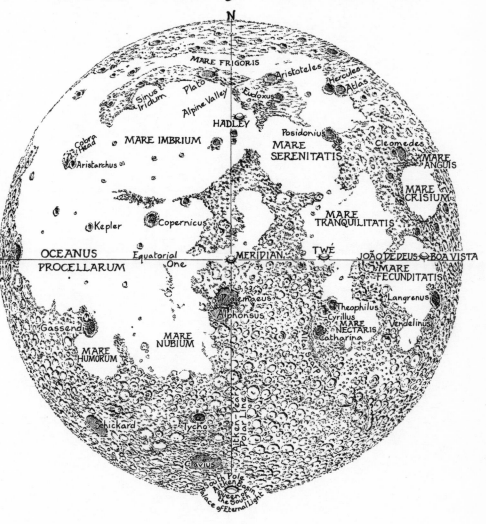

AFTER THE FALL: ARIES 2103

'Fly me to the Earth,' Lucas Corta said. The crew unstrapped him from the moonloop capsule and dragged him into the lock anoxic, hypothermic, dehydrated.

'You're aboard the VTO cycler *Saints Peter and Paul*, Senhor Corta,' the lock manager said as she sealed the pressure doors.

'Sanctuary,' Lucas Corta whispered, and vomited. He had held firm for five hours while the capsule fled the destruction of Corta Hélio. Five hours, while targeted strikes destroyed his industry out on the seas of Luna, while attackware iced his finances, while Mackenzie blades gutted his city. While his brothers drew blades to defend the house of Corta, and he fled, across the Sea of Fecundity, up and away from the moon.

Save the company, Carlinhos had said. *You have a plan?*

I always have a plan.

Five hours, spinning away from the destruction of Corta Hélio like blast debris. Then the comfort of hands, the warmth of voices, the solidity of a ship around him – a *ship*, not a bauble of aluminium and plastic – relaxed the bands of tight muscles and he threw up. The VTO dock crew moved in with portable vacuum cleaners.

'It helps if you orient this way, Senhor Corta,' the lock manager said. She wrapped a foil blanket around Lucas's shoulders as the crew turned him upright and manoeuvred him into the elevator. 'We'll get you back under lunar gravity very soon.'

Lucas felt the elevator move and the cycler's spin gravity take hold of his feet. *Earth,* he tried to say. Blood choked the words. Burst alveoli rattled in his chest. He had breathed vacuum, down on the

Mare Fecunditatis, when Amanda Sun tried to kill him. For seven seconds he had been exposed to the naked lunar surface. No suit. No air. Breathe out. That was the first rule of the Moonrunners. Empty the lungs. He had forgotten, forgotten everything except the airlock of the Moonloop station before him. His lungs had ruptured. He was a Moonrunner now. He should have the pin: Dona Luna, one half of her face black skin, the other white skull. Lucas Corta laughed. For a moment he thought he might choke. Bloody phlegm pooled on the elevator floor. He had to make the words clear. These Vorontsov women had to understand.

'Take me down to earth gravity,' he said.

'Senhor Corta,' the lock manager began.

'I want to go down to the Earth,' Lucas Corta said. 'I need to go to Earth.'

He lay on the med centre diagnostic bed in only a pair of shorts. He had always loathed shorts. Ridiculous and infantile. He had refused to wear them, even when they came into fashion, which they did as all fashions wheeled on the moon. Skin would have been better. He would have worn the dignity of nakedness well.

The woman stood at the foot of the diagnostic bed. Sensor arms and injectors surrounded her as if she were a deity. She was white, middle aged, tired. She was utterly in control.

'I am Galina Ivanovna Volikova,' the woman said. 'I will be your personal physician.'

'I am Lucas Corta,' Lucas croaked.

Dr Volikova's right eye flickered, reading from her medical interface. 'A collapsed lung. Multifocal cerebral micro-haemorrhages – you were ten minutes from a likely fatal brain haematoma. Corneal damage, interior bleeding in both eyeballs, ruptured alveoli. And a perforated eardrum. Which I fixed.'

She gave the smallest, tightest smile of dark amusement and Lucas knew he could work with her.

'How long…' Lucas Corta hissed. Broken glass ground in his left lung.

'An orbit at least, before I let you out of here,' Dr Volikova said. 'And don't talk.' An orbit: twenty-eight days. As a boy Lucas had studied the physics of the cyclers; the clever minimum energy orbits they wove around the moon, touching twice and then slingshotting back across the face of the Earth. The process was called a backflip orbit. Lucas could not understand the mathematics but it was part of the business of Corta Hélio and so he had to learn its principles if not its details. Loops around moon and earth as earth and moon described their own cycles around the sun and the sun and its worlds on its quarter-billion year dance around the galactic centre. Everything moving. Everything part of the great dance.

A new voice, a new figure at the foot of the bed, shorter, more muscular than Dr Volikova.

'He can hear me?' A woman's voice, clear and musical.

'He can.'

'And talk,' Lucas grated. The figure stepped into the light. Two worlds recognised Captain Valentina Valeryovna Vorontsova, yet she introduced herself formally to Lucas Corta.

'You're welcome aboard *Saints Peter and Paul*, Senhor Corta.'

Captain Valentina was solid, square built; Earth muscles, Russian cheek-bones, Kazakh eyes. Two worlds knew also that her twin sister Yekaterina was captain of *Our Lady of Kazan*. They were women of legend, the Captains Vorontsova. The first legend was that they were identical foetuses raised in separate host-mothers in disparate gravities. One space-born, one earth-born. The second enduring myth was that they shared an innate telepathy, an intimate identity beyond communication, no matter the distance that separated them. A quantum magic. The third myth was that they regularly switched command of VTO's two cyclers. Of all the legends of the Twin Captains, this was the only one that Lucas Corta believed. Keep your enemies guessing.

3

'I understand you have yet to be apprised of the situation on the moon,' Captain Valentina said.

'I'm prepared.'

'I don't think you are. Lucas, I have the worst possible new for you. Everything you knew has been lost. Your brother Carlinhos was killed in the defence of João de Deus. Boa Vista has been destroyed. Rafael died in the depressurisation.'

Five hours, alone on a moonloop transfer orbit, the pod wall staring back: Lucas's imagination had travelled into dark places. He had seen his family dead, his city crushed, his empire toppling. He had expected Valentina Vorontsova's news, but it still hit as hard and emptying as vacuum.

'Depressurisation?'

'Better not to talk, Senhor Corta,' Dr Volikova said.

'Mackenzie Metals blades blew the surface lock,' Captain Valentina said. 'Rafael got everyone to the refuges. We believe that he was searching for stragglers when the habitat depressurised.'

'He would do that. Something noble and stupid. Luna? Robson?'

'The Asamoahs have rescued the survivors and taken them to Twé. Bryce Mackenzie has already applied to the Court of Clavius to formally adopt Robson.'

'Lucasinho?' Now he had the emotional rigour, the physical control of his body, to say the name he wanted to cry out first. If Lucasinho was dead, he would get up from this bed and walk out of the airlock.

'He's safe in Twé.'

'We could always trust the Asamoahs.' Knowing that Lucasinho was safe and secure was a sun-hot joy: helium at fusion heat.

'Ariel's bodyguard helped her escape into the Bairro Alto. She's in hiding. As is your brother Wagner. The Meridian pack is sheltering him.'

'The wolf and the cripple,' Lucas whispered. 'And the company?'

4

'Robert Mackenzie is already assimilating Corta Hélio infrastructure. He has issued contracts to your former workers.'

'They would be idiots not to take them.'

'They are taking them. He has announced a new subsidiary: Mackenzie Fusible. His grand-nephew Yuri Mackenzie is CEO.'

'Australians all start to blur after the first two or three.' Lucas chuckled, deep and blood-filled, at his dark joke. To make a joke is to blow dust in the face of the overpowering. 'You know it was the Suns. They set us at each other.'

'Senhor Corta,' Dr Volikova said again.

'They make us cut each other's throats with delight. They plan in decades, the Suns.'

'Taiyang is exercising a number of options on equatorial real estate,' Captain Valentina said.

'They plan to turn the entire equatorial belt into a solar power array,' Lucas hissed. Pieces of his lung were breaking away in bloody sludge. He coughed up fresh blood. Machine arms moved to sop the red.

'That's enough, Captain,' Dr Volikova said.

Captain Valentina touched fingertips to thumb and dipped her head; a lunar bow, though she was a woman of Earth.

'I'm sorry, Lucas.'

'Help me,' Lucas Corta said.

'VTO Space and VTO Earth keep a distance from the VTO Moon,' Captain Valentina said. 'We have unique vulnerabilities. Protection of our Lagrange-point mass driver and our Earth-based launch facilities are paramount. Between the Russians, the Chinese and the Indians, we come under jealous eyes.'

The machine arms moved again. Lucas felt a sudden needling spray beneath his right ear.

'Captain, I need the moon to believe I'm dead.'

Captain and doctor, the slow worshipping arms of the medical unit, softened into a blur of white.

He could not identify a moment at which he became aware of the music but he surfaced into it like a swimmer breaking through a meniscus. It surrounded him like air, like the waters of birth and he was content to lie within it, eyes closed, breathing, painless. The music was noble and sane and ordered. A jazz of some kind, Lucas decided. Not his music, not a music he understood or appreciated, but he recognised its logic, the patterns it drew in time. He lay a long time trying to be conscious of only the music.

'Bill Evans,' a woman's voice said.

Lucas Corta opened his eyes. The same bed, the same medical bots, the same unfocused soft light. The same thrum of airconditioning and power that told him he was on a ship, not a world. The same doctor moving around the edge of his field of vision.

'I've been reading your neural activity,' Dr Volikova said. 'You respond well to modal jazz.'

'I enjoyed that.' Lucas said. 'You can play that any time.'

'Oh can I?' Dr Volikova and again Lucas heard the amusement in her voice.

'How am I, doctor?'

'You've been unconscious for forty-eight hours. I've repaired the most egregious damage.'

'Thank you doctor,' said Lucas Corta. He moved to prop himself up on his elbows. Flesh tore inside him as Dr Volikova gave a small cry and rushed to the bedside. She lowered him to the yielding surface.

'You need to recover, Senhor Corta.'

'I need to work, doctor. I can't stay here forever. I have a business to rebuild and limited funds. And I need to go to Earth.'

'You're moon-born. It's impossible for you to go to Earth.'

'It's not impossible Doctor. It's the easiest thing. It's just fatal. But everything is fatal.'

'You cannot go to Earth.'

'I can't go back to the Moon. The Mackenzies will kill me. I can't stay here. The hospitality of the Vorontsovs is not bottomless. Humour me doctor. You specialise in low-gravity medicine. Hypotheticals.'

A new tune now, loping and modal. Piano, bass, whispering drums. Such small forces. Such great effect.

'Hypothetically, with intensive training and medical support, a moon-born individual might survive two lunes under Earth conditions.'

'Hypothetically, would four lunes be possible?'

'It would take many lunes of physical conditioning.'

'How many lunes doctor? Hypothetically?'

He saw Dr Volikova shrug, heard the small sigh of exasperation.

'At least a year. Fourteen, fifteen lunes. Even then the chances of surviving lift-off would be no better than fifty per cent.'

Lucas Corta had never been a gambler. He dealt in certainties. As vice-chair of Corta Hélio, he had parleyed uncertainties into definites. Now iron certainties besieged him and the only hope was the bet.

'Then I have a plan, Dr Volikova.'

1: VIRGO 2105

The boy falls from the top of the city.

He is lean and lithe as a power line. His skin is the colour of copper, spangled with dark freckles. His eyes are green, his lips are lush and full. His hair is a shock of rust-coloured dreads frustrated inside a lime-green head-band. Two stripes of white gloss highlight each cheekbone, a vertical runs down the centre of his lips. He wears tangerine sports tights, cut low, and a white over-sized T-shirt. FRANKIE SAYS... declares the T-shirt.

It is three kilometres from the roof down to the floor of the great lava chamber in which Queen of the South stands.

The kids were running the top of the city; free-styling the old, automated industrial levels, swinging through the rigging of the world with breathtaking grace and skill; springing from rails and stanchions, bounding from wall to wall to wall, leaping, flipping, tumbling, flying across abysses, up and up as if weight were a fuel they burned to turn gravity back on itself.

The boy is the youngest of the team. He's thirteen; brave, agile, audacious, drawn to the high places. He limbers up with his fellow traceurs down on Queen of the South's forested floor, but his eyes are drawn towards the great towers, up to where they join the sunline. Stretch muscles, pull grip-gloves on to hands and feet. Practice jumps to loosen up, step up on to a bench and in a thought he is ten metres up. A hundred metres. A thousand metres; dancing along parapets and bounding up elevator gantries in five-metre bounds. To the top of the city. The top of the city.

All it takes is an infinitesimal mistake; a fraction of a second slow in reaction, a millimetre short in the reach, a finger light in the grip. His hand slips on the cable and he falls into empty air. No cry, only a small, amazed gasp.

Falling boy. Back first, hands and feet clutching at the gloved hands reaching down from the tangle of pipes and conduits along the roof of Queen. There is an instant of shock when the traceurs realise what has happened, then they explode from their perches, racing across the roof to the nearest tower. They'll never be fast enough to beat gravity.

There are rules of falling. Before he ever jumped, climbed, vaulted, the boy learned how to fall.

Rule one: You must turn. If you can't see what's beneath you, you are at best hurt badly, worst dead. He turns his head, looks down into the vast spaces between Queen's hundred towers. He twists his upper body; cries out as he wrenches an ab turning the rest of his body face down. Beneath him is a deadly lattice of crossing bridges, cable ways, catwalks and fibre-runs woven between the skyscrapers of Queen. He must navigate those.

Rule two: Maximise air resistance. He spreads arms and legs. Atmospheric pressure in a lunar habitat is 1060 kilopascals. Acceleration under gravity on the surface of moon is 1.625 metres per second squared. Terminal velocity for a falling object in atmosphere is sixty kilometres per hour. Impact the floor of Queen of the South at sixty kilometres per hour and there is an eighty per cent chance he will die. Impact at fifty kilometres per hour and there is eighty per cent chance he will live. His fashion T-shirt flaps in the gale. And FRANKIE SAYS: This is how you live.

Rule three: Get help. 'Joker,' he says. The boy's familiar rezzes up on the lens in his right eye, the implant in his left ear. True traceurs run without AI assistance. It's too easy for a familiar to map out the best route, locate hidden hand holds, advise on micro climate conditions. Parkour is about authenticity in a totally artificial world. Joker analyses the situation. *You are in extreme danger. I have alerted rescue and medical services.*

Rule four: Time is your friend. 'Joker, how long?'

Four minutes.

The boy now has everything he needs to survive.

The overstretched abs hurt like hell and something tears in his left shoulder as he pulls the T-shirt off. For a few seconds he breaks his spread-eagle position and accelerates alarmingly. Wind tears at the T-shirt in his hands. If he loses grip, if he loses the shirt, he dies. He needs to tie three knots while falling at terminal velocity. Knots are life. And the 77th cross bridge is there: *there!* He goes into spread, applies his teaching: tilts his upper body forwards, his arms, shifts his centre of gravity above his centre of hang. Tracking position. He slides forward and misses the bridge by metres. Faces look up at him. Look again: they've seen fliers. This boy is not a flier. He is a faller.

He knots neck and sleeves into a loose bag.

'Time.'

Two minutes. I estimate you will impact at . . .

'Shut up Joker.'

He gathers two fistfuls of T-shirt. This is about timing. Too high and he'll have limited manoeuvrability to clear the crosswalks and conduits webbed between the towers. Too low and his improvised parachute will not have brought him down to survive-speed. And he wants to land very much slower than fifty kilometres per hour.

'Let me know at one minute, Joker.'

I will.

The deceleration will be savage. It might rip the T-shirt from his grip.

Then he dies.

He can't imagine that.

He can imagine being hurt. He can imagine everyone looking down at him dead and crying at the tragedy. He likes that thought, but that's not death. Death is nothing. Not even not nothing.

He tucks his arms again to drift under the 23rd level cable-way.

Now.

He thrusts his arms forward. The T-shirt rattles and flaps in the gale. He ducks his head through the space between his elbows, thrusts his arms up. The knotted T-shirt balloons out. The sudden braking is brutal. He cries out as his strained shoulder is wrenched in its socket. Hold on hold on hold. Gods gods gods the ground is so close. The parachute leaps and tugs like someone fighting him, someone who wants to kill him. The strain in his arms, his wrists is agony. If he lets go now, he will hit hard and wrong: feet first, his hips and thighs shattered and driven up into his organs. Hold on, hold on. He cries, he gasps in effort and frustration.

'Joker,' he gasps. 'How fast...'

I can only estimate from...

'Joker!'

Forty-eight kilometres per hour.

That's still too fast. He can see where he will hit, it's only seconds away. A clear space between the trees, a park. People are running along the axial paths, some away, some towards the place where they estimate he will impact.

Medical bots have been dispatched, Joker announces. That bright thing, kind of big and bulky, what is it? Surfaces. Things poking out. A pavilion. Maybe for music or sherbet or something. It's fabric. That might minus the last few kilometres per hour he needs. It's also poky things; struts and stays. If he hits one at this speed it will go through him like a spear. If he hits at this speed, he might die anyway. He has to time this right. He tugs one side of the T-shirt parachute, trying to spill lift, trying to slide himself towards the pavilion. This is so hard so hard so hard. He cries out as he twists his agonised shoulder, trying to gain a last little lateral movement. The ground rushes up.

At the last second he lets go of the T-shirt and tries to tilt forward into spread to maximise his surface area. Too late too low. He hits the roof of the pavilion. It's hard, so hard. A split second of stunned pain, then he punches through it. His drift carries him clear of whatever is inside the pavilion. He throws his arms up in front of his face and impacts the ground.

Nothing has ever hit so hard. A swinging fist the size of the moon smashes every breath, sense, thought from him. Black. Then he is back, trying to gasp, unable to move. Circles. Machines, faces, in the middle distance his fellow traceurs racing towards him.

He inhales. It hurts. Every rib grates, every muscle groans. He rolls on to his side. Medical bots lift and flutter on ducted fans. He tries to push himself up from the ground.

'No kid, don't,' a voice calls from the circle of faces but no hand reaches to stop or aid him. He is a broken wonder. With a cry he gets to his knees, forces himself to stand. He can stand. Nothing is broken. He takes a step forward, a skinny waif in tangerine tights.

'Joker,' he whispers, 'what was my final speed?'

Thirty-eight kilometres per hour.

He clenches a fist in victory, then his legs fail and he stumbles forward. Hands and bots surge to catch him: Robson Mackenzie, the kid who fell from the top of the world.

'So, how does it feel to be famous?'

Hoang Lam Hung leans against the door. Robson had not noticed him arrive. He was occupied stroking his sudden celebrity. The word had gone twice around the moon while Robson was being transferred to the med centre. The boy who fell to Earth. He didn't fall to Earth. This isn't Earth. He fell to the ground. But that didn't fill the mouth as well. And it wasn't a fall. There was a slip. The rest was managed descent. He walked away. Only a step, but he took that step. But even if it was wrong the whole moon was talking about him and he had Joker scan the network for stories and pictures about him. He soon realised that the bulk of the traffic was the same stories and pictures shared and reshared. Some of the pictures were very old, from when he was a kid, when he was a Corta.

'Gets boring after half an hour,' Robson says.

'Does it hurt?'

'Not a bit. They've got me full of stuff. But it did. Like fuck.'

Hoang raises an eyebrow. He disapproves of the low language Robson learns from his traceur mates.

When Robson was a kid of eleven and Hoang twenty-nine they had been married for a few days. Tia Ariel had dissolved it with her legal superpowers, but their one night together had been fun: Hoang had made food, which is always special, and taught Robson card tricks. Neither of them much wanted to be married. It had been a dynastic match, to bind a Corta into the heart of Clan Mackenzie. An honoured hostage. The Cortas are gone; scattered, vanquished, dead. Now Robson has a different family status, as one of Bryce Mackenzie's adoptees. That makes Hoang a brother, not an oko. Brother, uncle, guardian.

Robson is still a hostage.

'Well come on, then.'

Robson's face says a *what*?

'We're going to Crucible. Or had you forgotten?'

Robson has forgotten. His balls and perineum tighten in dread. Crucible. Hoang brought Robson to Queen of the South to put him beyond Bryce's appetites and Mackenzie family politics but Robson's great fear is the twitch on the thread that pulls him and Hoang back to the citadel of the Mackenzies.

'The party?' Hoang says.

Robson collapses back on to the bed. Robert Mackenzie's one hundred and fifth birthday. A gathering of House Mackenzie. Hoang and Joker posted ten, twenty, fifty reminders but Robson's eyes were

14

on handholds and grip soles, traceur fashion and how to style himself on his first free run, maxing up his fitness and getting to his running weight.

'Shit.'

'I've printed you up something to wear.'

Hoang slings a suit pack on to the bed. Robson unseals it. Perfume of print-fresh fabric. A Marco Carlotta suit in powder blue, a black v-neck T-shirt. Loafers. No socks.

'Eighties!' Robson says with delight. It's the new trend, after the 2010s, after the 1910s, after the 1950s. Hoang smiles coyly.

'Do you need a hand dressing?'

'No I'm fine.' Robson flings back the sheet and swivels out of the bed. Diagnostic bots retreat. Robson drops to the floor. Goes pale. Cries out. His knees give. Robson steadies himself on the edge of the bed. Hoang is at his side, supporting him. 'Maybe not.'

'You're purple from head to toe.'

'Really?'

Joker accesses a room camera and shows Robson his brown skin mottled black and yellow, a blossom of bruises spilling into each other. Robson winces as Hoang slips his arms into the jacket sleeves. Pain stabs as he pulls on the loafers. A final touch; at the bottom of the suit bag, the last treat, is a pair of Ray Ban Tortuga Aviator shades. 'Oh, glorious.' Robson slides them up his nose, adjusts the sit with a tap of forefinger between the lenses. 'Ow. Even they hurt.'

There is one final touch. Robson rolls the sleeves of his Marco Carlotta jacket up to the elbows.

A dazzling light burns on the horizon: the mirrors of Crucible focusing the sun on to the smelters of the ten-kilometre-long train. As a child, Robson loved that light, for Crucible could only be minutes away. He would rush to the railcar's observation bubble, press his hands to the glass, anticipating the moment he would pass into the shadow of Crucible and look up at the thousands of tons of habitats and smelters and loaders and processors above his head.

Robson loathes it now.

The air had been foul – thick with CO_2 and water vapour – by the time the beams of the VTO rescue team came lancing through the frozen, empty dark of Boa Vista. The refuge was rated for twenty. Thirty-two souls were packed into it; shallow-breathing, conserving every movement. Cold condensation dripped from every edge, beaded every surface. *Where's paizinho?* he shouted as the VTO squad bundled him into the transfer pod. *Where's paizinho?* he asked Lucasinho in the moonship hold. Lucasinho looked across the crowded hold at Abena Asamoah, then took Robson to the head. These words must be private. *Wagner is in hiding. Ariel is missing, Lucas has vanished, presumed dead. Carlinhos is hung by his heels from a São Sebastião Quadra crosswalk. Rafa is dead.*

His father was dead.

The legal battles were furious and, for the moon, brief. Within a lune Robson was in a Mackenzie Metals railcar hurrying across the Oceanus Procellarum, Hoang Lam Hung in the seat opposite and a squad of blades deployed at a discreet distance, serving no other purpose than to embody the power of Mackenzie Metals. The Court of Clavius had ruled: Robson Corta was a Mackenzie now. At eleven-and-some Robson could not identify the look on Hoang's face. At thirteen he knows it as the face of a man who has been forced to betray the thing he loves. Then he saw the bright star on the horizon, the light of Crucible blazing in endless noon, and it changed from the star of welcome to the star of hell. Robson remembers the orixas of Boa Vista, their immense stone faces carved from raw rock a constant presence and reassurance that life resisted the cold brutality of the moon. Oxala, Yemanja, Xango, Oxum, Ogun, Oxossi, Ibeji the Twins, Omolu, Iansa, Nana. He can still name their counterparts among the Catholic saints and list their attributes. In the Cortas' private religion there was little divinity, less theology and no promise of heaven or hell. Endless return. It was natural, spirits recycled as the Zabbaleen recycled the carbon, water, minerals of the discarded body. Hell was pointless, cruel and unusual. Robson still cannot understand why a god would want to punish someone forever when there was no possibility that the punishment would achieve any good.

'Welcome back,' Robert Mackenzie said from the depths of the life-support system that kept him alive. The breathing tube in his throat pulsed. 'You're one of us now.' At his left shoulder, his familiar Red Dog. At his right, his wife Jade Sun, her familiar the customary Taiyang I-Ching hexagram: Shi Ke. Robert Mackenzie opened his arms, opened his hook-fingers. 'We'll look after you.' Robson turned his head away as the arms enfolded him. Dry lips brushed Robson's cheek.

Then Jade Sun. Perfect hair perfect skin perfect lips.

Then Bryce Mackenzie.

'Welcome back, son.'

Hoang has never spoken about the deals he made to relocate Robson from Crucible to the old family mansion of Kingscourt in Queen of the South but Robson is sure the price was heavy. In Queen he could run, in Queen he could be who he liked, hold the friendships he liked. In Queen he could forget that he would always be a hostage.

Now he comes again to Crucible. The glare of the great train's smelter mirrors swells until it blinds, even through the photochromic glass of the observation bubble. Robson lifts his hand to shade his eyes, then darkness. He blinks away after-images. On either side of him rise the bogies that carry Crucible above the Equatorial One mainline; a thousand of them stretching ahead of him, curving down over the close horizon. Traction motors, power cabling, service platforms and gantries, access ladders: a maintenance bot scurries up a support truss and Robson's eyes follow it. The stars of this sky are the lights of the overhead factories and accommodation modules.

A third generation moon kid, Robson doesn't understand claustrophobia – confined spaces are comfort, security – but today the windows and spotlights and warning beacons of Crucible press down like a hand and he cannot shake the knowledge that above those lesser lights is the white-hot focus of the smelter mirrors and crucibles of molten metal. The railcar slows. Grapples descend from the belly of Crucible. There is only the slightest tremor as the clamps lock and lift and slide the railcar towards the dock.

A touch on his shoulder: Hoang.

'Come on, Robson.'

There he is, there he is!

The tram lock opens on to faces, all turned to him. Within five steps Robson is surrounded by young women in their party dresses: short and tight, rah-rah and puffball; glossy hosiery, deadly heels, hair back-combed to halos. Fuchsia lips, eyes winged with liner, cheekbones highlighted with straight strokes of blusher.

'Ow!' Someone has poked him. 'Yes it hurts.' Laughing, the girls marshal Robson toward the end of the car where the young people gather. The conservatory – Fern Gully in Mackenzie lore – is large and complex enough in its winding paths and planting zones to allow a dozen sub-parties. Wait-staff with trays of 1788s – the Mackenzies' signature cocktail – sway between the arching ferns: all of a sudden a glass is in Robson's hand. He swallows it, bites back the bitterness, enjoys the warmth spreading through him. Ferns rustle; aircon units stir the humid atmosphere. Live birds pick at fronds, flit half-seen from bract to bract.

Robson is the centre of a circle of twenty young Mackenzies.

'Can I see the bruises?' asks a girl in a stretchy tight crimson skirt she keeps pulling down and dangerous heels in which she keeps testing her balance.

'Okay, yeah. Robson slips off his jacket, lifts his T-shirt. 'Here and here. Deep tissue trauma.'

'How far up do they go?'

Robson pulls the T-shirt over his head and there are hands all over him, boys and girls alike, eyes wide at the yellow mass of bruising across his back and belly, like a map of the dark mares of the moon. Each touch is a grimace of pain. A doodle of cool across his belly: one of the girls has drawn a smiley face in pink lip gloss on his abs. In an instant girls and boys pull out their cosmetics and assault Robson with pink and fuchsia, white and lime fluorescent yellow. Laughing. All the time laughing.

'God you're skinny,' a freckled, red-head Mackenzie boy says.

'Why didn't you break in bits?'

'Does this hurt? Does this, this; what about this?'

Robson cowers, back turned to the stabbing lip-sticks, arms wrapped around his head.

'Now now.'

A light tap on the shoulder from the titanium wand of a vaper.

'Leave him.'

The hands pull back.

'Put some clothes on darling. We've people to meet.'

Darius Mackenzie is only a year older than Robson but the kids step back. Darius Mackenzie is the last surviving son of Jade Sun-Mackenzie. He is short for a third gen, dark, his features more Sun than Mackenzie. No one on Crucible believes he is the product of Robert Mackenzie's frozen sperm. But he has the old master's tone of command.

Robson pulls on his shirt, rescues his jacket.

Robson has never understood Darius's affection for him – he is of the same blood that killed Darius's brother, Hadley, in the arena of the Court of Clavius. But if he has a friend in Crucible, it is Darius. On those occasions when Robson returns from Queen of the South – birthdays, Hoang's unspoken obeisances to Bryce – Darius always hears of Robson's arrival and finds him within minutes. It is a relationship that only exists in Crucible, but Robson appreciates Darius's favour. He suspects even Bryce fears Darius Mackenzie.

This is what Robson hates about Crucible; the fear. The naked, shaking fear that infests every gesture and word, every thought and breath. Crucible is an engine of fear. Lines of fear run up and down the ten kilometres of Crucible's spine, twitching and whispering, pulling and tugging on the hooks of secrets and debts buried in the skins of every one of the great train's crew.

'They're jealous really,' Darius says, drawing deep on his vaper and slipping an arm around Robson's waist. 'Now, come along. We have rounds to make. Everyone wants to meet you. You're a celebrity. Is it true none of the runners came to see you in med centre?'

Darius knows the answer to his own question but Robson says yes anyway. He knows why Darius Mackenzie asked it. The lines of fear run all the way from Crucible to the old quadras of Queen of the South. Even traceur kids know the legend that the Mackenzies repay three times.

'Robbo!'

Robson hates the chummy, Australianised contraction of his name. He does not recognise this coterie of high-fashion, big-haired young white women but they seem to assume some claim of kinship. Their hair is intimidating.

'Suit, Robbo. Marco Carlotta, classy. Got the sleeves right. Heard you had a bit of an accident.'

The coterie hoots with laughter. Robson recounts his story to appreciative oohs and eye-rolls but Darius has surveilled the next social group and, begging protocol, steers Robson on.

Under a canopy of fern fronds, 1788 cocktails loose in their hands, Mason Mackenzie and a group of young males talk handball. The Mackenzie way is for the women to talk in one group and the men in another. Mason is the new owner of the João de Deus Jaguars. He's signed Jojo Oquaye from the Twé All-Stars and he is boasting to his friends about how he put out the eyes of Diego Quartey in Twé. Robson hates to hear Mason talking about his team. It's not Mason's team, it never will be his team. They are not Jaguars; they never will be Jaguars – what is a Jaguar anyway? – they are the Moços. The guys, the girls. You can steal a team but you can't steal a name. The name is cut into the heart. He remembers his pai lifting him up on to the rail of the director's box, handing him the ball. It sat in his hand naturally, heavier than he imagined. *Throw it in.* All the players, all the fans and visitors in the Estádio da Luz were looking at him. For a moment he almost whimpered and wanted paizinho to lift him down from the rail, away from the eyes. Then he lifted the ball high and threw it with all his strength and it sailed out, much further than he had thought it could, over the upturned faces of the people in the terraces below, towards the rectangle of green.

'The Moços will never win for you,' Robson says. The men break off their conversation at the interruption. A moment's anger, then they recognise the kid who fell from the top of the world.

Darius links Robson's arm again.

'Okay. Enough.' Darius has spotted bigger game among the frond-shadows. 'Sport is crass anyway.' Cousins and more remote relatives pass and compliment Robson on his clothes, celebrity and survival. None ask to see the lip-gloss-smeared bruises. A live band plays bossa nova. It's been bigger than ever since the fall of Corta Hélio; a global music. Guitar, acoustic bass, whispering drums.

Robson freezes. Clustered between the band and the bar are Duncan Mackenzie and his okos Anastasia and Apollinaire, Yuri Mackenzie the CEO of Mackenzie Fusion, Yuri's half-brothers Denny and Adrian and Adrian's oko, Jonathon Kayode, the Eagle of the Moon himself. Darius tugs gently on Robson's arm.

'Work the room.'

Anastasia and Apollinaire's delight at Robson's adventure is effusive. Hugs, kisses, making him stand and turn one way then the other to check injuries – *his complexion is better than yours, Asya*. Yuri is smiling and unimpressed, Duncan disapproves; a fall from the roof of the world is a blatant breach of family security, but his disapproval bears no weight. Duncan Mackenzie carries no authority since Robert Mackenzie took back control of Mackenzie Metals. Yuri is CEO of the helium-3 company Mackenzie Metals scavenged from the corpse of Corta Hélio. Denny is a tense, set-jawed twitch of energy as constrained as helium in a fusion pinch-field. Denny is a link in a chain of vengeance: Carlinhos killed his uncle Hadley in the Court of Clavius; Denny slit Carlinhos's throat in the sack of João de Deus. Seize your enemy's fallen weapon and turn it against them.

The Eagle of the Moon wants to know Robson's secret. *You fell three kilometres and walked away?* Robson is starstruck. He has never seen the Eagle in the flesh: he's taller than Robson imagined, almost as tall as a gen three but built like a mountain. His formal agbada robes only magnify his gravity.

The secret? Darius answers for tongue-tied Robson. *Try not to hit the ground.*

'Sound advice.'

The voice is quiet and refined, low in pitch and soft but it silences even the Eagle of the Moon. The Mackenzie men dip their heads. The Eagle of the Moon takes the offered hand and kisses it.

'Lady Sun.'

'Jonathon. Duncan; Adrian.'

From time beyond remembering, the Dowager of Taiyang has been Lady Sun. No one knows the true age of Sun Cixi – none would dare ask. Her years may rival even Robert Mackenzie. Not for Lady Sun 1980s retro. She wears a faux-wool day suit from 1935, skirt to below the knee, wide-lapel led hip-length jacket, single button. Fedora, wide band. Classic style is never out of fashion. She is a small woman, even by first generation norms; dwarfed by her bodyguard of handsome, smiling Sun boys and girls, fit and fast in their fashionable powder-blue Armani suits and killer Yohji Yamamoto coats. She compels every eye. Her every movement communicates will and intent. Nothing is unconsidered. She is poised, electric, crackling with potency. Her eyes are dark and brilliant, seeing all, reflecting nothing.

A hand extended, a cocktail arrives in it. A gin Martini, barely hazed with vermouth.

'I brought my own,' Lady Sun says, taking a sip. Not a lipstick mark on the glass. 'And yes, it is terribly rude but I simply cannot drink that piss you call a 1788.' She turns her needle eyes on Robson.

'I hear you're the boy who fell the height of Queen of the South. I suppose everyone's telling you how wonderful you are for surviving. I say you're a damn fool for falling in the first place. If a son of mine did a thing like that, I'd disinherit him. For a month or two. You're a Corta, aren't you?'

'Robson Mackenzie, qiansui,' Robson says.

'Qiansui. Corta manners there all right. You always were smooth, you Brazilians. Australians have no finesse. Take care of yourself, Robson Corta. There aren't many of you left.'

Robson purses his right hand and dips his head the way Madrinha Elis taught him. Lady Sun smiles at his Corta decorum. An arm around Robson's shoulders, a wince of pain. Darius steers him onward through the party.

'They're going to talk politics now,' Darius says.

Robson smells Robert Mackenzie before he sees him. Antiseptics and antibacterials barely mask the piss and shit. Robson catches the oily, vanilla perfume of fresh medical electronics; hair grease, caked sweat, a dozen fungal infestations and a dozen more antifungals fighting them.

Plugged and socketed into his environment unit, Robert Mackenzie inhabits the green, whispering-fern pergola at the centre of his garden. Birds chirp and whirl through the ferns, glimpses of flashing colour. They are brightness and beauty. Robert Mackenzie is a man old beyond age, beyond the limits of biology. He sits on a throne of pumps and purifiers, lines and monitors, power supplies and nutrient drips, a leather purse of a man at the heart of a pulsing tangle of pipes and lines. Robson cannot bear to look at him.

Behind Robert Mackenzie, the shadow behind the throne, Jade Sun-Mackenzie.

'Darius.'

'Mum.'

'Darius, that vaper. No.'

The thing in the chair croaks and convulses in a dry laugh.

'Robson.'

'Sun qiansui.'

'I hate it when you say that, it makes me sound like my great-aunt.'

Words now from the thing on the throne, so slow and creaking Robson does not at first realise they are addressed to him.

'Nice one, Robbo.'

'Thank you, Vo. Happy birthday, Vo.'

'Nothing happy about it, boy. And you're a Mackenzie so speak the fucking King's English.'

'Sorry, Pop.'

'Still, nice trick, falling three kays and walking away. I always knew you were one of us. You getting any off it?'

'Any?'

'Puss. Cock. Neither. Whatever it is you like.'

'I'm only...'

'You're never too young. Always capitalise. That's the Mackenzie way.'

'Pop, can I ask you something?'

'It's my birthday, I'm supposed to be magnanimous. What do you want?'

'The traceurs – the free runners. You won't go after them?'

Robert Mackenzie starts in honest surprise.

'Why should I do that?'

'Because they were there. A Mackenzie could have died. Repay three times, that's the Mackenzie way.'

'It is, Robbo, it is. I have no interest in your sports mates. But if you want it official, I will not touch any of your free-runners. Red Dog, witness that.'

Robert Mackenzie's familiar, named after the town in Western Australia where he built his fortune, once wore the skin of a dog but over iterations and decades has changed like its owner to become a pattern of triangles: ears, a geometry that hints at muzzle, a neck; slash eyes: an abstraction of a dog's head. Red Dog tags Robert Mackenzie's words and forwards them to Robson's familiar, Joker.

'Thank you, Pop.'

'Try not to make it sound like sick in your mouth, Robbo. And give your pop a birthday kiss.'

Robson knows that Robert Mackenzie sees him close his eyes as he brushes his lips against the scaly, paper-crisp cheek.

'Oh yes. Robbo. Bryce wants to see you.'

Robson's belly tightens. Muscles clench painfully. His stomach seems to open on to nothing. He looks to Darius for help.

'Darius, give your mother five minutes,' Jade Sun says. 'I hardly ever see you these days.'

I'll find you, Darius messages through Joker. For a moment Robson considers hiding in Fern Gully's maze of paths and brakes but Bryce has anticipated that: Joker rezzes a path on Robson's lens through the short dresses and big-shouldered suits and bigger hair.

Bryce is talking with a woman Robson does not recognise, but from her height, her discomfort in lunar gravity, the cut of her clothing, he guesses she is from Earth. The People's Republic of China, he decides, from her confidence and aura of customary authority. The woman excuses herself. Bryce bows to her. For a big man, an immensely big man, he is light on his feet. Dainty.

'You wanted to see me?'

Bryce Mackenzie has eight adoptees. The oldest is thirty-three-year-old Byron, protégé of Bryce in the finance department. The youngest is Ilia, ten years old, orphaned after a habitat breach at Schwarzchild. He survived eight hours in a refuge coffin; corpses and rock piled on his faceplate. Robson can understand that. The refugee, the needy, the abandoned, the orphan: all swept into Bryce Mackenzie's family. Tadeo Mackenzie has even married, a woman too, but those same lines of power that Robson feels nerving the sun-bleached skeleton of Crucible are stitched through the skins of every adopted son. A tug and all are drawn together.

'Robson.'

The full name. The cheek offered, the filial kisses.

'I am very very cross with you, you know. It may take me a long time to forgive you.'

'I'm all right. Just a bit of bruising.'

Bryce looks him up and down. Robson feels eyes peeling away his clothing.

'Yes, boys are extraordinarily resilient creatures. They can absorb incredible amounts of damage.'

'I missed a hold. I made a mistake.'

'Yes, and physical exercise is so very important, but Robson, really. Hoang was responsible. I put you in his charge. No, I simply can't take the risk again. You're safer in Crucible.'

Robson thinks his heart might have stopped.

'I've bought you a present.' Robson hears excitement in Bryce's voice. He could vomit with fear and loathing.

'My birthday's not until Libra,' Robson says.

'It's not for your birthday. Robson, this is Michaela.'

She turns from the conversation in which she has been engaged, a short, tight-muscled white Jo Moonbeam. In her time on the moon she's learned Mackenzie etiquette: a brief dip of the head.

'She's your personal trainer, Robson.'

'I don't want a personal trainer.'

'*I* do. You need building up. I like muscle on my boys. You'll start tomorrow.'

Bryce breaks off, looks up. Robson sees it too, a shift in the angle of the light.

The light never moves. That's the power of Crucible: unwavering noon light focused on the overhead smelters.

The light moved. Is moving.

'Robson, come with me if you want to live.'

Light-footed Bryce is also fast. He snatches Robson by the arm and almost flies; great soaring lunar leaps as the alarms sound and every lens is over-ridden by the emergency alarm. General evacuation. General evacuation.

Sunlight touches Duncan Mackenzie's face and he looks up. Every Mackenzie in Fern Gully looks up, faces striped with the sudden shadows of fronds. Lady Sun lifts an eyebrow.

'Duncan?'

As she speaks, Esperance, Duncan Mackenzie's familiar, whispers the one word in his ear he has dreaded all his life.

Ironfall.

The apocalypse myth of Mackenzie Metals: the day the tons of molten rare earths in the smelters rain down. No one on Crucible has ever believed it possible. Everyone on Crucible knows the word.

'Lady Sun, we have to evacuate...' Duncan Mackenzie says but the Dowager of Taiyang's entourage has closed around her, pushing without hesitation through the startled party-goers. They shove Jonathon Kayode out of their path; the Eagle's guards drop into a tight phalanx, hands reaching for holstered blades.

'Leave that, get us out of here!' Adrian Mackenzie shouts. The swirl toward the lock to the next car is becoming a stampede. Shouts into screams. 'Not that way you idiots! The drop pods!'

'Adrian, what's happening?' the Eagle of the Moon asks.

'I don't know,' Adrian Mackenzie answers, crouching in the shelter of the ring of bodyguards. Knives drawn, the Eagle's guards push dazed, lost party-goers out of the way. 'It's not a depressurisation.'

Then his eyes go wide as his familiar whispers the same word to him: *Ironfall*.

'Mr Mackenzie.' Duncan Mackenzie's Head of Crucible is a short Tanzanian, Jo-Moonbeam-muscular. 'We have lost control of the mirrors.'

'How many?'

'*All* of them.'

'What?'

'Sir, in just over a minute the temperature will hit two thousand Kelvin.'

The light through the fern fronds is as bright and hot as fresh forged knives. Every bird, every insect in the fern jungle has fallen silent. The air burns Duncan's nostrils.

'My father . . .'

'Sir, I'm tasked with your protection.'

'Where is my father? Where is my father?'

Bryce Mackenzie's grip is steel. Beneath his mass lies muscle. He flings aside party boys and party girls – make-up smeared, heels broken – as he drags Robson towards the green flashing circles of lights that mark the drop pods.

'What is it, what's happening?' Robson asks. Around him voices ask the same question, clamouring louder as uncertainty becomes fear becomes panic.

'Ironfall, boy.'

'But it can't. I mean . . .'

The light grows stronger, the shadows shorter.

'Of course it can't. This isn't an accident. We're under attack.'

Hoang, Joker whispers and his face appears on Robson's lens.

'Robson, where are you? All you all right?'

'I'm with Bryce,' Robson shouts. The voices are terrible now. Hands tear at him, trying to rip him away from Bryce and his place in the drop pod. Bryce Mackenzie hauls the boy through the snatching hands and reaching arms. 'Are you okay?'

'I'm out, I'm out. Robson, I will find you. I promise. I will find you.' Hoang's face explodes in a puff of pixels. *Network is down,* Joker announces. A brief, terrible silence fills Fern Gully. Every familiar has vanished. Everyone is disconnected. Everyone is alone, against all others. Then the screams truly begin.

'Bryce!' Robson yells, hauling back on Bryce's hand. Like trying to move the moon herself.

A rearguard of blades defends the lock, two deep, knives drawn.

'Bryce, where's Darius?'

The blades part to admit Bryce and Robson. They push back the surging, panicked party-goers. The outlock is open, the ring of lights pulses green.

'Bryce!' Robson tries to slip his fingers free. Bryce stops, turns, eyes bulging in astonishment.

'Stupid, ungrateful brat.'

The slap stuns Robson. His jaw pops, stars explode in his vision. He feels blood burst from his nostrils. Every bruise on his body shrieks. Robson reels, then hands seize a fistful of Robson's jacket and haul him through the lock into the pod.

'Come on come on,' Bryce shouts. Head ringing from the blow, Robson falls on to the padded bench. Six blades tumble into the pod, then the door scissors shut.

Pod drop in ten, the AI says. Bryce buckles in beside Robson, crushing him against a bulky Ukrainian blade. *Nine.*

'Robbo. Robbie. Robson.'

Robson tries to shake clarity into his vision. Darius, strapped in directly opposite. His eyes are wide, his face is pale with terror. He clutches his vaper in a clenched fist.

'Darius.'

Two, one. Release.

The bottom drops out of the world.

The inner lock seals, the outlock opens. Jade Sun seats herself decorously in the drop pod. Robert Mackenzie's life-support unit manoeuvres in the tight lock. The inner door beats like a festival drum: fists fists fists. Mackenzie engineering is built for the moon: human hands are nothing to it, no matter how many, how desperate. In a few seconds the mirrors will turn their full focus on the Fern Gully, on every one of the thousand cars of Crucible. Twelve thousand mirrors, twelve thousand suns. Mackenzie engineering cannot withstand the light of twelve thousand suns.

Then the hammering on the door will end.

Fifty seconds to Ironfall, Jade Sun's familiar advises her. The network is down, but Robert Mackenzie's Red Dog will have told him the same. 'Jade, help me, woman. I can't get this fucking thing to move.'

Jade Sun-Mackenzie settles back on the padded bench in the sanctuary of the drop pod.

'Jade.' A command not a request.

Jade Sun-Mackenzie straps in. In the lock, Robert Mackenzie jerks and lunges with all his meagre, brittle strength, as if he might shift the massive life-support throne with his own sparrow weight.

'Why the fuck isn't this thing moving?'

'Because I don't want it to, Robert.'

Duncan Mackenzie's belly lurches as the locks release and the pod drops. Jonathon Kayode fixes eyes with him across the ring of seating. The Eagle of the Moon is grey with fear. His fingers are locked tightly with his oko's. Not one of his bodyguards have made it into the pod with him. For a few seconds the pod falls free on its cables, then the brakes cut in; a sudden deceleration that shakes a whimper of fear from the Eagle of the Moon. The pod lands soft and solid on its wheels. Explosive bolts detach the lines, each a small jolt. Engines whine; the pod races away from the dying Crucible. The great train is a line of blinding light curved along the horizon: a nova sunrise.

'Is my father safe?' Duncan Mackenzie demands. 'Is he safe?'

The chair will not move. Robert Mackenzie's wreck of a body shakes as he wills the life-support unit to obey him. His eyes, the muscles of his jaw that hold the final reserves of his dreadful will, the veins on his throat, his wrists, his temples, strain and bulge. The throne defies him.

'We hacked your LSU, Robert,' Jade Sun says. 'A long time ago. Sooner or later, we'd have shut you down.' The drop pod vibrates, soft concussions as other pods fall from their escape locks. 'The mirrors aren't our doing, but what kind of a Sun would I be if I didn't seize an opportunity?'

Thick drool ropes from the corners of Robert Mackenzie's mouth as he raises his hands towards the tubes lined into his neck.

'You can't disconnect, Robert. You've been part of it too long. I'm closing the lock now.'

Jade Sun's every breath burns. *Air temperature inside Crucible is four hundred and sixty Kelvin*, Shi Ke says.

The hammering on the lock door has stopped.

'I'm not. Trying. To disconnect,' Robert Mackenzie says. Claw fingers twitch at his collar. A blur of motion: Jade Sun reels back in her padded impact seat as a tiny buzzing object darts at her. She lifts a hand to the sudden needle of pain in her neck, drops it. Her face slackens, her eyes, her mouth open. AKA neurotoxins are swift and certain. Jade Sun slumps in her seat, held upright by the safety straps. The assassin fly hums on her neck.

'Shouldn't have waited to close the lock, cunt,' Robert Mackenzie hisses. 'Never trust the fucking Sun.' Then his croaking defiance becomes a terrible scream as the mirrors turn their full focus on him and flash the old man, every person and everything in Fern Gully into flame. Titanium, steel, aluminium, construction plastics

31

sag, melt, drip in the intense heat, then blast upwards and outward in a spray of molten metal as Crucible explosively depressurises.

When he fell from the top of Queen of the South, Robson Mackenzie had been afraid. More afraid than he had ever been in his life. He could imagine no greater fear. There is a greater fear. He is strapped into it while Crucible melts above him. In the big fall, life and death were his choice and skill. Here he is helpless. Nothing he can do here can save him.

Robson slams forward against his seat restraints. His stomach lurches. A moment of free fall, then the pod grounds hard. It is moving, trying to get to a safe distance, but to where, how fast, how soon Robson doesn't know. Something snaps him left, then right. Rattles, lurches. Creaks and cracks and whines. Robson has no idea where he is, what is happening. Noises, impacts. He wants to see. He needs to see. All Robson can see are the faces around him, glancing at each other but never letting those glances be caught, because then you would puke with fear.

The pod stops. There is a long low grinding noise. The pod starts again, very slowly.

Robson is in Boa Vista again, at the end, when the power went down and the light went out and there was nothing to see but the faces looking at each other in the green glow of the refuge's emergency biolights. Noises. Robson remembers the cracks of the explosives and how everyone closed their eyes at each blast, fearing that the next would smash the refuge like a dropped tea-glass. One great explosion, and then a terrible rushing noise, like the world tearing down the middle, the refuge shaking and shifting on its shock-springs, everyone too terrified to scream, the rushing mighty noise dying into silence and that was how Robson knew that Boa Vista was open to vacuum. That was how Robson knew his father was dead.

We're safe. Madrinha Elis had wrapped Luna tight in her arms, told her that over and over. *You're safe. Refuges can't blow. They've blown Boa Vista,* Robson thought but he didn't speak it, because he knew that one spark would send fear-fire tearing through the crowded refuge, burning all the oxygen in a flash.

Refuges can't blow. Drop pods can survive anything.

When the flashlight beams came waving through the dark, he didn't know if they were saviours or killers.

Robson slaps the release button over his chest. He pulls himself to the observation window.

He can't die in a steel bubble. He has to see. He has to see.

Crucible dies in slow eruptions; a line of molten light. The far end of the train is beneath the horizon but Robson can see glowing tears of molten metal, each the size of a drop pod, arcing kilometres high, spinning, tumbling and splitting. He shields his eyes against the light. The mirrors are still tracking, still moving, drawing their two-thousand Kelvin blades down the support piers and bogies. Undermined, the retorts fail. Trusses buckle, the converters twist and spill. Ironfall. Rare earths spill and run. Glowing floes of lanthanum, floods of cerium and fermium, long laps of glowing rubidium. Air pockets detonate; complex, beautiful machines explode. Molten metal rains on the Ocean of Storms.

Now the mirrors themselves are failing, their supports fatally undermined. One by one they twist and collapse, swinging their swords of light across the sky, across the mare, fusing arcs of glass out of the Procellarum dust. Robson sees a pod die, cut open by the deadly, inescapable focus of a furnace mirror, and another. One by one, the twelve thousand mirrors of Crucible fall. Mirror by mirror, darkness descends. The only light now is the glow of molten metal and the emergency beacons of the fleeing pods.

Robson finds he is crying. Full, helpless tears. His chest heaves, his breath quivers. This is grief. He hated Crucible, hated its scheming and secrecy and scuttling fear, its politics and the sense that everyone he met there had a plan that involved him as prey. But it was a home. Not in the way that Boa Vista was a home; nothing can ever be Boa Vista again; he can never go back. It was a home, and now it's gone, dead, like Boa Vista is gone. Dead. Killed. He's had two homes and both of them have been killed. What is the common factor? Robson João Baptista Boa Vista Corta. There must be something wrong with him. The boy who can't have a home. It gets taken away from him. Like paizinho, like his Mãe, like Hoang. His pai sent him to Queen, to Crucible where Hadley tried to make him a zashitnik. When he came back to Boa Vista, paizinho pelted handballs at him, hard enough to hurt, hard enough to bruise, to make him hate. Everything. Always. Is taken away.

The steel rain has ended. The drop pod races across the metal-spattered mare, co-ordinating rescue centres and mining bases and habitats all across greater Procellarum. The mirrors stare burning eyes in their final falling places. The destruction of Crucible is bright enough to be visible from Earth. The sky is brilliant with moving constellations, flickers of light that Robson knows are manoeuvring thrusters. VTO has turned out every search and rescue ship on the moon. No need to search, nothing to rescue. You either live or the moon kills you.

Robson finds an object in his hand. Squared edges, rounded corners, a thickness and heft. He glances down. His cards, the deck Hoang gave him when they were okos, that he has kept with him ever since. He cuts the cards, slowly, deliberately. Here is comfort and certainty in the manipulations his fingers work on them. This he can master. Cards he can control.

2: VIRGO – LIBRA 2105

Bodies in every room and tunnel, every corridor and lock. Bodies sitting, squatting, lying, cross-legged, heads bowed. Bodies leaning against each other. Bodies in party clothes: Chanel, D&G, Fiorucci, Westwood. Bodies saying little, moving less, waiting. Bodies saving breath. The rooms, tunnels, corridors, locks of Lansberg hum with the synchronised, shallow breaths of survivors. Every few minutes a lock opens and more evacuees step out in their party clothes, take one deep breath of the moist, reeking, re-breathed air; then their chibs click into emergency response and close down the breathing reflex to a susurrus. Wheezing, trying to gasp, they find places among the huddles and knots of survivors to sit and wait.

Lansberg is VTO's Equatorial One Central Procellarum mainline maintenance depot; a redoubt scooped under Lansberg crater for bots and service vehicles and track teams on two-lune rotations. Its environment unit is designed for fifty in an emergency. Twenty times that many are crammed into its dank chambers. Eight hours after Ironfall drop pods are still crawling into the lock on reserve power to disgorge anoxic, dehydrated, terrified survivors. Lansberg engineers are printing up CO2 scrubbers but now the water recycling system is failing. The toilets gave in hours ago. There is nothing to eat.

Darius Mackenzie hisses in frustration and sends the cards showering across the corridor. *I can't get it,* he says through Adelaide, his familiar. Robson gathers up the cards. He squares the pack and slowly shows Darius the move again. The flick with the thumb, the slide into the Tenkai palm. He shows his hand, spreads his fingers. See? The precision of the trick is the relative angle of hand and card so that none of the card is visible. It's one of the more difficult sleights of hand. He practised in front of a camera hour after hour. Body memory is dull and slow to learn; only repeated rehearsal will drive the move, the flow, the timing into the fibres of the muscle. Sleight of hand is the most rehearsed performance art. A conjurer will practise a move ten thousand times before braving an audience.

Bryce had briefly checked on Robson's well-being before commandeering a VTO moonship to take him to Queen of the South. Crucible had fallen, Mackenzie Metals must endure. That was five hours ago. For the first hour Robson and Darius held each other, numbed by the enormity of the destruction. Then Robson dared the network. Horrors flooded in. Numbers, names. Names he knew, names who had smiled and talked to him and poked innocently at his bruises and drawn their names in lipgloss on his ribs, names with big hair and party clothes. Eighty dead; hundreds missing. He sat, weighing every breath in his shallow chest, unable to comprehend what he was hearing. Three hours he listened to the news reports. Then he took out his cards.

I want to teach you how to palm a card, he whispered. *Palming is like the heart of conjuring. It's there, but it's hidden, right in front of everyone, and any time I want, I can call it back.*

He showed Darius the classic, the Hungard and the Tenkai palms, while new refugees picked paths over their outstretched legs and VTO water and medic teams worked their ways up and down the corridors.

You try it again.

Darius takes the deck, lifts the top card between his first and second fingers, makes the fake toss and folds his fingers down to lodge it between the tip and ball of his thumb. Something catches his eye: the trick is never completed. The cards fall from his hand. Robson squints into the damp, dusty haze. Lady Sun and her entourage, stepping carefully over the prone refugees. She breathes free and deep from a mask, one of her guards carries her oxygen tank. She takes the mask from her mouth.

'Darius. Up up.'

She waves her fingers: rise. Darius wobbles to his feet. A bodyguard steps in on either side to steady him. They seem untroubled by the reduced breathing. Lady Sun embraces him. Robson's jaw tightens at her famine-thin arms, her long, bone fingers around his friend.

'Oh my dear boy. My dear dear boy. I am so sorry.'

'Mum...' Darius says. Lady Sun presses a long forefinger to his lips.

'Don't talk.' She presses the breath-mask to her face, then to Darius's. 'There's a railcar waiting. You'll be safe in the Palace of Eternal Light.'

The handsome girls and boys form a guard around Darius. He glances back at Robson and for the first time Lady Sun notices him.

'Senhor Corta, I'm glad to see you safe and well.'

Robson purses his fingers, dips his head in his family's gesture of respect. Lady Sun smiles. A fast, conjurer's sleight and Robson offers half his deck to Darius. Darius slips the cards inside his jacket. The guards are already propelling him down the corridor, clearing a path through pushing, jostling Mackenzies who overheard the word *railcar*. Darius gives one final look back, then Lady Sun's entourage bustle him through the lock into the station approach.

I'll never see you again, will I? Robson whispers.

Body by body Lansberg empties. Robson's lungs expand, breath by breath. Train announcements, people getting up and leaving. VTO staff ask, Are you going? *Not going. Waiting.* Who are you waiting for?

Now Robson is the only one in the corridor. But he stays there because it's the way from and to the station. *He* has to come this way. And in the end, he sleeps because waiting is a dull sick ache, like a tinnitus of the soul.

A kick to the sole of his shoe. Another one.

'Hey.'

Hoang, crouching in front of him. Real true Hoang.

'Oh man oh you oh...' Robson throws himself on Hoang. They sprawl back across the empty corridor. 'Where have you been? Where have you been?'

'There was a train, I got taken to Meridian. It took so long to get a train out to Lansberg. So long.' Hoang hugs Robson tight, joint-dislocating love. New bruises over old.

'I was so scared,' Robson whispers in Hoang's ear. 'Everyone...' Words are not enough.

'Come on,' Hoang says. 'Let's get you cleaned up. When did you last eat? I brought food.'

When words are not enough, stuff suffices.

Old women should sit in the sun. Each seat around the table is illuminated from above by a beam of sunlight. Dust floats in the light. The game is venerable yet worth playing; tracing the spot back to mirror through mirror to mirror, to the hundred sun-bright dots of mirror in the perpetual shadow of Shackleton basin, to the high, blazing beacon of the Pavilion of Eternal Light. Eternal darkness to eternal light. Flummery with mirrors, for the amusement of those who know how the trick is done, but she still feels a prickle of old awe when the mirrors move through the dark, catch the light and burn.

When the mirrors move, the Board of Taiyang is in session.

'Lady Sun?'

Twelve faces, each lit by its own personal sun, turn to her.

'We tear them apart.'

You thought I wasn't listening, you thought I was a silly old lady, only allowed to sit in the light out of respect for my age, a senile old woman with the warmth of the sun on her face.

'I beg your pardon, Great-Aunt?' Sun Liqiu says.

'The brothers have always detested each other. All that held them together was the company, and their father. Robert is dead and Crucible is a pool of molten metal on the Ocean of Storms. We have a perfect opportunity to steal business for the solar belt.'

'Bryce has opened negotiations over Mackenzie Fusibles' L5 stockpile,' says Sun Gian-yin, Yingyun of Taiyang. The strong down light casts every face with deep, hard shadows.

'Oh, we can't have that,' Lady Sun says. 'We need some leverage over Bryce.'

'A man in debt is a well-behaved man,' Tamsin Sun says. She is Taiyang's Head of Legal Services. Lady Sun very much admires and very much mistrusts her honed, ambitious intellect.

'Any arrangement would be secure,' Sun Liwei says. 'Nothing could be linked to us.'

'Everyone will guess,' Amanda Sun says. The down light is more severe on her than the other board members. The shadows in her eyes, beneath her cheekbones say *killer*. You work it well, Lady Sun thinks. I don't believe you. You haven't the talent or the quality to kill Lucas Corta. No no, little killer, the one you really want, have always wanted dead, is me. You have never forgiven me for that cruel nikah that shackled you to Lucas Corta.

'Let them,' says Lady Sun.

Now the heads turn to Sun Zhiyuan, Shouxi of Taiyang.

'I agree with my grandmother. We divide and conquer. Like we did with the Mackenzies and the Cortas.'

The Cortas had flair. Lady Sun often regrets destroying them for something as inelegant as profit.

Abena Maanu Asamoah won't take his voice calls. Won't message, won't interact in any of the social forums. Won't recognise Lucasinho Corta as existing in the same universe. He contacts friends and friends of friends. He asks family. He sends hand-written letters on scented artisan paper to her apt. He pays his niece to write them. Lucasinho Corta can't hand-write. He posts apologies. He posts cutenesses and kawaii and emojis. He sends flowers and scented butterflies. He gets maudlin, he gets pathetic, he combs his hair down over his eyes and slightly purses his full lips in the way he knows is irresistible, he gets angry.

Finally he goes round to her apartment.

Of all the cities of the moon, Twé is the most bewildering; the least structured, the most organic, the most chaotic. Its roots were a cluster of agriculture tubes sunk into Maskelyne that, over years and decades, sent tunnels and power lines and pipes reaching out through the rock, linking, connecting, blowing habitat bubbles and driving new shafts and cylinders up towards the sun. It is a city of claustrophobic corridors that open into soaring silos, brilliant with mirrors turning the sun on to tier upon tier, level upon level of crops. The mirrors send stray shafts of light far through Twé's labyrinth, on to walls, into apartments, stairwells at certain moments of the day. In the long lunar night the magenta light of the LED arrays leaks from the tube farms into the labyrinth of tunnels and crosswalks. Lucasinho loves that dirty, sexy pink. It turns every tunnel, every shaft into an erogenous zone.

Public spaces are few and jammed with kiosks, food stalls, print shops and bars. Too narrow for motos, Twé's tunnels and streets are perilous with powerboards and scooters. Everyone sounds their buzzer, rings their bells, yells. Twé is a cacophony, a rainbow, a banquet. Graffiti, mottoes, adinkra, Bible verses adorn every surface. Lucasinho loves Twé's din, its purposefulness, the way that a deliberate wrong turn can bring him to new places and faces. Most of all he loves the smell. Damp, mould, growth and rot, sewage and deep water. Fish, plastic. The unique tang of air that has had much strong light shone through it. Perfume and fruit.

In the eighteen months since Lucasinho Corta came to Twé he has been a prince in exile, enjoying the protection and favour of the Asamoahs. Lucasinho loves Twé. Today, Twé does not love Lucasinho Corta. Friends look away; refuse to make eye contact; dissolve their groupings as he approaches; disappear into the crowd; flip up their powerboards, switch direction and surf away.

So everyone knows about Adelaja Oladele.

Abena's colloquium apt is on the twentieth level of Sekondi habitat; a half-kilometre deep cylinder of housing encircling a vertical orchard of apricots, pomegranates and figs. A mirror array beneath the glass roof sends long shards of light down through the leaves. Abena moved here when she joined the Kwame Nkrumah Colloquium. It's Twé's leading political science colloquium but Lucasinho liked her old apt better. It was private. Fewer people, and those that he did bump into weren't constantly judging him for some defect of ideology, privilege or politics.

He had a lot more sex in the old place.

The door won't answer me, his familiar Jinji says. Lucasinho checks his image in his lens, runs a comb through his hair, adjusts the knot of his white tie against his black shirt. He has all his piercings in their proper holes. She likes them. He raps a knuckle against the door.

Movement within. They'll know who's out there on the gallery.

He raps again. Again.

'Abena!'

Again.

'Abena, I know you're there.'

'Abena . . .'

'Abena, talk to me.'

'Abena, I only want to talk. That's all. Just talk.'

By now he is leaning against the door, cheek pressed to the wood,

41

tapping lightly with the knuckle of the middle finger of his right hand.

'Abena...'

The door opens wide enough to show eyes. They're not Abena's.

'Lucas, she doesn't want to talk to you.' Afi is the colloquium-mate least sneering at Lucasinho. *This is progress*, Lucasinho thinks.

'I'm sorry. Really. I just want everything to be right.'

'Well maybe you should have thought that before you fucked Adelaja Oladele.'

'I didn't fuck Adelaja Oladele.'

'Oh? You came five times in three hours. What's that then?'

'It was edging. You should know that he is insanely, insanely good at edging.'

'So edging isn't fucking.'

Why does he have the idea that Abena is feeding Afi lines?

'Edging isn't fucking. Edging's edging. Hand stuff. It's not intimate, like fucking.'

'Having Ade's hand on your dick for three hours isn't intimate?'

Adelaja Oladele has the hands of an angel, Lucasinho must admit. Three hours. Five orgasms.

'It's ... just playing. Guy stuff.'

'Guy stuff. Fine.'

Lucasinho can't win here. Get out with as little damage as possible.

'It's not like I—'

'Like you what?'

'Love him, or anything like that.'

'And you love me. Her. Her.'

'I don't love Adelaja Oladele.'

From inside the apt comes a sob. Afi glances around.

'Lucas, just go away.'

'I'll just go away.'

I could have coached you, Jinji says as Lucasinho stares at the closed door.

42

'You're an AI,' Lucasinho says. 'What do you know about girls?'

More than you, obviously, the familiar says.

But Lucasinho has a plan. A brilliant flawless romantic plan. By the time he hits the Level 12 access tunnel he is running full pelt. The flaps of his Armani jacket fly. Jinji puts a hire in and the powerboard meets him at the junction of 8th and Down. Lucasinho crouches low, arms outspread for balance, trouser pleats flapping in his own slipstream. The board dances through the streams of pedestrians and machines. He pulls up outside Tia Lousika's apt, arms folded, nonchalance in Armani.

He's naked by the time the kitchen space has unfolded.

'Luna, let's go get sherbet,' Madrinha Elis says. Tia Lousika objects to Lucasinho's enthusiastic nudity but Tia Lousika is hardly ever at home now: her commitments as the new Omahene of the Golden Stool keep her in Meridian. Luna has grown up comfortable with her cousin in his skin. What drives her and her madrinha out is Lucasinho in a kitchen. He is a diva.

Lucasinho pads naked to the worktop. He has the recipe, he has the ingredients, he has the talent. Lucasinho takes a deep breath, rubs his hands over his firm abdominals, the concavities of his incredible tight ass, the taut muscles around his lower spine. This will slay you, Abena Maanu Asamoah. He flexes his biceps and cracks his knuckles. Lifts the flour in its plastic sifter and lets it snow slow down into the work bowl. Miraculous stuff. Lucasinho knows its cost and its rarity. This is a work of love, an art beyond artisanal. Lucasinho plunges his hands into the bowl and delights in the silky flow of the flour; almost liquid, eddying around his fingers. He scoops it up and watches it descend, drips and drops falling out of the cloud where the powder has clumped.

Lucasinho dips a forefinger into the still-settling flour and draws a line along each cheekbone. A line down the centre of his forehead. A dab of flour on each nipple. A last white circle on the brown skin of his svadhishthana chakra. Creativity, sex, passion, desire. Interaction, relationships, sexual memory. He's ready.

'Let's bake.'

With cream he adorns her. A dab on the throat, one on each nipple, the belly, the navel. She stops his cream-laden finger midway between the wreckage of the cake and her vulva.

'Are you creaming my chakras?' says Abena Maanu Asamoah. Lucasinho leans in and places the blob of cream on the hood of her clitoris.

Abena gasps at the cold and the bold. She takes Lucasinho's hand and sucks the remaining smears of cream from his fingers.

'Now what am I going to eat?' Lucasinho says and Abena giggles deep and dirty and wiggles to offer her breasts to him. She growls a little in her throat as he licks her nipples.

'Anahita, manipura, svadhishthana,' Abena says. She puts her hand gently, firmly on the back of Lucasinho's head and directs him between her opening thighs. 'Muladhara. Leave room for seconds.'

He had waited, silvered with drizzle from the vertical orchard's hydration system, for fifteen minutes outside the door. Water condensed and dripped from the cake box he held in his hands. Water dewed and depressed his high-combed quiff. Water moistened his Issy Miyake suit and worked its way into the creases. Water ran from every silvery pierce he had put through his skin. When the door opened Abena was behind it.

'You'd better come in before you catch something.'

Was she hiding a smile?

She tried to ignore the cake on the lounger beside him.

He tried not to notice that all her colloquium-mates were gone.

'I made you cake.'

'You think that's the answer to everything? You just go off and make a cake and that makes everything all right?'

'Most things.'

'Why did you fuck Adelaja Oladele?'

'I didn't fuck him.'

'It was a hand job...'

'Edging...'

'Yes, he's fantastic at edging. Everyone says.'

'Legend. It's not a thing to be missed, so I'm told. And it's like you're...'

'I'm what?'

'Well, you're always busy...'

'Do not. Make this. About me. Do not. Try and say. That you only had sex with Adelaja Oladele because I was working.'

'Okay. But we agreed. You agreed. This isn't exclusive. We can see other people.'

'Because you insisted.'

'That's me. You knew that before we got together.'

'You could have asked,' Abena said. 'If it was all right to session with Ade. I might have wanted to watch. Boy on boy, you know.'

Lucasinho never stopped being surprised how Abena could surprise him. The Moonrun party, just before the assassination attempt on Rafa, when she had placed the special pierce in his earlobe and relished the taste of his blood. The wedding, when he exercised the power hidden in that pierce and claimed the protection of the Asamoahs rather than face marriage to Denny Mackenzie: Abena was waiting behind the pressure glass at Twé station. When Boa Vista fell, she suited up without hesitation, walked with him out to the waiting VTO ship, held his hand the whole flight. Went down into the lightless, empty hell that had been his home.

She was a hero, a goddess, a star. He was a cake-baking fool.

'Can I get out of these wet things?'

'Not yet. Not for a long time yet, Senhor. I know you. One flash of the abs and you think you're forgiven. But I might take a bit of cake.'

Lucasinho opened the box.

'It's a berry whipped cream cake.'

'What kind of berry?'

'I only know the word in Portuguese.'

'Say it.'

He did. Abena closed her eyes in pleasure. She loved the music of Corta Portuguese.

'Strawberry. I do like strawberries. I would definitely like a piece of your strawberry cake.'

'And cream.'

'Don't push it, Lucasinho.'

In the food space – so much larger than even Tia Lousika's, so much less well equipped – he cut precise slices – small portions, he's hopeful – and made mint tea.

'Are you shivering?'

Lucasinho nods. The precipitation has chilled him bone deep.

'Let's get you out of those wet things.'

It was then he had the great idea about the whipped cream.

After the cake and the play and the making-up sex Abena spooned close to Lucasinho, warming the last chill out of his marrow. Her cold absence wakes him.

She's taken the cake with her.

Lucasinho finds Abena sitting cross-legged on the common room floor, back hunched in concentration. She has pulled on a baggy T and tiny shorts and pulled her hair back in a green woven band. Lucasinho observes her pure and intense focus. If he allowed Jinji to link to her familiar he would see the room full of ghosts and politicians; her forum. She's explained it; a group of engaged people exploring new futures for everyone. Lucasinho can't think about futures. From where he lies, his looks the same in every direction, bleak as the Sea of Tranquillity. Abena's every hour outside colloquium seems spent talking in the back of her jaw with her political friends. Stuff going on, she tells him; *down there. Earth.*

Cortas don't do politics. They tried once. It killed them.

He places a hand between Abena's shoulder-blades, the other in the small of her back and corrects her spine. Abena gives a cry of surprise.

'You have the worst posture.'

'Luca . . .'

He loves it when she calls him that most intimate family name.

'Come back to bed.'

'It's still unfolding.'

'Crucible.'

'The death toll is up to one hundred and eighty-eight. Robert Mackenzie and Jade Sun are missing.'

'They burned. I'm glad.'

'The forums are insane. The markets are going crazy. I'm tracking panic buying on the helium markets.' Then Abena realises what Lucasinho has said. 'You're glad? People died, Luca.'

'They DPed Rafa. They hung Carlinhos by his heels. They broke Ariel's spine. Wagner's in hiding and my father, no one knows if he's alive or dead. They sent blades after me. Do you remember that? They burned. I can't be sorry about that. You saw Boa Vista. You saw Rafa, out there.'

'He's safe.'

Lucasinho shakes his head at the discontinuity, tripping over an emotional crack in the world.

'What? Who?'

'Your cousin. Robson.'

'Robson is in Queen of the South.'

'Robson was at Robert Mackenzie's party. He's safe, Luca. But you didn't know that.'

Lucasinho collapses back on to the lounger. Abena dismisses her forum.

'Luca, he's your family.'

This is an old conversation, its tracks deeply rutted, its emotional turns well-marked.

'Don't you think I know that? Don't you think I wanted to stop Bryce Mackenzie taking him? I couldn't do that. I'm nineteen years old. I'm the heir. The last Corta. I couldn't even keep Robson with me. I couldn't keep him safe.'

'Luca, you're not a lawyer.'

'Abi, shut up. You're always right. All you Asamoahs, you're always right and wise and have the answer: bim bam. Shut up and listen to me. I'm scared. When the Mackenzies start looking round for someone to blame, where will they look first? Cortas. I'm scared all the time, Abi. That session with Adelaja, it wasn't about the sex. It was about three hours not being scared. Do you know what it feels like, being scared all the time?'

Abena understands that she inhabits a world she can touch and shape, where her words and thoughts have power and agency. Lucasinho lives in a world for which he is responsible and yet powerless to change, where he carries blame for things he did not do. The distance will widen and split them apart in the end. Abena sees that clearly. She sees also a maimed, vulnerable boy who has experienced things beyond her imagining. A boy she can't help, and so understands him, because in this she's responsible and powerless too.

Abena puts her arms around Lucasinho.

So Afi finds them when she weaves in post-cocktail in search of cleansing tea. Better than tea: cake. She cuts herself a slice. The boy will have made it. They're cute together on the lounger, sleeping against each other. He's very pretty in that self-conscious Brazilian way but she could never invest in something so heavily damaged.

His cake, however, is outstanding.

Mackenzie Metals' house mixologist has created a memorial cocktail. Old-school industrial vodka, hibiscus syrup, lime, sprigs of wattle and a ball of cinnamon-myrtle-flavoured gel, slowly releasing orange tendrils into the pink. It commemorates the epochal life of Robert

Mackenzie in a glass. Waiters with trays of the things lurk by the doors, pressing them into hands.

'And this is?'

'Red Dog, Ma'am.'

Lady Sun takes the glass, sniffs, sips, passes it to one of her entourage. Tasteless, from the glass to the mix to the name. So Mackenzie. One of her guards pours her a thimble glass of her own private gin. Fortified, she sweeps into the salon to join the wake.

The mausoleum surprised her. No Mackenzie has ever shown any religious impulse, but the heart of Kingscourt, the old palace at Queen of the South, enfolds a small shrine: a pure white room, a perfect cube, three metres on a side. Duncan entered alone, then invited family and guests to pay their personal respects. Curiosity sent Lady Sun in. The chamber was small, large enough for three people at the most, pure white. The white walls were dotted with coloured discs, ten centimetres in diameter. Lady Sun stood in a polka dot chamber. Each disc was the familiar of a dead Mackenzie, frozen in ceramic circuitry. The body was recycled, the electronic soul endured. Here was Robert Mackenzie, a crimson disc at the centre of the far wall. Red Dog was his familiar, Lady Sun recalled. She touched Red Dog, half expecting a thrill of data, an echo of the old burning anger and ambition. It was a disc of doped glass, napped like velvet to the touch, nothing more.

After the obsequies the important event: the reception. Lady Sun drew up her conversation card on the tram ride from the Palace of Eternal Light. Pecking order is important.

First on the tour is Evgeny Vorontsov, his daughters around him. Good boned but inbred and stupid. Too much radiation woven into their DNA.

'Evgeny Grigorivitch.'

The CEO of VTO Luna is a great hulk of a man, long-haired, heavily bearded, immaculately dressed and groomed. Lady Sun particularly admires the damask of his shirt. There is a glass of neat vodka in his hand. The hand shakes. Lady Sun's informants whisper that his drinking problem is chronic, and that the command of VTO has passed to a younger, harder generation. Passed, been taken.

'Lady Sun. I'm sorry for your loss.'

'Thank you. It seems every house has been touched by this tragedy.'

'We've borne our own losses, Lady Sun.'

Jade Sun had been a work of a lifetime, decades of careful manoeuvring and manipulation undone in a drop of blazing sun. Jade was the honed weapon: Amanda had never the edge, the subtlety, the patience of her older sister. Lucas Corta out-thought Amanda Sun in every way. She should have married Amanda to Rafa, even as a third oko, but the Three August Ones insisted that that Lucas Corta would one day rule Corta Hélio.

'Sour times, Evgeny.'

Evgeny Grigorivitch Vorontsov knows a dismissal when he hears one.

To Lousika Asamoah now, elegant and lethal in Claude Montana. AKA politics are inscrutable to Lady Sun, but she understands Lousika is currently Omahene of the Kotoko, which is some kind of board, and that the position rotates around the Kotoko and that members come and go constantly. It seems fearfully elaborate and inefficient to Lady Sun. The Asamoahs keep everyone's secrets. That is all Lady Sun needs to know.

'Ya Doku Nana.' Her familiar informs her that this is the expected form of address to the Omahene.

'Lady Sun.'

They talk of families, of children and grandchildren and how the moon turns each generation stranger than the last.

'Your daughter is at Twé,' Lady Sun says.

'Luna, yes. With her madrinha.'

'I've never understood that Corta tradition, let alone why you'd import it wholesale into Twé. Forgive me, I'm an old woman and therefore forthright.'

'It's what she's used to.'

'I suppose. I can see how the child-care duties are very useful when you're away from Twé as much as you are since taking the Golden Stool. Tell me, how does it make you feel? You conceive the child, another woman bears it, births it, nurses it.'

Lady Sun spies a prick of irritation on Lousika Asamoah's perfectly composed, perfectly made-up face and takes pleasure at the little drop of blood she has drawn. Asamoahs keep secrets, I find them out. Some day, when the need comes – and it may never come – she will work an edge into this tiny wound and use it to splinter Lousika Asamoah apart.

Lady Sun has manoeuvred Lousika Asamoah to the edge of Bryce Mackenzie's space and effortlessly transfers social orbit. Lady Sun has not been in Bryce Mackenzie's physical presence for years now and she can barely contain her disgust. He is a horror. An obscenity. She can only tolerate his proximity by believing that his size is some form of perverse body art. Only two of his catamites today. Well-groomed boys. The taller one must be too old by now.

'Bryce.' She lays her hands on his. She is glad she is wearing gloves. 'There are no words. No words at all. A terrible, terrible loss.'

'And for you.'

'Thank you. I still can't quite believe that I was there – we were both there. A tragedy – an atrocity. Someone caused this. There are no accidents.'

'Our engineers are investigating. Physical evidence is hard to obtain and VTO wants to reopen Equatorial One as soon as possible.'

'But Mackenzie Metals goes on. It always did. We were the first, your father and I. You have the helium business at least. Far be it from me to tell a man how to run his affairs, but sometimes a quick, authoritative statement calms a nervous market. Until your father's will is made clear.'

'Mackenzie business is Mackenzie business, Lady Sun.'

'Of course, Bryce. But, for the old affection between our families, do not be a stranger at the Palace of Eternal Light.'

'The Palace of Eternal Light,' Bryce says. 'That is where you've taken Darius?'

'It is, and there he will remain,' Lady Sun says. 'I'm not having the boy ending up as another one of your little puppies.' Bryce's adoptees shuffle uncomfortably. Their society smiles tighten.

'He is a Mackenzie, Lady Sun.'

'Darius is a Sun first and a Sun always. However, we might be prepared to offer some recompense?'

Bryce dips his head, the shallowest of bows, and Lady Sun moves on to her final target. Duncan Mackenzie leans on the balcony, his Red Dog cocktail balanced on the rail. Queen of the South's towers are decked in flags and colours, banners and balloons and mythological creatures: preparations for the great celebration of Zhongqiu. In the chaos of Ironfall and its aftermath, Lady Sun had forgotten. At the Palace of Eternal Light, lasers will compete in the traditional Mooncake Festival ice sculpture competition.

'I've always envied you Kingscourt,' Lady Sun says. 'We let your father have the central site. I should have fought harder.'

'With respect Lady Sun, what my father had, he took.'

She remembers when Robert Mackenzie stood on that stone floor and declared that here he would make his headquarters. The lava chamber had not even been sealed for atmosphere when he moved in constructors and began building the first levels of Kingscourt. Queen of the South had been the logical place to drive roots into the moon – a lava chamber five kilometres long by three high, close by the ice of Shackleton crater – but the Mackenzies had moved quickly, to Hadley where they built their first smelter, then the insane ambition of Crucible, ever-circling beneath the hammer of the sun. Kingscourt remained the womb of the Mackenzies, where children were born and nurtured, dynasties engineered. Over the decades

Lady Sun had watched it grow to meet the ceiling and now it stood as the central spine of a forest, a cathedral of pillars.

'I'm sorry, Duncan.'

Duncan Mackenzie wears his habitual grey, and grey his familiar Esperance, but to Lady Sun's eye it looks less a hue, more a draining of colour from his soul, a hardening of spirit.

'Robert Mackenzie.' Duncan sets down his cocktail. 'I can't raise a glass of this piss to my father.'

Through her familiar, Lady Sun summons a bodyguard. The young woman produces two thimble glasses. Lady Sun slips the flask from her purse.

'That, I think, is worthy.'

They clink dewed glasses and throw back the gin.

'I see that even in the midst of calamity, it's business as usual for Mackenzie Metals. Your father would have been proud. Bryce is stabilising the price fluctuations on the terrestrial helium-3 markets. Very astute. It'll be some time until the rare earth division is producing again. Clever to make money on helium.'

'Bryce has always been a pro-active Head of Finance,' Duncan says. Lady Sun refills the glasses.

'A strong hand on the wheel. Any hand on the wheel. The terrestrials like that. They think we're a rabble of anarchists, criminals and sociopaths. The markets do so detest uncertainty. And the succession is unsecured. We know far too well how slowly the wheels of Lunar law turn.' She hands Duncan the second glass of pure gin.

'I am the heir of Mackenzie Metals.'

'Of course you are. That's not the question.' Lady Sun raises her glass. 'The question is, who's in charge, Duncan? You or your brother?'

Lady Sun circles back into the reception. A greeting here, a compliment there, a snub or a sigh. After a respectable interval she drifts up to Sun Zhiyuan.

'Satisfactory, nainai?'

'Of course not. This place stinks of laowai.'

'The drinks are atrocious.'

'Wretched.' Lady Sun leans close to her sunzi. 'I've set the fuel. Now you touch the fire.'

The Mackenzies of Kingscourt will feast in this salon. Piñatas filled with gifts hang from the ceiling. The bar is set up. Here is the stage for the band. In a few days it will be Zhongqiu and girls in puffball skirts, guys in shoulder pads, asexuals in elegant gowns will drink dance drug make out in this room. Mackenzies will arrive from all across the moon over the coming days, pay their respects and come to the bar. Memories are short. The dead bury the dead.

Now Bryce Mackenzie plots. He has summoned four Mackenzie Metals executives. They have power, experience, authority. They are all male. Twenty levels below, Robert Mackenzie's memorial performs its convolutions of respect and hypocrisy.

'You're here because I know and trust you,' Bryce Mackenzie asks. 'I've firm bids on our L5 helium-3 reserve.' Bryce maintains a stash in the gravitational limbo of the L5 libration point, hedging against price movements.

'How much?' says Alfonso Pereztrejo, Mackenzie Fusible Head of Finance.

'All of it.'

'It will force the price down,' Alfonso Pereztrejo warns.

'That's what I'm hoping,' Bryce Mackenzie says. 'I don't want terrestrial helium-3 extraction profitable. We are in no shape to take on competition. Output is still only at thirty per cent.'

'Fecunditatis, Crisium and Mare Anguis are still unproductive,' Jaime Hernandez-Mackenzie says. He is Mackenzie Metals' Head of Operations, a veteran jackaroo, lungs half turned to stone from decades of dust. Rare earths, helium, organics, water; he can take the moon in his hands and wring profit from it. 'The old Corta

Hélio heartland. There's evidence of sabotage. Those Brazilians hold grudges.'

'Then I want João de Deus tamed,' Bryce Mackenzie says. 'Whatever it takes. I want MH back at full production in two lunes.'

'MH?' says Rowan Solveig-Mackenzie. He is Mackenzie Metals' chief analyst; young and clever and ambitious; a model of the capitalist virtues.

'My father is dead,' Bryce Mackenzie says. 'Mackenzie Metals – the Mackenzie Metals my father built, the one we knew – is dead. The age of the family corporation is over. Metals are done. We are a helium company now.'

'The succession is settled, then,' Rowan Solveig-Mackenzie says dryly.

'If we wait for the lawyers, this company is fucked,' Bryce says.

'With respect, if the succession is not settled, we can't refinance,' Dembo Amaechi says. He is Head of Corporate Security; the quiet one, the one who has not spoken so far. 'There is no authority to make contracts.'

'I have finance,' Bryce says. 'Sun Zhiyuan has talked to me already.'

'Outside money,' Jaime says.

'Bryce, your father never ...' Dembo says.

'Least of all from the Suns,' Rowan adds.

'Fuck my father,' Bryce explodes. He quivers with frustrated passion. 'MH. Mackenzie Helium. Are you in or out?'

'Before we start filing contracts,' Dembo Amaechi says 'I have information on the mirror malfunction.'

No one misses the weight he lades on the word *malfunction*.

'We were hacked,' Dembo says.

'Obviously,' Bryce Mackenzie says.

'It was a clever piece of code. It integrated itself into our operating system, masked itself from our security, updated when we updated.'

'And you want to get into bed with the Suns?' Jaime shouts at Bryce. 'This has Taiyang written all over it.'

'There's the unusual thing,' Dembo says. 'It'd been there for a long time. Sitting. Waiting.'

'How long?' Bryce Mackenzie asks.

'Thirty, thirty-five years.'

'East Procellarum,' Bryce Mackenzie whispers.

Bryce had been eight when the Cortas struck Crucible. Duncan had grown among the heat and ugliness of Hadley, Bryce the intrigues and politicking of Kingscourt. Robert Mackenzie's policy was to keep the heirs separate. No one catastrophe could decapitate Mackenzie Metals. One day his mother Alyssa said, *It's ready. We're going to a new home.* The train ride from Queen was long, the one from Meridian longer, but when his mother called him to the window of the railcar he saw the burning star on the horizon and knew emotions he had never experienced before. Awe and fear. His family – his father – could hook a star out of the sky and shackle it to the moon. This was power beyond an eight-year-old's conceiving. He stared up at the rows of mirrors, filled with captured sun. Everything new, print-fresh, smelling of plastics and organics. New rover smell, a whole city of it. *I'm going to live there, in the greatest machine in the universe.*

Then the Cortas struck, cut the rail before and behind. Bryce watched the sun set on the crucible of eternal light and felt two new emotions: affront and humiliation. The Cortas had defiled a purity and beauty beyond them. They could never attain such power and wonder and so had struck in pettiness and envy. Unlike his brother, Bryce had never known a world free from the shadow of the Cortas. Unlike his brother, Bryce was an ungainly boy, dyspraxic and uncoordinated, poor at the sports his father and uncles adored, but from his earliest days in the growing spire of Kingscourt he took an interest in his family's business. By the age of seven he understood the principles of rare earth extraction, refining and marketing. Crucible was an extension of himself, a third hand. His pain at its shaming was physical.

Thirty-five years the code had hidden inside Crucible's AI, growing it, adapting, expanding.

'Our initial findings are that it was remotely triggered,' Dembo says.

'A Corta,' Bryce Mackenzie says. 'We should have exterminated them down to the last child.'

'We're businessmen, not blades,' Rowan says. 'The Cortas are three kids, one of those so-called werewolves and a washed up ex-lawyer. So, the Cortas destroy our home. We go one better: we take their machines, their markets, their city, their people, every thing they owned and held precious and in five years no one will remember the name of Corta. Remember what your father always said, Bryce? "Monopolies are terrible things".'

' "Until you have one",' Bryce answers.

Robson wakes screaming. His face, there is something over his face, he can't raise his hands to push it away from him. Hard, unyielding surfaces on every side of him. And the knock knock knocking, knock knock knocking. He's dead, in a silo. Awaiting reprocessing. The knock knock knocking is the Zabbaleen, rolling his casket over the joints in a corridor floor. With their knives they'll cut out everything useful; then the bots will hang him up in the kiln and dry every last drop of water out of him and suck it up with their tube-mouths. Then they will take the leaf and leather that is left and drop it into the grinding mills. And he can't move can't speak can't do anything to stop them.

'Robson.'

Light. Robson blinks. He knows where he is now, in a sleeping capsule in a dormitory at VTO Lansberg.

'Robson.' A face in the light. Hoang. 'You're okay, Robson. It's me. Can you move? You need to move.'

Robson grabs the handles and heaves himself out of the capsule.

The dormitory is a rack of capsules, ladders, cables. Hot beds and sleep pods warm with body odour.

'What time is it?' Robson is still stupid from clinging nightmares.

'Oh four,' Hoang says. 'It doesn't matter. Robson, we have to go.'

'What?'

'We have to go. Bryce thinks your people destroyed Crucible.'

'My people what?'

Hoang reaches inside the capsule and pulls a wad of crumpled clothing out of the netting. Robson's Marco Carlotta suit.

'Get dressed. The solar furnaces were hacked. It looks like Corta Hélio code.'

Robson pulls on the suit. It smells almost as bad as he does. He ducks into the capsule and slips his half-deck of cards into the pocket closest to his heart.

'Corta code?

'No time.' Hoang touches forefinger to forehead. *Familiars off.* 'Come on.'

Lansberg Station jostles with bodies and baggage. Track teams from Meridian and Queen and the great VTO marshalling yard at St Olga exchange places on the trains with Ironfall survivors.

'I've booked you to Meridian but you're not getting off there,' Hoang says, steering Robson towards the locks. 'You get off at Sömmering. It's a VTO place, like this. Someone will meet you.'

'Why not Meridian?'

'Because Bryce will have blades meeting every train.'

Robson stops dead.

'Bryce can't kill me. I'm a Mackenzie.'

'To Bryce, you're the closest Corta. And he won't kill you. Not until he's had his pleasure. You'll want to die long before then. Come with me.' Hoang extends a hand. VTO track-queens barge past, sasuits in heavy backpacks, helmets under their arms.

'Last time I ran away from Bryce...' Robson says.

He didn't see his mother die. *Don't look back*, she said. *Whatever happens, do not look back.* He was the good son and so he didn't see the bot, the blades that severed his mother's hamstrings, the drills whining through her helmet visor. *Launch it, Cameny. Get him out of here.* Her last words. Still he didn't look back. The BALTRAN capsule sealed, he grabbed for straps and then acceleration smeared out every drop of blood in his body. He went dark. Free fall. He fought nausea. Throw up in your helmet in free fall and you are dead. Then deceleration as brutal as the launch. The whole thing again. And again. And again. Grateful for the shock, the pain, the sickness and the discipline to control it because they clothed the truth that she was dead. His mama was dead.

'Stay close, Robson.' Hoang pushes into the crowd disembarking from the boarding locks, pushes through. An announcement, barely audible over the roar of the crowd. Something thirty-seven. All stops. All stops.

'What about you?' Robson says to Hoang.

'I'm taking a later train.'

Hoang scoops Robson up in an embrace as great as the sky. Cheek to cheek.

'You're crying,' Robson says.

'Yes. I have always loved you, Robson Corta.'

Then Hoang shoves Robson into the lock.

'Who's meeting me?' Robson shouts back as the lock cycles him on to the train.

'Your uncle!' Hoang yells. 'The wolf!'

3: ARIES 2103 - GEMINI 2105

The cleaning bot found him collapsed in the corridor of the outer-most, Earth-gravity ring, three metres from the elevator door.

'Five minutes longer and you would have asphyxiated under your own bodyweight,' Dr Volikova said as she accompanied Lucas Corta's crash bed up through the half-gravity intermediate ring to the lunar levels.

'I had to feel it.'

'And how does it feel?'

Like every muscle weak and melting. Every joint lined with ground glass. The hollow of every bone filled with molten lead. Every breath iron in lungs of stone. Every heartbeat on fire. The elevator had taken him down a well of pain. He could barely lift his arms from the handrails. The doors opened onto the gentle curve of the g-ring. A hill of agony. He had to step out. On the second step he felt his hips swivel. The fifth and his knees buckled, unable to hold him up. Centrifugal gravity pinned him to the wheel, breaking him breath by breath. Gravity was a harsh master. Gravity would never weaken, never stop, never relent. He tried to push himself up from the floor. He could feel the blood pooling in his hands, his face, swelling his cheek where it lay against the floor.

'We talked about hypotheticals,' Lucas Corta said as his crash bed docked with the AI. Diagnostic arms unfolded 'I want to talk practicalities. I am a practical man. You said it would take fourteen months to prepare for Earth conditions. In fourteen months I will take a shuttle down to Earth. My passage is booked. In fourteen months I will be on that ship, doctor, with or without you.'

'Do not blackmail me, Lucas.'

His first name. A small victory.

'I already have, doctor. You are VTO's pre-eminent expert on micro-gravity medicine. If you say it's hypothetically possible, then it's physically possible, Galina Ivanovna.' Lucas had memorised the doctor's first name and patronymic the moment she introduced herself as his personal physician, at the foot of this bed.

'And don't flatter me,' Dr Volikova said. 'You are physiologically different from terrestrial humans in a thousand different ways. Effectively, you're an alien.'

'I need three months on Earth. Four would be better. Give me a training scheme and I will follow it religiously. I have to go, Galina Ivanovna. Why should anyone agree to help me take my company back if I'm not prepared to sacrifice?'

'It will be harder than anything you have ever attempted before.'

Harder than my brothers dead, my city burned, my family shattered? Lucas Corta thought.

'I can't promise success,' Dr Volikova added.

'I don't ask that. This is my responsibility. Will you help me, Galina Ivanovna?'

'I will.'

The bed's diagnostic arms moved towards Lucas's neck and arm. He raised slow, leaden hands to fend them off but the manipulators were quick, the pain of injections swift and sharp and clean.

'What was that?'

'Another abuse of my profession,' Dr Volikova said, reading Lucas's physiology from lens. 'Something to get you going. You have an appointment.'

Light burned along Lucas's Corta arteries into his brain. He came up off the bed as if it were electrified. His feet hit the deck. He was in no pain. No pain at all.

'I will need a suit printed,' Lucas Corta declared.

'You're properly dressed,' Dr Volikova said.

'Shorts and a T-shirt,' Lucas Corta said with leaden disdain.

'You'll be better dressed than your host. Valery Vorontsov has an idiosyncratic sense of fashion.'

You'll need these, the elevator crew said. *Practise. It's not as easy as it looks.*

Lucas Corta pulled on the webbed socks and gloves. He pawed air, trod air. Vorontsovs. Always that sneer at the incompetence and inability of people trapped on worlds. Lucas was sick of being the incompetent man. He launched himself from the elevator into the hub. Even lunar leg muscles were too strong for the fractional gravity of the core. Lucas spread his hands, caught air in the webbing, paddled backwards against his direction of flight. He flexed his toes and spread his flippers as an air brake. This was easy. Instinctual. He came to a rest in the centre of the cylinder. The ship's axis of rotation. Zero gee. Lucas spun slowly, a human star.

He kicked and pushed at air. He wasn't moving. He convulsed his entire body as if the power of spasm alone might break him free from the gravity trap. Lucas could hear laughter from the elevator door. He convulsed again. Nothing. Lithe figures in fluorescents dived sleekly towards him from the further lock. Two young women in tight flight suits, hair carefully netted, bracketed Lucas and came to abrupt stops.

'Do you need any help, Senhor Corta?'

'I can get this.'

'Hold this line, Senhor Corta.'

The woman in the pink suit fastened the line to her work belt and plunged away. The snap of the line almost tugged it from Lucas's grasp. He was moving. He was flying. He could feel air on his face, in his hair. It was thrilling. The second ship-girl swam beside him. He noticed the vacuum cleaner on her belt.

In the lock to Valery Vorontsov's private chamber he thanked the young women for the exciting ride.

'Mind the branches,' was their only advice.

Valery Vorontsov's audience chamber at the heart of *Saints Peter and Paul* was a cylindrical forest. Lucas floated in a tunnel of twigs and leaves. He could not see the walls, so densely packed were the branches. Down there must be trunks, roots, the aeroponics that sustained this free-fall forest. The humidity, the notes of growth and rot were familiar to Lucas – the intimate perfume of Twé – but there were new notes he only recognised from his bespoke gins: juniper, pine, florals and botanicals. The forest was lit from deep among the roots, but the trees were adorned with thousands of bio lamps. Stars above, stars on either hand, stars below. It took a few seconds for Lucas to acclimatise to the gloaming, then he saw that the leaf canopy had been sculpted into undulations and spirals, crests and waves. A tree scape. Occasional solitary branches lifted above the topiary, trained and gnarled, holding a precisely trimmed raft of leaves like an offering. Lucas's eyes adapted fully to the light and he saw a figure at the centre of the free-fall forest. Something glimpsed, half hidden by the leaves, slow moving, deliberate.

A line ran along the centre of the cylinder. Lucas hauled himself toward the figure. A man – no, he realised as he drew closer: a thing like a man. That had once been a man. His back was to Lucas, he worked diligently on the foliage with hand-held shears, clipping, snipping, shaping. A halo of conifer trimmings surrounded him. Lucas smelled fresh taints among the resin and leaf: urine. Fungal infections.

'Valery Grigorivitch.'

The man-like thing turned to confront the interruption. A life in micro gee had shaped his body as surely and irrevocably as he had shaped his forest. His legs were twisted spindles; ribbons of withered muscle. His chest was heroic in width and girth but Lucas could see from the way it filled the compression shirt that there was no depth, no strength in it. Ribs stretched the tight material. The breast bone was sharp as a blade. His arms were long and wire-sinewed. His head was enormous, a human face annealed to a skin balloon. A frieze of silver hair around the base of the skull only emphasised its size. A double tube ran from the occipital bones to a free-floating pump. A second set of tubes ran from his left flank to a cluster of full colostomy bags, turning in the zero gee.

This was what half a century in micro-gee did to a human body.

'Lucas Corta.'

'An honour, sir.'

'Is it? Is it?' Valery Vorontsov took a vacuum cleaner from his tool belt and with the deftness of decades sucked up the floating tree clippings. 'I've never met another Dragon. Did you know that?'

'No longer a Dragon, sir.'

'I heard that. Nonsense, of course. It's in the genes. This is a novelty for me. And for you.'

'Valery Grigorivitch, I need to ask...'

'Oh, hold your hideous asking. I know what you want. We'll see if the universe lets you have it. But that's the thing, isn't it? Always asking questions of the universe. Lucas Corta, have you ever seen such a thing as this?'

Valery Vorontsov waved his shears at the starlit forest.

'I don't think anyone has, sir.'

'They haven't. Do you know what this is? It's a question I asked the universe. How would a forest grow in the sky? That's a question to ask. Here is the answer. It never stops growing, never stops changing. I work on it; I shape it to my will. It's slow sculpture. It will outlast me. I like that. We are such self-absorbed creatures. We think ourselves the measure of everything. Time will take away everything we are, everything we have, everything we will ever build. It's good to think beyond our own lifetimes. Maybe my forest will last a million years, maybe a billion. Maybe it will end in fire when the sun burns. When I die my elements will pass into root and branch and leaf. I will become one with it. That gives me great comfort.'

Valery Vorontsov unhooked the collection bag from the vacuum and sent it flying down-cylinder. A Zabbaleen bot darted from the foliage to snatch the refuse and shepherd it to the lock.

'My mother was a supporter of the Sisterhood of the Lords of Now,' Lucas said. 'Their mission is worked out over decades, centuries even.'

'I am aware of the work of the Sisterhood. You're not a believer, Lucas Corta?'

'It involves supernatural agency. It's impossible for me to believe it.'

'Hm. I hear you want to go to earth. That's a desire, not a question. The universe does not owe us our desires, but it may grant a good question. What is your question?'

'How can I take back what was stolen from my family?'

'Hm.' Valery Vorontsov broke off a branch tip, sniffed it, offered it to Lucas. 'What do you think of that? That's real juniper. All you've ever smelled is synthetic. Those Asamoahs, I know what they can do. They play with DNA. They swap genes around. Childish. I create an environment and let life respond to it. I grow real juniper in the most artificial environment humanity has ever created. No no no, Lucas Corta, that question will not do at all. The right question is, *how* can a moon-born man go to Earth and survive?'

'Dr Volikova is developing a training scheme for me.'

'If the re-entry doesn't kill you. If your heart doesn't give out in the acclimatisation suite. If you don't die of sunburn. If a million allergies don't swell you up like a colostomy bag. If terrestrial gut bacteria doesn't turn you inside out. If the pollution doesn't tear out your soft little lungs. If you can sleep down in that gravity hole without apnoea waking you every five minutes; between the nightmares.'

'If we listened to ifs, we wouldn't be dragons,' Lucas said. The two men had subtly, unconsciously matched orientations to float face to face.

'As you said, you're not a dragon any more. You'll be less than that on Earth. The Moon is not a state. The Moon is an offshore industrial outpost. You'll have no papers, no nation, no identity. You will have no legal existence. You won't know the rules, the customs, the laws. There are laws. They will apply to you but you'll know nothing about how they work. They are like gravity. You are subject to them. You can't negotiate with them. You have no power to negotiate.

'No one will know who you are. No one will care that you're the man from the moon. You're a freak, a ten day wonder. No one will respect you. No one will take you seriously. No one needs anything from you. No one wants what you have. You're an intelligent man. You worked this out while you were still in the capsule. And yet I find you here, with your plan and the favours you need from me and whatever it is you have that you believe can persuade me to grant them to you.'

Each of Valery Vorontsov's refutations was a nail through a finger, through a foot, through a hand and a knee and a shoulder. Mortifications. Lucas Corta had never understood guilt or remorse. Pride was his virtue. Pride tugged against those nails, tore him free from them. Their pain was nothing to what he had lost.

'I can't argue with you, Valery Grigorivitch. I have nothing to offer and nothing to bargain with. I will need your support, your ships, your mass-driver and all I can do is talk.'

'The universe is full of talk. Talk and hydrogen.'

'The Asamoahs think you're inbred monstrosities. The Mackenzies marry you for shipping rights but they engineer your DNA out of their children. My own family thought you were drunken clowns. The Suns don't think you're even human.'

'We don't need respect.'

'Respect buys no air. I'm offering something more tangible.'

'You have a thing to offer? Lucas Corta, who has lost his business, his family, his wealth and his name?'

'Empire.'

'Let's have your talk, Lucas Corta.'

'All the way?' Dr Volikova said.

'All the way,' Lucas Corta said. The corridor curved steeply upwards before him. The ceiling was a low, close horizon. 'Walk with me.'

Dr Volikova offered an arm. Lucas pushed it away.

'You shouldn't even be on your feet, Lucas.'

'Walk *with* me.'

'All the way.'

'I am a systematic man,' Lucas Corta said. Even in the lunar gravity of the inmost ring, each step sent wrenching pain from his ankles to his throat. 'I have very little imagination. I must have a plan. A child walks before she runs. I walk the lunar ring, I run the lunar ring. I walk the intermediate ring, I run the intermediate ring. I walk the terrestrial ring, I run the terrestrial ring.'

Lucas's steps were sure and purposeful now. Dr Volikova was a touch away. Lucas noticed a betraying flicker in her eyes. She was reading data from a lens.

'Are you monitoring me, Irina Galinova?'

'Always, Lucas.'

'And?'

'Walk on.'

Lucas bit down his smile of small victory.

'Did you listen to that playlist?' he asked.

'I did.'

'What did you think of it?'

'It's more sophisticated than I thought.'

'You didn't say it sounds like mall music. I'm hopeful.'

'I hear the nostalgia, but I don't quite understand the saudade.'

'Saudade is more than nostalgia. It's a kind of love. It's a loss and a joy. An intense melancholy and joy.'

'I should think you would understand that well, Lucas.'

'One can have saudade for a future event.'

'You never give up, do you?'

'No I don't, Galina Ivanovna.'

His joints were loosening, the pain easing, the stiffness working free.

'Your heart rate and blood pressure are up, Lucas.'

He looked up the curving corridor.

'I'm going to finish this.'

'Okay.'

Another small win.

Lucas stopped.

On again, up the curve of the world. Lucas's lungs were tight, his breath caught, his heart ached as if seized in a fist. Twenty metres ten metres five metres to the door to the med centre. Finish it. Finish it.

'It's customary,' Lucas panted. His words were brief, tight gasps. He leaned against the door lintel and looked back up the curving corridor. 'When offered. A playlist.' He could barely speak. A hundred metres under his own native lunar gravity, and he was clinging, gasping, aching. The damage was deeper than he had imagined. Fourteen lunes of intensive training seemed insurmountable. 'To offer a playlist. Of your own in return.'

'The Bill Evans?' Dr Volikova said.

'And more in that style. I believe it's called modal jazz. Curate it for me. Take me on a journey through jazzland. I'll need something to get me through the training.'

He woke in his capsule, flicked the lights on. Creakings and rattlings. The sleep pod was shaking. The ship was shaking. The pod lurched. Lucas grasped the hand rails, gripped tight, tighter until his nails dug into his palm. The pod lurched again. Lucas cried out. He felt the world drop beneath him. There was nothing to hold on to. And this was no world. This was a ship, a spinning top of aluminium and construction carbon. He was a man in a pod in a wheel in a tiny ship out beyond the far side of the moon.

'Toquinho,' he whispered. 'What's happening?'

The ship dropped under him again. Lucas gripped the solid, useless hand rails. The voice in his implant was unfamiliar, strangely accented. *Saints Peter and Paul* was too small to run a full network.

I'm making a series of course correction burns, Toquinho said. *My orbit is stable and predictable up to eleven years. Small periodic corrections every ten or so orbits push that window of predictability forward. These occur around the second perilune in a two-encounter orbit. The process is fully controlled and quite routine. I can supply schematics if you wish.*

'That won't be necessary,' Lucas said and the shaking, the jolting, the terrible terrible feeling of falling into nothing forever ended. *Saints Peter and Paul* spun around the moon and the moon threw it towards the blue gem of earth.

Toquinho chimed. Files from Dr Volikova. Lucas opened them. Music: lunes-worth. A journey.

In the first three lunes Lucas explored hard bop; its language and instrumentality, its identity and tonality, its triadic harmonies and plagal cadences. He learned the names of its heroes. Mingus, Davis, Monk and Blakey: these were his apostles. He studied the key recordings, its Gospels and Acts. He learned how to listen, what to listen for, when to listen for it. He traced its roots in bebop and how it both revolted against that movement and sought to reform it. He ventured into heterodox realms where the distinctions between funky jazz and soul jazz and the divorce between west coast cool jazz and east coast hard bop became schisms in the musical cosmos. It was the worst possible music to train to. Lucas loved it. He despised training. It was difficult and boring. Carlinhos had evangelised muscle burns and dopamine highs and hormonal stress releasers. What lifted Carlinhos into the transcendental made Lucas paranoid and furious.

He came out of the gym blazing with rage, snappy with anyone who so much as glanced at him, went to bed aching and edgy and dreading the next day's routine. Five hours. Six truths sent him back in the gym, Art Blakey on play. Carlinhos and his endorphins was dead. Rafa was dead. Ariel was in hiding. Lucasinho was under the protection of AKA. Boa Vista was an airless ruin and this ship, *Saints Peter and Paul*, was carrying stolen Corta helium-3 containers to the fusion reactors of Earth. So he trained. Hard bop was a place beyond the endless track of the treadmill, the ticked-off repetitions of weights, the indignities of toning. Hard bop was a time beyond the tick of days tocking into lunes. A year of this routine was endless; it must be broken down into a succession, not of sessions, sleeps, days, orbits, but of acts. A thing conceived, begun, worked through, completed. Then another. Then another. Quantised. The year-and-some would be measured not by the gradient of ever-heavier weights, ever better personal bests, nor the growing strength and resilience of his body, but by quanta of new music. After hard bop he would learn modal jazz, then move through free jazz to Afro-Cuban and Brazilian jazz which would circle back into his adored bossa nova. The next time he would listen to bossa nova, his feet would be on earth under an open sky. But in those first few orbits hard bop was a high, clear horizon; further and wider than any of the moon.

After half a lune he ran the inmost ring. All the way. After a lune he walked the intermediate ring, half an Earth gee, three lunar gravities. He walked without aid or support or pause and it took him an hour to complete. After two lunes he ran the mezzanine ring. After three lunes, Lucas Corta slept there. The first night he felt a brass demon crouch on his chest and shit molten lead into his heart and lungs. The second night, the third the fourth. After fifteen nights he slept a full night with only nightmares of being trapped beneath the iron ice of a steel sea. After that he slept in three lunar gravities every night.

The second three lunes Lucas Corta explored modal jazz – Dr Volikova's passion. His steps into the music were more certain; he had glimpsed this terrain from another country and knew where its ranges stood, where its river flowed. Geographical metaphors had meaning for him now, for the progression to modal jazz accompanied Lucas turning his attention to Earth. Here was a subject to contain a lifetime. Geography, geology, geophysics. Oceanography, climatology and their daughter meteorology. The interrelationships of water, heat, spin, thermodynamics and the beautiful and chaotic systems spun out from such basic elements enchanted him. Rich, unpredictable, perilous. He loved to read the meteorological reports and see their predictions drawn out in white and grey across the blue eye of the planet before him. Lucas Corta was an avid Earth watcher. He observed storms and hurricanes wheel across oceans; dun plains change to green as rains swept them, deserts darken in blossom, marshes and sundarbans vanish under twinkling floods. He watched seasons creep out from the poles as he cycled around the planet, lune by lune. He watched snow come and snow retreat and the rich darkness of the monsoon spread across parched millions.

One thing he would not watch, and that was the Earth encounter, when the cycler exchanged personnel capsules with the orbital tether and dropped cargo pods for controlled splashdown. In his cabin he felt the shudder of capsules and attachments releasing, the jolt of transfer pods docking but he would never join the spectators in the observation bubble. He would not grace plunder with his attention. He never once looked back at the moon.

Early in the year of orbits Dr Volikova was transferred to Earth on leave to St Petersburg. Her replacement was Yevgeny Chesnokov, a cocksure thirtysomething who could not understand why Lucas disdained him. He was over-familiar, his manners would have had him knifed in any cafe in João de Deus and his taste in music was execrable. Beats did not make music. Beats were easy. Even Toquinho, in its limited state, could invent a new beat. Lucas had grown accustomed to the new, flat character of his familiar. One ship, one voice, one interface. If Toquinho now talked of itself as *Saints Peter and Paul* personified, its hesitations and pauses made that sound less than omniscient. The speed-of-light lag made real-time access to Earth's libraries difficult but the cycler's system held enough information for Lucas to structure his research. He let his geophysical and climatological knowledge of the planet lead him into the geopolitical. Earth was undergoing a climate shift; it underpinned every aspect of the planet's politics, from decades-deep drought in the Sahel and Western USA to the perpetual storms striking north-west Europe, flood after flood after flood. Lucas could not understand the folly of living on a world that was not under human control.

He learned the power of the helium that had built his family's fortune. Clean electricity, no radiation, no carbon emissions. Tightly controlled. Fusion reactors were few and expensive. Each nation guarded its power plants viciously – against other nation states, against the unconventional forces of the parastates and freedom armies and warlords dislodged by the droughts, the crop failures, the famines, the civil wars. At any time in the past fifty years, Lucas read, there were over two hundred micro-wars burning on the face of the earth. He studied long to try to comprehend nation states and the many many allegiance groups that challenged them. The moon survived by denying power to groups and factions. There were individuals and there were families. The Five Dragons – Four Dragons, he corrected himself, feeling that pinch of pain as a discipline to sentimentality – were family corporations. The Lunar Development Corporation was an ineffectual board of governors of an international holding company; designed to be at permanent loggerheads with itself.

States, with identities and sets of privileges and obligations and geographical boundaries where those stopped, seemed arbitrary and inefficient to Lucas Corta. The notion of being loyal to one bank of a river and the bitter enemy of the other was ludicrous. Rivers, Lucas Corta had learned, ran between banks. And there was no consent in any of this. Lucas could not understand how people tolerated their powerlessness. The law claimed to defend and oppress all equally but a cursory survey of the rolling news – Lucas had become an avid consumer of terrestrial current affairs, from religious wars to celebrity gossip – bared the old lie. Wealth and power bought a brighter class of law. Not so different from the moon in that. Lucas was no lawyer but he understood that lunar law stood on three legs: more law is bad law; everything, including the law, is negotiable; and in the Court of Clavius everything, including the Court of Clavius, is on trial. Terrestrial law protected the people but what protected the people from the law? Everything was imposed. Nothing was negotiable. Governments imposed blanket policies on the basis of ideologies, not evidence. How did these governments propose to compensate those citizens negatively impacted by their policies? Riddles wrapped in mysteries inside enigmas.

These things Lucas asked Dr Chesnokov at the timetabled check-ups where he reviewed the data from Lucas's many medical monitors. You love CSKA Moscow Football team and you love Russia. Which is the greater of those loves? You pay taxes, but the law doesn't allow you any say in how they are spent, let alone the option to withhold them when you want to influence Government policy. How is this a good contract? Education, the legal system, the military and the police are all under the control of the state; health and transport are not. How is that a consistent position for a capitalist society? Dr Chesnokov went quiet when Lucas asked him questions about his government and its politics, almost as if he feared being overheard.

In time Dr Chesnokov cycled down and Dr Volikova cycled back for another tour of duty. She started at the sight of Lucas Corta in her office.

'You're a beast,' she said. 'A bear.'

He had forgotten how much he had changed in the two lunes she had been down on Earth. He had broadened ten centimetres. His shoulders sloped to his neck. His chest was two slabs of hard muscle, his legs were curves and bulges. His thighs did not meet properly. Veins stood out like lunar rilles on his biceps and calves. Even his face was square and broad. He hated his new face. It made him look like a duster. It made him look stupid.

'Hate and Bill Evans got me there,' Lucas said. 'I want to walk the third ring.'

'I'll come with you.'

'No thank you, Galya.'

'Then I'll be monitoring you.'

A new gravity, a new music. In the elevator he ordered Toquinho to cue up a representative free jazz playlist. Instruments beat around his head, flurries and skirmishes of notes, horns and saxes sharpened and abrading. His mind reeled. Here were challenges. Ornette Coleman summoned storms of triplets and Lucas felt gravity take hold and tug and test and tear at his great, brutal body.

The elevator door opened. Lucas stepped out. Shocks of pain struck each ankle. His knee felt as if a rod of hot titanium had been stabbed up through it. Ligaments shifted and twisted and threatened to yield. He gritted his teeth. The chaotic music was the hand and voice of a mad guru. Move. Two steps three four steps five. There was a rhythm to be found to walking in earth gravity, not the loose-hipped swing of lunar motion; a lifting and pushing forward and laying down of weight. On the moon it would have sent him soaring. In the outer ring of *Saints Peter and Paul* it just about kept him from the decking. Ten steps twenty steps. He was already further than his first foolish attempt on Earth-gee. Now he could look back over his shoulder and see that point vanish behind the horizon of the ring. The cycler was on the outward curve of its orbit; the outermost ring was thronged with Jo Moonbeams and researchers at Farside and a handful of business visitors, corporate agents, politicians and tourists.

In a few days they would migrate up to the intermediate rim, then to the inner, lunar gee ring, where the spin and the low gravity and the effect of a new means of locomotion on the inner ear would flatten eighty per cent of them with motion sickness. They nodded to him as he strode past, arms swinging, face tight with determination. Steel bands compressed his swollen heart, blood pulsed red behind his eyes with every beat, his eyeballs felt as if they were sagging in their sockets.

He could do this. He was doing this. He would do this.

He could see the elevator doors up the curve of the ring. He calculated the number of steps. His heart surged with the small joy. Joy made him careless. The careful rhythm of his steps broke. He lost his balance. Gravity snatched him. Lucas hit the deck with a blow that drove every breath and thought from him except that he had never been hit so hard in his life. He lay paralysed by pain. He lay on his side, unable to move. Gravity pinned him to the deck. Earth people clustered around him. Was he all right? What had happened? He slapped away the helping hands.

'Leave me alone.'

A medical bot came skirling along the corridor. That humiliation he would not bear. He pushed his torso up on wavering arms. Drew his legs under him. The transition from crouch to stand seemed impossible. The muscles of his right thigh fluttered and he was not certain his knee would bear him. The red eye of the bot accused him.

'Fuck you,' he said and with a tearing pain that wrenched a cry from him, Lucas Corta got to his feet. The bot circled in behind him like an attention-seeking pet ferret. He would have loved to have kicked it away. Sometime, not this time. He took a step. Acid pain ran from his right foot to his right shoulder. He gasped.

The step was firm. It was only pain.

The bot tagged along in Lucas Corta's footsteps as he walked the final few dozen metres to the elevator.

'You were lucky not to break something,' Dr Volikova said. 'That might have been the end of it.'

'Bones heal.'

'Earth bones. Jo Moonbeam bones. There is no literature on moon-born bones, with Earth-type bone density.'

'You could do a paper on me.'

'I am,' Dr Volikova said.

'But my bone density is Earth-type.'

'Earth-type for a seventy-year-old suffering from osteoporosis. I'll have to up your calcium regime again.'

Lucas was already building a plan on the foundation of the words 'Earth-type'. Walk until his feet had the feel of it, his hips the sway of it. Walk more. Then walk three minutes, run one minute. Repeat until the pain was bearable. Walk two minutes, run two minutes. Walk one minute run three minutes. Run.

'How are you finding the free jazz?' Dr Volikova asked.

'It demands you come to it,' Lucas said. 'It doesn't compromise.'

'I can't approach it. Too much jazz for me.'

'You have to work to find the beauty.'

Lucas didn't like this music, but he did admire it. It was the ideal soundtrack for what he had to do now. The hard stuff. The stuff he did best, the stuff he had always done best, his one gift and talent. Scheming.

The governments would always be the most difficult so he worked them first. China of course, because it was China, and because of its long war against the Suns. The United States of America, for its wealth, its historic animosity to China and because no empire is quicker to defend its honour than a decaying one. Ghana. Not a major player, but it had seen what a handful of its bold citizens had built on the moon and wanted some. And Accra perennially wanted to one-up its larger and more powerful neighbour, Lagos. India, which had missed the moon-rush and still smarted from that failure. Russia, because of the deal he had done with VTO and because some day he might have to betray the Vorontsovs. To the governments of these nations the fall of Corta Hélio was a local fracas, only important in its effect on helium-3 prices. He would have to teach them to listen to him. There were channels, names to talk to who would give access to other names. Chains of names, the slow ascent of the political hierarchy. This would be difficult and entertaining. Ornette Coleman best sound-tracked this work.

While exploring the recording legacy of John Coltrane Lucas worked his way into the terrestrial corporates. Robotics, yes, but they were ten-a-bitsie and he wanted a business that understood his offer, in both short term and the long. Banking and venture capitalism: here he trod warily, for though he knew money and its ways he had never understood the frenetically complex instruments of finance and the ways they intersected in the global markets. These meetings were easier to set up, the people he talked to genuinely interested – delighted even – in the daring of the scheme. They would have researched him, known of his downfall. The destruction of Corta Hélio would have touched them. They would listen to a moon man prepared to give a year of his time and health to come down out of the sky to talk to them.

Every day, as the wheels of *Saints Peter and Paul* spun around the moon, he talked to power. Name by name he hauled his way into conferences and one-to-ones. In his berth he played off investors against speculators, government against government. Who to trust, and how much, and when to end it. Who to betray, and when, and how. Who was susceptible to bribery, who to blackmail. Whose vanity could he stroke, whose paranoia could he stoke? Meeting after meeting fell into place. He would need at least three lunes on Earth.

'I'd prefer four,' he said again to Dr Volikova. He was running the third circle every day now. He was a middle-aged man, past his prime, taking on a physical challenge that would give pause to a man half his age. That might yet kill him, or cripple him beyond even the power of lunar medicine to heal.

'You need another month,' Dr Volikova said. 'Preferably two.'

'I can't afford two. I remember I told you I would leave for earth after fourteen months. There's a window, one tiny window.'

'A month.'

'One terrestrial month from now, I take the orbiter down. And I will never get Ornette Coleman.'

The final month, as he had planned, he relaxed into Afro Cuban jazz. Here were sounds and rhythms warm to his heart, that made him smile. From here he could reach out and catch hold of the hand of bossa nova. He enjoyed the insouciance of the play-listed tunes but soon found the rhythm too prescriptive, too forward. When he exercised in the outer ring gym it forced him to its beat, which he hated. It seemed too frivolous for the work which engaged his last days: his own identity and security. Valery Vorontsov had made him an employee of VTO Space: VTO Earth's judicious bribes had secured him a Kazakh passport. What little remained of his wealth was moved into forms he could access quickly and easily. Earth was suspicious of money in motion. At every step there were checks, questions, enquiries about money laundering. Lucas was affronted. He was not some petty narc baron or graceless minor despot. All he desired was his company back. Niggling, irritating work that was never done but always seemed to require some further identification or clarification.

'My mother came up on this ship,' Lucas said to Dr Volikova at his final pre-flight assessment.

'Fifty years ago,' Dr Volikova said. 'It's changed a lot since then.'

'It's just additions. Re-engineering. You haven't got rid of anything.'

'What do you want, Lucas?'

'I'd like to sleep in the same berth as my mother.'

'I won't even begin to go into the psychiatry of that.'

'Humour me.'

'It won't be the same.'

'I know. Humour me.'

'There will be a record somewhere. The Vorontsovs never forget.'

Ring three, blue quadrant, 34 right. Dr Volikova opened the private cabin. It was little bigger than the pod in which Lucas had arrived on the cycler. He pulled himself into it, lay in his clothes on the pad, for the struggle in taking them off was too much for now. The pad was soft and supportive, the cabin well-equipped and at every moment the only thing he was conscious of was gravity. Months of this to come. On the ship he could escape to the centre ring, even the inner, moon-gee ring when gravity grew too much to bear. There would be no escape on Earth. That scared him. The pod was close and comfortable. Lucas was a creature of small spaces, nests and chambers; he had lived his whole life closed in under roofs. That world down there had a sky. Open to space. Agoraphobia scared him. Everything scared him. He wasn't ready. He would never be ready. No one could be ready. All he could do was trust the talents that had brought him here, that had saved him from the fall of Corta Hélio.

That would be enough.

Before he fell into hard sleep, he recalled the faces. Lucasinho. So pretty, so lost. Ariel, in the crash bed in the med centre, after a blade came within a nerve of killing her. Carlinhos at Lucasinho's Moonrun party, big and broad as the sky and smiling as he strode across the lawns, sasuit helmet under his arm. Rafa. Golden, always golden. Laughing. His children around him, his okos at his side; laughing. Adriana. Lucas could only picture her at a distance, in the doorway of the crèche, in her favourite pavilion among the stone faces of the orixas of Boa Vista, at the other end of a board table.

He slept then, and for the next four nights, in the old cabin. His dreams were heavy, sweat drains, scream dreams. They always would be, under alien gravity.

On the fifth morning, he went down to Earth.

*

The lock crew balked at his tie. It would float, it would choke him, it would be a hazard to others. Lucas drew the knot sharp and tight until it was a knife tip at his throat, in the late twenty-tens style. Three piece single breasted Thom Sweeney suit in mid grey. Narrow cut, three centimetre turn-ups.

'I'm not arriving on Earth like some Bairro Alto up-and-out,' he declared. He undid the bottom button of his waistcoat.

'You will if you throw up all over it.'

The lock sealed. It seemed to take an age for the pressure to equalise with the transfer capsule. Dread beat in Lucas's ribcage. The suit had been a distraction, a way to assert himself against the dread. A way to be Lucas Corta again. Thirteen lunes between worlds – one less than he had budgeted – thirteen lunes of geopolitics and global economics, of deal brokering and precisely manipulated bribes, of discerning and exploiting antagonisms, of relentless training, had focused down to this. The tip of the blade. Ship to capsule. Capsule to tether. Tether to SSTO. SSTO to Earth. In less than four hours it would be over. There was no consolation in that.

The lock opened. Lucas seized a handhold and kicked into the capsule.

Farewell indignity, functional clothing and mid 20th Century jazz.

The transfer capsule was a twenty-metre cylinder, windowless, completely automated. Ten rows of seats. Dr Volikova grabbed a handle and buckled in beside him.

'You'll need your physician.'

'Thank you.'

Five more passengers, then the lock sealed. Always fewer going down than coming up. Safety announcements, either superfluous or ineffectual. Toquinho, linked to the capsule AI, offered Lucas views through the exterior cameras. He took one look at the blue world huge beneath him and switched them off. He cued up a long-curated play list of classic bossa. Tunes he knew, tunes he loved, tunes he had asked Jorge to play for him, in the best sound room in two worlds.

A series of bangs; lurches. Silence. The capsule was free from *Saints Peter and Paul*, a pellet of lives falling across the face of the blue world. He had studied this. He knew how it worked. It was all controlled falling. He asked Toquinho to show him a model of the transfer tether wheeling around the limb of the planet. The schematics comforted him.

Lucas had drifted into a doze when he was woken by a clank he could feel through the hull. The tether had connected. The floor dropped out of his stomach, gee forces took hold as the tether accelerated the capsule into a docking orbit with the SSTO. Lucas had made a tether transfer once before, escaping from the moon, when the Moonloop had snatched him from the top of the tower and slung him into a transfer orbit with the cycler. Acceleration had peaked at three, four lunar gravities. This was far beyond the Moonloop. Lucas felt his lips peel back from his teeth, his eyes flatten in their sockets, the blood pool in the back of his skull. He couldn't breathe.

Then he was in free fall again. The tether had released the capsule and now Lucas was falling towards rendezvous with the SSTO. Toquinho showed him the orbiter; an improbable beauty of wings and streamlines like a living thing, quite alien to Lucas's aesthetic of machines designed to operate solely in vacuum. The spaceplane opened its cargo hatches. Pulses from the attitude thrusters nudged the capsule. Lucas watched the manipulator arm unfold from the orbiter and latch with the docking ring. Lucas felt a tiny acceleration, as gentle as a domestic elevator, as the arm pulled him in. Space travel was tactile; clicks and thumps, soft jerks and brief jolts. Vibrations through his arm rests.

Lucas counted the numbers in his head. One hundred and fifty. The height of the SSTO orbit in kilometres. Thirty-seven. The number of minutes until de-orbit burn. Twenty-three. The number of minutes the ship would be in transit through the atmosphere. Fifteen hundred. The degrees Celsius which the ceramic hull of the orbiter would reach on re-entry. Three hundred and fifty. The speed in kilometres per hour at touch-down. Zero. The number of crew who could take the controls if anything went wrong.

The cabin shook, shook again, shook for a long time. The de-orbit burn. A fist of gravity seized Lucas's head and tried to pull him into the ceiling. The deceleration was savage. The ship jolted. Lucas Corta's fingers hooked the armrests but there was nothing to hold, nothing true and immovable. His heart wanted to die. He couldn't take this. He had been wrong all along. He had been a vainglorious fool. A moon-man could not go to Earth. The killing Earth. Cries of deepest fear fluttered in his throat, unable to break the crushing gravity.

The shaking intensified; bounds and skips that threw Lucas into momentary free fall and then slammed him against his restraints hard enough to leave bruises, then a high-frequency vibration as if the ship and souls were being grated into powder.

He found a hand and seized it so tight he felt bones shift in his grasp. He held that hand, held it as the only sure and solid thing in a shaking, roaring world.

Then the shaking stopped and he felt gravity, true gravity under him.

We are in atmospheric flight, Toquinho said.

'Show me,' Lucas croaked and the seat backs and warning signs of the grey capsule were overlain by a window. He was high enough to see the curve of the planet. It went on forever, subtle and vast as a life. The sky above him deepened to indigo. Beneath lay veil upon veil of cloud, merging into a dull yellow haze. He glimpsed dusty blue. *That is an ocean*, he thought. It was so much bigger, so much more grand and aloof than he had imagined. The SSTO arrowed down through the highest cloud layer. Lucas's breath caught. Land. A line of brown half-seen through cloud.

Lucas knew from his research that he was coming in across the coast of Peru, two thousand three hundred kilometres from touch-down. Beyond the brown of the coastal desert would appear the sudden dark of mountains; the spinal chain that ran the length of the continent. The Andes. Sun flashed from snow and Lucas Corta's heart surged. Beyond the mountains lay the remnants of the great forest; patches of deep green among the lighter greens and golds of crops and the swatches of buffs and duns where the soil had died. Those plumes, strangely low and truncated to his eyes, would be smoke, not dust. Towering clouds boiled up from the baking land. Below lay the final cloud layer. Lucas held his breath as the orbiter dropped toward, then through them. Grey, blind. The ship jolted. Holes in the air. Then out, and Lucas Corta's breath caught. Sun silver, then gold: the great river, yellow with silt. The SSTO followed the line of the river east, along a trellis of tributaries, tributaries of tributaries. Enchanted, Lucas tried to discern a pattern to the loops and meanders of the lesser waters. An alert from Toquinho, what had it said? He had not been paying attention. How many minutes to landing?

Another great river, black meeting gold, and at their junction, a blur of human activity. Thousands of sun-flashes as the shuttle passed over: a city, Lucas realised. His breath caught. A city, between the twin rivers, lidless, open to the universe, spilling across the earth. Huge beyond his imagining. Those webs of light when the clouds did not cover the Earth gave no hint as to the sprawl and appalling magnificence of the planet's cities.

The spaceplane banked. Lucas gritted his teeth as gee forces played with him. The SSTO was circling, dumping speed for landing. He could hear the air out there, like hands on the hull. He glimpsed the long strip where this ship would touch down, the city, banked at an alarming angle, the meeting of the rivers. Black and gold waters side by side without mingling for many kilometres. Lucas found the effect charming. He did not understand enough terrestrial hydrodynamics to know if the effect was commonplace or spectacular. What were those moving objects on the waters?

Ten minutes to landing, Toquinho said.

'Lucas,' Dr Volikova said.

'What?'

'You can let go of my hand now.'

Over the city and the rivers once more, lower now. The spaceplane levelled out. They were committed. The landing strip was straight and true before him. Luca felt the wheels go down and lock. The spaceplane lifted its nose and dropped solidly on to its rear wheels, a lesser shock as the nose came down.

Earth. He was on Earth.

Dr Volikova stayed Lucas's hand as he went to open his seat harness.

'We're not there yet.'

For what felt an aeon to Lucas Corta the SSTO rumbled over taxiways. He felt it stop. He could hear movements through the hull, feel inexplicable thumps and vibrations.

'How do you feel?' Dr Volikova asked.

'Alive,' Lucas Corta said.

'I've arranged for a medical team and a wheelchair.'

'I'm walking off this ship.'

Dr Volikova smiled and then Lucas felt the unmistakable lurch that meant a crane had lifted the capsule free from the orbiter.

'I'm still walking,' he said.

Lugs locked, locks spun. The hatch opened. Lucas blinked in the light of Earth. He took a deep breath of the air of earth. It smelled of cleaning products, plastics, human bodies, ingrained dirt, electricity.

'Can I help you?' Dr Volikova called from the hatch. The other passengers had left, as casually as shift workers sauntering off the Peary-Aitken express.

'I'll let you know.'

'The clock is ticking, Lucas.'

When he was alone Lucas placed his hands square on the armrests. He took a breath of the breathed, cleaned air. He took his weight on his forearms, leaned forwards, pushed up. Thigh muscles took over: a crazy move. On the moon, it would have sent him soaring, crashing into an overhead bin. On the Earth, he stood. First the right hand, then the left. Lucas Corta let go of the arm rests and stood free. Only for a moment – the space was confined and he needed his hands to negotiate his way into the aisle. The weight was terrible, irresistible, relentless, waiting for him to lose balance and smash him down to earth. *Falls will kill you*, Dr Volikova had said.

And he did almost fall on that first step down the aisle. Gravity was not the spin-gee of *Saints Peter and Paul*. He had learned to walk in earth gravity under the Coriolis force of spinning habitat rings. The spin threw everything a fraction off. Lucas put his weight onto his foot and it was not where it needed to be. He staggered, grabbed the armrest, steadied himself.

He made it to the lock. The light blinded him. Beyond was a boarding tube. At the end of the tube, Dr Volikova, medics, a wheelchair.

He would not be wheeled into his new world. He inhaled a mighty draught of earth air. He could breathe. Breathe freely.

'Lucas?' Dr Volikova called.

Lucas Corta walked on, one slow wavering step at a time, up the boarding tube.

'Cane,' Lucas Corta said. 'Print me a walking cane. Silver tipped.'

'We don't have your level of printing sophistication,' a solemn young man in a bad suit said. Lucas squinted to make out his name from the badge clipped to his pocket. It ruined the line of the jacket, but it was a poor and cheap suit. Abi Oliviera-Uemura. VTO Manaus. 'We might be able to find one by tomorrow.'

'Tomorrow?'

Lucas stopped in front of a window. Heat buzzed from the grooved concrete of the apron and runway. The SSTO was a black dart, beautiful and lethal, a weapon, not a spacecraft. At the far edge of the field, further than any horizon on the moon, was a line of irregular darkness above a line of liquid. Toquinho would have magnified them for Lucas but Toquinho was a dead lens in his eye, dead air in his ear. Trees, Lucas surmised, rising out of heat haze. How hot was it out there? The light was painful. And the sky. Going up forever, so much sky, high over all. That blue. The sky was terrifying, dizzying. Lucas would be a long time reckoning with the agoraphobic sky of Earth.

He squared himself up.

'So,' Lucas Corta said. 'Brasil.'

From the quarantine suite's one window, Brasil was water tanks, comms dishes, solar panels and a slot of dun concrete, a hyphen of trees and a shaft of sky. Sometimes clouds broke the abstraction of blue, green, buff. This was the Amazon, the rain forest. It looked drier than the Ocean of Storms.

VTO refused to let Toquinho link with its network so Lucas was dependent on old fashioned, remote access to information. His contacts were messaging him daily; calls, conferences, physical meetings. *I am safe, I am well,* Lucas replied. *I will be in touch very soon.*

The daily fitness sessions were as dull and dispiriting as ever. He had been assigned a personal trainer, Felipe. His conversation was limited to moves, muscles, reps. The surgical mask he wore may have restricted his chat. The mask was at Dr Volikova's insistence. Lucas's immune system fizzed with a dozen inoculations and phages but he was still vulnerable to a hundred infections and pandemics. The sessions took place in the centre's pool. *Water is your friend,* Felipe said. *It will support body weight. It gives a good workout to all major muscle groups.*

Lucas slept oppressed by the smell of chlorine. The gravity was tough, the gravity was relentless but he knew this enemy. The minor afflictions fought with attrition. The deep, phlegm cough that brought up dark, dust-laden catarrh. The diarrhoea from the change in water and diet. The rhinitis and itchy red eyes from one allergy after another. The way he had to get up slowly to keep the blood from rushing from his head. The way his feet swelled inside his shoes. The wheelchair. The agony of having to bend down. How he couldn't understand a word anyone said. It was not the Portuguese he understood, inflected with Spanish, loaned a hundred words and phrases from thirty languages. The accent was odd and when he tried to speak Globo, eyebrows raised and heads shook.

The meat in his meals, that gave him terrible cramps.

The sugar in the sauces, the drinks, the bread.

Bread. His stomach rebelled at it.

The certainty that his trainer, his valet, his young and charming VTO personal assistants were spying on him.

'I need to work,' he complained to Dr Volikova.

'Patience.'

The next morning the valet told him to shower and shave and helped him dress in a decent suit. The valet arranged him comfortably in the wheelchair. At the door Lucas snatched up his silver-handled cane he had demanded. Once he swallowed his pride and accepted the wheelchair when he needed it, the cane assumed a theatrical character. The valet wheeled him along windowless corridors and down a boarding tunnel to a cylinder full of seats.

'What is this?' Lucas Corta asked.

'An aircraft,' the valet said. 'You're going to Rio.'

The clouds stunned him. They lay along the ocean edge of the world; stripes and layers that broke into bars, stipplings, hatchings, all moving on the very limit of his perception of change. He glanced away, to the lights coming on block by block, street by street, and when he looked back the clouds had changed shape. Skeins of lilac edged with purple; purple deepening to the colour of a bruise as the light bled from the sky, to indigo and blues for which he had no name and no experience. Why would anyone do anything else than watch clouds?

In the evening the heat will be tolerable, the hotel staff told him. The suite was comfortable and well appointed. Toquinho interfaced smoothly with the local network, though Lucas had no doubt that a dozen surveillance systems reported his words and actions to a hundred watchers. He worked solidly and productively, setting up conference calls and face-to-face meetings, but his attention strayed to the window, to the street and the heat haze that turned it and the vehicles speeding along it to quicksilver, to the ocean and the islands and the march of waves on the beach. He had never felt claustrophobic on the moon. This corner suite in the legendary Copacabana Palace hotel was gilded oppression.

Evenings, when the heat was less, he spent in the spa pool. *Seek water*, Felipe had told him. Lucas felt gravity slide from his shoulders as he shucked clothes that had never been weighty before and slipped into the balcony pool. He was out, in the air, in the world. The view was magnificent. If he shifted position to his right, he could see the favelas rising up behind him on the hills. In the waning dusk their lights, from windows and streets and staircases, were a straggling web of colours; a chaotic contrast to the strict pattern of the Copa, prim and tight between Tabajaras and the ocean. The web of lights was broken by patches of darkness where the slope defeated even the ingenuity of the builders of the informal shanty town. Or the power had outed. A million people lived in a handful of square kilometres. Their close presence comforted Lucas. The favelas, pressing closer every day by a house, an apartment, an extension, reminded him of the tiered quadras of João de Deus; the vast canyons, kilometres deep, of Meridian.

The waiter brought him a Martini. He took a sip. It did what a Martini should do obediently, obviously. It was the hotel's rarest gin but it was still standard, mass-produced; a small-batch Martini but still a commercial vermouth. Mass drinks for mass markets. He could not enjoy it in the knowledge that nowhere else in the two worlds was anyone drinking what he was drinking.

The light was almost gone in deepening indigo. Lucas's glass froze at his lips. Light on the eastern edge of the world, spreading from beneath the horizon. A silver lip kissed the ocean. Lucas watched the moon rise out of the sea. Every myth, every superstition and goddess: he believed them. Here was true divinity. A line of light reached across the ocean from moon to moon-man. The moon rose clear of the sea. She was in her waxing crescent: Ole Ku Kahi. The days of the lune were imprinted on Lucas as they were on every moon-born, but he had never understood them as he did now; as they were named, from the Earth, looking at the moon in her changing phases.

'You are so small,' Lucas whispered as the moon rose clear from the distraction of the horizon and stood alone in the sky. With his thumb he could blot out his crescent world, everyone he had ever known or loved. Lucasinho; gone. The seas, the mountains, the great craters; the cities and railways; gone. The billion footprints of humanity's seventy years on the moon. Gone.

Lucas saw Lady Luna as his mother had seen her, almost a century ago: Yemanja, her personal orixa, throwing down a silver path across the sea and space. And this was all Adriana had ever seen, this one face of Dona Luna, ever changing but never turning away. His understanding flipped upside down. Earth was relentless, crushing hell. The moon was hope. A small, dim hope, blotted out with an upraised thumb, but the only hope.

A thread of cloud moved across the crescent moon, fringed silver. The sky expanded around Lucas Corta. The moon was not a bauble on the edge of the world. She was distant and untouchable. Cloud across the moon was beautiful and desolating.

Full dark now and the moon stood high and Lucas's dark-adapted eye could make out the features of the reclining crescent. The mitt and thumb of Fecunditatis and Nectaris, the palm of Tranquilitatis, part of the wrist of Serenitatis. The suit glove, in lunar lore. The dark pupil of Mare Crisium, and how bright the south-eastern highlands. He could make out a bright ray from the crater at Tycho. These places, these names he looked at dispassionately, from an astronomical distance. Now he saw that tiny lights sprinkled the dark part of the moon. Sparks clustered along the equator; the settlements and habitats that followed the line of Equatorial One. That tangle of lights was Meridian at the centre of Nearside, the closest point to Earth. His eye moved south: a handful of sparkles in the darkness of the pole. Queen of the South. Scattered lights along the pole to pole line. With magnification he could discern individual trains. There, on the edge of the sun zone; those sharp lights in the dark would be the mirror farms of Twé. Crucible, the brightest feature on the surface of the moon, would not be visible in this phase, under the full sun around the shoulder of the moon.

Neck deep in sustaining water, Lucas Corta drank his inferior Martini under the lights of the cities of the moon.

4: LIBRA 2105

In this black pyramid squatting on the Marsh of Decay he was born, fifty-three years ago. Duncan Mackenzie draws his finger through the dust that lies thick on the desk. Here are his skin flakes; with every dust-filled breath he inhales his childhood. Adrian wears a dust mask; Corbyn Vorontsov-Mackenzie sneezes theatrically; but there was no other place Duncan could assemble his board than Hadley. The first forge of the Mackenzies.

Duncan Mackenzie lays his right hand flat on the surface of the desk. Esperance sends the silent order running out through the nervous system of the old city. Duncan smiles at the vibration beneath his feet; systems waking, checking, powering up. Lights switching on, corridor by airless corridor. Pressure seals closing, atmosphere rushing into the vacuum. Buried elements and headlamps raising the temperature from lunar cold. Chamber by chamber, system by system, Duncan Mackenzie builds his capital. When the family is safe, when the company is secure and rooted, then he will let the full weight of Crucible's fate rest on him. Until then, someone must bear the roof beams on his back. Someone must share air until everyone has escaped from the rover.

'Bryce is relocating to João de Deus,' Yuri Mackenzie says.

'Tranquillity Ops Managers have received orders to surrender the control codes.'

'That fucker has no right,' Denny Mackenzie says.

'My brother is mounting a coup,' Duncan says. 'He has to go for helium. We have the only rare earth smelter on Nearside. If we move fast, we can kill this before it breathes. Who have we got on the ground in Tranquillity and East Fecundity?'

Denny Mackenzie lists teams, dusters, resources. Duncan is distracted by his new gold teeth. He lost two in the flight from Crucible. Duncan hopes the poor bastard who lost his place to Denny died on the bend of his blade, quick and clean.

'How many can we trust?' Duncan asks.

The list is shorter by half.

'Take twenty solid jackaroos and get me those extractors. Deny them to Bryce. Whatever means you think appropriate.'

'Use their weapons against them,' Denny says. Duncan remembers that maxim. Hadley Mackenzie, his half brother, had been teaching Robson Corta how to fight among the shafts of blazing light in Crucible's Hall of Knives. In three moves he disarmed the kid, pinned him and brought the tip of Robson's own knife within a hair of the boy's throat. An eleven-year-old boy. Lady Luna is fickle. She loved the Cortas; the lucky, flashy Cortas. She has never been kind to the Mackenzies. Hadley Mackenzie died on the edge of Carlinhos Corta's knife. Carlinhos died on Denny's blade, when João de Deus fell. Lady Luna tests who she loves.

'And send teams to Crisium,' Duncan says. 'Yuri, take charge of that. I'm not losing Mare Anguis twice.'

Denny is already in the elevator. He will be putting out contracts, assembling squads and materiel to strike hard, strike fast. Bryce's flaw is that he has never understood the physical. Codes, orders, commands, analyses is his way. Dusters in the field, boots on the regolith win every time. Duncan will plunge his knife into that flaw and twist it until the blood pours free.

'Adrian.'

'Dad.'

The Eagle of the Moon has flown back to his eyrie in Meridian but Adrian came to Hadley. Family is what holds when the iron falls.

'I need you to give us the LDC.'

Adrian Mackenzie hesitates. Duncan reads a dozen emotions in the muscles around his mouth.

'The Eagle's influence over the Lunar Development Corporation is not as sure as it used to be. Eagle and LDC differ on certain issues.'

A turn-tongued, diplomat's-oko answer.

'What does that mean?' Duncan says but the voice of Vassos Palaeologos, once steward of Crucible, now steward of Hadley, cuts in.

'Mr Mackenzie.'

The perfect retainer, Vassos would only interrupt with the most important news.

'Go ahead.'

Vassos is a small man, balding, sallow skinned. His familiar is the concentric blue rings of the matiasma, the eye that banishes evil.

'A report from Meridian Station. Wang John-Jian is dead.'

John-Jian was the best production engineer on the moon. Duncan had secured his loyalty at the memorial at Kingscourt. This is a deep wound.

'How? What happened?'

'On the platform. A targeted insect.'

Cyborg drone-insects, armed with fast-killing toxins, are the signature weapons of the Asamoahs but no one in Hadley's small control room believes for an instant that AKA sanctioned this assassination. It was chosen because it was small, silent, precise, cruel and involves no expensive collateral that might demand damages. A very Bryce Mackenzie murder.

Strike hard, strike fast. Strike fast. Bryce has gone in one smooth power curve from rivalry to war. Esperance calls Denny's familiar.

Denny is in motion, accelerating out from under Hadley's half-kilometre tall black pyramid down the Aitken-Peary polar line.

'I've got five full squads. Staunch jackaroos.'

'Good work. Denny. I want this over fast. Gut the fucker.' A rumble of approvals and murmured *yeahs* from around the control room. Duncan holds out a hand.

'Does anyone here deny that I am Chief Executive of Mackenzie Metals?' Duncan Mackenzie asks.

Yuri is the first to take the offered hand. Corbyn, Vassos. Adrian is last.

'I'm staunch, Dad.' But he won't look at his father, won't hold eye contact when Duncan seeks eye contact. *Are you with me, son? You aren't with Bryce, but who are you with? You shake my hand, but do you pledge allegiance?* Bryce may have the company, Duncan has the family.

One last piece of theatre. Duncan Mackenzie likes to search out the theatre of the everyday, turning presentations into productions, finding the melodrama in meetings. His signature head-to-toe grey, the shimmering grey sphere of Esperance, are all calculated effects. A silent command and behind him the long-shuttered windows of Hadley Control slide open. The heavily glassed slots in the thick sloping sinter walls of Hadley yield enormous views over the Marsh of Decay and the thousands of dark objects waiting there.

The mirrors wake.

Hadley rises from an array of five thousand mirrors. At Duncan Mackenzie's command, long-stilled mechanisms jar and creak, grind dust in their motors and actuators. Juddering, the mirrors turn their faces to catch the sun. The mirror field blazes so bright the men in Control throw their hands up in front of their eyes before the photochromic glass reacts and brings the shafts of blazing, dusty light down to bearable levels. The power of the Mackenzies has always been the sun. Hadley's mirror array had been the envy of two worlds, the summit of solar-smelting technology, but it had not been enough for Robert Mackenzie. For the fourteen days of the lunar night, the mirrors were dark, the smelter cold. He had conceived a smelter that would never go dark, that would always have the high noon sun pouring into its mirrors. He built Crucible. The Suns boast of their spire-palace, the Pavilion of Eternal Light. A cheap boast, a fortune of location and selenography. The Mackenzies engineered their endless noonday. They shaped the moon itself to create it.

The mirrors lock into position; five thousand beams focused on the smelters at the apex of the dark pyramid. Even in the light of a full moon, it will be visible from Earth; a sudden star kindling in the grey of Palus Putridinis.

Duncan Mackenzie closes his eyes but the light still sears his eyelids red. He shuts them the better to feel. Subtle, but unmistakable once he has isolated it from the background hum of the awakening city. An old body-memory; the all-pervading tremor of Hadley under production; the vibration of liquid metals pouring from the smelters down the refractory gullet at the centre of the pyramid.

He turns to his board.

'Mackenzie Metals is back in business.'

Glass Crew Lucky Eight Ball gets the distress call five hundred kilometres out from Meridian. The glassers have been out for a lune in the highlands east of Tranquillity. The crew has been working the northern edge of the solar array, checking the performance of the sinterers, maintaining and repairing, reporting and analysing. Glass work is well paid and boring boring boring. For the past three days the crew has been repairing damage from a micrometeorite shower over the Dionysus region. A thousand pinholes; ten thousand cracks, a whole sector of the solar belt gone dark. Painstaking, detailed work that can't be hurried, that can't be done any faster or more efficiently. Glass Crew Lucky Eight Ball is impatient to get back to Meridian. None more than Wagner Corta, laoda of Glass Crew Lucky Eight Ball. The Earth grows round. Changes sweep over him. His crew has no problem working with a wolf – both the boundless energy and ability to think three different thoughts at the same time of his light aspect and the intense focus and concentration of his dark aspect are valuable talents on the surface. The times between, when the Earth waxes and wanes, are the difficult ones, when he becomes restless, moody, unpredictable, irritable and unapproachable.

Crew Lucky Eight Ball. Wagner gives the same speech at the start of each tour of duty. Some veterans have heard it seven times. *That's our name.* The new workers look at each other. Lady Luna is a jealous queen. To call a thing lucky, fortunate, favoured, blessed is to invite her wrath. *And we are.* The old hands stand with arms folded. They know it's true. *Do you know why we're lucky? Because we are boring. Because we are diligent and attentive. Because we focus and concentrate. Because we are not lucky. We are smart. Because on the surface you have a thousand questions, but only one question matters. Do I die today? And my answer to that is no.*

No one has ever died on the Little Wolf's squad.

Out on the glass, forty kilometres south of Dionysus, a spinning red asterisk flashes up in Wagner Corta's lens: SUTRA 2, the penultimate of the five levels of surface threat. The ultimate level is white. White is the colour of death on the moon. Something has gone very bad out in the sinterlands. Wagner checks atmosphere, water and battery levels, flicks command of the rover to his junshi Zehra Aslan while he acknowledges the emergency and briefs Glass Crew Lucky Eight Ball. His light-aspect familiar, Dr Luz, flashes up the rescue contract. Mackenzie Metals. Memories flock to him – huddling afraid and alone at Hypatia Station while his family fell, slipping home to the pack feeling a knife in every shadow, hiding among the bodies of the wolves, hating himself for surviving.

Wagner signs the contract, flashes it to the Palace of Eternal Light for executive authority. There is memory and there is survival. He works for the Suns now. They tried to kill him, when he lifted the corner of their intrigue to set Mackenzies and Cortas at each other.

The Magdalena wolves of Queen of the South saved him that time. When the House of Corta fell, the Meridian pack sheltered him, paid his Four Elementals, until he realised that with Corta Hélio destroyed the Suns no longer held any animosity towards him. Wagner applied for a glass crew and got a contract the next day. He has worked Taiyang for over a year. He is the good wolf.

They find the first body twenty kilometres west of Schmidt crater. Glass Crew Lucky Eight Ball flick up their safety bars and drop to the regolith. The rover's medical AI searches for vital signs but, to the glassers, it's clear there is no life inside the suit. The tight weave has been opened throat to balls.

'Clean edges,' Zehra Aslan says.

Wagner crouches to study the slash. Lady Luna knows a thousand ways to kill, none of them clean. A blade did this. Glass Crew Lucky Eight Ball leaves a tag for a Zabbaleen recycle team: carbon is precious, even abandoned in the boulder fields of West Tranquillity. Emergency beacons lead the rover along a string of corpses. By the tenth the crew no longer leave the rover. Wagner and Zehra photograph, report tag, move on. Stabbed, slashed, amputations. Beheadings. Death by a blade's edge.

Zehra crouches to closer examine a tangle of four bodies.

'I don't recognise this suit design.'

'Mackenzie Helium,' Wagner says. He stands up, surveys the close horizon. 'Tracks.'

'Three rovers, and something much bigger.'

'A helium extractor.'

In the shadow of the western wall of Schmidt crater, Wagner finds a rover. Its spine is broken, its axles snapped. Wheels lie at crazy angles, aerials and comms dishes bent and crushed. Every seat bar is up. The crew tried to escape their stricken vehicle. They didn't make it. Sasuited bodies litter the crater floor. Glass Crew Lucky Eight Ball investigates the corpses. Wagner plugs Dr Luz into the dead rover's

AI and reads its logs, voice and data records. He needs to patch together the events that ended here, in the cold shadow of Schmidt.

Zehra Aslan stands up and waves.

'We've got a live one here!'

Barely. A sole survivor in a ring of bodies. A golden sasuit. Wagner has heard of this suit. Half of Glass Crew Lucky Eight Ball has heard of this suit. Wagner's medical AI identifies a score of traumas, a dozen violations. Crush and heavy impact injuries, multiple lesions and abrasions, a deep puncture wound between the seventh and eight ribs. The golden suit has healed over the puncture; the tension of the weave will hold the wound shut.

What do you think? Zehra asks on Wagner's private channel. *Call in a moonship?*

We're forty minutes from Hypatia, Wagner says. *We'd be there before any moonship. They've got full medical facilities.*

The survivor's sasuit is low on power and O2. How long has he been out here, waiting? Hoping? Wagner has often thought, out in the tedium of the pristine black glass, of what he would do if Lady Luna deserted him and left him wounded on the surface, air running down, power too low even to call for help. The long look at death, advancing with every breath one step across the dead regolith. Nothing surer, nothing more true. Open the helmet. Look Lady Luna in the face. Take the dark kiss. Would he have the courage to do that?

Wagner runs a jack into the golden suit.

'We're going to move you now.'

The man is unconscious, verging on comatose but Wagner needs to speak.

'This may hurt.'

Wagner's crew lift the survivor and strap him to the carry rack. Zehra runs lines from the air and water processors into the suit.

'His core temperature is way too low,' she says, scanning readouts on her helmet. She patches a connector to the environment pack. 'I'm going to cycle his suit with warm water. I'm shit scared I'm going to drown him in his own suit but if I don't the hypothermia will kill him.'

'Do it. Willard, get Hypatia. We have a casualty incoming.'

The man stirs. A groan in Wagner's helmet speakers. Wagner presses hands to his chest.

'Don't move.'

Wagner winces at the sudden cry of pain in his earphones.

'Fuck…' An Australian accent. 'Fuck,' he says again, in deep bliss as the heat bathes him.

'We're taking you to Hypatia,' Wagner says.

'My crew…'

'Don't talk.'

'They jumped us. They had it all planned. Fucking Bryce knew we were coming. We ran straight on to his blades.'

'I said don't talk.'

'My name's Denny Mackenzie,' the survivor says.

'I know,' Wagner says. Wagner knows the legend of the man in the golden suit. In the dark time, when the light of the Earth is dim, Wagner has tried to imagine Carlinhos's final vision: the face of Denny Mackenzie holding his head up by the hair, baring his throat, lifting the knife to show Carlinhos the thing that will kill him. He's always been as faceless as he is now, behind the reflective faceplate. *And I am as faceless to you.* 'You killed my brother.'

Glass Crew Lucky Eight Ball's chat on the common channel is silenced as if with a knife. Wagner feels every faceplate turned to him.

'Who are you?' Stabbed and pierced, hypothermia, exhausted and reeling from industrial painkillers, at the mercy of the man with every reason on the moon to kill him. Still defiant. The Mackenzie Way.

'My name is Wagner Corta.'

'Let me see you,' Denny Mackenzie says.

Wagner retracts his sun visor. Denny Mackenzie clears his faceplate.

'You killed my brother with his own knife. You drove him to his knees and tore his throat open. You watched him bleed out, then you stripped him and ran a cable through his Achilles' tendons and hung him from the West 7 crosswalk.'

Denny Mackenzie does not flinch, does not look away.

'So what are you going to do, Wagner Corta?'

'We're not like you people, Denny Mackenzie.' Wagner silently gives the order for Glass Crew Lucky Eight-Ball to strap in and move out. Seat bars fold down, sasuits link to the rover's life support.

'My people owe you,' Denny Mackenzie croaks as the safety bars descend around Wagner Corta.

'I want nothing from your family,' Wagner Corta says. He flicks control of the rover to Zehra.

'Doesn't matter, Wagner Corta.' Denny Mackenzie groans as the rover jolts over battle debris. 'The Mackenzies will repay three times.'

'Marina!'

No answer.

'Marina!'

No answer. Ariel Corta swears under her breath and reaches for the grab-rope. She pulls herself up from the empty cool box.

'We're out of gin!'

Ariel grabs the ceiling net and swings from the kitchen alcove past her shameful hammock to the consulting cubby. Three short swings and a much-practised drop at the end into what she calls her Justice Seat. The apartment is too small for two women and a wheelchair. It's been a lune since she last deprinted the wheelchair and left the occupancy at just two women. She needed the carbon allowance. She's since drunk ninety per cent of it.

'Let's see me, Beijaflor.'

Her familiar hooks into the cubby camera. Ariel studies her working face. Cheekbones highlighted with gradated powder. Orange eyeliner, black mascara. Her eyes widen, Beijaflor zooms in. This new crease, where did that come from? She hisses in exasperation. Beijaflor can edit it out for clients. Your familiar is your true face. She pouts her lips. Fuchsia, deep Cupid's Bow. If Ariel can afford one thing on trend it's cosmetics. And her top: Norma Kamali, bat wing and funnel-neck, in carmine. Still in the game.

The upper half of Ariel Corta is professional. The bottom, out of camera shot, is slouch. From the waist down Ariel is a disgrace, swinging around the place in whatever pair of basic-print leggings Marina isn't wearing. She always steals, never asks to borrow. That would be surrender. She could manage her caseload as easily from her hammock as the Justice Seat but that too would be surrender.

'Beijaflor, get Marina to get some gin.' There's a good little printer down on Level 87. She takes folding, material cash.

You have only ten bitsies of data.

Ariel swears. She'll need every bit of bandwidth for her clients. Now that she can't have it, breakfast gin is the roof and the ground, the Earth and the sun, the background hum of the universe. She takes a drag on her long titanium vaper. It supplies nothing but hauteur and oral satisfaction. Ariel checks her hair. It's fashionably big.

'Let's have the first one.'

The Fuentes Nikah. Beijaflor calls Aston Fuentes up on Ariel's lens and she quickly runs down the twenty-seven clauses in the contract with the potential to turn around and rip her client's heart out of his chest. His mouth opens a little more with every legal point.

'You're gaping, Aston.'

Client two. The Wong divorce. The only way he can get custody is by having his daughter file a separate petition effectively divorcing her co-father – failure to thrive or to provide an optimal domestic environment are the obvious paths, though the easiest for Lily to argue would be personal disgust at remaining with Marco in a parental role. Ariel recommends going deep and dirty – there will be something, everyone has something. Even if she succeeded, it would be the girl's decision to contract parenting to Brett. And it would effectively destroy Marco's name and reputation – for which he could seek legal redress. So what Brett has to ask himself is: Is the price worth paying?

The Red Lion amory. By now the image of gin is as precious as the rare rains that sweep the dust from the air of Orion Quadra. No no no no no, darling. Ariel will always advise against partnering into an amory with too heavy a contract.

'Amory's are light, open, flitting and fleeting things, darling. You don't crush them beneath heavy nikahs. Send me the contract, I'll take it apart and put...'

And gone.

We're out of data, Beijaflor says.

'Fuck!' Ariel Corta swears. She smashes a fist edge-on against the white wall. 'I fucking hate this. How can I get any fucking work done? I can't even talk to my clients. Marina! Marina! Get me some connectivity. I've ascended into the fucking proles.'

She hears movement outside the street door.

'Marina?'

Marina has warned Ariel time and again not to leave the door open. She's not safe. Anyone could walk in. That's the idea, darling. Law is always open. To which Marina answers: *Who carried you up here on her shoulders? You may never be safe.*

Movement in the lobby space.

'Marina?

Ariel pushes herself up from the Justice Seat and hooks her fingers into the netting that lines the ceiling of the tiny apartment. She swings herself out into the main room.

A figure turns.

She first feels a fist, and then a kick.

She's up in a cross-tube, one of the forgotten access tunnels that run through the bare rock connecting one quadra to another. They're old, dusty, scary with radiation. Behind her is midnight in Antares Quadra, before her is morning in Orion. She's got a belt of old dirty printed money from clients, some curry noodle and moon-cakes for the festival and she's on her way home to Ariel.

The cross-tubes are long and shadow-filled. The moon abandons its obsolete infrastructure. Kids, rebels and up-and-outs all find their own uses for it.

They were waiting. They were practised, they knew her routines and what she was carrying. She never saw them. Of course she never saw them. If she had seen them, they would never have hit her. The first took her in the middle of her back. A fist, from the dark, into a kidney that knocked breath and thought from her and sent her crashing to the mesh.

Then the kick. She sees it through the red pain and scrambles away. The shoulder, not the head.

'Hetty,' she gasps. But she is alone. She has shut down her familiar to donate her data to Ariel for her consultations.

The boot again raised over the side of her head. She reaches for it, tries to push it back before it crushes her skull against the titanium mesh. The boot comes down on her hand. Marina screams.

'Got it got it,' a voice yells. A knife nicks her money belt.

'I want to kill her.'

'Leave her.'

Marina gasps, bleeding. Boot heels on the walkway. She can't make out if they are women or men. She can't stop them. She can't touch them. They take her money, her curry noodle and her moon-cakes.

She couldn't touch them. That makes her scared beneath the blood, the beating, agonised kidney, the cracked ribs, the black fingers. Once she threw Mackenzie Metal dusters around the lock of Beikou habitat like toys. Two muggers up in a cross-tube at midnight, and she couldn't touch them.

*

'I'd offer you gin but we're out of gin. I'd make you tea but I don't do making and I'm in the only chair,' Ariel Corta says. 'Sorry. There are hammocks, or you can perch.'

'I'll perch,' says Vidhya Rao. E positions erself on the edge of Ariel's desk. E has put on weight since Ariel saw er last, in the faded decor of the Lunarian Society. E is a bulb of a human; waddling and ungainly, swathed in layers of fabric. E has jowls, bags under the eyes.

'I'm sorry to find you in reduced circumstances,' Vidhya Rao says.

'I'm happy simply to find myself breathing,' Ariel says. 'You still work for Whitacre Goddard?'

'Consulting,' Vidhya Rao says. 'I have a portfolio of clients. And I still dip my fingers in the markets, see what I can stir up. I've been following your recent cases. I can understand why you practise matrimonial law. There is no end to the entertainment.'

'That entertainment is people's hopes and hearts and happinesses,' Ariel says. Gin. She wants a bloody gin. Where is her gin, where is Marina? Ariel twists a capsule into her vaper and flicks a fingernail against the tip. The element glows, she inhales a cloud of customised tranquillity. Calm floods her lungs. Almost gin.

'Your reputation still precedes you,' Vidhya Rao says. 'I have state of the art pattern recognition software but in all honesty, I didn't need it to find you. For a woman in hiding, you show a distinctive flair. Most theatrical.'

'I never met a lawyer who wasn't a frustrated actor,' Ariel says. 'Courts and stages: it's all performance. I remember you saying, when I was a member of your little political glee club, that your software had identified me as a mover and shaker.' She gestures with her vaper, a curl of smoke taking in the whole three and a half rooms of her empire. 'The moon remains unshaken. Sorry to disappoint your August Ones.'

'And yet it shook,' Vidhya Rao says. 'We live among the aftershocks.'

'You can hardly connect me with what happened at Crucible.'

'But there are patterns,' Vidhya Rao says. 'The hardest ones to spot are the ones so large they seem like a landscape.'

'I can't say I was overly upset when Bob Mackenzie took the thousand degree shower,' Ariel says with a flourish of vapour. 'Living under a million tons of molten metal is tempting, if not Providence, certainly something with a sense of irony. Oh, don't look at me like that.'

'Your nephew was there,' Vidhya Rao says.

'Well he's obviously all right, otherwise you wouldn't have said that. Patterns. Which nephew?'

'Robson.'

'Robson. Gods.' She hasn't thought about her nephew since the word distilled through old legal contacts that the boy had been made a ward of the Mackenzies. Lucasinho, Luna, any of the kids, the survivors. She hasn't thought about Wagner the wolf, or Lucas, whether he is alive or dead. She hasn't thought about anything but herself, her life, her survival. Ariel inhales sharply to mask the tic of loss and guilt. 'Do the Mackenzies still hold the parenting contract?'

'He is a ward of Bryce Mackenzie.'

'I should get him out of it.' Ariel taps her fingers together. You could always tell a Mackenzie contract. Sloppy work.

'More important, since Ironfall, the terrestrial commodity markets are in turmoil,' Vidhya Rao says. 'Helium-3 and rare-earth prices hit an all-time record yesterday and will set a new one today. The G10 and G27 groups are calling for action to stabilise prices and production.'

'In vacuum no one can hear you shout,' Ariel says.

'Moon and Earth are bound by more than gravity,' Vidhya Rao says. Ariel exhales a long plume of vapour.

'Why have you come here, Vidhya?'

'To bring you an invitation.'

'If it's the festival, I'd sooner stick needles in my eyes. If it's politics; Cortas don't do politics.'

'It's an invitation to cocktails. The Crystaline, Mohalu, thirteen hundred Orion Quadra Time.'

'The Crystaline. I'll need a dress,' Ariel says. 'A proper cocktail dress. And accessories.'

'Of course.'

Beijaflor whispers, *Credit transfer*. It's enough for the dress and the accessories, for a new wheelchair, a moto. Gin. Beautiful beautiful gin. Before any of those: data. Beijaflor reconnects to the network. The sensation of world, the inrush of information, message, chat, gossip, news at the same time as her curiosity rushes out like a child into morning light, is powerfully sensual.

'Beijaflor, get me Marina,' Ariel commands. Already Beijaflor is opening catalogues and pattern books. 'I need her to pick an order up from the printers.'

'You can afford to get them delivered,' Vidhya Rao says from the door. 'Aren't you curious about whom you're meeting?'

'It doesn't matter. I'll stroll it.'

'The Eagle of the Moon.'

Marina stumbles through a kilometre of cross-tube to Orion Quadra. She hits the call button for the service elevator and cries aloud at the blaze of pain through her bruised, blackened fingers. As she rides the elevator cage down from the top of the city she remembers all the people she saw die on the moon, how sudden and arbitrary their deaths. Head caved in by an aluminium beam in the training bay. The edge of a knife pulled out through a throat. Impaled through the skull by the silver spear of a vaper. She never stops seeing that death. She never stops seeing that man's eyes change from living to dead. She never stops seeing the moment he realises that this fraction of a second is all he has remaining of life. Edouard Barosso. He crippled Ariel, would have killed her if Marina had not seized the only weapon to hand and stabbed it up through the softness of his jaw, out through the top of his soft, moon-born skull.

How easily she could have joined that roster of the dead, up there in the cross-tunnel. They hurt her. They wanted to kill her. They should not have been able to hurt her. Two third-gen punks should not have been able even to touch her.

She swears as she wrenches open the gate with her black, rigid fingers, slumps against the safety grilles. Every breath is a slow, deep knife. She reels out on to West 17th, staggers across traffic to seize the balustrade. The chasms of Orion Quadra open before her. She hauls herself along the edge of the drop, stanchion by stanchion. The clinic is a kilometre north on the vast cylinder where the five wings of Orion Quadra meet. Stanchion by stanchion she hauls herself to help. It takes her ten minutes to make a hundred metres.

Almost, she whispers the command to reboot Hetty. Call for help. Call Ariel. Ariel can help. That's what everyone up in the Bairro Alto says. She can't. She failed. She let them take Ariel's money. How can she claim to protect Ariel when she can't even protect her money? Since that day Corta Hélio fell in fire and blood and she climbed up to the roof of the world, hand over hand, rung over rung, Ariel Corta on her shoulders, she has kept her safe against enemies many, harsh and patient.

Hand over hand, Marina hauls herself along the railing.

Call her. Don't compound idiocy with pride.

Hetty boots up. There are three messages. Two about gin, one to inform that their data credit limit has been exceeded. Marina Calzaghe smashes her wounded fist on the handrail. The pain is intense, justified and purifying.

It isn't that they beat her that scares her. It's how they were able to beat her.

The moto swings in and unfolds.

'You work with Ariel, don't you?' The fare is a middle-aged man, hair and skin greyed by years of slow radiation.

Marina manages a nod.

'Get in. Gods you look like shit.'

He helps her to the clinic door.

'I used to work for Corta Hélio,' the man says. 'I was a duster, then.' Then he adds in Portuguese, 'Piss on Bryce Mackenzie's contracts.'

'Of course Ariel's credit is good.' Dr Macaraeg's clinic on Orion Hub 17th is glossy and well-equipped. Gleaming bots, shiny clients. Real flowers on the reception desk, where Marina leaves blood smears on the white plastic. Dr Macaraeg is the former medic of Boa Vista, personal physician of Adriana Corta. She tended Ariel in João de Deus med centre, after Edouard Barosso severed her spinal column with a knife grown from his own bones. She huddled with the family in the over-crowded, fetid refuge when Boa Vista was destroyed; she tended to the survivors, the last thing she could do for the Cortas. She came to Meridian and set up her high-end practice on Orion Hub, close to the centres of society and power. Dr Macaraeg remembers honour and loyalty, family and duty. 'Just not good enough for a patch up and a scan.'

Dr Macaraeg is not a charity.

'I'll take the scan,' Marina says.

'I would advise...' Dr Macaraeg begins but Marina cuts in.

'The scan.'

The scanner is cheap and perfunctory; two sensors that snap-fit to universal arms, but sufficient for the task. Marina stands on the footprints and the bot moves its arms over her, intimately mapping every centimetre of her body. She doesn't even need to take her clothes off.

'How long?'

'One, maybe one and a half lunes.'

Hand over hand, rung over rung, Marina had borne up Ariel Corta into the roof of the world, to Bairro Alto where the up-and-outs go; the poor, the out-of-contract, the refugees, the sick and the ones whose lungs are turning to stone after thousands of dust-filled breaths. The hunted. Up the ladders and the staircases, to the cubicles and cells and caves pushed into the gaps between the old environment plants and power units, lighting grids and water tanks. Marina knew this world. Six weeks on the moon, scarcely able to walk straight, a cancelled contract had sent her up to Bairro Alto. Selling piss. Breathing short so some air-buyer, down there, could breathe long. She never thought she would return. But she knew it and knew how to survive it. And she knew that Ariel Corta did not know it, and that her ignorance would kill her quicker than any Mackenzie blade. She found the cubby, scavenged hammocks and the ceiling netting, and, as she gathered in the bitsies, the paraphernalia of a life with some comfort. Reliable data. A reliable print shop with an idea of fashion. Cosmetics. A refrigerator and gin to put in it. As Marina wove a life for Ariel, she forgot her own. She forgot her own body. She forgot what the moon was doing to it; leaching the calcium from her bones, the strength from her muscles, sucking away the Jo Moonbeam strength that allowed her to throw those Mackenzie dusters around the lock at Beikou like rags, until a couple of skinny punks could smash her to the ground, rob her, beat her to nothing.

Marina pulls the scanner display panel to her.

'It's not going to contradict me,' Dr Macaraeg says. It doesn't, but Marina has to see the numbers that tell her Moonday is coming, and soon. The day when she will have to decide whether to go back to Earth, or remain on the moon permanently. One, maybe one and a half lunes. Thirty, forty-five days. *Days.*

'Don't tell Ariel.'

'I won't.'

This she must tell Ariel face to face. Tell her that Moonday is rising. Tell her that she hates the moon, has always hated the moon, hates what it makes people, hates the fear and the danger and the smell of dust that gets into everything, every blink and breath, the smell of death. That she aches for open skies, horizons, free air in her lungs, free rain on her cheeks. Tell Ariel that the only reason she stays, serves Ariel, protects Ariel, cares for Ariel, is because Marina can't abandon her.

Then tell her nothing.

'Thank you doctor.'

Dr Macaraeg presses fingers into her bruised ribs, forcing her by pain down on to the examination trolley.

'Sit there and keep still. Let's get you fixed up.'

It is the night of Zhongqiu in Meridian. Aquarius Quadra is decked in red and gold; fork-tailed banners, prayer flags and cascades of lamps tumble from levels and galleries and bridges, and every staircase and ramp twinkles with lights. Enormous festival lanterns waddle up toward the darkened sunline. Flocks of helium-filled Jade Rabbits skip through the middle air, dodging flotillas of red balloons that have escaped from children's hands. There is a flying drone-dragon, undulating between the bridges and cable ways. Here biolights gleam through the trees and glimmer from the cafés and tea booths and Mooncake kiosks that line Tereshkova Prospekt. Look: cocktail stalls! Listen: a dozen musics competing with jugglers and street magicians and bubble blowers! On the moon, bubbles reach titanic dimensions. Parents tell their children that bubbles can trap naughty kids and carry them up to Bairro Alto: a venerable lie. There is face painting. There is *always* face painting. *I'm going to turn you into a tiger*, the face painter says lifting her brush. *What's a tiger?* the children ask.

Everyone in Aquarius Quadra has turned out in fresh printed party clothes. Streets, levels, walkways are thronged. Kids run from stall to stall, unable to choose between the wonders on offer. Teenagers and young adults move in groups, disdainful of the populism of it all. They all secretly love Mooncake festival. Some have worked it in each of Meridian's three quadras. Zhongqiu is the festival to hook up with the someone you've been lusting for all year but never had the nerve to approach. There! Did you see that? Those girls, those guys – Were they guys? Were they girls? – running and laughing through the crowds in nothing but body paint. Ten Lady Lunas, one half alive and black, the other bone and white. Zhongqiu is a time for skin and sass.

Zhongqiu rightly belongs to Chang'e, Goddess of the Moon but Lady Luna – usurper, pretender, thief – stole it. On this night Our Lady of Love and Death permits other, lesser saints and orixas, gods and heroes, to share her honours. A hundred perfumes and incenses spiral up to her. Yemanja and Ogun accept flowers cakes and gin. Street shrines to Our Lady of Kazan glow with a hundred luminescent votives. A trillion in paper money will go into the shredders tonight.

And Mooncake! Mooncake. Round and fluted, stamped with mottoes or adinkra, shaped like rabbits and hares and unicorns and little ponies, cows and rockets. Everybody buys it. No one eats it. *It's so rich. Too dense. Too sweet. I just look at it and my teeth ache.*

The helmet bears a crest on its brow, just above the plate: a face half-living, half-bone. Not a woman's face, not the face of Lady Luna; an animal face; the mask of a wolf. Half wolf. Half wolf skull. The helmet is strapped to the back of a suitpack, the suitpack is slung over the shoulder of Wagner Corta. Through Mooncakes and music, saints and sex, he's coming home. Bone tired but elated, pulled in every direction by the sights, the sounds, the smells, the spirits, as if by fine hooks in his skin.

He moves through the festival like the wolf in his heart, working his way upward by ramp and staircase and escalator. He feels light, lighted, enlightened. His heightened senses pick up a dozen conversations, touch a hundred moments. *I love this tune. Try this, go on just a bite.* A startled kiss. A bulge-eyed sudden vomit: too much Mooncake. *Touch me while I'm dancing. Can I have a balloon? Where are you?* His peripheral vision catches on a familiar, one familiar among the host of digital assistants, then five, ten, a dozen others moving through the crowd toward him. Wagner breaks into a run. His pack has come to meet him.

Amal, leader of the Meridian pack, launches nerself into Wagner, wrestles him, tousles his hair, bites his lower lip in the ritual assertion of pack authority.

'You you you.'

Né lifts him, sasuit and helmet and all and swings him round and by then the rest of the pack has gathered in kisses and embraces and small, affectionate bites. Hands ruffle his hair, play-punch his belly.

The cold death of West Tranquillity, the plain strewn with sasuits, the horror that left him numb; all are burned away in the intensity of the pack kiss.

Amal looks Wagner up and down.

'You look like death, Lobinho.'

'Buy me a drink for gods' sake,' Wagner says.

'Not yet. You're needed at Sömmering.'

'What's at Sömmering?'

'A special delivery for you, Little Wolf, from Hoang Lam Hung-Mackenzie. And because it's the Mackenzies, we're going with you.'

Early, before the other wolves wake, Wagner disentangles himself from the sleeping pack. He shakes the dream out of his head. Shared dreams are heavy, adhesive, haunting. It was an effort to unplug himself from pack sleep. Clothes. Remember clothes.

The pile of blankets on the lounger where he put the boy to sleep is empty. The space where Robson slept has a distinct, alien smell. Honey and ozone; sweat and sleep-drool. Greasy hair and skin spots. Over-worn clothes, under-washed skin. Foot fungus and arm-pit. Back-of-ear bacteria. Teenage boys are rank.

'Robson?'

You all sleep together? Zhongqiu was ebbing in crushed lanterns and spilt vodka and trampled Mooncake when the pack returned to Meridian. *Wolves,* people whispered, moving out of the path of the tight, purposeful guard of dark-faced people, a boy in a pale suit, sleeves rolled up, at the centre. Robson was dead on his feet but he doggedly, thoroughly, explored the packhouse. Wagner understood what the boy was doing: embodying the territory. Learning the wolf-world.

I'll make you something up, Wagner had said. *On the lounger. We don't really have separate beds.*

What's it like, all sleeping together?

We share dreams, Wagner said.

He finds Robson in the food area, hunched on a high stool at a serving bar, sheets draped around him. He cuts a deck of cards – a half deck, Wagner notes, sharp-eyed – one handed, dexterously, lifting the top of the pack, swivelling out the lower cards, swapping them over, closing the pack; again and again.

'Robson, you okay?'

'I didn't sleep that good.' He doesn't look up from his compulsive card-cutting.

'I'm sorry, we'll try and print you up a bed.' Wagner speaks Portuguese. He hopes the old tongue will be sweet and comforting to Robson.

'The lounger was fine.' Robson answers in Globo.

'Can I get you something? Juice?'

Robson taps a glass of tea on his small table.

'Let me know if you need anything.'

'I will, sure.' Still Globo.

'There'll be people moving around here soon.'

'I won't get in their way.'

'You might want to think about putting something on.'

'Will they?' The cards divide and flip.

'Well, if you do need anything...'

Robson looks up as Wagner turns away. Peripheral vision catches the flicker of eyes.

'Can I print some clothes out?'

'Sure.'

'Wagner.'

'What is it?'

'Do you guys do everything together?'

'We like to be with each other. Why?'

'Could you take me out for breakfast? Just us?'

Twenty days on the glass never left Wagner Corta as exhausted as three days of Robson Mackenzie. How can thirteen-year-old boys demand so much time and energy? Nutrition: the kid never stops eating. He is a perfect mass-energy conversion machine. The things he will and won't eat; and where he will or will not eat them. Wagner hasn't been to the same hot-shop twice.

Respiration. The adoption contract with the Mackenzies guarantees the boy's Four Elementals. Bryce Mackenzie is not beyond spiteful breach of contract. It's an hour's work for the pack, in full gestalt mode, to discreetly link Robson's chib to a secondary account through a network of nested false companies. Breathe easy, Robson.

Education: the contracts are far from simple. Is it to be individual tuition or a colloquium group? Specialism or generalism?

Masturbation: finding a private place in the house of wolves to do it. That's if he's doing it at all. Wagner's sure he wasn't doing it at that age. Then there's the whole question of where the kid stands on the spectrum: what he likes, who he likes, who he likes more than others he likes, if he likes anyone at all.

Financialisation: gods but the boy is expensive. Everything about thirteen-year-olds costs.

Isolation: the boy is sweet and serious and funny and cracks Wagner's heart a dozen times a day but every moment spent with him is one spent away from the pack. It's different for wolves; the need to be together is physical, burned into the bones by blue Earthlight. Wagner feels the ache of separation every moment he's with Robson and he knows his pack mates feel the disruption. He's seen the looks, felt the shift in the emotional climate. Robson's sensed it too.

'I don't think Amal likes me.'

They're lunching at Eleventh Gate. Robson wears short white shorts, neat creases; a sleeveless cropped white T-shirt with the word WHAM! printed large. White-framed Wayfarers. Wagner is in double denim. Some packs only wear their own style; invariably Gothic. Meridian is always on-trend.

Eleventh Gate is a noisy wun sen noodle bar. It's quiet in the lull after Zhongqiu but Wagner is wary. Wolf-senses on the diners and tea-drinkers. Of all the issues Robson brought with him from Sömmering, security is the greatest.

'You make ner feel uncomfortable.' *You make a lot of us feel uncomfortable.*

'What do I do?'

'It's not what you do, it's what you can't do. Ekata.'

'I've heard that word.' They speak in Portuguese now. Ekata is a wolf word, taken from Punjabi and made their own.

'I can't really translate it. It means the togetherness. Christians would say the fellowship, Muslims the ummah I think, but it's much more intense than that. Oneness, unity. More than that. You open your eyes and I see through them. We understand without understanding . . . I'm a wolf; I'm not sure I can explain it to anyone who isn't.'

'I love the way you say that. "I'm a wolf".'

'I am. It took me a long time to own it. I was your age when I realised what all those mood swings and personality shifts and the rages meant. I couldn't sleep, I was violent, I was hyperactive and then at other times – the dark times – I wouldn't speak to anyone for days. I thought I was sick. I thought I was dying. The doctor gave me meds. My madrinha knew what it was.'

'Bipolar disorder.'

'It's not a disorder,' Wagner says, then realises he has spoken too quickly, too sharply. 'It doesn't have to be a disorder. You can push it down with meds or you can push it in another direction altogether. You can make it into something more. What the wolves have done is given a social frame to it, a culture that accepts and supports it. Nourishes it.'

'Wolves.'

'We're not really wolves. We don't physically change at the turn of the Earth. Well, the brain chemistry does. We take meds that change our brain chemistry. *Werewolves* is a rich and emotionally fulfilling framing narrative for the fact that we cycle from one psychological state to another. Reverse werewolves. Werewolves inverted. Howling by the light of the Earth. Though photosensitivity isn't unknown in bipolar people. So the light might have something to do with it. Listen to me, I'm probably talking really fast and staccato?'

'You are.'

'That's the light aspect. I take a lot of meds, Robson. We all do. Madrinha Flavia knew what I was and she put me in touch with the packs, back when she was still at Boa Vista. They helped me, they showed me what I could do. They never put any pressure on me. It had to be my decision. It is a rich life. It's a tough life, becoming someone else every fifteen days.'

Robson sits upright, startled. Noodles and prawns fall from his chopsticks. 'Every fifteen days. I never knew . . .'

'It takes a toll. At Boa Vista, you only ever saw one me; dark-me, and you all thought that was Wagner Corta. There is no Wagner Corta; there's the wolf and his shadow.'

'I never saw you much at Boa Vista,' Robson says.

'There were other reasons,' Wagner says and Robson understands that those questions are for another time.

The boy asks, 'Wagner, when you stop being the wolf. When you turn in to the shadow. What happens to me?'

'The pack breaks up. We go to our shadow lives and shadow loves. But the pack never ends. We look out for each other. I'm a wolf, but I'm still a Corta. You're a Corta. I'll be there.'

Robson pokes with his chopsticks in his bowl.

'Wagner, do you think I could see my friends from Queen?'

'Not yet.'

'Okay.' Another Wayfarer glance. 'Wagner, I should tell you, I tried to find my traceur équipe.'

'I know. Robson...'

'Be careful on the network. I couldn't find them. I'm scared for them. Bob Mackenzie said he wouldn't hurt them...'

'But Bob Mackenzie's dead.'

'Yes. Bob Mackenzie's dead.' Robson looks around him. 'I like this place. I'd like to come here regularly.' It's a rite of adulthood, finding a customary hot-shop. 'Would that be okay?'

'It would.'

'Wagner, I take up a lot of your time. I take you away from them. Is that a problem?'

'It's a tension.'

'Wagner, do you think I can learn Ekata?'

The moto leaves the two women in the door of the Crystaline. Marina slaps a button and the wheelchair unfolds. Ariel swings herself into it. Staff turn and stare, unsure what to do, how they should serve. They are young, they have never seen a wheelchair.

'I can push you,' Marina says.

'I push myself,' Ariel says.

Ariel rolls across the polished sinter floor of the bar and in booths and at tables heads turn. *She's back; look at her, I thought she was dead.* Marina maintains a steady, dignified pace two steps ahead, clearing people from her path but Ariel sees the limps and winces of concealed hurt. Dr Macaraeg had strapped, patched, bound, anaesthetised the grosser wounds; Ariel covered the rest with fabric and make-up.

'Thank gods they left your face,' Ariel said. Marina grimaced as Ariel pulled the lace glove over the swollen fingers. 'You're going to lose a couple of nails. I'll print you some new ones.'

'I'll grow some new ones.'

'How long have we been together and you're still so terrestrial?' Ariel had felt a reaction in the hand she held, one not caused by any physical damage. 'There.' Now a final blend of the eye-liners, a last back-comb to big up the hair. Cocktail ready.

The Eagle of the Moon waits in the private room beyond the private room. The table is set among dripping stalagmites and stalactites, the whole a trickling, gurgling water park. Ariel finds it rather crass. The water smells fresh and pure. She inhales deep.

'Darling, if discretion is paramount, don't parade me the whole length of the Crystaline.'

The Eagle of the Moon booms with laughter. Drinks await: water for him, a dewed Martini for her.

'Ariel.' He stoops and takes both her hands in his. 'You look wonderful.'

'I look like shit, Jonathon. But my upper body strength is truly formidable.' Ariel places her elbow on the table, forearm upright, the classic arm-wrestler's challenge. 'I could take you, and probably everyone else in this bar except her.' She nods her big hair to Marina. 'Adrian not with you today?'

'I didn't tell him where I was going.'

'Conspiracies, Jonathon? How delicious. It won't do any good. Word will have made it round to Farside by now. And Adrian always was such a diligent Mackenzie.'

'He has more pressing concerns right now,' the Eagle says.

'And whose side is he on, his father's or his uncle's?'

'His own. As ever.'

'Eminently reasonable. And where does the Eagle of the Moon stand on the Mackenzie civil war?'

'The Eagle of the Moon stands for free contracts, economic growth, responsible citizenship and uninterrupted rental revenue flows,' Jonathon Kayode says, at the same time touching a finger to his right eye; the signal that this conversation will now be conducted without familiars. Pixels swirl and fizz in lenses. Bare. The Eagle of the Moon inclines his head the barest nod to Marina.

When Marina has closed the door to the softly lit, trickling stalactite room Ariel says, 'Do you know what I enjoy most about my work? The gossip. I hear the board of the LDC isn't happy with you, Jonathon.'

'The Board of the LDC want me gone,' the Eagle of the Moon says. 'I've been lucky that they're too mistrustful of each other's candidates to table a no-confidence motion. Earth is flexing its muscles. It has been since the collapse of Corta Hélio.'

'Collapse,' Ariel says. 'That's my family, Jonathon.'

'You once told me the Cortas kept the lights burning up there. Earth fears power shortages, dark cities. The price of domestic electricity has trebled. I was at Crucible, Ariel. I watched it burn. Duncan and Bryce are at each other's throats. They are hiring mercenaries from as far away as Earth. Blades battle on the Prospekts of Meridian. Commodity prices are soaring. Industries are closing. The old Earth looks up at the moon and it sees a world falling apart. It sees an Eagle who cannot fulfil his contract.'

Ariel takes a sip from her Martini. The Eagle knows her too well. It is perfect: cold, astringent, fabulous.

'Jonathon, if the LDC really wanted rid of you, they'd have bought up your bodyguards and gutted you in your sleep.'

'As you enjoy my protection, so I enjoy the protection of the Dragons. None of them wants to see an LDC stooge take over from me. The Suns fear another attempt by the People's Republic to seize control. Moscow will never admit anything, but the Vorontsovs have been regularly uncovering its agents and sending them out of the lock. The Asamoahs have no love for me but less much less love for Moscow and Beijing. The Mackenzies are wrapped up in their little war but the winner will side with whoever offers Mackenzie Metals the most freedom to wheel and deal.'

'And the Cortas?'

'Have no power, no wealth. No status to defend, no family to protect. Nothing to hold, nothing to fear. Which is why I want to hire you as my legal counsel.'

Can the Eagle detect the minute tremor of shock that runs across the meniscus of her thirteen-botanical gin?

'I do marriage contracts. I take human passion and human lust and human stupidity and give them as many escape routes as possible.'

'You can have it all back, Ariel. Everything you lost, everything you had taken from you.' He inclines his head to the wheelchair.

'Not everything, Jonathon. Some things are not in your gift.' But Ariel sets the glass down before the shivering gin betrays her. She never believed in her mother's personal style of umbanda – never believed in belief. She was thirteen when Adriana brought her to the new palace at Boa Vista. She had stepped from the tram station and been almost overwhelmed by the size, the light, the perspectives. She smelled rock, new humus, green growth, fresh water. She held up her hand to shield her eyes from the sky-glare, squinted, tried to focus on objects more than a few dozen metres distant. João de Deus had been close and cramped. This was endless. Then the faces of the orixas came into view, each a hundred metres tall, shaped from the stuff of Boa Vista and she knew she could never believe. One should never meet gods eye to eye. They looked stupid and stony. Dead and unworthy of faith. Embarrassments: these things wanted her trust?

But Madrinha Amalia had always told her the saints are subtle and Ariel has taken truths from the orixas that have kept her all her life. No heaven, no hell; no sin, no guilt; no judgement or punishment. One opportunity, once given, is all they offer. This is the grace of the saints. She deserves the Marc Jacobs dresses and the Maud Frizon shoes, the low-level Aquarius hub apartment, the place on the party circuit, the entourage of the adoring. She deserves to be famous, she deserves to be feted. She deserves to walk again. 'What do you want me to do, Jonathon?'

'I want you to be my lawyer of last resort. I want you to be my counsel when everyone else has abandoned me. For that I need someone with no vested interests, no family loyalties, no political ambition.'

She can feel the orixas around her like a cape; insubstantial yet crowding, eager to see if she takes the gift they offer. Not yet, you saints. The seal of a good lawyer – of this lawyer – is to put everything on trial. Even the saints. The fly move, the cheap trick, is a pillar of lunar law. Malandragem.

'A counsel of despair,' Ariel says.

'I have other counsellors. My enemies expect no less. I don't trust them.'

'They are your contracted counsels.'

'Lady Luna never made a contract she didn't break.'

'I won't be hidden away, Jonathon. I won't whisper in small rooms. The whole moon has to know that Ariel Corta is advising you.'

'Done.'

Ariel takes the last of her cocktail. Love me, says the spiral of lemon peel in the empty glass. Love me again. Have me. Her fingers touch the stem, ready to twist the glass a quarter-turn, the acknowledged sign for another. The table would sense it, a server would bring it to her, pure and dewed and cleansing. Almost. And release.

'What is Vidhya Rao's role?'

'With someone who claims to be able to predict the future, it's better to have er with you than against you.'

'With someone who can predict the future surely it doesn't matter which side e's on.'

'Our relationship has shifted. We were adviser and advised. Now we find ourselves allies.'

'Vidhya once told me er machines pegged me as a great mover and shaker in the affairs of the moon. What did they say about you, Jonathon?'

'The Eagle will fly.'

'Don't you just love prophecy? I'll do it. One condition. I go to every meeting. Beijaflor gets every report. I need to see their faces.'

'Thank you, Ariel.'

'That was my condition. These are my riders. Marina is my security. I want a clothing budget. I want a lovely apartment, one hundred square metres minimum, on a hub. No higher than 15th street. I want my legs back. Soon. But first...'

She flicks out her vaper to its full length and locks it. Then twists the stem of her Martini glass.

The wolves are dancing but Robson Corta doesn't dance. The moves are simple for him – most of the wolves are bad movers and poor dancers, he could out-funk any of them, and the music – musics; they can follow two different beats at the same time – not too painful, but Robson won't join the boogie. Wagner nods to him; Amal holds ner hands out in invitation, Robson shakes his head and drifts away from the beats and the bodies out on to the balcony. Amal the top wolf tried to bite Robson that morning. He shied away and avoided ner for the rest of the day but now he thinks it might have been a compliment. Wolves: there is so much to work out.

The club is on the 87th level on east Krikalev, the end of the prospekt; unfashionably far from the hub, disreputably high up. Robson hadn't wanted to go but a pack is hard to refuse. The wolves like to congregate at full-Earth. The Meridian pack is congregating with the Twé pack: pack members swap in, swap out. There will be a lot of sex.

Robson leans over the rail. Krikalev Prospekt is a canyon of lights, Antares Hub a distant glowing galaxy. Cable cars form chains of swaying lanterns; bikers down-hilling on 75th are streaks of light hurtling down the levels and staircases so fast so thrilling. Robson holds his breath. He did things like that once, when he was the boy who fell to Earth.

Robson holds his cocktail over the drop. There's more in it than alcohol. Hoang had been strict about psychotropics. Wagner doesn't have a clue about what's appropriate for kids. Hoang was strong on boundaries; always enforced but always negotiated. Wagner has no boundaries. Not in Wolf form. Robson misses Hoang. Robson thinks often about Hoang's last lie, outside at the lock at Lansberg Station. Wagner still won't let him contact Hoang, or Darius, or the traceurs.

Robson sets down his cocktail glass untouched. Another night, another party he might have wolfed it down and loved the buzz but for what he needs to do now he must be bright in head and bones. He reaches into a leg-warmer for the paint-stick. Robson suspects his 1980s workout gear was not originally designed for guys. Guys would have put in more pockets and pouches. But it looks good on him and feels better. He draws a thick band of white down his lips. Slash left slash right and there is a line of white along each cheekbone.

No one sees Robson Corta leap on to the railing, two kilometres of glowing space on his left, and run light and sure to the end of the balcony. The company of wolves wheels on. The two beats drift in and out of phase.

This place is easy. This place is like a climbing frame. It's a simple tic-tac to the balcony above. Robson takes a short stride, plants a foot on the wall, pushes himself up and back. Soars. Turns. Seizes the rail of the higher balcony and uses his momentum to clear the rail in a saut-de-bras, legs between arms. Run, bounce, a somersault that no one but him can see – that no one but Robson needs to see – and he is among the trusses that support the level above; running from girder to girder until he finds a place, a crotch where beam and strut meet, from which he can survey the whole club. Robson crouches, wraps his arms around his knees.

He had a pack once. Baptiste, teaching him the shapes and names of the moves. Netsanet who drilled him, again and again and again, until those moves became as close to him as breath and heartbeat. Rashmi who showed him the possibilities within his body. Lifen who opened his senses to see with more than eyes, feel with more than skin. Zaky who made him a traceur. His pack. His Ekata.

Amal comes out on to the balcony below. Né goes to the rail and the vista beyond. As if né can scent him – and Robson knows he has only seen the least part of what the wolves can do when they enter the group consciousness – Amal looks up. Eyes lock. Né nods to Robson, clinging to the ribs of the world. He returns the slightest acknowledgement.

Now Wagner joins Amal on the balcony. Robson watches unseen from his high perch. Cocktails fall in slow blue arcs from their hands, their fingers tear at each other's clothing. Amal has ripped Wagner's Guarabera shirt open to the navel. Né tugs at a nipple with ner teeth. Robson sees blood. Robson sees the alien joy on Wagner's face. Né leaves bloody bite marks all the way down his tight belly. Wagner's teeth are hard on ner ear lobe and né murmurs with hurt and pleasure.

Robson watches. The blood, the passion, the secrecy of his hidden perch, all excite him but Robson watches to understand. Blood runs from a dozen bites, flows down Wagner's dark skin, and Robson understands that being a wolf is not an understood thing. You can't learn to be a wolf. You are born a wolf. Robson can be in the pack, sheltered, protected, loved, but he can never be of the pack. He can never be a wolf. He is, he always will be, utterly alone.

Robson's table is at the back of the Eleventh Gate, hard against the glassy wall of the gas-seal. He twists an untouched glass of mint tea, a quarter-turn right, back, a quarter-turn left, back.

'You shouldn't be here alone,' Wagner says, dropping on to the chair.

'You said it was an important stage in socialisation, choosing your hot-shop,' Robson says. 'I like it here. And I'm not alone; now.'

'You have to think about security.'

'I know where the exits are. I'm facing out. You're the one with your back to the street.'

'I'm not happy you being away from the pack.'

'It's not my pack.' The boy reaches across the small table to jab the edge of a thumb nail into a bite mark on the side of Wagner's neck. 'Does that hurt?'

'Yes, a little.' Wagner does not flinch, does not move Robson's hand away.

'Does it hurt when né bites you?'

'Yes.'

'Why would you let ner do that?'

'Because I like it.' Wagner reads a dozen minute distastes flicker on Robson's face that would be invisible to any non-wolf. The boy conceals his emotions well. Growing up on Crucible, living in Queen of the South fearful of the call home, control would be a necessary skill.

'Do you love ner?'

'No.'

Again, the tightening of the jaw line, the tension of the corner of the mouth, the flick of the eyes away.

'Robson, I have to go away.'

'I know. It's the time of the lune. You're going dark.'

'Yes, but that's not why I'm going. I have work. I would love to stay more than anything, but I need to work. I'm taking a crew out on to the glass. I'll be gone seven, maybe ten days.'

Robson leans back against the cool glass wall. Wagner can't look at him.

'Amal will look after you,' Wagner says. 'Someone has to stay to mind the packhouse. But né'll change. Like I'm changing.' Wagner reads distrust, apprehension, fear in the tiny play of muscles beneath Robson's brown skin. 'I know you don't like Amal, but you can trust ner.'

'But it won't be the same Amal. Né will go away. You all go away. You all become someone else. Everyone goes away.'

'It's only seven days, Robson. Maybe ten. I will come back. I'll always come back. I promise.'

*

The delegation will arrive by train, the word went. *14:25 at João de Deus station, direct from Queen of the South. Private railcar.*

The notice was short, the expectations high. None other than Bryce Mackenzie is to inspect the new headquarters of Mackenzie Helium so João de Deus must honour him. Squadrons of bots clean the streets and prospekts and scrub anti-Mackenzie graffiti from the walls and apartment-fronts. Crews print banners and pennants and hang them from roof trusses and crosswalks. The conjoined letters of Mackenzie Helium's sigil stir in the constant light breezes of the air plants. Hoardings and posters cover up those scars and empty, smoke-stained shells that still stand derelict eighteen months after the battle of João de Deus. Squads of blades and cheap enforcers patrol the prospekts; immaculately dressed, more immaculately armed.

The train is prompt to the second. Bryce Mackenzie, his entourage and bodyguard, step from the emptied station on to Kondakova Prospekt. Jaime Hernandez-Mackenzie and his blades meet the honoured CEO. Bryce dismisses the fleet of motos that are to convey him to his João de Deus headquarters.

'I'll walk.'

'Of course, Mr Mackenzie.' Jaime Hernandez-Mackenzie dips his head, orders his private guard to fall in with Bryce's escort.

'Figures, Jaime. Reassure me that you have this place running smart and Mackenzie-style.'

Jaime Hernandez-Mackenzie reels off extractor deployments, estimated reserves, processing and output figures, reserves and delivery schedules, shipments to orbit and de-orbits to Earth. Information that could be faster and better transmitted familiar to familiar. Information Bryce could read in his office high on Kingscourt without coming within a thousand kilometres of João de Deus. This is the conqueror showing the vanquished his right and power. *I walk among you and you cannot touch me.*

'Your initial personnel problems have been resolved?' Bryce asks. His narrow, fat-girdled eyes flash left, right. No detail is lost to Bryce Mackenzie.

'They have, Mr Mackenzie,' Jaime says. 'And without blood.'

'Glad to hear it. Waste of good human resources. You've got the place looking smart. Cleaner than it ever was under those Cortas.'

Jaime knows that Bryce has never before been to João de Deus.

'On the surface, Mr Mackenzie. A lot of the infrastructure needs replacing to bring this place up to modern standards.' He ventures: 'As Head of Production, I would be reassured to know that it's safe to move extractors back into Mare Crisium. Without threat to my jackaroos.'

'Your jackaroos can work safely,' Dembo Amaechi, Head of Corporate security, says. 'I've cleared out Anguis, Crisium and East Tranquilitatis. And without blood too.' He smiles. 'Much blood.'

'And the head of Denny Mackenzie,' Alfonso Pereztrejo says. 'That's a coup.'

'Not quite,' Rowan Solveig-Mackenzie says, with evident pleasure. 'Some Taiyang glass-crew hauled him out of Schmidt Crater with ten minutes of O2 in his pack.'

'He always was a tough little dunny rat, my nephew,' Bryce says. 'But, as long as my brother is back pouring hot metal, I'm content. For now.'

Bryce stops dead, his entourage a heartbeat behind him.

'Jaime, this city is under your control?'

A rope hangs from the centre of West 7 crosswalk. The loose end is dyed red.

'I'll have it removed.' Blades are already in motion.

'Do that.'

Bryce Mackenzie sweeps on. His guard check the arcades and side alleys. The small, bloody reminder of what the Mackenzies did to João de Deus was a quick, furtive act. The culprit cannot have got far. Someone's familiar will have captured the deed. Bryce may even want to interrogate the culprit personally.

Mackenzie Helium's João de Deus office smells of new-printed furniture and flooring. The small human staff has the look of people who need to seem competent but don't yet fully know the terrain. There are fresh flowers, a touch Bryce admires with a sniff. No perfume. The Asamoahs breed for visual beauty, not olfactory.

Bryce settles his vast bulk behind the desk. It's been built to his body shape. He does not doubt that it will be deprinted the moment his railcar pulls out of João de Deus station. He studies the desk, the walls, the comfortable and stylish chairs arranged in front of his desk. It takes a moment for his staff to realise their error. A junior junior scurries to the kitchen area. A printer whines, water thunders to a boil for mandatory tea.

'I'm irked,' Bryce Mackenzie declares, pouting in displeasure. His chair creaks under his shifting weight. His feet kick in unconscious irritation. Everyone notices his small feet. A Mackenzie legend, Bryce Mackenzie's dainty feet. 'The boy. It is an affront to me, that I can't keep my own safe and secure.'

'He's under the protection of the Meridian pack,' Dembo Amaechi says.

'The Meridian pack!' Bryce roars. Backs stiffen, from the kitchen comes the sound of dropped glass. 'Fucking kids playing fucking games. You bring me my property, Dembo.'

'I'll arrange that, Mr Mackenzie,' Dembo Amaechi says.

'Be quick about it. Ariel Corta is back. Give her enough time and she'll drive a helium extractor clean through my adoption contract.'

Rowan Solveig-Mackenzie and Alfonso Pereztrejo exchange glances. This is news – unwelcome news – to them. This is a failure in corporate intelligence.

'Mr Mackenzie, I could hire assassins...' Dembo Amaechi ventures.

'You will not touch a hair on her cunt. Half of Meridian saw her doing cocktails with the Eagle of the Moon. He's contracted her.'

'The Eagle needs a D-list marriage lawyer?' Rowan says.

'Big men are not necessarily fools,' Bryce says and everyone in the room hears the steel in his voice.

'Mr Mackenzie?' The intern stands in the door, tray of tea-glasses in hand, plotting a course of grace and caution between the men packing the room. Bryce waves him in.

'Bring me Robson Mackenzie,' Bryce commands. 'If you're afraid of the big bad moon-wolf, wait until the pack dissolves.'

Dembo Amaechi conceals the flare of anger in his eyes inside a short, obedient bow.

'I'll make it my personal responsibility.'

'Good. No need for any particular gentleness.' Bryce lifts the freshly-printed tea-glass to his full, pursed lips. He sips, grimaces. 'Tasteless. Bloody tasteless. And far too hot.' He sets the glass on the white desk. The rest of his entourage set their untasted glasses on the tray. The intern is grey with fear. 'I think everyone in this shit hole who needs to see me has seen me? Then take me back to Queen.'

5: LIBRA – SCORPIO 2105

Wagner Corta has always thought gold cheap. Its colour is tawdry, its shine mendacious, its heft a fiction that equates weight with worth. Up in the sky hangs an entire planet hypnotised by the lie of gold. The acme of wealth, the spirit of greed, the final measure of value.

The moon is profligate with gold. Corta Hélio helium extractors threw away tons of gold every year in their exhaust plumes. Gold was not even worth the cost of its own sifting. Adriana Corta owned no gold, wore no jewels. Her wedding band was steel, forged from lunar iron. The steel ring on the Iron Hand.

The Church of Theotokos of Konstantin is a womb of gold. Gold the low door through which all must stoop to enter the presence of the holy icon, gold the walls and dome of this tiny chapel, gold the rails and lamps and censers, gold the frame of the tiny icon. The background of the icon is beaten lunar gold. Gold the cover over the lady and the child, only their faces and hands exposed. Gold the holy crown. The mother's skin is dark, her eyes downcast, looking away from the needy, pressing infant in her arms. Wagner has never seen such sad eyes. The child is a monster, too old, a tiny old man; greedily reaching a hand across the mother's throat, face pressed hard against the mother's cheek. Browns and golds. The legend is that Konstantin Vorontsov painted his icon in orbit, his wood and paints brought up over many launches from Kazakhstan with the materials to build the first cycler. He finished it on the moon with a backdrop of gold dust from the Sea of Tranquillity.

The Church of the Theotokos is the perfect place to meet Denny Mackenzie.

And here is the golden boy, ducking under the low lintel, squinting as he adjusts to the bioluminescence. Wagner is disappointed that he is wearing a black Helmut Lang suit. Denny Mackenzie grins at the decor. Gold teeth gleam.

'Tasteful.'

There is room enough in the Church of Theotokos of Konstantin for two men, no entourages.

'So where have you hidden your wolves, Wagner Corta?'

'Same place as you're hiding your blades.'

'I don't think so.' Denny Mackenzie opens his jacket to show the knife hilts, one in either holster. The hand grips are gold.

'I don't think so either,' Wagner says.

'Of course not. Do you think I'd come here without a bodyguard? You won't see them, Wagner.'

Meridian is free and disputed territory in the Mackenzie civil war. Factions skirmish, blades are drawn, fights sprawl across the prospekts, Zabbaleen wash blood from the streets. Denny Mackenzie buttons up his jacket. He bends to peer at the icon.

'Pretty.'

'The theory is that the image has always existed. The artist just found it,' Wagner says. 'You see that patch where the gilding is worn away? Lips did that. Thousands of lips. Maybe millions of lips. You kiss the icon, the love is transferred to the Lady.'

'Those Vorontsovs believe some weird shit. Three claims, Wagner Corta. You used one of them getting me here.'

'Keep him safe.'

'The boy?'

'Would I claim for anything else? Keep him safe from Bryce. In the dark time. When the pack breaks up. When I'm away. Watch over him.'

'I can do that, Wagner Corta,' Denny Mackenzie says. 'I give you my word on that. That's two claims. You have one more.'

'No,' Wagner says. 'Not yet. I'll know when I need it.'

'So be it. Our business is done, Wagner Corta?'

'Done.'

Wagner remains in the tiny chapel. The icon of the Theotokos of Konstantin is set low, to bring to their knees everyone who would revere it or marvel at it or be baffled by it or simply seek solace from it.

I have made a deal with the man who killed my brother, Wagner tells the little icon. *I have placed the boy I'm sworn to protect in the hands of my enemy. Do you condemn or do you forgive, Lady?*

The icon says nothing. Wagner Corta feels nothing.

Lady Sun sighs at the castles and dragons. Banal. She rolls her eyes at the manhua princesses and great moments in handball. Technical but tedious. She walks through the grove of woven trunks and branches without a sideways look.

'Now,' she says, 'this.'

The hollow cube is suspended from the dome by invisible lines. It seems to float in the air. The cube is hollow, its faces have been pierced with geometric patterns inspired by the Moorish architects of the Alhambra Palace. A light source hangs at the centre of the cube and casts a web of woven shadows across the two visitors standing before it. Lady Sun's breath hangs in the air and in turns becomes a surface for the interplay of shadows from the worked cube.

'Precision lasers,' says Sun Zhiyuan. 'Thaw, freeze action.'

'I don't want to know how the trick is done!' Lady Sun snaps but takes her grandson's arm and draws him close to her. Condensation from her breath is already freezing on the fur of her hooded cape. She shivers, though the cold is nowhere near as deep as when the ice field was first discovered. Water held as ice for two billion years in the perpetual shadow of Shackleton crater, while the peak of Malapert Mountain burns in eternal light. Ice and fire, darkness and light, the opposing elements out of which the Suns built the moon, lying next to each other. Three quarters of the ancient ice is gone, what remains is more than enough for the annual ice sculpture festival; for a hundred Zhongqiu. Castles and dragons. Dear gods.

This cube in its simplicity and geometric elegance pleases her.

'Who made this?' Lady Sun asks.

Her grandson names three kids Lady Sun cannot tell from the woman who hand stitches her shoes. Lady Sun walks around the Alhambra cube, through changing shadow-scapes, and thinks about her warm, softly lit apartments.

'I believe that Lucas Corta is alive,' she says.

'That would be important news,' Zhiyuan says.

'For many reasons,' Lady Sun says, continuing her orbit around the ice cube. 'I had discreet enquiries made. Amanda tells me that the rover in which Lucas Corta died was never found. No body, one's suspicions are naturally aroused. I had my agents run a satellite scan mapped against the range of a surface rover. They found it adjacent to the Central Fecunditatis Moonloop tower. The Vorontsovs are an endless trial of frustrations and obfuscations but my agents did find a record of a capsule launch at a time commensurate with an escape by rover from João de Deus.'

Lady Sun takes her grandson's arm again and draws him round to the third face of the ice lantern.

'Understand that discretion is everything. The evidence was slight, but evidence nonetheless, that Lucas Corta escaped off world by Moonloop. There is only one place he can go. If the Vorontsovs have been sheltering him, they are invested in keeping it secret. Too heavy a touch might alert them.'

'Nevertheless...'

Lady Sun squeezes Zhiyuan's arm. 'I am a nosy old woman. It was quite irresistible. The Vorontsovs are certainly keeping something secret, in space and on Earth. Money is moving. Money walks with a heavy tread. Terrestrial corporations are forming new venture capital groups. VTO Earth has come to an agreement with the Russian government.'

Zhiyuan lets go his grip on Lady Sun's arm.

'That's impossible.'

'More than that. My whisperers inside the Chinese Communist Party have gone quiet. That concerns me. They are afraid. Conspiracies assail me. Earth contrives and the Eagle of the Moon finds his board turn against him? Lady Luna allows no coincidences.'

'What do you suspect, nainai?'

'Lucas Corta is coming to take back what was stolen from him. He will have his revenge on those who destroyed his family.'

'Can the Three August Ones give us a foresight?'

'I am reluctant to involve them.' A tug on her grandson's sleeve draws him on to the final facet. Lady Sun closes her eyes in the broken light streaming from the cube of ice. 'We cannot act openly on this. Amanda will suspect that we know she lied to us about killing Lucas Corta. Her position on the board would be finished. She's been humiliated by Lucas Corta once: that divorce. Twice she will not allow. Involve the Three August Ones, and the whole board will know.'

'We have to know who we can trust. I will proceed discreetly and correctly. There will be no error.'

'Thank you, Zhiyuan.' Lady Sun links arms again. The frost is thick on the fur of her hood. 'Now, I've had quite enough of this frozen hell. Take me back for a nice warm glass of tea.'

It's a fantastic opportunity.

It's true. Nothing more true. How is it then that the greatest truth sounds like the feeblest lie?

I have a chance – one chance Luca – to study at the Cabochon.

And he'll say, Cabochon? And she'll have to explain again that it's the foremost political colloquium working on alternative models of lunar governance. And he'll say *What*? and that will blunt it, blur it. Cuts should be fast, sharp, clean.

It's a year. It sounds like forever, but it's not. And it's only Meridian, that's an hour on the train. It's a year, it's not the end.

But it is the end. Colloquium relationships don't work, her friends all say. Never have, never will. Break it off. He could come with me. Hands go up in horror. Are you insane? That's worse. He'll follow you round to all the political salons and cocktail parties and at some point you'll catch him out of the corner of your eye and for a moment you won't see Lucasinho Corta; you'll see a pet; and beyond that a point when you're ashamed of him and beyond that a point where you stop inviting him and a point where he no longer cares that you don't invite him.

So it has to be over and it is over. That is settled. The next question then: How to tell him it's over?

Familiar, her friends say. It's the modern way. I can't do that. He deserves better. Deserves better? He's moody, he's needy, he has no ambition and no self-respect and he'll fuck anything with a pulse – and he has – and good sex and better baked goods do not compensate for that. And she says: Yes, and add infuriating, vain, trivial, bored, demanding, insensitive and emotionally illiterate. And hurt hurt hurt. Hurt more than anyone she has ever known, more deeply. Scarred to the bone. He needs her. She doesn't want to be needed. She doesn't want a dependant. You can't let your life be trapped by another's.

When the tiny package had been delivered to her hand, brought by BALTRAN from Meridian, when she had found the two halves of the ear-spike inside, she had called the council of her abusua. They had not hesitated. The metal was the contract. She gave it back to Lucasinho and without a thought he slipped it through his ear, though its magic was used up. He still wears it. When he annoys her, when she hates him, she thinks he wears it to remind her that she owes him for her brother Kojo. That she will go on owing. That the debt is his to discharge, or hold. It is a small titanium hook in her freedom. She wants to shout: *It's our debt, not my debt.*

She hates him now. Then she sees his eyes; those Sun cheekbones; his full, lovely boy-lips. The swagger, the sly smile that hides and displays so many fears.

Can he read? she asks her familiar. A card, a piece of writing would be personal but keep the necessary distance.

He has a reading age of six, her familiar replies.

What did those Corta madrinhas teach their kids?

No letter, no familiar-to-familiar fuck off. It will be face to face. She dreads it, she is already running the script in her imagination. He is faithless and needy and annoys her more than anyone else she has ever known but this much she owes him.

Book me a table at Saint Joseph, she orders. It's classy and neutral and far enough away from her social orbit for friends not to be there.

She's going to miss the cakes.

The bar on the train refuses to serve him. First he won't accept it. The bar is polite but insistent. Then he shouts, *Do you know who I am?* The bar does but train bars have no facility for social status. Last he punches it, so hard he cracks the fascia. The bar reports damage and prepares a small legal claim.

I think you should go back to you seat, Jinji says. *Passengers are staring.*

'I want another drink.'

I'd advise against that. Your blood alcohol is two hundred milligrams per hundred millimetres of blood.

He refuses out of petty defiance but it is a worthless rebellion, defying a familiar. On the way back to his seat he glares down anyone who dares make eye contact.

This is the third day of Lucasinho's binge. The first day was chems.

A dozen custom houses, twice that many narcotic DJs. His mind, his emotions, his senses spun from high to low to out to in; colours and sounds expanding and contracting. Chems and sex: armed with a bagful of erotics he went to Serpent House, where Adelaja Oladele the Master Edger lived, and a house of cute boys who welcomed his bag of sexy-highs like Yam festival.

His aunt Lousika called him, messaged him, implored him to come home until he shut down Jinji and locked himself into a bubble of bodies, sweat and cum. Taking himself offline was the only thing that stopped him abuse-bombing Abena over the social network. The second day, still descending ten different paths from ten different highs, he took what was left in his bag of treats round to Kojo Asamoah. Kojo made him tea, put him to bed, folded himself around Lucasinho while they shared out the last of the pharmaceutical treats and fended off all the questions about why his sister had gone to Meridian, why she didn't think enough of him to stay, why nobody stayed, ever. By morning Lucasinho was gone. Kojo was relieved. He had dreaded having to blow him all night.

The third day Lucasinho went drinking. Twé was an ecosystem of tiny drinking places, from thatch shacks to pool bars to cubbyholes carved out of old rock, so small the clients fitted into them like segments of tangerine. Lucasinho was not a drinker. He did not know that there was a strategy to bingeing so he drank fast and freely and catholically. He drank spirits and stuff not made from printers; hand-made drink, banana beer and yam beer, pumpkin beer; Twé cocktails that were unlike anything else on the moon. He was a terrible, amateur drunk. He bored people. He forgot sentences. He stood too close. He took off his clothes in company. Twice he threw up. He didn't know alcohol could do that. He fell asleep on a potential lover and woke with a headache he was certain, *certain,* would kill him until Jinji, in offline mode, told him it was dehydration and a litre of water would ameliorate it.

Then he woke up and found himself folded up in the seat of a high-speed train. Wanting another drink. Which the bar refused him.

'Where am I going?' Lucasinho asks but before Jinji can answer he hears a man's voice speaking to a child, and the child answering, both in Portuguese and at the sound of the hummed nasals and burnished sibilants Lucasinho pulls his knees in to his chest and sobs silently, convulsively.

João de Deus. He is going back.

He's the last off the train, the last through the passenger lock; the last standing, unsteady, on the platform of João de Deus station. So many times across this shining floor. To friends and amors and the great cities of the moon. To his wedding. To Meridian, when he ran away from the boredom and confinement of Boa Vista and he discovered that on a world as small as the moon all running away from is running to and that all he was exchanging was a small cave for a larger one.

'How's my eye make-up?' Lucasinho asks. He remembers now, putting on the slap in Kojo's toilet. Not the full ensemble; something to make him feel wild and fierce, something to mark that Lucasinho Corta is returning to João de Deus.

I'm offline so I can't see, but your last application was three hours ago so I recommend a little touch up.

The washroom has old-fashioned mirrors. Lucasinho works as deftly as the alcohol in his brain will allow. He admires one profile, then the other. This 1980s retro really suits him.

The smell. He had forgotten it, but smell is the lock of memory and the first breath is all his nineteen years of being a Corta. Raw stone and the tang of electricity. Overworked sewage and the perfumes used to mask it, piss, cooking oil. The vanilla greasiness of printer plastic. Bodies. They sweat differently in João de Deus. The fresh sweetness of bots. Dust. Everywhere, dust.

Lucasinho sneezes.

So small. The prospekts are narrow, the roof so low he cringes from it. Twé obeys an architecture different from any other lunar settlement. It is a city turned on its end; clusters of slim silos a kilometre high, filled with green and true light bounced down cascades of mirrors, not the false sky of the sunline. Twé is a city of hidings and discoveries: João de Deus is open. Kondakova Prospekt, crossed by bridges and catwalks, stretches true before him the city's hub.

They came through here, on the night of knives. Off the train, through the locks, across that wide station plaza. Ghost soldiers march past Lucasinho, hands on knife hilts. Scorch-marked walls and building fronts; the old Corta Hélio offices hollow like punched-out teeth. His father's apartment; the finest sound-room in two worlds a mass of fused audio equipment and charred wood.

Santinhos hurry past on foot, scooter, motos. Eighteen months ago the whole moon knew his face. Wedding of the year! Stylish and cute Lucasinho Corta. Some faces turn, some double-take, most don't even spare him a glance. Is it that they don't recognise him, or that it is safer not to recognise him?

West 7 catwalk. Lucasinho stands and looks up. The Mackenzies hung Carlinhos's stripped body by his heels from those girders. Arms and long hair and dick hanging down. Throat opened. They drove him to his knees with tasers, they closed in around him. So many blades. He could not escape. While Lucasinho hid in Twé, protected by the knives and living weapons of the Asamoahs.

Mackenzie Helium logos on office fronts, bots, the banners that drape fifty metres from the higher levels. A duster in a sasuit passes, fingers hooked through the faceplate of a helmet that carries a small MH on its brow. There are more white faces than he remembers. The hot-shops and tea-houses and bars chalk up their daily specials on the wall in Portuguese and Globo. English on the streets; Australian accented.

I can't protect you if I'm offline, Jinji says, as if reading his thoughts. Perhaps it is. Perhaps its circuitry has worked its way through his skull into the folds of his brain, reading the spark of neurons. Perhaps it just knows Lucasinho so well that it has become an echo of his mind.

Lucasinho stops at the entrance plaza to the Estádio da Luz. New lettering, new name, new corporate identity. Ballarat Arena. Home of the Jaguars.

'Jaguars,' Lucasinho says.

Terrestrial members of the cat . . . Jinji starts.

A voice calls from a higher level; a *hey!* Lucasinho knows is directed at him. A second call, more doubtful. Lucasinho walks on. His destination is clear now.

The Boa Vista tram station has been screened off with sheeting, sealed with Do Not Cross tapes and the suit-helmet symbol of depressurisation warning. Even without the shuttering, Lucasinho couldn't have gone there: Boa Vista is dead, depressurised, open to vacuum; locked behind many pressure seals. The foot of the wall is a rippling pool of coloured lights. Biolights, hundreds of them; some fresh and new, some pulsing fitfully on the edge of death. The minuscule lights – red, gold, green – catch on a host of small objects huddling along the lanterns. Closer, Lucasinho sees that they are cheap plastic prints of the orixas and their attributes – both their umbanda and their Christian aspects. The blade of Ogun, the thunderbolt of Xango, the crown of Yemanja.

The four icons are arranged in a triangle; Adriana at the centre. Rafa the apex, the lower points occupied by Carlinhos and Lucas. The images are small, hand-sized, devotional; the frames heavy and decorated with paint, jewels, more plastic votives. The luminescents cast a wavering light over the triangle of faces, over Lucasinho's face as he squats to examine the other offerings left at the shrine.

A Moços shirt, '03 season. A T-shirt, contemporary cut, carrying the image of a dust-bike: Serenitatis Endurance Race. Many knives, their tips snapped off. Music cubes which, when Lucasinho lifts them, play the old bossa nova his father and grandmother loved. Pictures, dozens of pictures: dusters and handball fans and wonderful pictures of the old days of the moon, when Adriana built a world. Lucasinho lifts them: the images are old but the pictures smell freshly printed. This bearded, smiling man is the grandfather he never knew, who died before even his father was born. Here are madrinhas with children in their arms and at their sides. Here are the faces of Boa Vista half-carved. These are gods that speak to Lucasinho, things found inside stone, emerging from raw rock. Here are two young women; one his grandmother, the other unknown to Lucasinho. Their heads are together, they smile for the lens. His grandmother wears a compression shirt with the Mackenzie Metals double-M logo. The other woman's shirt carries a Ghanaian adinkra.

They are gone. He remains, kneeling drunk among the votives. He is disgusting. He loathes himself. The icons reproach him.

'Not you.' Lucasinho tries to rip the picture of his father from the wall but it has been glued in place. He scrabbles to find an edge he can tug. A hand on his arm, a voice.

'Leave it.'

He turns, fist balled to drive it deep into a face, a snarl on his face.

The old woman steps back, hands raised, not defensively, not in fear, but in wonder. She is knife-thin, dark, swathed in white robes, a white turban on her head. She wears a green and blue stole, many rings, more necklaces. Lucasinho knows her but cannot remember where. She recognises him.

'Oh you, little mestre.'

She darts her hands forward, fast as a knife-fighter's stab, and folds Lucasinho's hands in her own.

'I'm not...' He can't pull away. Her eyes are dark and deep and paralyse him with fear. He recognises those eyes. He has seen them twice; once at Boa Vista with his Vo Adriana, again at his grandmother's eightieth birthday feast. 'You're a sister...'

'Irmã Loa, of the Sisterhood of the Lords of Now.' She kneels before Lucasinho. 'I was your mother's confessor. She was generous to my order.' She rearranges votives where Lucasinho's feet have scattered them. 'I chase the bots away – they know no respect, but the Zabbaleen remember the Cortas. I always knew someone would come. I hoped it would be you.' Lucasinho snatches his hands from her dry, hot grasp. He stands up, and that is worse. This old woman kneeling in front of him horrifies him. She looks up into his eyes and it is like supplication. 'You have friends here. This is your city. The Mackenzies don't own it, they never could. There are people here still regard the name of Corta.'

'Go away, leave me alone!' Lucasinho yells, backing away from the sister.

'Welcome home, Lucasinho Corta.'

'My home? I've seen my home. I went there. You've seen nothing. You feed lights and chase bots and dust the pictures. I was there. I went down and I saw the plants dead and the water frozen and the rooms open to vacuum. I got the people out of the refuges. I got my cousin out. You weren't there. You saw nothing.'

But he swore he would come back. His sasuit boots crunching the flash-frozen debris of a great house, he vowed he would bring it back. This was his.

He can't. He doesn't have it in him. He is weak and vain and luxurious and stupid. He turns and runs, sobered by shock and adrenaline.

'You are the true heir,' Irmã Loa calls after him. 'This is your city.'

By the second, Lucasinho knows that Blue Moons are terrible cocktails. He finishes it and orders the third and the bartender knows the right way and does the trick with the inverted tea spoon, the tendrils of blue Curacao dispersing into the gin like guilt. Lucasinho picks it up and tries to catch the bar lights in its blue cone. He is back drunk again, where he wanted. His Tio Rafa created the Blue Moon but he knew nothing about good cocktails.

The bar is small, smelly, dim, booming with loud chart music and louder conversation and the bartender recognises Lucasinho but keeps professional discretion. The girl does not. They came in halfway through his first; two girls, two boys, one neutro. They've been glancing over from their booth carved from raw rock, glancing away when he catches their eyes. Heads down, furtive. She waits until the fourth Blue Moon to make her approach.

'Ola. You're, ah . . .'

Pointless to deny. He would only spark rumours, and rumours are legends that have only just learned to crawl.

'I am.'

Her name is Geni. She introduces Mo, Jamal, Thor, Calyx. They smile and nod from their booth, waiting for a sign to join him.

'Do you mind if I?' Geni gestures to the stool, the empty bar space.

'Yes actually.'

She either doesn't hear or doesn't care.

'We're, Urbanistes?'

Lucasinho's heard of this. Some extreme sport; suiting up and exploring old abandoned habitats and industrial plants. Abseiling down agriculture shifts. Crawling along tunnels with your O2 gauge running down in the corner of your eye. No interest. History, sport and pointless danger. He hates all of those. Too much like effort. Lucasinho slides back on his stool until he rests his chin on his hands, studying the half-drunk fifth Blue Moon. The bartender catches his eye; the flicker of silent communication says *give the nod and I will get rid of her.*

'We've been out there. Three times.'

'Boa Vista.'

'We can take you.'

'You went to Boa Vista?'

She looks less certain now; she glances over at her friends. The gulf beyond booth and bar is stellar.

'You went to Boa Vista?' Lucasinho says. 'You went to my home? What did you do, go along the tram line? Or did you go down the surface shaft? Did you feel really proud when you touched down; like you'd really done something? Did you all do high-fives?'

'I'm sorry, I just thought...'

'My home, my fucking home.' Lucasinho turns his fury on the young woman and it is hot and pure, fuelled by shame and self-loathing and Blue Moon. 'You went to my home and you walked all over it and took your pictures and your movies. Look, here's me in the São Sebastião Pavilion. Here's me in front of Oxala. Did your friends love them and say that's so amazing, you're so daring and brave? That's my home. My fucking home. Who said you could go to my home? Did you ask? Did you think maybe you had to ask? That's there a Corta left to ask?'

'I'm sorry,' the young woman says. 'I'm sorry.' She is scared now and Lucasinho is so mean with alcohol and shame he adds her fear to his combustion. He smashes his Martini glass down on the bar, shattering the stem, spilling blue liquor over the glowing counter. He staggers to his feet.

'It's not yours!'

The barman has caught the woman's eye but her friends are already leaving.

'I didn't mean...' the young woman calls from the door. She is in tears.

'You weren't there!' Lucasinho shouts after her. 'You weren't there.'

The bartender has mopped up the breakage and set a glass of tea on the counter.

'She wasn't there,' Lucasinho says to the bartender. 'Sorry. Sorry.'

'So there he is.' Lucasinho had given no more than a glance to the duster on the far side of the bar but now she looks up from her caipiroshka and speaks. The bar throws strong shadows up from her features. Her dark face is spotted white with radiation-induced vitiligo. 'Mão de Ferro.'

'What?' Lucasinho snaps.

'The Iron Hand. The Corta name. I gave your family twenty-five years of my life. I'm owed.'

Owed? is on Lucasinho's tongue but before the word can be spoken the tiny bar is full of big women and men in fashionable suits and bulges in their jackets that hint at bladed weapons. Three surround Lucasinho, two cover the bar, one on each shoulder of the duster. Adinkra familiars. AKA security.

The squad leader sets a titanium ear-spike on the glowing white bar.

'You forgot that,' he says. The duster looks at Lucasinho, shrugs. 'Come with us please, Senhor Corta.'

'I'm staying...' Lucasinho says but the guards haul him to his feet. A firm hand on his right forearm, another in the small of his back.

'Sorry,' the duster says as the Asamoah guards hurry Lucasinho out on to Kondakova Prospekt. 'I mistook you for the Iron Hand.'

'I thought you'd like the room with the window.'

Ariel wheels from the living space into the bedroom and around the bed. A bed, not a hammock. A free-standing bed. A bed wide enough to spread out every limb. A bed with space all around it. Space enough to move properly, freely. Compared with the moss-damp wooden home, rain dripping from its shingles, in which Marina grew up, the apartment on Orion Hub is a clutch of cubbyholes, intimate as a wasp's nest. By Meridian standards, it is the pinnacle of desirability; low enough to be fashionable, high enough to escape the grosser smells and sounds of the prospekt. By the standards of the holes up in Bairro Alto, it is paradise.

'Give me the traffic noise, right,' Marina says. She sees Ariel crest-fallen and regrets the jibe. The apartment is magnificent.

'Show me more,' Marina says with what she hopes sounds like enthusiasm. Ariel's court-room senses have been dulled by the excitement of the new apartment. On any other day she would have heard the insincerity like a temple bell.

There are two bedrooms, a living space and an auxiliary social space which can be closed off. An office, Ariel declares. There is a small separate room for whatever purposes require a small separate room.

'That could be your new sex room,' Marina declares, putting her head around the door to check the dimensions. 'Soft flooring, new wall covering.'

Sex had been problematic up in Bairro Alto. Her disability and reduced station in life had not touched Ariel's autosexuality. Times and spaces were negotiated. Marina donated her pittance of a carbon allowance to print up Ariel's sex toys. Sex became a household joke, a third character in the family, with its own nicknames and vocabulary and code: Senhora Siririca and Ribbed and Exciting. Sister Rabbit – Marina had to explain what a rabbit was – was the household trickster deity and Senhor Girth kept up an ongoing rivalry with Senhor Depth. The conversation became easy but it never once crossed to Marina's side of the tiny apartment. Who she was doing it with; who might she do it with; was she doing it all? Marina had in time accepted celibacy as the pledge of her watch over Ariel Corta. Most of the time she was too tired to even remember sex, much less engineer a fantasy. Now, as she closes the door on the small room in the vast new apartment, the possibility opens. She can think about herself.

A private banja. A separate spa, in which the water keeps running until you shut it off. Marina still can't believe that the Four Elamentals graphics on her chib are gold and remain gold. There is a house printer. There is a food space and a chiller. The chiller is stocked with designer gins and vodkas, the food space with twists and mixers and botanicals, and the work surfaces with appropriate glassware.

'Marina coracão, I'd adore a Martini.'

'It's just gone ten.'

'Where's your sense of celebration?'

Bairro Alto had been lean in pleasure. Anything that tasted of victory – a case, a deal, a new thing around the house – Ariel celebrated. Marina had recognised the point at which celebration slumped into dangerous drinking. It would have to be faced, some day, some place. Not in Bairro Alto. This is the place, but Marina cannot make this the day. This is a worthy celebration. She mixes two breathtakingly dry Martinis from a twenty-two botanical from Cyrillus. Ariel levers herself out of the wheelchair and drops into the yielding expanse of the lounger. The wheelchair scurries to a corner and folds itself down to a flat box.

'What do we think?' Ariel lifts her legs on to the couch, one at a time, sprawls out, Martini glass in hand.

'I'm thinking, who lived here before?' Marina says.

'You nortes are such Puritans.' She raises her glass. 'Saude!'

Marina tips glass against glass. It has the ring of good crystal. 'Tim tim.'

'Since you ask, it belonged to Yulia Shcherban. She was a special economic adviser to Rostam Baranghani.'

'The LDC Board Member?'

'The same. She was recalled. There's been a spate of recalls among the LDC ancillary staff.'

'You'd think...'

'I have mentioned it to the Eagle.'

'And?'

'He thanked me for my due diligence.'

'Well, I do know it's a seller's market in personal security,' Marina says. 'Above and beyond the Mackenzies. If you've got any kind of history with the Dragons, you can name your price.'

Ariel sits up.

'Where did you hear this?'

'While you're listening, we're talking.'

'Why didn't I hear that?'

'Because you're sitting on Jonathon Kayode's shoulder trying to work out if his lawyers will stab each other before they stab him.'

'I should be on that,' Ariel insists. 'I'd have been on that. Anyone as much as belched in Meridian, I used to know it.'

'You've been out...'

Ariel cuts in.

'He's fucked. His board is against him. His legals are trying to save their own asses. I'm the only one he trusts.' Ariel takes a long draw at her Martini. 'It's all so polite and formal and discreet, but I read the faces. The LDC was constituted so that no terrestrial government could gain overall control. They're unified now. Something has changed. The board will act to remove him soon.'

'If he jumps before he's pushed?'

'The board will still put their stooge in.'

'Fucked if he does, fucked if he doesn't. What did he do to piss off his board so mightily?'

'The Eagle of the Moon is a great big stupid romantic. He believes that the office of the Eagle of the Moon should be more than just rubber-stamping the edicts of the LDC and mincing around cocktail receptions. He believes in this world.'

'When you say, he believes in this world...'

'Self-government. Turn us into a state, not an industrial colony. He's become political, the dear thing.'

'That would piss them off,' Marina says.

'Yes,' Ariel says. 'I whisper in his ear and I take his money and his apartment and there's not a thing I can do.' Ariel throws herself back down on the lounger and stretches her arms wide. Marina scoops up the Martini glass as Ariel's fingers lose their grip on the stem. 'Which is a pity, because I rather like the big idiot. Enough politics. I want the vodka this time.'

'Ariel, do you think...'

'Get me a fucking vodka Martini, Marina.'

The glass, the ice, the chill-thick liquid. The homoeopathic drip of vermouth. Ariel's casual arrogance never fails to wound. Never a pause, never a thought for what Marina might want. Never the consideration that Marina wouldn't want the bedroom with the window. Never the notion Marina might not want to move into the apartment. Never the question about Marina's life. Marina's hand shakes with tight rage as she stirs the Martini. She does not spill a drop. Never a drop.

'Sorry,' Ariel says. 'That was inelegant.' She sips the Martini. 'This is a thing of beauty. But tell me, what do you really think?'

'I think that if the Eagle falls, try not to be underneath him.'

'No, not the Eagle, enough of the fucking Eagle,' Ariel snaps. 'And the fucking LDC and lawyers and advisers and every little gimcrack political club and debating society and activism group. Now, tonight, I need you. There's a Lunarian Society meeting I want to go to.'

'You want to go to the Lunarian Society?'

'Yes. The Cabochon political science colloquium is delivering papers on models for lunar democracy.'

'Well, I've got your excuse. I've a ticket to go and hear a band.'

'You've what? You never told me.'

Marina bridles. 'I need permission to go and hear a band?'

'What do you need to go and hear a band for? Do we even have bands any more?'

'We do and I like them and I want to see one.'

'Is this that rock stuff?'

'I need to justify my taste in bands?' Marina had learned quickly that Ariel, unlike her brother, had no appreciation of music and camouflaged her ignorance as disdain.

'Here's what you do. Drop me off, go and get yourself a cup of tea and have Hetty stream this ... band. It'll be just like being there. Better. You won't have all those ghastly sweaty rock people in your face.'

'Ghastly sweaty people in your face is what makes it rock,' Marina says but Ariel's incomprehension is so total, so manifest, any further defence of guitar-led music will only confuse. 'You do owe me.'

'I owe you so much that there is no possible hope of me ever repaying it. But I need to go to the Lunarian Society. I've no interest at all in ghastly zealous student idealism. No, I want to go because Abena Maanu Asamoah is delivering a paper and the last thing I heard she was fucking my nephew Lucasinho. And I'm concerned about the little fucker. So, will you?'

Marina nods. Family wins.

'Thank you, sweetie. Now, third time of asking: What do you think?' Ariel gestures expensively to the wide white room and sends vodka slopping on to the lounger.

'I'm thinking how do I rig it?'

'Ropes and nets? Handles on everything?'

'I think of them more as mobility aids.'

'I plan not to need them.'

There is only one scenario under which Ariel will not need Marina's rigging of nets and lines to move around the apartment.

'You didn't tell me.'

'I should tell you every detail of my deal with the Eagle?'

'Walking is a bit more important than wanting to go and see a rock band.'

'Do you think I would have agreed if walking wasn't part of the deal?' Ariel says.

'I remember Dr Macaraeg said it could take months,' Marina says. 'That spinal nerves were a slow and painstaking job.'

'It takes as long as it takes. But I'll be mobile, Marina. I won't need that.' Ariel slops vodka toward the recharging wheelchair. 'I won't need you. No, yes, I will. You know what I mean. I will always need you.'

The hands over his eyes disgust him. Hot, dry, skin papery, rustling. He holds his eyelids tightly shut. The idea of those palms, that skin touching a naked eyeball brings a retch to his throat.

Motion ceases, doors open. The hands impel him a few steps forward, then fly from his face.

'Open your eyes, boy.'

His first thought is to refuse; irked by the tone of command in the old woman's voice, the touch of the old woman's controlling hand on his shoulder, though he is a head taller than her. He had prickled with small rebellion when she ordered him to close his eyes and keep them closed the whole ride up in the elevator, as he had bristled when she snatched the vaper out of his hand. *A ridiculous affectation.* But rebellion costs, and more, he knows she will wait until he obeys her.

Darius Mackenzie opens his eyes. Light. Searing light. He closes his eyes. He beheld the light of Ironfall, the light of destruction. This light is so bright he can see the capillaries in his eyelids.

The pavilion is a glass lantern atop the slender elevator tower atop Malapert Mountain. Darius stands at the centre of the hexagonal floor. Tiles, struts, vaults and ribs, the glass itself looks blasted and weary, their structural integrity pecked away photon by photon. The ideograms on the elevator call panel are bleached almost to illegibility. The air tastes scorched, strained, ionised.

'Every Sun is brought here at the age of ten,' Lady Sun says. 'You're late being a Sun, but you're no exception.' Darius lifts his hand to shade his eyes, lets it fall. No child of the Palace of Eternal Light would ever do such a thing.

Not a lantern, Darius realises. The light of a lantern comes from within. This light comes from without; from a blinding sun perched on the very rim of Shackleton crater. Low midnight sun casts huge shadows up behind Darius like wings. Every dust mote dances. The Pavilion of Eternal Light is not a place where you observe the sun; it's a place where the sun observes you.

'Yeah, we had this in Crucible,' Darius says.

'Don't be clever with me,' Lady Sun says. 'The difference is profound. Crucible had to forever follow the sun. The sun comes to us. Go, go on. Look at it. Go as close as you dare.'

Darius is not to be dared by old women. He walks without hesitation to the glass, presses his palms to it. The toughened glass pane feels frail. It smells of dust and time. He looks full on the sun, rolling along the edge of the world. The Pavilion is a Peak of Eternal Light, one of those legendary places across the worlds, all at the poles, where the sun never sets.

'Fifty years ago a message came in the night. It was on another world, in another city in another country. I had awaited that message for years. I was ready for it. I got up and left everything and went down to the car that I knew would be there. The car took me to a private plane. Aboard it were my aunts and uncles, my sisters and cousins. The plane took us to VTO Kazakhstan, and then to the moon. Do you know what that message said, boy?'

Darius wants very much to lick the window, taste the glass.

'It said that a faction in the government was moving to arrest my family,' Lady Sun says. 'They wanted hostages they could use to leverage my husband. Even a Mackenzie must have heard of the name of Sun Aiguo. Sun Aiguo, Sun Xiaoqing, Sun Honghui. They built Taiyang. They built the moon. Learn history, boy: the Outer Space Treaty bars Earth's national governments from claiming and controlling the moon – this is why we are administered by a corporation, not a political party. The terrestrial states have always envied our freedom, our wealth, our achievements. What they fear is someone else taking the moon, so they watch each other. Jealousy is an honest emotion, easy to manipulate. Jealousy has kept us safe for fifty years.

'Every family has a fear; every one of the Five Dragons. The Cortas feared that their children would destroy their inheritance. The Mackenzies...'

'Ironfall,' Darius Mackenzie says, without thought.

'Do you know what the Suns fear?' Lady Sun says. 'That the sun will go out. That one day it will dip below that horizon and never rise again and we will go down in the cold and dark. The air will freeze. The glass will shatter.'

'That can't happen,' Darius says. 'It's astronomy, physics: science.'

'So ready with glib answers. The day the sun goes out is the day the rules break. The rule that has protected us for fifty years; the day the terrestrial states realise they have more to gain by acting together than stalking each other with knives. This is my family's fear, Darius; the call in the night. When it comes, everything we have built, everything we have achieved, will be taken from us because we have nowhere to run.'

'Is this what you tell all the others you bring up here?'

'Yes. I tell them that; the ones I think need to hear it from me.'

'And you think I need to hear that from you?'

'No. What you need to hear from me, Darius, is that Ironfall was no accident.'

He turns from the glass. Lady Sun's face is impassive – Lady Sun's face is always perfect, discreet – but Darius knows his obvious shock has pleased her.

'Crucible was sabotaged. There was code embedded in the operating system for the smelter mirrors. A simple but effective routine. But you saw what it did.'

'You are the coders,' Darius says. Dust dances in the hot light around Lady Sun.

'We are. Pre-eminently. Information is our business. But this was not our code.'

'Whose was it?'

'You're not the Prince, Darius. You're not the last heir of Robert and Jade. Duncan and Bryce are at each other's throats, do you really think there's a seat at their tables for you? Do you think you're safe?'

'I...'

'You're safe here, Darius. This is the only place you can be safe. With your family.' Lady Sun has been moving step by unnoticed step, subtly steering Darius so that now she stands between him and the slow-rising sun. Darius squints into the painful light. Lady Sun is a heavy silhouette.

'Do you think we'd let those Australian barbarians decide the succession? You're not a Mackenzie, Darius. You never were. They know it. You wouldn't have lasted six lunes. The Ironfall code, Darius; it was old code. Older than you. Much older.'

'I don't understand.'

'Of course you don't. It was the Cortas who killed your mother.'

Abena Maanu Asamoah accepts the applause with a coy smile. The Lunarian Society's Erasmus Darwin Salon is full; the faces close. The audience was easy to read: the sitter-back-with-arms-folded in the front row, the sitter-forward-with-the-constant-frown in the second row; the head-shaker second row far right, the mutterers in the second row centre, the stifled yawner in the third row. The Lunarian Society printed out extra chairs but there are still listeners perched on the arms of the big old-fashioned seats, leaning against the back wall. She can barely see through the host of hovering familiars.

Abena is the last to present and the room has broken into private discussion as she comes down from the dais. Her colloquium mates press in to congratulate and adulate. Wait-staff offer drinks: small vodka, genever, cocktail tea. Abena takes a glass of chilled tea. As she receives compliments, accepts offers to speak, fields the questions of one persistent young man, she notices a disturbance in the room, as if people are making space for an object moving through them. A woman in a wheelchair: the wheelchair incredible, the woman unbelievable. Ariel Corta. Abena's colloquium mates part to admit her to the circle.

'Nicely done,' Ariel says. She looks to Abena's classmates. 'Would you mind?'

Abena nods: *Catch you later when we go on to the club.*

'Let's go on the balcony. The decor in here nauseates me.' Ariel rolls towards the pavilion above West 65th. 'A few notes. Always have something to do with your hands. Lawyers and actors know this. You're not about truth, you're about persuasion. People believe body language when they won't believe spoken language.' She scoops a genever from a tray and thanks the waiter. 'Second note. Work your audience. Before you open your mouth, pick your targets. Who looks frightened, who looks over-confident, who catches your eye when you check out the room, who would you most like to seduce. Target them with what you have to say that they want to hear. Make them feel like you are speaking to them personally. If they nod, if they adjust their body posture to mirror yours, you have them.'

Ariel pats a low padded bench by the balustrade. Abena accepts the invitation to sit. Voices burble from the rooms beyond, laughs and interjections spike drama into the susurrus of networking. The sunline dims to indigo. Orion Quadra is a canyonland of lights, the glowing nave of a stupendous, godless cathedral.

'You take me away from my friends and then tell me everything I'm doing wrong,' Abena says.

'I know, I'm an arrogant monster.' Ariel takes a sip of her genever and grimaces. 'This is hideous stuff.'

'How did you find my paper?'

'You're taking a terrible risk, asking me that. I could say I found it banal, naive and jejune.'

'I'd still stand by it.'

'I'm very glad to hear that.'

'So what did you think of it?'

'I'm a lawyer. I see society as sets of individual but interacting contracts. Webs of engagement and obligation. Society is this' – she lifts her thimble of genever up to the cross-town lights – 'in a Nicole Farhi dress. My problem with democracy is that I think we already have a more effective system. Your argument from terrestrial small states was fascinating, but the moon is different. We're not a state; we're an economic colony. If I were to make a terrestrial analogy, it would be with something enclosed and constrained by its environment. A deep sea fishing boat, or perhaps an Antarctic research base. We're clients, not citizens. We are a rentier culture. We don't own anything, we have no property rights, we are a low-stakes society. What's my motivation to participate?

'The problem with a democracy – even as elegantly constructed a direct democracy as yours – is free-riding. There will always be those who don't want to participate, yet they share the benefits of those who do engage. If I could get away with free-riding, I certainly would. I only agreed to join the Pavilion of the White Hare because I thought it would give me a hand up to the Court of Clavius. Justice Ariel Corta has a nice ring to it. You can't compel people to engage politically – that's tyranny. In a society with low benefits to participation you end up with a majority of free-riders and a small engaged political caste. Leave democracy to those who wish to practise it and you always end up with a political class. Or worse, a representative democracy. Right now, we have a system of accountability that engages every single person on the moon. Our legal system makes every human responsible for their life, security and wealth. It's individualistic and it's atomising and it's harsh but it is understood. And the limits are clear. No one makes decisions or assumes responsibilities for anyone else. It doesn't recognise groups or religions or factions or political parties. There are individuals, there are families, there are corporations. Academics come up from Earth to Farside and tut and roll their eyes about us being cut-throat individualists with no concept of solidarity. But we do have what they would call a civil society. We just believe it's best left to negotiation, not legislation. We are unsophisticated grudge-bearing barbarians. I rather like it.'

'So: banal, naive and jejune,' Abena says. 'You didn't come here to listen to political science students deliver naive banalities.'

'Of course not. Is he well?'

'We will keep him safe.'

159

'That wasn't what I asked.'

'He's with Madrinha Elis. Luna's with her too. Sometimes Lousika, when she's not up in Meridian.'

'That wasn't what I asked either.'

'Okay.' Abena sucks in her lip; a tell of emotional discomfort. 'I think I broke his heart.' Ariel raises an eyebrow. 'I had to come here. A chance to study in Cabochon?' Ariel's eyebrow arches higher. 'You don't rate it, but it's the best political science colloquium on the moon. And he got so clingy. And needy. And unfair. It was fine for him to have sex with someone if it made him feel better but if he needed me, he thought taking off his clothes and baking cake would solve everything.'

'He is a spoilt little prince,' Ariel says, 'but he is very easy on the eye.'

The tenor of the voices in the room beyond shifts; the traffic tones from below change: people making farewells and taking leaves, arranging meetings and rendezvous, extracting favours and promises: motos arriving and opening to receive fares, groups setting out on foot to the nearest elevator, heading on.

'I've kept you long enough,' Ariel says. 'Your friends look impatient.' She pushes the wheelchair away from the balustrade back toward the mill of guests. The glass of genever stands half-drunk on the rail, perilous above the luminous drop to the trees of Gargarin Prospekt.

'I can push you,' Abena offers.

'I push myself.' Ariel pauses, half turns. 'I could use a legal intern. Interested?'

'Is it paid?' Abena asks.

'Of course not. Expenses. Tips. Access. Politics. Interesting times. Visibility.' Ariel pushes on, throws back over her shoulder without waiting for Abena's response, 'I'll get Marina to arrange it.'

'It will hurt,' Preeda the facilitator says. 'It will hurt more than anything in your life.'

At the sight of the sixteen people in a circle of seats, Marina almost turns her heel in the door and walks away. It looks like a rehab group. It is.

Marina has come late – dawdling late – but the facilitator has done this many times and has sharp corners to her eyes.

'Marina?'

Caught.

'Yes. Hi.'

'Join us.'

Sixteen people watch her take the seventeenth seat.

The facilitator rests her hands on her thighs and looks around the circle of faces. Marina dodges eye contact.

'So, welcome. First of all I have to thank you all for making the decision. It's not an easy one. There's only one harder decision and that's the one to come here in the first place. And this will be difficult. There's the physical element, and everyone knows about that. That will hurt. It will hurt more than you think. But there are mental and emotional elements. Those are the ones that really hurt. You will question everything you think about yourself. You will walk that long dark valley of doubt. I offer only this: we're there. We'll pledge that: when any one of us needs that, we'll be there for each other. Yes?'

Marina mumbles her response with the others. Her gaze is fixed on her knees.

'So, shan't waste time. Last in first up. Tell us something about yourself.'

Marina swallows her nerves and looks up. Everyone in the circle is watching her.

'I'm Marina Calzaghe and I am going back to Earth.'

Marina's first thought is that burglars have ransacked the apartment. The furniture is upended. Every glass and fast food container, every utensil is smashed or on the floor. The bedding is strewn far and wide, toiletries scattered. The place has been trashed. Marina's second thought is that there are no burglars on the moon. No one owns anything to steal.

Then she sees the wheelchair on its side just inside Ariel's bedroom door.

'Ariel!'

Ariel is on her back amongst a pile of bedding.

'What the fuck is going on here?' Marina asks.

'What the fuck have you done to my gin?' Ariel shouts.

'I poured it down the shower.'

'And the printer?'

'I hacked it.'

Ariel props herself up on her elbows.

'There is no gin in the house.' It's an accusation.

'No gin, no vodka, no alcohol of any kind.'

'I'll go get some.'

'I'll hack your chair.'

'You wouldn't dare.'

'Wouldn't I?'

'I'll unhack it.'

'You know jack shit about coding.'

Ariel collapses back into the pile of bedding.

'Get me a drink. One drink. That's all.'

'No.'

'I know, I know. But it's always Martini hour somewhere.'

'Don't beg. It's not classy. Here are the rules. There's no alcohol in the house. I can't stop you when you're out, and I wouldn't because that's a lack of respect.'

'Well thank you for that. Where were you anyway? Another one of your bands?'

'Training.' It's not a complete lie. 'Gracie Jiu jitsu. You never know when I'll need to save you again.'

'This, always this.'

'Give me a fucking break, Ariel.'

'Give me my fucking gin! Give me my fucking legs! Give me my fucking family!' After a silence in which neither of the two women can look at each other, Ariel says, 'I'm sorry.'

'You scare me. I saw the state of the place, I saw the wheelchair on its side, what am I supposed to think? I thought, what if I find her lying dead?'

Now Ariel can't look at Marina.

'Marina, can you do something for me?'

'I won't get you a drink, Ariel.'

'I don't want you to get me a drink.'

'Call yourself a lawyer? That was a damn lie even to me.'

'I want you to get in touch with Abena Asamoah.'

'She delivered the paper at the Lunarian Society?'

'The paper was simplistic democratist nonsense. But she's smart and she's ambitious.'

'And she's fucking your nephew.'

'And her aunt, my erstwhile sister-in-marriage, is Omahene of the Golden Stool. And, while the patronage of Eagle gets me into LDC meetings, the patronage of Dragons comes with an altogether sharper set of claws.'

'What do you want me to do?'

'I mentioned to her that I was looking for an intern. She'll be an idiot to accept it, but I intend to seduce her. There's a LDC meeting scheduled for Ku Kola. Invite her to it as my guest. Tell her it's an opportunity to see how politics really works. Arrange the clearances, would you?'

'Why do I do this?'

'Because I have people now,' Ariel says. 'Tell her to dress better. And give me a hand up and help me clear up this mess.'

Every face in the lock looks up. Thirty, fifty faces, Wagner estimates as he descends the ramp. Wagner's helmet is under his arm, Zehra Aslan, his junshi at his shoulder. Some faces down there are familiar, some over familiar. Most new. More new than he has ever seen before. Sombra runs through their résumés. A couple claim to have worked for Corta Hélio. Nice try.

The crowd parts. Wagner and Zehra walk to the front of Rover Lucky Eight Ball.

'I can take four,' he announces.

No one moves.

Wagner turns to the tall Igbo man whose sasuit is covered in Manchester United patches.

'You. Jo Moonbeam. Leave.'

The big man's eyes widen in rage, he draws himself up. He is a head taller than second-gen Wagner.

'I'm surface certified.'

'You're a liar. The way you stand, the way you set your shoulders, the way you carry your weight, the way you smell, the way you wear that suit, the way you hook your fingers into the helmet, the way the seals sit. No. You're a danger to yourself; worse than that, you're a danger to my crew. Leave now, get surface hours and maybe the next time I see you, I won't throw you out. And do not ever lie on your résumé again.'

The Jo Moonbeam locks eyes with Wagner, tries to stare him down but Wagner has the eye of the wolf. The big man sees the fury that burns there, turns and pushes his way through the crowd.

Nice touch of theatre, wolf, Zehra says through her familiar. But he is wolf no more, not now the dark is on the face of the Earth. It is his dark-side focus that spotted that the Jo Moonbeam was a liar.

'Ola, Mairead, Neile. Jeff Lemkin.' Wagner has glassed with the first three names before, the fourth is new to him but comes with exemplary recommendations from the VTO track teams repairing the destruction after the fall of Crucible. 'The rest of you, thank you.'

When only his fresh Glass Crew Lucky Eight Ball remain in the dock, Wagner runs through the mission assignment – glassing out east of Meridian on the Sea of Tranquillity.

'Laoda?' Zehra's voice. 'The speech?'

'Sorry.' Jeff is the only one who hasn't heard it before but even he can tell that Wagner is rolling it out by rote. The speech, the specs, the order to suit up and strap in. The names of his crew rez up on his lens, the roll bars fold down over him and lock; the numbers wind down to zero pressure. Red light and green.

'Zehra.'

'Wagner?'

'Take her out for me.' He flicks her the drive HUD.

'Sure.'

Zehra Aslan has been Wagner's junshi for ten tours now and their relationship is as close, familiar and efficient as a well-contracted marriage. She runs system checks and files traffic plans while the crew of Lucky Eight Ball hook up to the inboard life support. Wagner has Sombra open a private call.

'Wagner.'

He's in Eleventh Gate, with tea, wearing apricot sports shorts with blue trim and a baggy T, his hair piled up.

'Just making sure you have everything.'

'I have everything.'

'And everything's all right?'

'Everything's all right.'

'Well, if you do need something...'

'I don't.'

'But if you do...'

'Amal's on it.'

Wagner remembers how he saw Robson last, under the canopy of the packhouse, Amal at his side. Amal's arm around him. Wagner experiences again the stab of an emotion equal parts loss, jealousy and longing.

'Well, that's good.'

The dock is evacuated, the outlock door slides up. Zehra guns the motors and sends the rover up the ramp into the expanding slot of darkness.

'Wagner, why did you call?' Robson says.

'Just to make sure. Nothing really. Well, I'll be back in ten days.'

'Okay. Be careful, Lobinho.'

Robson and his tea vanish from Wagner's lens and as the rover rolls off the ramp on to the surface and throws up plumes of dust from its fat wheels, Wagner flays himself. Why didn't he say it say it say it?

Love you, littlest wolf.

He snuffs out the bio light and sits in the deepest shadow at the furthest table. Hunched shoulders, downcast eyes challenge anyone, even the hot-shop owner, to talk to him. The horchata went cold long ago.

His thoughts march a tedious circuit. Nauseating shock. Scarlet humiliation. Shrieking outrage. Cold injustice. His mind rolls from one emotion to another, round and round like the stations of a pilgrimage.

You killed my parents.

Darius had rejected call after call. Fifteen. Twenty. That should have been the clue. Robson persisted. Naive Robson, stupid Robson, calling and calling, wondering why his old friend, his best friend, wasn't picking up; imagining all kinds of businesses or sicknesses or family commitments that prevented him from picking up when the truth was that his friend, his *best* friend, had been turned.

I'm only answering this to tell you I hate you.

When Darius did pick up after twenty-five calls: naive Robson stupid Robson smiling, saying, *Hey Darius, what's going on?*

That stupidity he hates most. The humiliation of it feels like something kicking its way into his stomach, to claw and eat things there.

Betrayers and murderers.

He is still trembling from the shock. He hears two things: Darius's words and Darius's voice. They are not the same. The words tumble in his head, the voice goes on and on. Darius spoke for less than thirty seconds and Robson has played it endlessly in remembering.

I will cut your eyes and lying tongue out, Robson Corta.

Joker cut the link and Robson ran from the packhouse.

His friend has turned against him.

'I thought I'd find you here.'

Robson's shoulders stiffen. He glances up. Ner.

'I do not want to talk to you.'

'Robson . . .'

'You're shit with me, you know?'

Amal pulls up a chair and positions it at an angle to Robson. No direct eye contact, nothing confrontational. Robson would stare ner to death if he could.

'I will sit and I will wait.'

'So sit.'

Né doesn't sit.

Né snatches the glass of horchata and throws it. Né picks up the chair né is about to sit on, swings and lashes out with it at the figures that have arrived behind ner close and fast and without Robson seeing. Né tips the table over, throws Robson from his seat and pushes him down behind it.

The glass strikes a man in a Reebok tracksuit and sends him reeling. The chair trips another two men in Adidas. Amal head-butts the fourth assailant. The woman reels, shakes it off, seizes Amal by a fistful of clothing and hoists ner one-handed. Amal's dark-senses alerted ner to the attackers but this woman has Jo Moonbeam strength. She balls her gloved right hand into a fist: strikes. Fused glass gas-seal cracks and chips. An Iron Fist. Robson has heard of these things: supple fabric that polarises on impact into a carbon hard as steel. The woman raises the fist again, drives it into Amal's stomach. Things burst. Robson is already on his escape route.

The snatch squad has recovered and follows fast and close. Robson darts through the kitchen, tips over woks, pans, hot liquids. He hears the whine of a taser charging. He ducks through the vent and in a heartbeat is up the access ladder at the back of the kiosk. Taser darts clang against metal. He's on the roof, now swinging hand-over-hand up the service pipe to Level One. Only a kid, only a traceur, can follow Robson's escape route. He's worked it out, he's timed it but he's never tested it with his body until now. He jumps, soars, grabs rail and swings himself up on to the safety rail of Aquarius West One. His escape won't be complete until he's three levels up, but he takes a moment, perched on the rail, to look down at his hunters, furious and impotent down on the hot-shop roof.

The drone bobs down into his eyeline.

'That's not fair,' Robson says, then the taser barbs take him in the belly and send him flying into the middle of East One. He can't breathe. Every muscle is dipped in molten lead, pulled so taut his tendons could shear from his joints. He's pissed his shorts. The drone hovers an arm's reach above his face. He could tear it down, if he could move even an eyelid.

Figures arrive on powerboards and carve to a halt.

'Nimble little fucker,' says the big man Robson recognises as Bryce's head of security. The drone drops its taser wires and flies up. Robson can't move, can't breathe. Dembo Amaechi walks towards him. Robson is locked rigid.

Then bodies come down from the roof, over the railing, out of the side alleys. In a flicker of steel two of Bryce's blades are down. The third drops his knife, shouts, 'I'm not contracted for this.' Turns, runs.

'How are you, Dembo?'

Robson can't turn his head to look but he knows the voice. Denny Mackenzie.

'Rowan said you weren't dead.'

'Very much undead. Or is that non-dead?'

'An oversight I intend to remedy now.'

'That's a smart line, Dembo,' says Denny Mackenzie. Still, Robson tries to move. He can push himself away, skin scraping raw on the roadbed. 'You always had a facility for the language. Me, I'm an undereducated jackaroo. Handy with a knife though.'

Away, away. The two blades clash. Away. Robson struggles to his feet. His legs won't hold, he goes down hard on his hands. Up. Away. All eyes are on the fight. Mackenzie versus Mackenzie. This time Robson's feet hold him. He limps to the next stage of his escape route. Aquarius Quadra wears its engineering on the outside; it's one giant climbing frame. Robson hooks his fingers into pipework. They are numb but there is enough strength to hold him. He hauls himself up. And again. And again. It is the most difficult thing he has ever done. He rests a moment in the elbow of the Level Two pier and shakes the tingle out of his hands and feet.

A great blood cry. Robson glances down. One figure on the ground, one figure walking towards his hiding place.

Denny Mackenzie grins up at him, opens his arms.

'Robson, come on down, mate. You're safe now.'

Robson levers himself out of the elbow and squirms through the gap where the cable cluster pierces the Level 2 roadway.

'Don't make me come up there after you.'

You can't, Robson thinks. *It's too tight for adults.*

The voice rings up from below. Denny looks up the cable shaft. 'Wagner asked me, Robbo. *Look after him when I can't.*'

Robson climbs. Maybe if Denny had not used the hated nickname. Maybe if he hadn't heard things break inside Amal that could not be put together again. Maybe if he hadn't felt the spit and bile of Darius. Maybe then he might climb down. But he can't be a Mackenzie and he can't be a Sun and he can't be a wolf. Two levels up, his escape route will take him to the East 4th Elevator. He can drop on to the car and ride that elevator up past the gardens of the rich all the way to the top of the world. There will be people up there for him.

'I will find you,' Denny Mackenzie calls. 'You're my debt, Robbo. And I pay my debts.'

He has always shaved his body hair, since puberty and his first hairs around his penis disgusted him. Total, from the crown of his head to the hair on his toes. Back crack sack. He works his body over again with the razor until he is perfectly smooth. He dries, lets his familiar show him himself. He slaps his belly. Still tight, the abs packed, the inguinal crease pronounced. Still got it. Last the oil. It is his own personal mix, from expensive organics, not synthesised. He works it slowly and painstakingly into every muscle fold and crease. The back of the neck, the head, the backs of the knees and the soft pucker of the perineum. Between the fingers. He gleams, he is golden. He is ready.

Hoang Lam Hung takes a deep, huffing breath and jogs on the spot, loosening muscles.

The shower cubicle door opens. Three Mackenzie Helium blades wait.

'You've come to take me home to Queen of the South!' Hoang says. 'Have you any idea how bored I am of Lansberg?' He shows his naked body. 'I've shaved for Bryce.' The blades look confused. 'A joke.' A bitter one, too.

'Bryce isn't happy,' the first blade says. She is a short, well-made Jo Moonbeam, she carries a taser stick. 'He wanted the boy.'

'I'd never let Bryce have him,' says Hoang Lam Hung.

'It would be really better if you didn't talk,' the second blade says.

'He breaks everything he touches. I couldn't let the boy end up like me.'

'Please,' says the third blade. He carries cleaning equipment.

'Sorry mate,' the woman says and jabs the taser in Hoang's belly. He goes down, jaws, fists, spine and sinews locked. Every muscle and nerve burns as if intaglioed with acid. He's pissed himself. He's shit himself. The woman grimaces in disgust as she and the second blade lift Hoang to his knees and drag him down the corridor. Cleaning blade moves in to deal with the mess. The Vorontsovs are meticulous in their cleanliness. Theirs is a world where a stray hair, a skin scale can bring down a space ship.

Hoang is fragrant and slick with body oil. The blades lose their grip on his sleek skin as they drag him to the outlock. His feet and shins leave oily marks on the soft-impact flooring. He can't move. He can't speak, can't breathe.

Robson is in Meridian, with the pack, with Wagner. He's protected. Hoang regrets lying but if he had told Robson the truth, that he had to stay, that he had to offer himself as a price, the boy would never have boarded the train.

The second blade punches code. The lock opens. Bodies surge forward; kids, five boys, three girls, all naked. Lips and cheeks are ornamented with smears of white. Through the pain Hoang recognises those streaks of battle-paint. Traceurs. Free-runners. Robson's crew. Screaming, hands reaching, pawing, grabbing. The blades push them back with tasers and knives, shove Hoang in among them. A few stabs of the shock stick, a few kicks, smashed fingers and faces, then the second blade seals the lock. Green light. Dull, distant hammer of fists on metal. Counts ten. Hits the switch. The green light turns red.

In the antechamber the third blades sasuits up. He'll go out there in a while and clear up the mess. The Vorontsovs and their clean environments.

The security woman looks into Abena's right eye and Abena almost giggles at the cool thrill that runs down through her body as she nods her through. Elite access. This will never tarnish. The penultimate Gate of Anxiety is passed. The first Gate of Anxiety was whether Ariel's offer on the balcony of the Lunarian Society was genuine. Her familiar, Tumi, called Marina Calzaghe. True. Abena thought Marina's response terse. Perhaps she should have called in person, but that was so old. The second Gate of Anxiety was whether the LDC had a record of her in Ariel's' entourage. Tumi checked with the Lunar Development Corporation. Abena Muusa Asamoah. Assistant to Ariel Corta. Yes, you really are on the team.

The third Gate of Anxiety was the dress. Was Christian Lacroix suitably professional for a meeting of the Lunar Development Corporation, sufficiently fashionable to impress Ariel Corta? For dress read shoes make-up hair. Her colloquium mates had spent two hours that morning working on her hair.

The fourth gate she has just breezed through, into the lobby of the Lunar Development Corporation headquarters. It is all wood and chrome. Abena can't begin to calculate the carbon budget. The lobby is crowded with the great of the moon, loud with their voices and customised perfumes. Big shoes and bigger hair, shoulder pads and eye shadow. The middle air flocks with familiars: the adinkra of the Asamoahs, the I-Ching trigrams of the Suns. The Vorontsovs seem to be favouring Heavy Metal imagery this season: umlauts and rust. Board members skin their familiars in the simple dot-and-orbiting-satellite of the LDC. She spots the Triple-Goddess sigil of the Lunar Independence movement before it is lost in the host of icons. Live wait-staff serve glasses of tea and small edibles which Abena declines, fearful of grease marks on her Christian Lacroix. She has chosen well; shoulders not the widest, waist not the narrowest. Now: Ariel. Abena scans the crowd looking for a gap in the social skyline that would indicate a woman in a wheelchair. No. She works the room again, and then again, and then finds Ariel at the centre of a knot of lawyers and judges, vaper in one gloved hand. Ariel beckons her with a wave of the vaper.

Abena recognises every member of Ariel's entourage. Her stomach lurches in dread. These are the moon's sharpest lawyers, the most respected judges, the most astute political theorists. Abena hesitates. Again Ariel beckons. Abena knows she won't beckon a third time but what Ariel cannot see is that between her and Abena stands the

Fifth Gate of Anxiety, the one she has never passed before. The Gate that asks, *And who exactly are you? What do you think you are doing here?* The Gate of the Impostor.

Abena swallows hard and steps forward. A hand touches her sleeve. She almost drops her tea-glass, turns to see the Eagle of the Moon. Jonathon Kayode is one of the few terrestrials who can stand eye for eye with her generation-3 height.

'Delighted delighted!' He pumps Abena's hand. He is unaware of the strength of his grip, and he does not let go as he says, 'New talent is everything, isn't it?' This he directs to Adrian Mackenzie, a pale shade at his side. Adrian does not shake Abena's hand.

'A pleasure, Madame Asamoah.'

'I have Senhora Corta to thank...' Abena begins but the Eagle of the Moon has moved to other greetings and salutations.

'Darling.' Ariel kisses her three times, then, to her party, says, 'Let me introduce Abena Maanu Asamoah, of the Cabochon Colloquium. An able young politico. I hope to knock some sense into her.' The entourage laughs and Ariel names them one by one. Abena recognises the names but hearing each one spoken is like a physical blow. 'You've all got assistants, so why should I be left out? And she dresses better than yours. And is very much smarter.'

Social tides sweep the crowd toward the open doors of the council chamber.

'Passable.' Ariel scrutinises Abena Maanu Asamoah's clothes and make-up. 'Sit on my left, look interested and say nothing. You can lean towards me from time to time and pretend to whisper. And this.' Ariel touches her left forefinger between her eyes but Abena can see the familiars wink out as the councillors enter the chamber. She can't remember the last time she was without AI assistance. She feels as if she has no underwear.

The council chamber of the Lunar Development Corporation is a series of tiered rings. The Eagle and Board members occupy the inmost, lowest circle. Advisers and legal representatives, experts and analysts occupy increasingly higher rings by their status and importance. Ariel directs Abena to the second tier. Importantly low. Abena's name shines from the surface of the desk next to Ariel. Her seat is high backed and expensively comfortable. Ariel occupies her wheelchair. Abena frowns at the pad of paper and the short wooden rod on her desk. The Eagle's other representatives file in on either side of Ariel and Abena, but the Eagle, in the seat immediately beneath the two women, turns to nod only to them. The council chamber fills rapidly. The room buzzes with soft conversation; lawyers confer with their clients, lean over desks or crane round in their seats to greet colleagues and rivals. It looks quaint and archaic to Abena. This could surely all be conducted through the network, like the Kotoko.

'We'll get going in a couple of minutes,' Ariel explains. 'Jonathon will open with the formalities, there will be the minutes of the last meeting and the current agenda. It's quite tedious. Watch the advisers. That's where you really see what's going on.'

'What's the mood?'

'A little too friendly.'

'What does that mean?'

'I have no idea.'

Jonathon Kayode turns again in his seat.

'Ready?' he asks his advisers. Mumbles of assent.

'Any last questions?' Ariel says to Abena.

'Yes.' Abena holds up the paper pad and the stylus. 'How do these work?'

In a Caron peplum suit, Marina sits at the end of the tea-bar where the bodyguards go and twirls her glass of mint tea. It's the worst spot at the bar, but it's at the bar. The tables are social death. The guards rate the LDC bar highly though Marina has no understanding of the points of lunar tea. She lifts the glass to study the twist of leaves within. Lunar economics and sociology in one glass. Unfeasible to grow tea or coffee economically in lunar tube farms. Mint runs rampant. You need chainsaws to keep it down. Impossible to make decent mint tea without true tea so AKA cut a few *Camellia sinensis* genes into the mint. Now AKA genetic science is sufficiently advanced to design a true tea that would grow luxuriantly in lunar conditions – even coffee – but the moon now has the taste for mint tea.

Marina always has loathed and always will loathe mint tea.

She sits among the bodyguards and dreams of coffee. Strong, sharp-roasted arabica, steaming hot, bitching with caffeine; good north-west coffee made slowly and with affection: the water poured from height to achieve perfect aeration, stirred – fork, not spoon – and left to sit and settle. It will tell you when it is ready. Lightly pressed. Two hands cupped around a craft-made mug, the steam of her breath mingling with the steam from the mug in a cold morning on the porch with the grey rain rattling in the gutters and sheeting down the galvanised chains the house uses for downpipes. The mountains hidden for days by deep cloud, the mist closing down perspectives and bringing the tree right to the edge of the house. The windsock limp and dripping, rain running from each end of the washing line to merge in the centre and drip. The shuffle and grunt of a dog. Music from three rooms away.

The creak of the boards under the wheels of Mom's chair. Her asking questions questions questions at every television show: *What's happening, who's that, why is she there, who's that again?* The atlas of car tyres: their unique sounds on the dirt out front; those they recognised and would open the door to, those they did not and hid from. The pentatonic voice of a solitary wind-chime placed to catch the east wind, the same wind that spun a flake of multiple resistant tuberculosis up over Puget Sound and into the lungs of Ellen-May Calzaghe. The east wind, the plague wind. Thick white coughing, endless, racking.

Marina's attention snaps back to the LDC tea-bar. She drops the glass of mint tea. Every glass falls. Every bodyguard rises from their seats. Marina runs for the door.

Go to Ariel, Hetty shouts in her ear. *Ariel needs you.*

Armed mercenaries pour through the doors and down the steps on to the council floor. They swarm the LDC board, knives drawn, tasers aimed. A second wave bursts into the chamber and takes positions threatening the advisers, hands on hilts and taser holsters. A third squad of hired blades secure the doors. The council chamber is a roaring pit: board members, legal advisers, armed invaders.

'What's going on?' Abena shouts.

'I'm going to find the hell out.' Ariel swings her chair away from her desk. A mercenary shoves the crackling blue tip of a shock stick at Ariel's face. Ariel locks eyes with her, stares her down, defies her.

'I can't raise the network,' Abena shouts. The invaders yell, the delegates yell, the LDC members struggle at the strong arms that restrain them. There is a centre, a still heart. Jonathon Kayode sits in his chair, hands in lap, eyes downcast. He turns to catch Ariel's eye.

Sorry, he mouths. Then a detonation silences the council chamber like sudden vacuum. Chipped sinter falls from the ceiling, everyone ducks. A gun. Someone has fired a gun, a real gun. The gun-woman stands in the centre of the pit, weapon raised, aimed at the roof. It's black and stubby and alien. No one in the council chamber has ever seen a real gun.

Now Jonathon Kayode rises heavily to his feet.

'My fellow citizens. My dear friends. By the power vested in me as Chief Executive Officer of the LDC, I dissolve the board of the Lunar Development Corporation and place its members under house arrest as clear and present dangers to the stability, security and profitability of the moon.'

Voices from the pit and the tiers above bellow objections but the mercenaries have cuffed the board members and herd them towards the emergency exits. Faces are taut from screaming, tendons tight as torsion bars, mouths speckled with rage-spittle.

'Can he do that?' Abena whispers to Ariel.

'He just has,' Ariel says. She wheels into the centre of the pit. In an instant two mercenaries are on her, knife and taser. 'I demand access to my client.'

The mercenaries are stone but the Eagle of the Moon halts two steps from the emergency exit. His face is grey.

'Can I trust you, Ariel?' Jonathon Kayode says.

'Jonathon, what have you done?'

'Can I trust you?'

'I am your lawyer...'

'Can I trust you?'

'Jonathon!'

Four mercenaries cover Jonathon Kayode's retreat through the emergency exit as the second tumult that has been building in the lobby breaks. Bodyguards, escoltas, blades and warriors overwhelm the mercenaries on the door and storm the council chamber. Shock sticks duel and parry, stab and shock. Bodies spasm and go down in gouts of body fluid. Guards and mercenaries slip and fall in vomit and blood and piss. It's a dirty, chaotic fight where a dozen different contracts and interests clash and no one is certain which side is which. The delegates duck under desks, slide over chairs and huddle at the centre of the pit. Ariel seizes Abena's hand.

'Do not let go.'

Ariel glimpses Marina at the back of the fight. She carries a shock stick in each hand and sufficient sense to know when she is over-matched. Another gunshot, then a third. The room freezes.

'This is not your fight,' the woman with the gun shouts. 'Disengage and we will release the bystanders.'

Abena's grip tightens on Ariel's hand.

'They won't hurt us,' Ariel whispers. Mercenaries and bodyguards separate, the mercenaries retreat to the emergency exit. The woman with the gun is last to leave. The episode is over within one hundred seconds.

Marina powers down her shock sticks and conceals them in the clever holsters inside the jacket of her Caron suit.

'What the hell happened?'

'My client just staged a coup.'

6: GEMINI 2105

The bundle of plastic pipes was light but after forty flights of steps it felt cast from pig iron. The pipes were contrary fucks to wrangle around the corners, booming and mooing like desolate musical instruments as they clattered against the steps. Add a tool belt and welding mask, top off with the bag of working lights slung across her back and by the time she kicked open the door and hauled her pipework out on to the top of Ocean Tower her thighs and forearms were burning. A moment in the swift lilac twilight to taste the sea in the gloaming, listen to the crump of waves on Barra beach beyond the rumble of traffic along Avenida Lucio Costa and the chug of air conditioners. A dozen musics and voices from a dozen apartment windows. The twilight heat was tolerable. She rigged her lights. Her sodium glare highlighted and shadowed things unnoticed in the day sun. Needles and patches, cigarette butts. Panties discarded behind the satellite dishes. The rustle of roosting fowl in their hutches. The skunk garden, lusciously night-fragrant.

Later. Repair woman's perk.

She donned the welding mask, keyed open the hatch of the water steriliser and checked the UV array. Nothing wrong with it. Last forever, these modern UV guns. UVc was harsh. With every installation she would call the community together, explain how ultraviolet made the water safe, tell horror stories of UV-induced conjunctivitis 'like having sand in your eye, forever'. Then she showed the photographs of eyes burned red and ulcerated by photokeratitis and everyone went *whoa*. No fingers strayed near her sterilisation plants.

She disconnected the UV array and took off the mask. Full dark now. She inspected the pipe run. Good thing she had turned off the supply; her finger went through the first u-bend, plastic falling into translucent crumbs. Ultra-violet ate polyethylene.

She would have to replace every pipe. She had brought plenty.

The pipes crumbled as she removed them. The steriliser was hours – perhaps minutes – from failure. Loud voices from below, complaining that the water was off. Not everyone had got the message that the Queen of Pipes was working on Ocean Tower's supply. *What do we pay her for?*

For running taps into the Barra main and keeping up the payments to the FIAM officers so that they never find them. For laying and running pipe down the hill and up the sides of the towers and connecting them to the defunct plumbing in each and every apartment. For the pumps, and the solar panels that powered them, and the rooftop tanks and filtration units and this sterilisation unit so that the water you give your children is clean and bright and fresh. That's what you pay me for. And if I spend what you pay me on a trustworthy secondhand Hawtai pick-up or football boots for the boy or a new hub for the apartment or an intensive manicure and nail rebuild for me, would you begrudge me? Because water engineering is hard on the nails.

She flicked up a playlist on her ear bud and set to her work. Night deepened, and on the third set of tubes Norton tried to booty call her.

'Working.'

'After you're working?'

'You're working.'

As she tightened the connectors, she played with the idea, as she often did, that maybe she should have a better boyfriend. Norton was toned, honed and carried himself with a ripped nonchalance softened by a self-awareness that she found charming. He was proud to be a boyfriend of the Queen of Pipes, even if he could not understand why she did what she did. It annoyed him that she earned more than him. It annoyed him that she worked at all. She should let him keep her, support her, spoil her; like a man ought. Norton was security; security was the thing, security was important. You met celebs and rich people but security could get your ass killed.

She never said what everyone knew, that the best security, the most expensive security, was robotic. D-listers hired humans. But he had plans, aspirations for them both. A beach side apartment, and a proper car. Not that Hawtai pick-up; it made him look bad, her riding around in that. An Audi; that was a proper car. *Can I get my gear in the back of an Audi?* she asked and he would answer, *When you're with me you won't need any gear.*

She didn't want Norton's future. Time would come when she would have to get rid of him. But he was sweet and the sex, when their diaries connected, was good.

She hooked up the last pipe, turned on the water, checked the joints, drained any air locks. She listened to the gurgle and thrum of the water in the pipes. Then she flipped on her welding mask, reactivated the UV array and closed and locked the hatch.

There's your clean water, Ocean Tower.

Her ear bud pinged again. Not Norton this time. An alert. She tapped up her lens and the app dropped a reticule over the arrival point. South-south-east, twenty kilometres out. She grabbed a fistful of buds from the skunk farm and sat on the edge of the parapet, legs dangling over the eighty-metre drop, kicking the backs of her heels against the concrete and looking out across the ocean. The power was out again, the streets were dark. Good for drop-watching. Not so good for community safety. Generators chugged from the roofs of the surrounding apartment blocks. The booths and shops glowed with harvested solar. Three hundred kilometres out, her reticule said. One hundred and fifty up. She let the digits guide her and gazed into soft, warm night. And the sky lit. Arcs of fire; three of them, looping down from the thermosphere in golds and crimsons. Her breath caught. Her breath had been catching for twenty years, since the night a seven-year-old went up with Tio German to see the moon.

See the moon? See those lights? Those are your cousins. Family. Cortas. Like you. Your Great-Aunt Adriana went there and became very rich and powerful. She is Queen of the Moon, up there. Then she saw stars fall, streaks of fire across the stars, and nothing else mattered. She knows now that they are freight packages; rare earths, pharma. Helium-3. Corta Hélio lights the lights. Fusion was supposed to end the brown-outs. Fusion was cheap and limitless, the ever-bright and humming saviour. All saviours fail. Fusion was never about the power that could be delivered, it was always about the wealth that could be extracted by buying and selling on the electricity markets. The three packages fall, cloaked with re-entry plasma, in slow, incredible beauty. She preferred the time of innocence and wonder, when her great-aunt threw stars down to her like candies.

Adriana Corta had sent money to the brothers and sisters she left behind on Earth. The Brasil Cortas had lived high and comfortably; then one day, the money stopped. Adriana Corta had closed the sky but her great-niece still watched the lines of fire drop down from the moon and felt her heart crack.

Dark now. The show was over. Out there on the dark ocean retrieval ships were picking up the capsules. Alexia Corta picked up her tool bag and welding mask. Someone else could clean up the old pipework. She had sensimilla in the pocket of her cut-offs. She would savour its giggly blurring of her cheap and tattered world. Every time she saw the packages fall in blazing stars, she suffered a stab of resentment, of opportunity blighted. She was Barra's Queen of Pipes, but what more might she have been, in that world up there?

At the front door the security kid handed her an envelope of cash.

'Thank you, Senhora Corta.'

She counted it in the pick-up. Another term of Marisa's school fees. Pharma for grandma Pia, a night out with Norton. Nail art and money in the savings account. The Queen of Pipes steered out into the flow of tail-lights along Avenida Lucio Costa and the betraying moon was a blade thrown into the sky.

Like most apps, Alexia used the police siren twice: once when she bought it, once to show off to her friends, then forgot about it. Several times when cleaning out her ware she thought of deleting it but always its little smiling cop-cruiser icon jiggled and said, *When you need me, you will need me.*

This morning, on Avenida Armando Lombardi, auto-drive off and eleven-year-old Caio and fourteen-year-old Marisa and Sister Maria Aparaceida from Abrigo Cristo Redentor in the back, she needed it.

Her air horns blasted emergency. Her hazard lights flashed blue: another little car-hack, as was the police traffic network tag that made every car in Leblon think she was an emergency vehicle. Whatever got them out of her road. She shot through the intersection of Avenida das Americas and Avenida Ayrton Senna.

Sister Maria Aparaceida in the back banged on the roof and leaned over the cab to bellow through the driver's window.

'Where are you going? Holy Mothers is left.'

'I'm not going to Holy Mothers,' Alexia yelled over the howl of sirens. 'I'm taking him to Barra D'or Hospital.'

'You can't afford Barra D'or.'

'I can,' Alexia shouted. 'Just not anything else.' She bounced the heel of her hand off the horn and plunged through the intersection. Automated vehicles fled like gazelles.

She sent him off smart and fed. Every day, clean, clothes ironed, shoes bright. Smart and fed, and a proper lunch, with stuff he would eat and stuff he could trade. Money for the security guys, money for the savings scheme; Alexia on emergency dial, in case. He would never be A-grade, that was not the way his intelligence worked, but he was always presentable and a credit to the House of Corta.

School security called Alexia when Caio was half an hour late. She dropped her tools. The neighbourhood had already found him, in a shallow concrete culvert clogged with corn-starch water bottles and tied plastic bags of human excrement. A community sister from the Holy Mothers was with him. Alexia slid down the concrete slope. His head was a mess. A mess. His lovely head. Everything was wrong. She didn't know what to do.

'Get the pick-up down to the steps!' Sister Maria Aparaceida yelled. Neighbours hauled Alexia up the rough cast culvert. She backed the pick-up to the low curve where street crossed culvert. Hands passed him into the back of Alexia's truck, where Maria Aparaceida had set down some foam packing. Maria Aparaceida arranged Caio in the recovery position and snatched an offered bottle of water to wash the wound. So much blood.

'Well, drive!' Sister Maria Aparaceida shouted.

'Where's his backpack?' Alexia asked. He had pestered and pestered and pestered her for the Capitan Brasil backpack and when she relented and bought it for him he had been so pleased and proud he had almost slept inside the thing. It was gone.

'Alexia!' Sister Maria Aparaceida shouted. Alexia swung into the seat. Sirens.

She swung into the ambulance bay at Barra D'or. Armed security surrounded the pick-up.

'Get a gurney!' Alexia screamed at the solid, well-fed security faces. Hands stayed other hands reaching for weapons. They knew the Queen of Pipes. Alexia burst into the Emergency Room reception. She leaned over the reception desk.

'I've got an eleven-year-old kid in the pick-up, half his head is in. He needs immediate medical attention.'

'I'll need your insurance details,' the receptionist said. She had flowers on her white desk.

'I don't have insurance.'

'Barra Day Hospital does offer Medicare services,' the receptionist said. Alexia snatched the pay terminal, held it up to her eye, pressed her thumb to it, swivelled it back to the receptionist.

'Will that cover it?'

'Yes.'

'Get him in.'

The nurses called security to prise Alexia away from Caio as the crash nurses wheeled him.

'Lê, let them do their work,' the security men said. 'As soon as it's safe, the doctor will let you see him.'

She sat. She fretted. She curled up one way on the uncomfortable waiting room seat, then another, then another and none of them was right for her bones. She went back and forth to the vending machines. She glared death at anyone who so much as turned an eye on her. After two and a half hours the doctor came for her.

'How is he?'

'We've stabilised him. Can I have a word?'

The doctor took her to a private consulting room. She laid a piece of stained paper on the bed.

'We found this in his pocket. Is this his writing?'

'He writes better than that.'

'It's addressed to you.'

An address, and a signature. Alexia did not recognise the signature but she knew the name. An infant's hand-writing, an adult implication.

'Can I take this?'

'That depends if you want to involve the police.'

'The police don't work for people like me and Caio.'

'Then take it.'

'Thank you, Doctor. I'll be back, but I have a piece of business to conduct first.'

*

Only the new boys stared as Alexia walked into the gym. The older men, who knew who she was, paused at their weights and punch-bags and nodded in respect. She strode past the desk and the sign that said Men Only, all the way past the sauna, the whirlpool and the dark maze to the office at the rear. Two escoltas in gym T-shirts stepped in front of her.

'I would like to see Seu Osvaldo.'

The younger escolta was about to open his stupid mouth and refuse her; the older laid a restraining hand on his shoulder.

'Of course.' The guard mumbled into a concealed microphone. A nod. 'Please go in, Senhora Corta.'

Seu Osvaldo's office was as cosy and compact as the cabin of a sailing schooner. Brass and polished wood. Framed photographs of MMA fighters covered the walls. A well equipped bar stood beneath the shuttered window. Chinese electro-pop hovered in the air, present but not so emphatic as to break Seu Osvaldo's concentration. He was a great bear of a man, tall and heavy, spilling out of his chair behind his desk, where he studied MMA matches on an array of old desk monitors. The air was conditioned cool and faintly mentholated but he sweated heavily. Seu Osvaldo could not tolerate heat and daylight. He was dressed in a pair of well-pressed white shorts and the T-shirt of his gym.

He tapped one of his old school screens.

'This boy, I think I might buy him. He's a vicious little fuck.' Seu Osvaldo's voice was luxuriant and deep, thickened with the rattle of childhood tuberculosis. The legend in Barra was that he once trained to be a Catholic priest. Alexia believed it. 'What do you think?' He swivelled the screen to show the fighters in the cage.

'Which one am I looking at, Seu Osvaldo?'

He laughed and with one graceful gesture folded all his screens flat to his desk.

'You'd have made a good fighter. You have the discipline and the focus. And the rage. What can I do for you, Queen of Pipes?'

'I have been wronged, Seu Osvaldo.'

'I know that you have. How is your brother?'

'His skull is fractured in three places. There's been severe concussion and significant blood loss into the brain. The doctors say damage is inevitable. The question is how much.'

Seu Osvaldo crossed himself.

'How will he be?'

'He may require care for the rest of life. The doctors said he may never fully recover.'

'Shit,' Seu Osvaldo muttered in his deep, rich voice. 'If it's money . . .'

'I'm not asking for money.'

'I'm glad. I would not want to charge you interest.'

'The Gulartes have sent me a message. I would like to send them one back.'

'It would be an honour, Alexia.' Seu Osvaldo leaned forward. 'How emphatically would you like your message delivered?'

'I want them never to threaten my family or anyone ever again. I want their water empire wiped out.'

Seu Osvaldo sat back again. His chair creaked. Oily sweat beaded on his bald head, though the office was chill to Alexia.

'You are the Iron Hand.'

'Pardon?' Alexia said.

'You've never heard that? It's a Corta family name. My family and yours are old friends. My grandfather bought Mercedes from your great-grandfather.'

'I know we had money once.'

'It's a Minas Gerais nickname, from the mines. The one with the grip and the will – and the ambition – to take what they want from the world. The Iron Hand. Your great-aunt, the one who went to the Moon, she was a true Miniera. The Mão de Ferro.'

'Adriana Corta. She cut my family off. All the money in the moon, and she cut us off.'

'And you forgot you were ever called Iron Hand. Maybe she's just waiting. I will do this for you, Alexia Corta. I am very upset about Caio. A kid . . . Rules have been broken. I will make sure the Gularte brothers enjoy real pain before they die.'

'Thank you, Seu Osvaldo.'

'I do this for the respect I bear to the Queen of Pipes. We all owe you. But, please understand, I can't be seen not to require a payment for my services. Even from you.'

'Of course.'

'My mother – Jesus and Mary be kind to her – is very comfortable in her old age. She has a nice apartment, she has a sea view, she has electricity almost all the time. She has a veranda and a chauffeur to take her to mass or cocktails or to play bridge with her friends. She wants one thing. I think you can address that want.'

'Name it, Seu Osvaldo.'

'She has always wanted a water feature. Fountains and cherubs and those things that blow horns. Shells and baths for birds. The sound of falling water. This would complete her life. Can you arrange that, Rainha de tubos?'

'It would be an honour to bring a little water into an old lady's life, Seu Osvaldo. Can I ask one more favour?'

'If you can start within a week.'

'I want Caio's Capitan Brasil backpack.'

Norton came to the apartment.

'You don't come to the apartment,' Alexia said, the bar on the door and her left eye to the gap. She let the concealed taser slip down behind the door and toed it away. In this time between asking the favour of Seu Osvaldo and his execution of it, uninvited hammering on the door met an armed response. The corridor cams showed only Norton. That meant nothing. The Gulartes could be holding his family hostage. Marisa, pressed close to the wall, scooped up the taser. Always have back-up.

'I need to talk to you.'

'You don't come to the apartment.'

'Well, where can I talk to you?'

The gazebo. Marisa put a message out on the tower network and the rooftop nest was empty by the time Alexia and Norton made it to the stop of the stairs. A whisper of wind down from the hills made the evening air tolerable. Alexia curled up on the divan. She had thrown six Antarcticas into a cool sack and casually opened one on a wooden rail. She offered it to Norton. He looked away. The tendons of his neck, his throat, the veins in his forehead were tight with anger. Alexia took a swig from the bottle. Dear cold sacramental beer.

'Why did you come to the apartment?'

'Why did you go to Seu Osvaldo?'

'It's business. You don't ask me about business.'

Norton paced. He was a pacer. *Do you know how restless your hands are when you're angry?* Alexia thought.

'And I don't come to the apartment,' Norton said. 'Was there a contract I should have signed?'

'That's glib, Norton.' Alexia had never been able to bear others' laughter. Norton understood this: never make a joke out of Alexia Corta.

'I know why people go to Seu Osvaldo. Why didn't you come to me?'

A true, spontaneous laugh burst from Alexia.

'You?'

'I'm in security.'

'Norton, you're not in Seu Osvaldo's league.'

'Seu Osvaldo has a price. I don't want you owing Seu Osvaldo.'

'Seu Osvaldo's eighty-year-old mamãe is going to have the best water feature in Barra on her balcony. Cherubs and everything.'

'Don't laugh at me,' Norton snapped and the dark flash of his anger, the knife-quick turn of his passion stole Alexia's breath. He was beautiful-angry. 'How do you think it makes me look if every time you need help, you go running to Seu Osvaldo? Who's going to hire a man who can't look after his woman?'

'Norton, be very careful here.' Alexia set the beer bottle down half drunk. 'You don't look after me. I am not your woman. If your security-jock friends disrespect you for that, either you get new friends or a new me.'

As the words were spoken, Alexia wished them unspoken.

'If that's what you want,' Norton said.

'If that's what you want,' Alexia mimicked, knowing what she was saying was the worst of all possible words, unable to stop saying them. Junior, when he was alive, used to say she would fight with her own shadow. 'Why don't you just make your own decision for once?'

'Well what I want is to go someplace else,' Norton yelled. He stormed off.

'Fine!' Alexia shouted at his back. The roof door slammed. She would not follow him down. She would not even indulge in a killing riposte down the stairwell. Let him come to her. 'Fine.'

She waited three minutes, four. Five. Then she heard the sound of a scrambler bike engine in the parking lot below. She didn't need to look over the parapet to know it was Norton's. The infantile engine-rev sound he had patched over the electric motor was unmistakable.

'Fucker,' she said and slung the half-drunk bottle of beer the length of the roof top. It smashed against the concrete coaming. 'Fucker.'

The roof door creaked open.

'Lê?'

Marisa joined Alexia in the gazebo. They watched the half-moon rise out of the Atlantic. On the avenida the street lights flickered and went out.

'Hope he crashes,' Alexia said.

'No you don't.'

'Don't I?'

'You won't let anyone laugh at you but you laugh at him.'

'Shut the fuck up, irmazinha.'

Marisa swung her legs. Alexia reached up a dewed beer from the cooler.

'Open it for me.' Marisa had been drinking beer since she was ten. The bottle cap spun in the moonlight.

She loved the feel of Norton's fresh shaved balls. She loved the smooth suppleness of the skin, the softness of the oil; how they felt like something independent from his body, like a small, nuzzling animal. How they lay heavy in her palm, the way she could circle the scrotum with her thumb and forefinger, the yield and tightening of his body in surprise when she gently stretched them. She loved their fullness and vulnerability; how with a shoelace or some rubber bands or hair ties she could turn them into two glorious swollen apples of lust. She liked to flick her fingernail against his tight tied balls. The first time she did it he almost concussed himself on the headboard.

Alexia folded her hand around the shaved shaft of his cock. Norton was big; smooth and oiled, his cock was a vain monster, a rain forest giant standing proud from cleared undergrowth. Big and elegantly curved. She had worked out long ago how to keep him on edge, bringing him to the brink of orgasm only to pull him back, by the manipulation of her closed hand over his glorious cock. She folded his head into the palm of her hand, ran her thumb along the thick line of his corona. He moaned and lolled back on to the pillows.

This was how she knew it wasn't goodbye sex. He had shaved for her.

She pressed the ball of her thumb to the little triangle where the two curves of the cock head – like a heart, she thought – met the pee slit. Coraçãozinho was her name for it. She didn't know if it had a scientific name but she did know that when she touched him there, rubbed him there, flicked him there, vibrated him there, this square centimetre of nerve endings gave her absolute power over him.

The rest of the guys in his security team must have seen that he shaved for her.

They could pick up an idea or two.

She had a fantasy that one day she would lather him and shave him, then oil and work him closely over with an old-fashioned cut-throat razor until he was so smooth she could take each ball into her mouth like a doce. She imagined the fear and trust and delight on his face.

She bent low and touched the tip of her tongue to coraçãozinho.

Norton jerked as if mains voltage had run through his urethra. His abs tightened, his ass cheeks clenched. Now she had his attention. Alexia guided him to where she really wanted his Little Heart to go.

Afterwards she rolled out of his bed and padded to the bathroom, then to the fridge.

'Any guarana?'

'Behind the Bohemia.'

The fridge light flickered as she squatted in the blue glow, shuffling beer cans. A man's fridge. Beer, coffee, soft drinks. Sex always affected her fluid balance. Liquid out, liquid in. She popped the can and slid back under the black sheet.

Black bed linen. New, for her. Clean bedsheets for back-together-again sex. Jesus and Mary. Little silver archipelagos.

He lay on his side, one leg folded, the other stretched straight, hugging the sheet to him. He knew it made him look cute. His skin was three shades darker than hers – castana-escura to her canela. She liked to look at him.

The lights went out.

'Shit. Give me a minute.' Crouching naked, Norton scuttled around the room lighting the aromatic candles Alexia brought him. They kept the stale male smell down. Alexia preferred Norton's apartment by candlelight. She did not like to see it in too high a resolution.

She really needed to get herself a better boyfriend.

'Caio's back home,' she said. The guarana was working now. Sugar and caffeine.

'How is he?'

'He'll be two months out of school. I'm arranging tutors. His right side is affected. He'll have to learn to become left handed.'

'Shit. I'd like to see him.'

A thing she liked about Norton: how he treated Caio like a kid brother. A thing she did not like about Norton: that he tried to teach Caio to be like him. A malandro.

'You can call at the apartment to do that.'

'Thank you. I appreciate that, Lê.'

He made her melt when he dropped the man-theatre and spoke what he felt.

'What happened to the Gulartes?'

'You don't want to know.' Bodies in the concrete footings of the new commuter rail viaduct. 'No one will be threatening Caio again.'

'Lê...'

Alexia rolled on to her side. Norton was shy of her eye contact. It was another tool by which she could control him.

'We used to have another family name. Did you know that? Mão de Ferro. It's an old Minas Gerais name for the big one, the serious one. The one who does what needs to be done. I was the Iron Hand. So shut up and never ask me again.'

Norton sat up abruptly, jostling Alexia's arm and slopping sticky guarana over her breasts.

'Fuck, Norton...'

'No, listen listen listen. I'm working for a Corta. New contract, started yesterday. Thanks for asking. You always said there weren't many of you, no one knows where the name comes from, no one really knows where you came from. Well, this is a Corta and he comes from the moon.'

'No one comes from the moon.' Alexia felt around for a tissue that wasn't creamy with cum. *This man needs to learn the necessity of wet wipes.*

'That's not quite right, Lê. Milton came from the moon.'

'Okay, workers come back from the moon.' Barra had cheered

when one of their own made it to the moon to mine helium-3. He came back to Earth before gravity withered his bones with enough of a fortune to buy his way out of Barra, settled in Zona Sul and was murdered a year later. All his wealth was electronic. The killers didn't get a centavo.

'He's not a worker. He was born there.'

Alexia jerked upright. The can of guarana spilt over Norton's black sheets. She rolled over Norton to straddle him, pushed her vaj hard against his cock.

'Who is he? Tell me.'

'Something Corta. Lucas Corta.'

'Lucas Corta's dead. He was killed when the Mackenzies took out Corta Hélio.'

'Maybe that was a different—'

'There is only one Lucas Corta. Do you know anything about the moon?'

'I know they play handball and you can fight people to the death but other than that I don't really care what goes on up there.'

Alexia ground again. Norton groaned.

'Up there is my family. You're sure he's Lucas Corta?'

'Lucas Corta from the moon.'

'How is he... never mind.'

'He's pretty sick. A wreck. Doctors all over him.'

'Lucas Corta on Earth.' Alexia lifted herself off Norton's cock and showed him her full magnificence. 'Norton Adilio Daronch de Barra de Freitas, if you ever want in here again, you will get me in to talk to Lucas Corta.'

The maids' uniform was a size too small. Buttons gaped on the shirt. The skirt was too tight, too short. She constantly pulled it down. The gusset on her panty hose rode low. She constantly pulled it up. Ridiculous that staff were expected to work in such stupid shoes.

She had bribed the hotel manager heavily: at least she could have supplied a uniform that fitted.

Half of Barra worked in service but Alexia had never seen the interior of a five-star hotel. The paying parts were marble and chrome, over-polished and tired of standing to attention. The kitchen and service were concrete and stainless steel. She suspected this was universal. The corridors smelled of much-breathed air and tired carpets.

The Jobim suite.

The fear hit her at the doorbell.

What if there was security beyond the security Norton had fixed?

She would think of something. She rang the bell. The door buzzed open.

'Turn-down service.'

'Come in.'

His voice surprised her. When he spoke, Alexia realised she had no idea how a man from the moon should sound, but it was not this. Lucas Corta spoke with the voice of a sick, sick man. Tired, weighed down, struggling for breath. His Portuguese was strangely accented. He sat in a wheelchair by the panoramic window. Against the brightness of beach, ocean and sky he was a silhouette: Alexia could not tell if he was facing her or turned away.

She went to the bed. She had never seen one so wide, smelled one so fresh. Five different medical bots attended it, a dozen medications stood on the bedside table. She touched the sheets: the bed undulated. A water bed. Of course.

Something twitched on the side of her neck. Alexia raised her hand.

'Touch that insect, you die,' Lucas Corta said in his old sick man voice. 'Who sent you?'

'Nobody, I'm ...'

'Unpersuasive.'

Alexia flinched to the touch of insect feet, tip-tapping as they crawled around to the soft spot behind her left ear. The urge to flick it away was overpowering. She did not doubt Lucas Corta. She had read about cyborg insect toxin delivery systems. On the moon they were the preferred weapon of the Asamoahs. And she was thinking this, appreciating this, with neurotoxic death in a pool of her own piss and vomit a millimetre from her skin.

'I'll try that again. Who sent you?'

'Nobody...'

She whimpered as she felt the tiniest prick of needle snag skin.

'I am the Iron Hand!' she shouted.

And the insect was gone.

'That's a name to live up to,' Lucas Corta said. 'What's the rest of it?'

Alexia dry retched, hands trying to find support and certainty in the seascape of the waterbed, shivering with frayed fear.

'Alexia Maria do Céu Arena de Corta,' she gasped. 'Mão de Ferro.'

'The last Mão de Ferro was my mother.'

'Adriana. Luis Corta was my grandfather. He was named after his grandfather Luis. Adriana was named after her great-aunt. She had an electric organ in her apartment.'

A hand lifted against the searing blues of ocean and sky.

'Come into the light, Iron Hand.'

She saw now that he had not once looked at her. He had sat throughout with his back to her. The light collapsed his shadowy bulk, withered him, made him translucent and sick, a spider caught in the light. His hands were gnarls of sinew and swollen joints. The skin of his throat, his cheeks, under his eyes, his lips, sagged. He looked something crueller than old, more terrible than death.

Lucas Corta looked up into the sun, his eyes black with polarising lenses.

'How do you live with this?' he asked. 'How does it not continually dazzle and distract? You can see it move. You actually believe it moves... and that's the trap, isn't it? It blinds you to reality. You can only understand if you look away.'

He glanced at Alexia and she felt the black lenses peel the skin from her face, the flesh from her cheekbones, flense every nerve to the fibre. She did not flinch. The heat radiating from the triple-layered glass was palpable.

'You have the look.'

Lucas Corta spun away and wheeled away from the window to the dim cool of the interior.

'What is it you want, Senhora Corta? Is it money?'

'Yes.'

'Why should I give you my money, Senhora Corta?'

'My brother . . .' Alexia began but Lucas Corta cut her off.

'I'm not a charity, Senhora Corta. But I reward merit. See me tomorrow. Same time. Find a new way in. This way is closed to you. Show me you're the Iron Hand.'

Alexia picked up her hotel bag of turn-down goodies. Her mind still reeled, vertiginous. She could have died on that bed. She had come within a needle's-point, a fractional instant of everything ending.

He hadn't said yes, he hadn't said no. He said, *Show me.*

'Senhor Corta, how did you know?'

'The uniform is two sizes too small. And you smell wrong. Room service has a particular aroma. Chemicals get into the skin. It seems we on the moon are more olfactorily sensitive than terrestrials. On your way out, please send up the real turn-down service. I am sleeping stupid hours.'

Alexia stripped off the maid's uniform the moment the service door swung behind her: too tight blouse, too short skirt. Stupid stupid shoes. In underwear and sag-crotch hose, Alexia Corta pushed past Norton and into his car in the Copa Palace's underground garage.

'It's on my skin, my fucking skin,' she shrieked at Norton as he drove her back to his apartment. 'I can feel it.'

She plunged straight into his shower.

'I should kill him,' Norton said, watching the silhouette behind the water-beaded fabric.

'Don't touch him.'

'He tried to kill you.'

'He didn't try. He defended himself. But I feel dirty. It was on me. An insect, Nortinho. I'm never going to feel clean again.'

'I can help with that,' Norton said and slipped through the curtain. Clothes dropped to wet tiles. He stepped out of pants, shook off shorts. 'So what was he like? You were so freaked by that insect bot you never told me.'

'He creeped the fuck out of me, Norton,' Alexia said. Her back was turned to him; water ran down her skin, down the glass. 'It was like something pretending to be a person. It looks okay from a distance but when you get up close everything is just that little bit off. Uncanny valley. Nothing was the right shape. Everything was too long or too big or top heavy. An alien. I heard people born there grow up different; I never thought . . .'

'You don't get to pick your family,' Norton said and stepped into the shower. He pressed against Alexia's warm, wet flank and she gasped. 'So where is this dirty bit?'

She scooped her hair away and tilted her head to show him the soft places on her neck and beneath her ear where the assassin insect had nuzzled. He kissed them.

'Cleaner now?'

'No.'

'Now?'

'A little.'

He moved his hands to cradle the perfection of her ass. She pressed muscle-close, curled a leg around his thighs, hooked him in to her soft dark skin.

'So are you going to see him tomorrow?'

'Of course.'

*

'Handsome boy.'

'Here he is on the futsal team.' Alexia flicks him the picture of Caio grinning in singlet and shorts and long socks into Lucas Corta's eyes. He lolls in the pool, cool water roiling gently. He has invited Alexia several times to join in. The idea repels her. She sits on a pool chair in the shade of the canopy. The sun is brutal today. The sea looks like it is dying.

'Is he good?'

'Not really. Not at all. They only pick him because of me.'

'My brother had a handball team. They weren't as good as he thought they were.'

Alexia flicks him another picture of Caio, trying to look big on the beach; stripes of blue sun block on his nose, cheekbones, nipples.

'How is . . . Caio?'

'He's walking. He knocks things over a lot and he needs a stick. Futsal is over for him.'

'If he wasn't very good, maybe it's a blessing. I was terrible at any kind of sport. I couldn't see the point. One of my uncles was called Caio.'

'Caio is named after him.'

'He died of tuberculosis shortly before my mother left Earth. My mother taught me the names of all my aunts and uncles, the ones who never came. Byron, Emerson, Elis, Luis, Eden, Caio. Luis was your grandfather.'

'Luis was my grandfather, Luis Junior was my father.'

'Was.'

'He walked out when I was twelve. He left three of us. My mother just threw her hands up.'

'On the moon we have contracts for that sort of thing.'

Now. Ask him for the money. Claim kinship. He let you get in to the hotel. She had tracked down Dr Volikova, asked her to pass Alexia off as Lucas's locum masseuse. Alexia had dressed the part.

She sat by his pool in sports leggings and a crop top. Ask him. An image appeared on Alexia's lens. The moment was lost.

'This is Lucasinho, my son.'

He was a very pretty boy. Tall in that weird moon way but well proportioned. Thick glossy hair that she knew would smell clean and fresh. An Asian turn to the eyes that made him look withdrawn and beautifully vulnerable, cheekbones to fall in love with, lips you could kiss forever. Not her type – she preferred her men muscled and with no overt signs of intelligence – but so so cute. He was instant heartbreak.

'How old is he?'

'Nineteen now.'

'And how is ... Lucasinho?'

'Safe. As far as I know. The Asamoahs are protecting him.'

'They're at Twé.' As Lucas researched Alexia, she researched him and his world. 'They run agriculture and environment.'

'They have traditionally been our allies. The legend is that every Dragon has two allies...'

'And two enemies. The Asamoahs' enemies are the Vorontsovs and the Mackenzies, the Suns' enemies are the Cortas and the Vorontsovs, the Mackenzies' are the Cortas and the Asamoahs, the Vorontsovs' are the Asamoahs and the Sun, the Cortas' are...'

'The Mackenzies and the Suns. Simplistic, but like all clichés, with an element of truth,' Lucas Corta said. 'I fear for him all the time. It's an elegant fear, of many parts. The fear that I haven't done enough. The fear of not knowing what is happening. The fear that there's nothing I can do. The fear that, even if I could, whatever I did would be wrong. I heard what you did to the men who hurt your brother.'

'I had to make sure they would never go near Caio, or any of us, ever again.'

'My mother would have done that.' Lucas took a sip of tea from the glass balanced on the edge of the pool. 'She always wondered why none of you ever came. I think it was the great disappointment of her life. She built a world for her family and no one wanted it.'

'I grew up believing that she turned her back on us. Took back her wealth and power and left us to fall.'

'You still live in the same apartment, I believe.'

'It's falling apart, the elevators haven't worked since before I was born and the electricity is more off than on. The plumbing is good.'

'When we were twelve years old my mother took each of us up on to the surface at Earth-dark. She showed us continents all lined in lights and the webs of lights across them, and the knots of lights that were the great cities and she told us, *We light those lights*.'

'They make more money trading that power than using it,' Alexia said. 'But Corta Agua does supply reliable and clean water to twenty thousand people in the Barra da Tijuca area.'

Lucas Corta smiled. It was a heavy thing, costly for his body and the more valuable for that.

'I would like to see that. I would like to see the place my mother grew up. I don't want to meet your family ... that wouldn't be safe. But I wish to see Barra, and the beach where the moon fell across the sea like a road. Arrange that for me.'

The hire MPV was a glassy bubble, all doors and windows, and made Alexia instinctively uncomfortable. Like something the Pope rode, waving and blessing. Nowhere to duck and hide, only faith and toughened glass to save you. She itched on the seat facing Lucas Corta as the car cruised down Avenida Lucio Costa.

Dr Volikova had been adamant in her refusal to allow Lucas Corta out of the hotel until a short, sharply worded argument that startled Alexia with its passion and ferocity. Patient and doctor argued like lovers. Dr Volikova followed in a pick-up stacked with emergency treatment bots.

'This is my home,' Alexia said. In the lilac cool, with the eastern ocean indigo and the lights coming on street by street, level by level,

Barra could strut its old glamour. If you overlooked the potholes, the sidewalk tiles missing like broken teeth and the trash in the gutter, the parasitic power cables and the cell masts, the white plastic water pipes scrambling up every vertical like strangling fig.

'Show me,' Lucas said. Norton ordered the MPV to pull in to the crumbling curb. Alexia had no intention of letting him drive, but relaying commands to the auto-drive gave him sufficient purpose and agency.

'I'd like to get out,' Lucas Corta said. Norton scanned the street theatrically. He could be so adorably bad ass. Alexia opened the door and unfolded the elevator. Lucas Corta travelled the few centimetres to touch down on planet Barra. 'I'd like to walk.'

'Are you sure?' Alexia said. Dr Volikova was at hand even before the car had opened.

'Of course I'm not,' Lucas said. 'But I want to.'

The two women helped him from his wheelchair and passed him his cane. Lucas Corta clicked along the sidewalk. At every moment Alexia was in fear of a loose tile, a stray can, a kid on a bike, blown treacherous sand, anything that might trip him and send him crashing to earth.

'Which apartment?'

'The one with the Auriverde windsock.'

Lucas Corta stood a long time on his cane, looking up at the lights of the apartment.

'We've remodelled it since your mother's time,' Alexia said. 'It used to be a rich neighbourhood, so I was told. That's why we're near the top. The richer you are, the higher you lived. Now it just means the more steps you have to climb. If you have any choice, you live as low as you can afford. I read the moon's like that.'

'Radiation,' Lucas Corta said. 'You want to be as far from the surface as you can afford. I was born in João de Deus and lived there until my mother built Boa Vista. It was a lava tube; two kilometres long. She sealed it and sculpted it and filled it with water and growing things. We lived in apartments carved out of the giant faces of the orixas. It was one of the wonders of the moon, Boa Vista. Our cities are great canyons filled with light and air and movement. And when it rains ... It's beautiful beyond your imagining. You say Rio is beautiful, the Marvellous City. It's a favela compared to the great cities of the moon.' He turned away from the tower. 'I'd like to go to the beach.'

The light was gone now and the beach was the preserve of guy-gangs and teenagers making out or vaping drugs. Norton's jaw twitched in displeasure but he helped Lucas down the steps on to the beach. Lucas's cane sank into the sand. He recoiled in horror, tried to tug it free.

'Careful, careful,' Dr Volikova admonished.

'It's in my shoes,' Lucas said. 'I can feel it filling up my shoes. This is horrible. Get me out of this.'

Alexia and Norton carried Lucas to the sidewalk.

'Get it out of my shoes.'

Alexia and Norton steadied Lucas while Dr Volikova removed Lucas's shoes and poured out streams of fine sand.

'I'm sorry,' Lucas said. 'I hadn't thought I would react that way. I felt it and thought *dust*. Dust is our enemy. I have no control over these things. It's the first thing we learn.'

'The moon is up,' Norton whispered. A waning crescent stood over the eastern horizon. The lights of the cities of the moon twinkled like diamond dust. *Oceans of dust*, Alexia thought and it thrilled and horrified her at the same time. This man, this frail man, dying of gravity in every step and movement, came from there. A Corta: her blood, and utterly, implacably alien. Alexia shivered, tiny and mute under the far moon.

'My mother told me that the whole family used to come down at New Year and set paper lanterns into the sea,' Lucas said. 'The ocean would somehow draw them out until no one could see them any more.'

203

'We still do that,' Alexia said. 'The Reveillon. Everybody dresses in white and blue, Yemanja's favourite colours.'

'Yemanja was my mother's orixa. She didn't believe it, but she liked the idea of orixas.'

'I find the idea of religions on the moon strange,' Alexia said.

'Why? We are an irrational species, and profligate at exporting our irrationality. My mother was a benefactor of the Sisterhood of the Lords of Now. They believe that the moon is a laboratory for social experiments. New political systems, new social systems, new family and kinship systems. Their ultimate goal is a human social system that will endure for ten thousand years – which they consider the time it will take us to become an interstellar species. I could believe in the orixas more easily.'

'I think it's optimistic,' Alexia said. 'It says, we won't blow ourselves up or die in climate collapse. We will get to the stars.'

'*We* may. The Sisterhood says nothing about you here on Earth.' Lucas Corta looked out again at the now-dark ocean. The moon drew a shiver of light across the black waters. 'We fight and we die up there; we build and we destroy, we love and we hate and live lives of passion beyond your comprehension and not one of you down here cares. I'd like to go now. The sea is making me anxious. I can bear it in the light, but in the dark it has no end. I don't like it at all.'

Norton and Alexia manoeuvred Lucas into the MPV. The car closed and Alexia saw relief on Lucas's face. Norton ordered the car into the traffic. A couple of motorbikes had passed twice and made him nervous. Alexia glanced over her shoulder to make sure they hadn't woven in between the MPV and Dr Volikova in her medical pick-up.

'Senhora Corta,' Lucas said. 'I'd like to make you an offer.' Lucas touched the glass partition and muted the car microphones. Norton was deaf in the front. 'You are a talented, ambitious, ruthless young woman with the intelligence to see an opportunity and take it. You've built an empire but you can do so much more. This world has nothing for you. The offer my mother made to your predecessors, I make to you. Come to the moon with me. Help me take back what the Mackenzies and Suns stole from me and I will reward you so that your family will never be poor again.'

This was the moment. For this she had bribed, blackmailed, lied her way into Lucas Corta's bedroom. She had prised open the door to the wealth and power of Corta Hélio. Beyond it was the moon.

'I will need time to think about it.'

'Of course. Only a fool would heedlessly step off for the moon. You have your water empire; that's why I didn't ask you to work for me. I asked you to come to the moon with me. I want it to cost you. You have two days to decide. My time on Earth is short, I have maybe three, four weeks left before surface-to-orbit will kill me. As it is, the odds are that I will suffer permanent damage to my health. Come to the hotel when you are certain. No more lies and disguises.'

7: LIBRA - SCORPIO 2105

The Eagle of the Moon serves exceeding good Martinis but Ariel leaves hers untouched on the polished stone table on the edge of the drop.

'I thought it was always Martini hour in some quadra,' the Eagle says.

'I don't have the taste for it this morning.'

They sit facing each other across the small stone table beneath the sculptured canopy of the Orange Pavilion, on the very edge of the stupendous vault of Antares Hub. Late traffic hums across the bridges and crosswalks, up and down the cable ways, bobbing through the air. The sunline deepens to evening, the street lights blink on as the daylight recedes along the sun lines to the furthest ends of the quadra's prospekts. It was morning the last time Ariel sat here, in this belvedere, by this stupendous vista. The last time she sat in this Eyrie, the Eagle of the Moon had commanded a dynastic marriage. Corta and Mackenzie. Lucasinho and Denny. The bergamots on the ornamental trees still bear traces of silver paint from the wedding decorations.

'I'm owed an explanation, Jonathon.'

'The board was about to table a motion of no confidence. I forestalled that.'

'You took them hostage.'

'I arrested them.'

'Our legal system has no process of arrest. You kidnapped them and you're holding them hostage. Where are they?'

'They're under guard in their apartments. I've taken the precaution of dialling down their breathing. It works wonders with compliance.'

'There is nothing in the LDC articles of incorporation that permits you to abduct and hold the board of the Lunar Development Corporation.'

'This is the moon, Ariel. We do what we like.'

'Do you want me to quit, Jonathon? I will if you shit me. There are eight thousand writs out there and I'm the only thing between them and you.'

'I was tipped off that the board would try and remove me from office at that meeting.'

'Vidhya Rao.'

'E predicted the attempted No Confidence motion. The board's move to unseat me was orchestrated from Earth. The terrestrial nation states are moving against me.'

'Why did you contract me, Jonathon?'

'Vidhya Rao's machines make guesses through finding patterns, often indiscernible to humans. E tracked the financial flows back through a bewildering array of shell companies to sovereign wealth funds. At the centre is someone you know well. Your brother.'

Ariel tucks her Oscar de la Renta clutch bag under her arm and turns her chair away.

'Fantasy, Jonathon. Paranoia. I'm out. This contract is terminated. I no longer represent you.'

Jonathon Kayode reaches across the table to seize Ariel's wrist; a swift move for a big man.

'Lucas survived the Suns' assassination attempt, escaped the moon and found refuge with VTO.'

'Let me go, Jonathon.' She meets Jonathon Kayode's eyes. The grip on her wrist releases. The Eagle is also a strong man; his fingers have left pale imprints on her brown skin. 'You hired me as a shield.'

'Yes.'

'Fuck you, Jonathon.'

'Yes. So will you walk?'

Ariel eyes the Martini. Cold and potent and holy. She lifts the glass from the table and takes a sip. Sanity, certainty. Glorious.

'Am I safe, Jonathon?'

'I forestalled his attempt to oust me.'

'Jonathon, you're a fool if you think my brother has only one plan.'

The other worshipper dropped out at the 8th Street West ladeira. Marina has run lone for an hour ten now. She will keep running until someone joins her. That's the faith of the new Long Run. Someone will always join you. The Long Run never stops.

Marina rattles, a caged thing, in the new apartment. Her life is more now than hand to mouth and her new comforts and securities are not enough. The physicality of her return-to-Earth program gives her a hunger for other vocabularies for her body. She remembers the Long Run: the bodies, the painted skin, the coloured threads and tassels of the orixas, the absorption into a unity, an unconscious consciousness where time and distance evaporated and physical limits dissolved, the many-legged beast that runs in the outer darkness, singing.

She remembers Carlinhos. The sweat streaking the fluorescent paint on his pecs and thighs. The coy self-consciousness when they came out of the run-rapture. The dark velvet softness of his skin against her in her bed the night before he fought. How she saw him last raging and exultant in the blood of Hadley Mackenzie on the floor of the Court of Clavius.

She heard whispers through the sports and fitness channels, through her Gracie Jiu Jitsu instructor, through the santinhos who had left João de Deus after Bryce Mackenzie made it his capital. The

Long Run had come to Meridian. It required a critical mass. From the start it had to be eternal. There would always have to be a body in motion. Meridian was different from João de Deus; it did not have the orbital service tunnel far from the main prospekts, where bodies could flow and chant ceaselessly. A route was devised, a complex loop of service roads through seven levels of Volk Prospekt: seventy kilometres. Then the five prospekts of Aquarius Quadra: three hundred and fifty kilometres. In the end it would cover all three quarters: one thousand and fifty kilometres.

The New Long Run would take sixty hours to complete: the longest continuous run in the two worlds. The danger was that such an endurance run would become fashionable and the Long Run was not a competition or a challenge. It was a discipline and a transcendence. A system of alerts made sure there was always a body in motion. Marina is not a founder; she is a maintainer: she crews the long empty stretches, the hour that becomes two. She finds private transcendence up in the long empty stretches. She thinks about Earth, she thinks about her bones withering, her muscle mass growing. She thinks about No Running. She will be wheelchair bound for weeks, she will need crutches and sticks for months. It will be a year before she dare pull on something small and stretchy and run. Even then, it will only be running. There will be no saints, no voices, no communion.

She thinks this not to think about Ariel.

Meet point in sixty seconds, Hetty says. Marina can see the runner coming up the West 26th ladeira. They'll meet at the entrance to the 18th Street bridge.

Que sues pes correm certeza, the woman says. She is dressed and painted in red. Her shorts and top carry the lightning bolt of Xango. Marina admires the look. It wouldn't work with her colouring.

Corremos com os santos, says Marina and the woman switches to Globo. The old tongue has never sat comfortably between Marina's lips. The two women fall into a pace and cross the street bridge. It is night and they run between two endless walls of lights.

'You work with Ariel Corta?' the woman says.

'Sort of.'

'I thought so. I've seen you around. Ariel sorted out an amory for me that veered bad. Revenge and stalking and everything. I was the only one didn't end up with a restraining contract. Everyone says amories are the easiest to get out of. Don't you believe them. When you see her, thank her from me. Amara Padilla Quibuyen. She won't remember me.'

'You'd be surprised what she remembers,' Marina says. And here she is, thinking about Ariel again.

In the green of Ogun and the red of Xango, Marina Calzaghe and Amara Padilla Quibuyen drink cocktails. The Long Run has passed to other feet and, like a pair of dusters in after a six-week contract, the two women have gone straight to a bar. It is Amara's secret, a couple of scoops out of the wall of East 35th, seats and tables sculpted from sheer rock; a place where the barkeep knows everyone's name because it only holds eight people.

'I have a confession,' Marina says. 'I never liked Blue Moons.'

'Me neither. I like fruit and sweet stuff.'

Marina clinks her caipiroshka against Amara's guava batide.

'Eternamente.' The Long Runner's farewell.

'Eternamente,' Marina says in her execrable Portuguese. Drinks after run. That breaks every one of Marina's professional and running protocols. Ariel needs her more than ever since the Eagle of the Moon's coup. But she can't face the claustrophobia of the big, airy apartment; Ariel swept up in her host of legal AIs swatting down squadron after squadron of writs, Abena assisting in silent intensity, hunting down cases and precedents and rulings, aware that this is work at the very edge of her ability and stamina and that it will make her career at Cabochon. The kid has slung a hammock in the kitchen, but her eyes are on the Golden Stool.

'Were you at João de Deus or out in the field?'

'Payroll.' Amara raises her glass. 'Don't fuck with the accountants.'

'You look like a duster.'

Amara dips her head coyly.

'I kind of like duster style.'

'Works for you.'

'So, you and Ariel?'

'I kind of backed into working for her. My doctorate was in computational evolutionary biology in process control architecture. I had a wait-staff job at Lucasinho Corta's Moonrun party when someone tried to kill Rafa Corta. More qualifications than all the Cortas put together and I end up as Ariel's bodyguard, personal assistant and bartender.'

How did that caipi disappear so quickly? Dmitry at the bar is already preparing a second.

'You do want another?' Amara says.

Why not replace all her lost body fluid with alcohol?

'I majored in custom logics for artificial intelligences,' Amara continues. 'Ended up as payroll clerk. At least there's work. People will always need to be paid.'

The second caipiroshka is as sharp, delicious and generous as the first.

'Here's to payroll.'

'How long have you been on the moon?' Marina asks.

'Does it show? I was hoping you'd think I was gen 2. I'm considered unfashionably tall in my family. I'm Filipina originally. Luzon. Mother is an orthodontist, father is in banking. I know. Good upper-middle-class nuclear family upbringing. All expected to excel, all went to good US universities, all got good degrees, then the bad tall one catches a rocket, waves goodbye and heads off to the moon. They still can't understand it. Three years eight months...'

'One year eleven months. Four days.'

'That's why that second caipi went down so fast.'

The second empty glass startles Marina. Dmitry swipes it away. The makings of the third are already laid out on his bar.

'Tell me: what made you stay?'

'What's there to go back to? Bad government, cheap terrorism, rising sea levels and the next person you kiss could breathe a killer disease into your lungs.'

'Family?'

'Family is what works. Where are your people?'

'North-west. Olympic Peninsula. Just inland from Port Angeles. You're going to say, that's beautiful, mountains and forests and the sea. It is. I saw snow, once. There was some freak of the weather and suddenly up there, on the very high peaks: white. Snow! We took the car and drove up the old park road just to walk in it. It was pretty much all gone by next day. Rain on snow is an ugly thing.'

'You're going back, aren't you?'

'I can't live here. My ticket's booked. Got my seat on the Moonloop, got my berth on the cycler.'

Amara finishes her first cocktail. Dmitry brings fresh: second for Amara, third for Marina. She must be cuing him through their familiars.

'Have you told Ariel?'

Marina shakes her head.

'If you can't even say that to me, what chance do you have of saying it to her?'

Marina looks up from her glass.

'You have an awful lot to say about me and Ariel.'

'I've been buying you cocktails all night.'

'And two hours ago we were running-mates.'

'I think you've been wanting to tell someone about this for a long time, and I am prepared to buy you another caipiroshka.'

'What is this, caipi therapy?'

'It's runners, coming off the high.'

'Buy me another caipiroshka.'

Caipiroshka four arrives as gorgeous as all its predecessors. Marina shivers as she sips, feels the warmth and closeness of this tiny troglodyte bar around her, comforting and clothing like a stone suit.

'I can go suddenly but I can't go cleanly. Understand?'

Amara frowns as she sips batide through her straw.

'There will always be a connection.'

'There will always be something she needs me for. The moment of supreme need will come, and I will have abandoned her.'

'If you tell her, she'll ask you to stay.'

'She wouldn't ask. She would never do that. But I would know. And I might stay, and then I would hate her.' Marina stands up. 'I have to go. I have to get back. I'm sorry. Thanks for all the cocktails.'

'At least finish that one.'

'I shouldn't. I'm trying to keep her off the gin and if I roll in half in the bag…'

'You've earned it.'

'No, I can't. Hetty, get me a moto.' Marina bends to kiss Amara goodnight. Amara pulls Marina close and whispers.

'Oh, I'm so sorry. You see, I had a plan for this evening. I've noticed you. Been noticing you. I moved schedules to get to run with you. My evil plan was to lure you here and fill you with cocktails and try and seduce you or at least get a date and I have no chance of that. I never will. Because all the talents I possess are powerless against love.' She kisses Marina tenderly. 'Eternamente.'

The higher profile the AKA executive, the more discreet the security, until it merges with the world and passes from human perception. Ariel does not doubt that that insect thrum, that flicker of bird wings, that skulk of fur and glint of eye in the low foliage can kill her without her ever knowing. Never trust living creatures. She is her mother's daughter. But the shade beneath the branches is cool and scented with the spice notes of decomposing leaf-litter and the paths of the park empty as only the power of the Golden Stool can command.

'Is she any use at all?' Lousika Asamoah asks. The two women amble and roll along crunching pink gravel paths. This is the first time they have met since the fall of Corta Hélio, the destruction of Boa Vista and the death of Rafa Corta.

'I may have ruined the girl as a career politician,' Ariel says. 'She's going to think every issue can be solved with the liberal application of mercenaries.'

Lousika Asamoah's laughter is generous, full and light as a bell. Ariel negotiated the nikah with Rafa and from the start it was evident that love lived in this relationship as it never had in Rafa's other marriage to Rachel Mackenzie.

'I should send her straight home to Twé,' Lousika Asamoah says. 'Gods know what she'll land in next.' The words are glib but Ariel hears the undertone of concern. Political violence has impacted Meridian's staid, dull administration and no one knows how deep the trauma will be or how far the debris will fall.

'She's not a player,' Ariel says.

'I think everyone is a player now,' Lousika Asamoah says. She stops on the gravel path. The small movements through the branches, the leaves, the ground ivy, stop with her. Ariel feels a dozen venomed eyes on her. 'Our families have always been close, but I'm here today as the Omahene of the Kotoko. The Eagle's action is unprecedented. We can't forecast the consequences. This alarms us.'

'All the Eagle asks is for a commitment.'

'A commitment I can't give. AKA is not like the other dragons. Our governance is complex and many-layered. So many opinions to seek, so many votes to secure. Some see it as slow and unwieldy and inefficient but we've always believed that power is best placed in as many hands as possible. AKA moves slowly but it moves surely. We simply have not had time to reach a consensus.'

'The Eagle would appreciate even a private indication . . .'

'I don't have the authority to offer that. The Golden Stool has no voice.' Lousika walks on. Ariel's chair matches speed. The watchers in the wood follow. 'Our families have always been close. Like you, we aren't the richest or most powerful of the Dragons. We've bought our position by keeping out of the rivalries between the other families and where we can't, by judicious alliances. The Kotoko will watch but we won't be rushed into a commitment.'

'You'll side with whichever faction wins,' Ariel says.

'Yes. We must. VTO, the two Mackenzies, Taiyang to a lesser extent, all depend on a relationship with Earth. We don't. The moon is all we have. But, as we say, everyone eats, everyone sleeps.'

'Shall I tell that to the Eagle?'

'That is the answer of the Golden Stool.'

Movement in the trees; a sudden thrill of wings. Birds rise, butterflies skirl past Ariel's face and small fast low things dash and dart along the borders of the paths. The guardians are leaving, the cordon is lifted. Ariel understands that she is to remain while the Omahene takes leave. She listens to dead leaves tumble across the gravel on the unpredictable winds of Aquarius Quadra's microclimate. Crunch of footfalls and tyres: runners and sweet-eat sellers' carts.

Lady Sun pulls the sleeves of Darius's suit down to cover his wrists. Darius pulls them up again.

'It's the fashion,' he says.

Lady Sun concedes but snatches the vaper from his fingers.

'This I will not tolerate.'

Darius's shoes click on the polished stone. The Great Hall of Taiyang is an open, empty cuboid sculpted to millimetre perfection from the raw rock of Shackleton crater rim. Its proportions and acoustics are engineered to induce physiological awe. The Suns favour it to receive guests and clients.

'That's Ariel Corta,' Darius says. In a red Emanuel Ungaro dress,

Ariel Corta is the bright sun of an orbit of Taiyang dignitaries. Even chair-bound she commands every eye. Ariel Corta is not one to be cowed by architectural trickery.

'Who are those people with her?' Darius asks.

'The younger woman is Abena Maanu Asamoah.'

'A niece of the Omahene,' Darius says. The perspectives in the Great Hall deceive. He feels he has walked for kilometres without drawing a footstep closer.

'You've paid attention,' Lady Sun says. 'Good. Significance?'

'The Asamoahs and the Cortas are traditional allies.'

'Half of their bloodline lives under Asamoah protection.'

'As I live under the protection of the Suns,' Darius says.

'Keep that sneer out of your voice or I will poison you myself, young man,' Lady Sun says. 'The third woman is her personal guard. She need not concern us.'

'She killed a man with a vaper,' Darius says.

'Did you research that, or have your familiar look it up?' Lady Sun says.

'I recalled it,' Darius says. 'That is what you want me to do?'

The huddle of executives opens. Heads dip to Lady Sun.

'Grandmother: Ariel Corta, representing the Eagle of the Moon,' Sun Zhiyuan says.

Lady Sun extends a hand. Ariel shakes it. You're not supposed to do that, Darius thinks. You kiss the hand of Lady Sun.

'Madam Sun.'

Darius studies Ariel Corta as introductions are made. From her chair she commands everyone in the room. Her attention is a favour she rations and even the executives of Taiyang crave it. Why does she not walk yet? She can easily afford the surgery. Is there power in the chair? Does it give her advantage? Everyone, even Lady Sun, must lower themselves to speak to her. Darius tries to understand the will that chooses disability and authority over ability and anonymity. There is a lesson here.

'And my ward, Darius.'

Darius dips his head to Ariel Corta.

'Charmed, Senhora Corta.'

The flare in the back of her eyes as they meet his sends a shock of fear through Darius. Was his tone too cute? Has she seen into him?

'A pleasure, Darius.'

She's suspicious of him.

'I wanted him to meet you, Ariel,' Lady Sun says. 'The young need to learn the value of perseverance. No great thing was wrought without it. A fall, a time away from the world, the rise to prominence and power: perseverance. Come Darius.'

Business resumes. Zhiyuan and Ariel are discussing the civil service, the operatives that keep the moon spinning around the Earth; from the recyclers of the dead to the administrators who bond the chib to every new eyeball. The human staff will work for whoever keeps them breathing. Who will Taiyang's administrative AIs serve: Eagle or Board?

'You were flippant,' Lady Sun chides as she guides Darius away from the conference.

'You were rude,' Darius says. 'To her face.'

'I am the Dowager of Shackleton,' Lady Sun says. 'Dowagers are rude. You've heard of the Three August Ones.'

'I've heard stories.'

'They are very much more than stories. They are quantum computers we constructed for Whitacre Goddard bank to make highly accurate guesses at future events. Prophecies, if you like. Of course we built a back door into them and they have been dealing us a measure of future insight ever since. They are wretched things; they obfuscate and they never totally agree. They have only ever been unanimous on one thing: that Ariel Corta will be a major figure in the story of the moon.'

'This is why she is our enemy.'

'She isn't, yet. She may be. I may well be dead and gone to the Zabbaleen by then, but you will be ready.'

'I will be, great-grandmother.'

Darius's feet tippy-tap on the polished rock. Coming or going, he heard not a sound from Lady Sun's footsteps.

Abena can't stop shivering. The air is warm, scented with a spicy tang of dust pleasing to anyone who grew up in Twé's ever-expanding maze of tunnels and agriculture tubes. The rock, the rock, the relentless rock, oppresses her. Hadley is rock and metal unrelieved by any fleck of life or colour. Dead metal, stifling and cold. Abena feels she has been trudging this corridor for years. It must have turned or branched but still Abena marches on, hand brushing the right armrest of Ariel's chair for reassurance, shivering with claustrophobia.

'They could have escorted us from the station,' Abena says.

'I will not be marched into the presence of Duncan Mackenzie by the blades who killed my brothers,' Ariel says.

'And who tried to kill you,' Marina says, at the left side of the silently rolling chair.

'I don't understand how you can even come here,' Abena says.

'That's because you don't understand the counsel/client relationship,' Marina says. 'Ariel represents the Eagle of the Moon. She's here as his counsel and representative. What she feels, her history with the Mackenzies, have no place here. Here she's not Ariel Corta. Duncan will respect that.'

'It still seems that she's erasing her personal integrity,' Abena says.

Marina stops dead.

'You have nothing to tell Ariel about integrity.'

'Both of you shut up,' Ariel snaps. 'I'm not fucking dead, you know.' Abena hears apprehension beneath the irritation.

And then there is a door. Behind the door, an elevator. Beyond the elevator, a golden-haired smiling Mackenzie Metals woman who could not say unarmed and harmless more clearly were she unclothed and hairless. Beyond her, a low-ceilinged room, rock and metal; windows like squints. Shafts of light stab down from slots in the low ceiling.

'Still the mirrors,' Ariel whispers.

Five figures stand arranged for effect in the strong down lights. Abena recognises them from her briefing: the board of the new Mackenzie Metals. All men, of course. Duncan Mackenzie is larger than Abena imagined. Signature grey, his familiar an oily ball of grey light. She finds herself awed by this man where the psychoarchitecture of the Palace of Eternal Light was stage magic. He has presence and gravity.

'Duncan.'

'Ariel.'

How can she shake his hand? How can she speak to him, how can she say his name? Abena is sure she could never debase herself so lowly. Professional objectivity is a career lesson she knows she must learn but there are principles which may not be compromised without losing all credibility and self belief. She admires Ariel's professional detachment; she is not certain she respects it.

'Thank you for coming to Hadley,' Duncan Mackenzie says.

'Testing me, Duncan?'

'Partly. And I no longer feel safe in Meridian.'

The Mackenzie Metals woman brings a tray of drinks. Ariel passes it without hesitation, without even a lingering look. It does not pass near Abena and Marina.

'What do you want from me, Ariel?'

'The Eagle of the Moon needs to know if he will continue to enjoy the support of Mackenzie Metals.'

'And where do my brother's loyalties lie?'

'You wouldn't let as petty a thing as that colour your judgement?'

'Three hundred and fifty deaths and two hundred and fifty million bitsies in materiel damage and lost revenue is hardly petty.'

'Your brother has yet to request a meeting with the Eagle's counsel.

I thought you would have known that, or has your back channel to the Eagle gone quiet?'

'Adrian remains resolutely unaligned,' Duncan Mackenzie says. He invites Ariel to a ring of seats. Abena notices there is no space for her or Marina. There is a lot of standing around in the job of intern to the Eagle of the Moon's counsel. She is glad of Ariel's advice on comfortable shoes. 'We need stability, Ariel. The Eagle's coup on top of my family's ongoing issues has not reassured the markets. Capital hates uncertainty and we're men of business. Mackenzie Metals will support whichever party offers us the most stable and secure environment to guarantee profits.' Duncan Mackenzie sits back in his chair. His board unconsciously echoes him. 'That's the position of Mackenzie Metals. The position of the head of the Mackenzie family is this.

'My father came to the moon to build a world. His own world, outside the controls and restrictions of governments, consortia, empires. Boards and investment funds. He sank every cent of his fortune into sending five robot prospectors to the moon, then a construction hub, then a production and shipping facility, then an inhabited base. Always reinvesting his own profits. He never took anyone else's money, he never let any outsider invest or buy a stake in Mackenzie Metals. He fought to keep terrestrial nation states from turning us into a colony. He fought to uphold the Outer Space Treaty – and strengthen it. He opposed the establishment of the Lunar Development Corporation, and when it was forced on him, made sure its power was so fractured and diluted that the politics of terrestrial states could never be imposed on free lunar workers. To his dying day my father stood for our freedom and independence. So, please tell Jonathon Kayode that Duncan Mackenzie supports him.'

Abena sees Ariel Corta ready her answer. Duncan Mackenzie raises a hand.

'If he supports me against Bryce.'

*

Ariel watches the drop of dew run down the under slope of the Martini glass. It hesitates at the junction of bowl and stem, gathers, fills, shivers under its weight and glides to the foot.

'Beautiful,' Ariel Corta says. 'The most beautiful thing in this Quartersphere.'

The train hits eight hundred kilometres per hour across Palus Putridinis. The Aitken-Peary Polar line was the first railroad to be built on the moon, serving the ice and hydrocarbon reserves at both poles, but its primacy has been usurped by Equatorial One. Ariel, Marina and Abena are the only passengers in the observation car of the Polar Express. Abena is uncomfortable in the glass blister. She feels exposed, too close to vacuum. Her skin itches from imagined radiation. The vista is of a landscape exhausted by the extractors of Mackenzie Metals. Every crater graded flat, every rille filled with spoil, and that waste scabbed by rover tracks, abandoned machinery, slat panels, abandoned caches and refuges.

It's more interesting than the usual gentle uplifts and soft grey moundings.

Ariel pushes the glass across the table to the waiter.

'Now take it away please.'

With a dip of her head, the waiter whisks the glass away. Not a ripple, not a bead of dew disturbed.

'If you ever do that again,' Ariel says to Marina, 'I shall put the glass through your face.'

'It worked, then.'

'The same applies if you congratulate me or try any of that motivational garbage, sweetie.'

Marina hides a tight laugh. Abena cannot understand the constant low-key aggression between the two women, or the laughter behind every cut and jibe. Ariel disrespects, belittles or outright insults Marina, yet back in Hadley when Abena questioned Ariel's personal integrity Marina had turned on her like a knife-fighter.

'Will he keep to it?' Marina asks.

222

'Duncan has some sense of honour,' Ariel says, catching the conversational shift like a handball ace. 'Unlike his shit of a brother.'

'I still don't see how it couldn't have been done through the network,' Abena says. 'We've been to Hadley, the Palace of Eternal Light – we would have gone to Twé if Sewaa Lousika hadn't been in Meridian.'

'Law is personal,' Ariel says. 'Personal contracts, personal agreements, personally negotiated. When you deal with Dragons, you must offer them a treasure. Maybe they will take it, maybe they will let you keep it. No greater treasure than your own life.'

'Do you know where we haven't been?' Marina says. Abena frowns. Ariel nods.

Realisation. 'The Vorontsovs!'

'I've had no request for a meeting,' Ariel says.

'Does VTO support the LDC board members?' Abena asks.

'Ariel would know,' Marina says.

'Ariel would,' Ariel says. 'And Ariel doesn't know where the Vorontsovs stand. Ariel doesn't like that. So Ariel's going to talk to someone who might be able to guess.'

The print really is very small, no larger than her two thumbs put together. Ariel must lean close to make out the minute figures standing on the upper limb of the curved world and the smaller third figure on the first rung of the ladder that rests on the limb of the crescent moon.

'*I want! I want!*' Ariel reads. There is an inscription beneath the print's minuscule title but it is in cursive and she cannot parse that form of writing.

'William Blake,' Vidhya Rao. 'Eighteenth-, nineteenth-Christian-century English artist and poet. Visionary, prophet and mystic. Uniquely, he excelled at all of them.'

Ariel has never heard of William Blake but she knows Vidhya well enough to commit no trespasses of false erudition. The lunch has been excellent, given the location. The Lunarian Society dining rooms are private and discreet – a suite that can be sealed off from the network – but in Ariel's experience members' clubs seldom have good kitchens. The ramen is as tolerable as noodles can ever be, the sashimi so fresh Ariel suspects it is cut from living fish.

'And our cocktail creator is as good as any in the two worlds,' Vidhya Rao said when e met Ariel in the Lunarian Society Lobby and took the handles of her wheelchair.

'Far too busy for cocktail hour,' Ariel said. Knowing now cocktail hour might never come.

At the small table in the discreet dining room, Ariel's attention is drawn back to the print. The style is simple, almost simplistic, the message a clear parable but there is a vigour, a power to the etching that draws the eye and captures the imagination.

'Crying for the moon,' Ariel says. Vidhya Rao's mouth twitches. Ariel has disappointed er.

'I do so adore Blake,' e says. 'There is always more to him.'

'The surface the figures stand on looks more like the moon than the moon does,' Ariel offers. She has noticed that every table has a small print on the wall, just above the lamp. Beijaflor enhances: they are all in the same style, by the same artist. Decorations, conversation starters.

'That's an interesting observation,' Vidhya Rao says. 'So in fact, from our point of view, it could be Earth, from the moon.'

'That would be beyond nineteenth-century imagining,' Ariel says.

'Not Blake,' Vidhya Rao says. E takes a wallet from er bag and places it on the table. Ariel looks inside.

'Paper,' Ariel says.

'I find it more secure.'

'What dark secrets are you sharing with me?'

'You wanted to know why VTO has not requested a meeting with you.'

Ariel has never been a strong reader. She concentrates to stop her lips moving as she works through the digest at the head of the document. That effort grows more extreme the deeper Ariel goes into the paper. Her mouth opens. She sets the paper on the table.

'They will cut us apart.'

'Yes. We aren't soldiers. We have no soldiers, we don't even have a police force. We are an industrial colony. We have private security and militias at best.'

'Your Three August Ones told you this.'

'With an eighty-nine per cent outcome probability.'

'Who else knows about this?'

'Who would we tell? We have no defences. Whitacre Goddard has started diversifying and strengthening its portfolio as a hedge.'

'Fuck you bankers.'

Vidhya Rao smiles.

'That is the very heart of the matter. We have no solidarity. We are individuals, families and corporations, all acting in our own self-interest.'

'You said the Suns have a back door into the Three August Ones. Do they know this?'

'I look at patterns. I try to draw inferences. From Taiyang's recent investments and disinvestments, I would infer not.'

'How could they avoid seeing something like this?'

'Quite simple. They haven't asked the right questions.'

Ariel spreads sheets across the small table.

'This requires massive space-lift capability.'

'The terrestrial nation states don't have the capacity.'

'My question about VTO is answered. What I don't understand is why.'

'VTO is unique among the Dragons in having an Earth-based arm. That makes it vulnerable to political pressure.'

'Gods.'

'Yes. All of them, of whatever name and nature. I'm sorry, Ariel. Tea?'

Ariel almost laughs at the incongruity. Tea. Mashed mint leaves in a glass, steeped in boiling water. Sweeten to taste. The universal lubricant. A known thing, a comfortable thing. A fine thing, a small defiance in a glass. When the stars fall, when worlds collide, when seers and prophets cry: the only thing. A glass of tea.

'Thank you. I believe I will. One last question, Vidhya.' Ariel gathers up the scattered papers and squares them neatly into the folder. 'How long have we got?'

'Oh my dear. It's already begun.'

Tedium is the quiet killer of the glasslands. Kilometre after kilometre, hour after hour, of black glass black glass black glass. Attention softens and melts, the mind turns inward. Entertainments, distractions and games offer a focus for concentration but threaten a different trap: distraction. Taiyang rovers are equipped with multiple sensors and alarms to warn of any of the thousand internal and external accidents that could moon-wreck a crew, but no surface worker puts their entire trust in AIs. No surface worker who wants to keep living.

Wagner Corta has evolved his own way of working the glass. They accord with his two aspects. In his light aspect his brain accepts many simultaneous inputs and he can watch the glass, the horizon, monitor the rover systems, play a game of Run the Jewels and listen to two music streams at once. In his dark aspect, when his focus is monomaniacal and intense, he can stare at the black glass until he enters a state of deep presence and mindfulness. Above the glasslands, unmoving, the high blue Earth wanes and Wagner transforms to his dark aspect. In full light and full dark wolves are superlative laodas; in the transition they are vulnerable, they can make mistakes.

Message from Taiyang Tranquillity Control. Contact has been lost with the Armstrong grader squadron. The big bot moon-dozers are the grunts of the glasslands; ranked ten abreast, a samba-line can grade a hundred-metre wide strip of regolith to skin smoothness. Samba-line: an old Corta Hélio name.

Wagner blinks up the common channel. 'Change of plan. We're going off-glass. Armstrong has lost a dozer squad.' Derisive whistles from Glass Crew Lucky Eight Ball. The mis-mesh between Taiyang's public pronouncements on the magnificence of its solar belt project and the working day reality has passed beyond private surface-worker joke to lunar legend. 'We've been tasked to investigate, intercept and reboot.' Taiyang Tranquillity Control flicks co-ordinates on to Wagner's lens. Wagner sends them to the rover and locks in a long south-easterly curve across the solar panels. 'There's a bonus.' A small ragged cheer from Glass Crew Lucky Eight Ball.

We have images from orbit, TTC says. Wagner surveys the map overlay. A samba-line of moon-dozers is almost visible from Earth: ten sets of tracks, impeccably spaced, heading without deviation into the plains of East Tranquilitatis.

'Is that unusual?' Wagner asks.

They have a simple flocking algorithm, so they tend to stay together, Control says. *What is unusual is that they're headed straight for Kwabre.*

'Which is?'

A new AKA agrarium core. There's an ecosystem engineering team working on it. A pause.

'The dozers could go right through it.' Wagner pushes up the speed. It will still be tight. 'Have you alerted them?'

We're having trouble raising them. We've contacted AKA; they can't reach them either.

There are a hundred reasons why comms could fail. There are a dozen reasons dozers could turn rogue. The intersection of those reasons scares Wagner Corta.

'I'll try them on the local net once I get over the horizon.'

Kwabre lies forty kilometres beyond the southern edge of the solar belt. Ten kays out Wagner runs up the aerial and tries to contact the agrarium. Not even a whisper of a whisper. At five kays Rover Lucky Eight Ball sights the graders. In perfect choreography, the big machines, five times the height, twenty times the length of Rover Lucky Eight Ball, are pushing regolith over the transparent caps of Kwabre's agriculture tubes.

Wagner has never seen anything like this. None of his crew has. No one on the moon has.

Beyond the initial shock, Kwabre's silence becomes apparent. The comms tower lies toppled, the mirrors that beam light into the agriculture tubes are empty frames hanging from the booms.

'Laoda,' Zehra says. 'The graders could bring down the comms. But those mirrors were broken one by one.'

'I'm declaring SUTRA One,' Wagner says. The highest level of surface threat; human life in imminent danger, render all assistance. 'Zehra, notify Twé. Stand by for a Code 901 to VTO.'

'Twé is sending three squads,' Zehra reports.

Wagner edges the rover forward. Keep the senses open, see with more than sight, feel with more than touch. One of the graders turns to face Glass Crew Lucky Eight Ball. Wagner stops dead, then steers right. The moon-dozer turns on its tracks and moves to match the rover's speed and position.

'What the fuck?' Zehra says on the private channel to Wagner.

'Zehra, relay this to Control.'

Again Wagner moves the rover. Again the dozer matches him.

'I don't want to push this,' Wagner says.

'I don't want you to,' Zehra says.

A grader pushes up a great berm of dust which breaks like a wave over the final glass dome, smothering it, burying it. The squad forms up; the machine which has held Glass Crew Lucky Eight Ball at bay joins them. The samba-line heads north-north-east.

'Laoda, Tranquillity tasked us...' Zehra says.

'This is a SUTRA One,' Wagner says. 'Human life in imminent danger.' He edges the rover to the edge of the main lock. 'Neile, Mairead, Ola, with me. Zehra, relay Twé the feed from Neile's cameras.'

'Twé?'

'It's where the dozers are headed.'

Wagner's crew step from their seats on to the regolith. Zehra raises the lighting array and floods the area.

'Neile.' Wagner crouches by a set of marks in the regolith. 'Get this.'

'Machines?'

'Bot prints.' The sharp, three-pointed hoof-marks are faint, dainty but now he has identified them, Wagner sees that the surface around Kwabre is covered in them. 'Look.' A trail of prints is obliterated by grader tyres.

'Whatever made these were here before the dozers,' Neile says.

Wagner the wolf stands up.

'Zehra, please light up the main lock.'

The lighting array swivels and focuses on the slot of the outlook, buried by a hard brow of sinter. The lock is open. The hard light picks out an object on the ramp, just inside the lock doors.

'Do you want me to get a camera on it?' Zehra asks.

'No,' Wagner says. 'We're going in.'

'You be fucking careful in there, laoda,' Zehra says on the private channel. She doesn't say, doesn't need to say, that Wagner Corta's crew has never lost a member.

'Zehra, I want you ready to go at my command.'

Hard white bounces from the grey walls; lock mechanisms throw long shadows. Wagner beckons his team down slope to the rounded shape that has no place in lock schematics. Glass Crew Lucky Eight Ball's shadows fall long before them.

Zehra says, 'What does the wolf think?'

'The wolf is afraid.'

Helmet lights bob over the object on the ramp. Vacuum kills meanly, but it did not kill this dead man. The crew moves to allow Zehra's lights to fully illuminate the corpse. A young man in an agricultural worker's waterproof boots and vest-of-pockets, opened from breastbone to navel. Glisten of blood and intestines.

'Fuck,' Ola whispers.

'Are you getting this to Twé?' Wagner asks the rover.

'What could do that?' Zehra asks.

'I'll find out.' Neile squats in front of the dead man. 'There may be enough power left in his lens to read it through the near field.' Her faceplate touches his brow. Her light reflects from the frozen eyeballs. Wagner finds Neile's intimacy with the dead man chilling. Corpse kiss. 'Going to you now.'

The recovered scrap of memory is short and searing. Movement, running movement, then a turn and something leaps toward the lens, something short and fast and made of blades. Flash of silver, then the fall. Then the dying twitch. In the corner of the dying eye, tiny, pert steel hooves, trifurcated.

'Jesus Maria,' Mairead says, kissing the back of her gloved knuckles.

Wagner raises a hand. *Silence*. Something, on the edge of his wolf senses. Not a sound – there is no sound in vacuum – a tremor. A stirring.

'Zehra, get me light in the far left corner.'

Shadows shift and dwindle. In the darkness behind the agrarium rover, something that is not rover.

And Wagner's wolf senses scream.

'Run,' he says.

The machine explodes from its cover. Wagner catches an edge-of-vision glance of limbs, blades, sensor booms. Pert steel hooves. Gleam of floodlight on metal. No more. He's running. Mairead is beside him, Ola a stride ahead of him, Neile a stride behind him.

'Zehra!' Wagner yells. She's already in motion. The rover bounces over the edge of the outlock, lands halfway down the ramp. Zehra donuts on the dusty sinter. Wagner leaps for the crash bars as the rover slides towards him and swings himself into the seat.

'Neile?' Mairead shouts. On Wagner's HUD, Neile's familiar fades from red through pink to white. Wagner glances back to see Neile's body slide off three precision titanium blades. She drops on her front.

The blades have run her through, spine to breastbone, punching clean through the tight weave of her sasuit. Blood sprays, evaporates, freezes. That second of hesitation, that one pace slow of Wagner killed her. Wagner's fast senses read the thing behind the body. It is a bot made only for killing. Legs not wheels. Those sharp hooves double as weapons but also unfold into flat spades for dust running. Fast and sure on the moon's many terrains. Four arms, three bladed, one grappling. Blades are swifter and more certain than projectiles. Head a clutch of sensors. Heavy duty batteries. The bot steps over Neile's body, locks sensors with Wagner's faceplate. Sees him. Knows him. Leaps in pursuit.

Behind it, the inlock opens.

Rover Lucky Eight Ball hits the top of the ramp at full acceleration and flies: ten, fifteen, twenty metres. Two bots leap from the open inlock. The third leaps with them. Gods they are fast. The rover lands hard in a spray of dust, almost toppling ass over nose but Zehra saves it. Zehra drives better than AI. He flicks up a pane to watch the killers through the rear cameras. They hold themselves low, poised, seeking.

'I'm calling in a rescue,' Wagner says to Zehra on the private channel.

'It's quicker to get to Twé,' Zehra says.

'I don't want those things anywhere near Twé,' Wagner says. 'Rendezvous here.' He swipes GPSS code to Zehra and makes the distress call twice, once to VTO's emergency network, again to Taiyang Tranquillity. Wagner flicks up the status HUD. He must assume that the things hunting him have deeper power reserves than the rover. Batteries at forty per cent. The rover is lighter without Neile. He weighs a life against battery reserves, dispassionately, with a wolf's calculation. He sees again Neile's body sliding slowly from the killing blades. He's seen people die. He's seen people die accidentally, stupidly, hideously, cheaply, but he's only ever seen one other person die by act of will. That was in the polished wood and old-blood warmth of the Court of Clavius, not the outlock ramp of a dead agrarium. The killing blade had been Hadley Mackenzie's, the hand that ripped it out through its owner's throat Carlinhos's. *Brother, what do I do here?*

Batteries at thirty-five per cent. The hunters will catch them ten kilometres from the rendezvous point. Why hasn't VTO responded? Wagner asks Sombra for a spread of extraction zones that all return the same answer: he can't outrun them. He must fight them.

We're a Glass Crew. We patch solar panels. We have sinterers, panel lifters, circuit webbing and repair bots. Versus three killing machines.

Use their weapons against them.

'Zehra, give me control.' Wagner takes the drive HUD. 'Hold on.'

Zehra is the better driver but what must be done now, only the wolf can do. Wagner grits his teeth as he drifts the rover. Billion-year-old dust arcs out from the line of the skid. For a moment he thinks they might roll but Taiyang builds its rovers sure and stable. Wagner guns the motors and steers straight at the hunters. They scatter on sharp, fast legs. Not fast enough. Wagner catches one a glancing blow that sends it bowling in a flail of legs and blades across a hundred metres. His front left wheel catches a hoof and crushes it. The bot lurches. Wagner brakes, throws the rover into reverse. His ribs slam against the seat harness. Impact shakes the rover; the bot flips clear over the top in a rain of debris. Teeth gritted, Wagner donuts the rover again and bears down at full speed on the other damaged bot. It climbs unsteadily to its hooves, focuses sensors, levels blades. Too slow. Too too slow. The blunt prow smashes it down under the drive wheels. The rover jolts, Glass Crew Lucky Eight Ball shout and hoot.

'That's two,' Zehra says.

Then Jeff's familiar goes white.

'Zehra, take it!' He slings the drive HUD to Zehra. She snatches it up without a beat. Ola screams on the common channel. Wagner slaps the emergency release, stands up on his seat. Only his wolf senses save him from the blade that swings for the top of his helmet.

'It's on top of the rover!'

'Do you want me to stop, laoda?'

Ola is screaming but his familiar is solid red. Red is life.

'We stop we die.'

The rover jolts and bounces. Wagner hisses in concentration as he balances on the seat. His free hand unclasps the shovel from the utility rack beside him. He thrusts the shovel up. The blade impacts with a clang he feels through his wrist bones. In the split second between attack and recovery he hauls himself into a kneel on the top of the rover.

The killing bot clings there with him, legs spread wide, hoof-claws hooked into the rails and trusses. One blade is driven to the hilt down through Jeff's helmet and skull. One stabs down, down, down again at Ola, dodging in the cage of his crash bars. The last blade is for Wagner. The bot's blade is trapped in Jeff's skull. Therefore the bot too is trapped. A spray of black vacuum frozen blood on the sensor array. This is the machine that killed Neile. All this Wagner senses in the split second it takes to parry the one free blade with his shovel and, while the bot recovers, stab forward with the sharp edge to sever the cabling inside one of the hooves. The claws spasm and fly free. The bot locks all its sensors on him. It attacks in a blur of dancing blades, too fast for any human to parry. Wolf eyes see the decision in the machine lenses an instant before bot brain acts: Wagner throws himself flat and scrabbles out of range of the blade.

'Zehra, donut!'

Wagner grips with all his strength. And even that may not be enough as Zehra throws the rover into a vicious power slide. Spars and construction beams rattle hard under Wagner's ribs: he's slipping, slipping. Over. Wagner hangs from the side of the rover. He risks taking a hand off, reaches, seizes the shovel as it slides over the edge. Unbalanced, the bot topples. The wedged blade pulls free from Jeff's helmet. Wagner swings with the shovel, connects, hammers again and again. The bot falls, swords flailing.

'Zehra!'

The sudden acceleration almost wrenches Wagner's shoulder from its socket. He hangs from the crash bars, turning painfully to see the fallen bot rise, tuck the destroyed foot under its belly and launch itself after the rover.

'Die, just fucking die!' Wagner screams.

A rover explodes over a low crater rim, six wheels in the air. It lands, bounces. The damaged bot spins. Too slow. The rover takes it head on. Legs, arms, sensory pods explode. The rover drifts, throwing blinding dust over Glass Crew Lucky Eight Ball. When it clears the final bot is a tangle of metal on the regolith and the rover runs alongside Lucky Eight Ball. Its spars and panels are decorated with the intricate geometric designs of AKA. The AKA driver signals to stop. Wagner drops to the surface, then to his knees. He can't stand, can't speak. Can't stop shaking. A hand grips his shoulder.

'Lobinho.' Only Zehra is allowed to use his old Corta Hélio nickname. 'Steady, Little Wolf. Steady.'

'Report?' Wagner forces the word from chattering teeth. He is death cold.

'We're mobile.'

'I mean ...'

'Jeff is dead.'

'And Neile.'

'And Neile.'

'I never lost anyone,' Wagner says. 'Anyone. Glass Crew Lucky Eight Ball never loses anyone.'

The AKA squad boss squats in front of him.

'You okay?'

Sombra tags her as Adjoa Yaa Boakye. Wagner nods.

'What were those things?' Adjoa asks.

'Can't you see he's in shock?' Zehra snaps.

'I just want to be sure there aren't more of them out there,' Adjoa says. Her crew of blackstar surface workers drop from their seats to the regolith.

Wagner shakes his head.

'He needs help,' Zehra insists. Only her hands on his shoulder hold Wagner upright. 'Where the fuck is our ship?'

'VTO is not responding,' Adjoa says.

'That's not possible,' Zehra says.

Wagner is cold. Terribly terribly cold. Helmets, suits, bodies swim in and out of a blackness swirling red blood motes.

'Medic!' Adjoa shouts. One of her blackstars kneels beside Wagner, pulls a hypo from a calf pouch, strips it out, preps it.

'Hold him.' Zehra and Adjoa grab Wagner's shoulders. The medic punches the needle through sasuit, skin, flesh. Wagner spasms as if a power line has been run into his aorta, then a wave of well-being washes up him and his heart, his breathing, his surging blood settle into their familiar rhythms. 'That should stabilise him,' the medic says. Wagner feels Zehra and Adjoa lift him and bar him into his seat.

'Kwabre is dead,' Wagner whispers. 'The dozers are on their way.'

'What happened?' Adjoa asks.

'I still can't raise VTO,' Zehra says. 'What the fuck is going on?'

Then the flash.

Then the ground shakes.

Then the metal rain.

Lucasinho's cock is long and curved, belled with a thick rimmed glans. Abena's hands slide down the shaft to cup the smooth, full balls, then move up over his perfect belly to his breasts. They are firm, upturned, large nippled. Perfect.

Abena sighs.

She rolls Lucasinho's nipples between thumbs and forefingers. He purrs. His full glossed lips part. She closes, breasts to breasts, belly to belly. His cock is hard, its head resting in her navel. She runs her fingers through the dark, shiny hair that falls to his ass and draws him into a kiss.

She has been skinning him as a futanari for a lune now. The first time he lifted his adorable little maid tutu and stepped out of his girl pants and his cock slipped free from its bulge, she came. Ecstatic transgression. The second and third time she had network sex with Futa Lucasinho the spice was that he didn't know what she had done to his avatar. The fourth, fifth, sixth times the electricity was her control over Lucasinho. She could make him anything she wanted. Turn his skin to plastic. Give him a goddess's multiple breasts. Give him an alien cock. Her haptics would respond. This seventh time she notices that she's given him much better tits than hers.

She pushes Lucasinho down on to the pad and straddles him so she can watch his breasts jiggle as she fucks him. That dick is a cartoon dick, a manga dick. He's fantastic with it, all that way down the cable link in Twé, though he doesn't know what she's given him. She adores her cock-girl Luca.

When it is finally finished she rolls off him and lies on her side, studying her art.

'Kojo and Afi are right,' Lucasinho says. 'I do have better tits than you.'

'Shit,' Abena says.

'You might have asked.'

'Do you mind?'

'No, but that's not the issue.'

Distance sex, like every other style of human sexual expression, is about consent. By sculpting Lucasinho's avatar without his knowledge, Abena has transgressed.

'Kojo and Afi shouldn't have told.'

'Afi was pissed at you. Some colloquium thing.'

'That doesn't mean she can tell you my stuff.'

'So you would have told me?'

'Yes,' Abena lies. Now that he knows, the clandestine thrill has gone out of it. 'Did she show you?'

'She did.'

'Do you like it?'

'I love the cock.'

'You're welcome. What about the tits?'

'I'm still finding out about them. Do they excite you?'

Abena hesitates.

'I got the idea from Grigori Vorontsov. You know he used to be a big Vorontsov bear. Well, he's not anymore.' She nods at Lucasinho's avatar.

'Futa?'

'In real life.'

'Whoa,' Lucasinho Corta says. He sits up. *Oh gods, look at the ass I gave you,* Abena prays silently. *Like an apricot.* And again, 'Whoa. Since when?'

'Back in Capricorn. It took a while for the surgery to heal.'

'Grigori. I never would have thought.'

'He's gorgeous,' Abena says. Lucasinho's avatar sits on the end of the pad swinging his legs. Half the moon away, in a network sex cabin in Twé, his physical body will be doing the same. 'Luca,' Abena says, 'do you ever skin me?'

Grigori Vorontsova is stunning. Everything Abena said is true. The chunky red-haired Russian boy with the bottomless lust for Lucasinho Corta is a slim full-hipped manga-eyed red-haired futanari.

'Ola Luca,' she says. 'Nice to hear from you.'

'Um yeah,' Lucasinho stammers. 'You look...'

'Fantastic? That's so sweet. You're looking hot as ever, Luca.'

In his room in the Oyoko abusua house in Twé, a quarter of the moon away from Meridian, Lucasinho Corta blushes. Grigori Vorontsova always could get her fingers inside his head.

'So which do you prefer?'

'I don't know what you mean,' Lucasinho stammers.

'That Grigori or this one? Let me help you decide.' Grigori steps back from the lens. She wears a tutu dress with a bolero jacket. Fingerless gloves, sheer Capri leggings and pumps. Crucifixes and Theotokos of Konstantin icons around her neck and a golden bow in her hair. Layer by layer, Grigori strips. The bra unsnaps and falls to the ground as Grigori stares a challenge into the camera. Lucasinho gasps.

'You've seen nothing, Lucasinho Alves Mão de Ferro Arena de Corta.'

She hooks fingers in the waistband of her panties and peels them down.

Then the lights spasm and go off. Grigori Vorontsova blinks out of his lens. The room shakes, dust falls and outside the screaming starts.

Wagner peers out from under the rover. The rain of rock and metal ended several minutes ago, and now the ground is covered in a hail of small rocks and splashes of molten metal.

'Report,' Wagner calls.

Laoda, Zehra says. *Laoda* from Mairead, and from Ola.

Glass Crew Lucky Eight Ball scrambles out from cover. The rover is a mess; a hundred scratches and cracks. Zehra inspects the damage, rerouting damaged cable, patching holed life-support ducts. Wagner and his AKA counterpart meet on the pocked terrain between the two rovers.

'What was that?' Wagner asks.

'Twé reports an explosion at the Maskelyne G power plant,' Adjoa says.

'The fusion plant?' Wagner feels his belly and balls tighten, checks Sombra for radiation spikes. New instincts wired into the moon-born: protect the DNA from radiation.

'If Maskelyne G had exploded, we wouldn't be here,' Adjoa says.

'Something blew a hole down through to the fifty metres of regolith, clean through the outer and middle shells, and cracked the inner caisson.'

Murmurs on the common channel.

'An impacter?' Wagner asks.

'VTO would have warned us,' Adjoa says.

'VTO was supposed to come for us,' Zehra says from the top of Rover Lucky Eight Ball.

Mystery after mystery. Wagner does not like mysteries. Mysteries kill. There are too many deaths out here in East Tranquillity. The only safe place is deep, with your back turned to the sky and the rock pulled over you.

'That is one unluckily accurate impacter,' Zehra says, patching and plugging.

'Meaning?' Adjoa says.

'Meaning, Maskelyne was targeted,' Zehra says. 'I ran a few mass and velocity parameters. What hit it was either something big, in which case we would have seen it, or something small and fast-moving.'

'Did anyone see anything?' Adjoa asks. Negatives from her black-stars and Crew Lucky Eight Ball. Nothing on cameras.

'All I'm saying is, it wasn't us or AKA built those bots we took out,' Zehra says. 'The Mackenzies are fighting all over this Quartersphere but they've enough sense not to involve Sun or AKA. Maskelyne gets hit. VTO has a mass driver up there at the L2 point. Any way you point it, that's a gun.'

'Why would . . .' Adjoa begins. Zehra cuts her off.

'How would we ever know? We're just the grunts, the surface workers. Collateral.'

'Are we mobile?' Wagner says.

'Just,' Zehra says, jumping down from the top of the rover in contravention of all safety protocols to land lightly on the regolith.

'Lost a couple of solar panels. I wouldn't want to have to try to outrun anything.'

'Follow us to Twé,' Adjoa says and swings up into her command seat.

In the mid 2060s a troop of excavation bots ventured out into the southern Sea of Tranquillity. They unfolded solar generators and began to dig. They dug precisely and carefully, a helix cut into the sea floor of Mare Tranquilitatis. Where the regolith was fractured they sintered it, where it was the hard basalt of the lunar mare they ground forward, centimetre by slow centimetre. After two lunes the excavators had dug a hundred-metre-deep shaft west of Maskelyne crater with three helical ramps cut into the walls. They drove up the winding ramps and into the sun. Then they scooped out shelters and waited.

Over the horizon came Efua Asamoah and her caravan of short-contract workers. They parked their habitat trailers and bermed them over with regolith. From the flatbeds they unloaded universal construction trusses, an extractor that ran hydrogen through a bed of regolith to generate water, and two tonnes of Queen of the South's shit and piss.

Efua Asamoah sank her fortune into this rifle-barrel in the Sea of Tranquillity. The shit had been particularly costly. Now the work. The construction trusses were assembled into a pylon that ran the height of the shaft and another hundred metres above the surface. The sinterers shaped black-glass mirrors from the regolith: Efua Asamoah and her crew hung them one by one from the spine. The bots spread a cap of translucent impact carbon over the shaft and sealed it. Beneath this roof Efua Asamoah created an ecosystem. By hand she worked Queen of the South's shit into the pulverised spoil from the excavation until she had a tilth. On that day Efua Asamoah lifted a handful of her soil and tasted it and knew that it was good. Her workers spread it by hand along the helical ledges. They installed water plants and irrigation systems, a gas exchange to handle excess oxygen, motors to guide the mirrors and a pink-light array. Then Efua Asamoah hauled a caravan of seedlings all the way from Queen of the South and under the pink light she and her farmers laboured through the long lunar night, hand-planting the spiral ledges.

Build a farm, feed the world, Efua Asamoah had told her investors. The risk was enormous. Efua Asamoah was asking the money to accept that the moon would develop along the equator, not around the pole. That her radical design of farm, using sunlight and lunar regolith, would work, let alone prove cheaper and more efficient than the existing rack farms. Most walked. Only two came for the day that Efua Asamoah opened the shutters and sent the rising sun down the shaft on to the mirror array and woke a garden beneath the Sea of Tranquillity.

That walled garden became two, became five, grew roots and tunnels, became fifty, became the garden city of Twé: three hundred glass domes on the plains of Tranquilitatis.

And it is under siege.

Glass Crew Lucky Eight Ball and Adjoa Yaa Boakye's blackstars crest the low western rille and stop. Now Wagner Corta sees where his missing graders have gone. One hundred dozers are patiently burying the light-domes of Twé in lunar regolith.

Cut off the light, shut down the power to the artificial lighting arrays, and the crops will die. Wagner appreciates this at once. Kill a farm, starve the world.

Wagner joins Adjoa on the edge of the low overlook. His dark-side mind drills through ideas and strategies and discards them. Two rovers-full of surface workers against an army of kill-dozers.

'Maybe we could counter-hack the dozers, or plant demolition charges,' Adjoa says.

'You'd never get close,' Zehra interrupts. 'Laoda . . .'

Wagner is already swinging into his seat. From their scrapes and trenches and revetments encircling Twé, a line of twenty bots charges their position, blades raised.

8: SCORPIO 2105

The two rovers run silent and swift, west across the southern limb of the Sea of Tranquillity. Before them, beyond the horizon, is Hypatia. Behind them are twenty hunting bots.

Hypatia is a hope, a haven. They may reach it on the dregs of power. There may be something at Hypatia that can deal with a score of killing bots. There may be something between their current position and Hypatia that will save them.

Or their batteries may fail, despite the careful husbanding. Then the bots pounce and annihilate them. Every ten minutes Wagner runs up the radar mast to peep over the horizon. They are always there. They are always closer. No hope of losing them: the two rovers leave indelible fresh tracks, aimed like arrows at Hypatia.

Too many hopes and ifs, too many of which end impaled on a blade, but Wagner's fears and dreads fall around Robson. Death is nothing; that failure might be his last emotion almost paralyses him with horror. Comms are down all over the quartersphere, the sky is silent. He can't raise TTC. The moon has turned upside down; all parameters have been exceeded and all Wagner can think of is that thirteen-year-old he left behind in Meridian. He imagines Robson waiting, not knowing, waiting, asking Amal, not knowing, asking wider and wider, no one knowing.

Wagner's earplugs blast deafening noise into his inner ear. His visor blazes white: Wagner is light-blind. He feels Rover Lucky Eight Ball roll to a halt beneath him. Comms are down. He tries to call up Sombra. Nothing. His vision clears in blotches of glowing black and fluorescent yellow. His ears ring. Wagner tries to blink away one dead patch in the centre of his eye and can't. His lens is dead.

That can't happen.

He tries to flick up the HUD. Nothing. No read-out from his suit, his life support, his temperature and vital signs, his crew. Wagner tries to command Lucky Eight Ball to move, to report and, when those orders fail, to open the safety bars and set him down on the surface. Nothing. He is locked out of any and every control. Wagner glances at his crew. No names, no tags, no familiars.

There must be a manual release. Every device used on the surface of the moon carries multiple redundancies. Wagner tries to remember his training sessions on the Taiyang XBT rover. A hand reaches up and slaps a switch. The safety bar lifts, the seat drops ungently to the surface. Zehra presses her helmet to Wagner's.

'We're dead in the dust.' Zehra's voice is a distant, indistinct shout, muffled by air and helmet insulation.

'Those things are behind us,' Wagner bellows. 'What happened?'

'Electromagnetic pulse,' Zehra shouts. 'The only thing that could take everything out at once.'

Dust rises above the eastern horizon. Moments later a squadron of rovers arrives, customised in AKA geometrics. Blackstars drop to the surface. They wear long dark strung objects slung across their backs. When Wagner recognises them their incongruity renders them almost comical. Bows. Things from old madrinha stories of Earth and its heroes. Bows and arrows. The lead rover runs up an over-the-horizon radar mast while a dozen archers take up a perimeter, bows unslung, arrows nocked. The bows may be complex, mean devices, all pulleys and stabilising weights, but they are medieval terrestrial weaponry. The arrows are balanced and weighted and armed with a small cylindrical payload. Wagner's dark intelligence digs into the incongruity. The ballistics of archery are as precise as those of the BALTRAN. More: the effect of solar wind is lessened on a small projectile. Bows are easy to print: the delivery system is simple human muscle. AIs aim accurately: under lunar gravity AKA's archers can shoot over the horizon. A smart delivery system for electromagnetic pulse warheads.

Clever.

The colours of the archery squad leader's suit flow into words.

GET BACK.

The suit blanks, forms new words.

IN THE.

ROVERS.

Those of the AKA squad not on guard are already hitching the dead rovers to theirs. Wagner again fumbles for the manual override. Zehra hits it for him: he imagines a grin through her faceplate as he rides up and locks into the chassis and the safety bars drop.

THEY'RE NOT.

ALL DEAD, the suit says.

That's the weakness, Wagner thinks as the AKA archers run to their vehicles. Emps are effective at range, but inside their envelope, as he and his AKA counterpart had been, you are as vulnerable as your targets.

Wheels spin. Wagner jolts hard in his harness as the tow cables take up the slack and Lucky Eight Ball is jerked into motion. Insulated in his sasuit, isolated from his world, his crew, his familiar, his pack and his loves, his boy, Wagner Corta looks up at the crescent Earth. He lets its small light pour through his visor. Without anyone knowing, without any declaration or draft, he has become a soldier in a dubious war.

A kiss.

'Aren't you coming with us?' Luna Corta says. Despite the cramp in her old calf muscles, Madrinha Elis crouches, eye to eye with Luna.

'There aren't enough places on the train, anjinho.'

'I want you to come.'

The berçário quakes again. Up there, the machines pile ton after ton after ton of regolith over Twé's windows, burying it, smothering it. The power has come and gone three times in the same number of hours.

'Lucasinho is going to look after you.'

'I will. Luna, I'll get you there.'

Lousika Asamoah parlayed all the influence of the Golden Stool to book Luna and Lucas on to the train. Madrinha Elis knows that to find those seats, she had bounced two other refugees to a later train. This she will never tell Luna, or even Lucasinho.

'I'm scared, Elis.'

'So am I, coracão.'

'What's going to happen?' Luna asks.

'I don't know, coracão. But you'll be safe in Meridian.'

'Will you be all right?'

'We should go now,' Lucasinho says and Elis could kiss him forever for that. She kisses him twice. Love and luck.

'Go. Lucasinho?'

He is so vulnerable. Here lie the borders of care; a cold land of events and powers impervious to dedication or love.

'Look after yourself.'

As she closes the berçário door Twé quakes again. The power flickers, comes back in half-light.

'Lucasinho,' Luna says. 'Hold my hand. Please?

The lights go out. Twé roars. One hundred and twenty-five thousand voices, trapped underground in the dark. Lucasinho snatches Luna to him and holds her tight, cheek to chest, as panicked parents and children push past in the narrow tunnel, trying to find the station, the train, the saving train. The roar does not stop. Bodies large and small crash into him. Why are people moving when the sensible thing is to stay still and wait for the emergency lights? The emergency lights will come on. The emergency lights can only fail if the back-up power fails. He learned that from Madrinha Flavia. And if the back-up power fails? He spins Luna to the wall, puts his body between her and the stampede.

'Lucasinho, what's happening?'

'The power's out again,' Lucasinho says. He holds Luna to him, buffeted and beaten by bodies, trying not to feel the darkness as a solid, crushing thing. If the power has failed, what about the air supply? His chest tightens, he fights an involuntary gulp of panic. Reaches a decision, in the suffocating dark.

'Come on…' He seizes Luna's hand and draws her behind him, against the flow of people down the pitch-dark tunnel. Voices call the names of missing children, children and parents call for each other. Lucasinho forces a path through the press of blind, confused bodies.

'Where are we going?' Luna asks. Her hand is so small and light in his. It could slip free so easily. He firms his grip. Luna yelps with pain.

'You're hurting me!'

'Sorry. We're going to João de Deus.'

'But madrinha Elis said we were to get on the train to Lousika.'

'Anjinho, no one's getting on a train. No train's going anywhere. We're going to take the BALTRAN to João de Deus. The Sisters will look after us. Jinji, go to infrared.'

I'm sorry Lucasinho, but the network is currently unavailable.

Blind in a darkness deeper than dark Twé.

'Jinji,' Lucasinho whispers. 'We need to get to the BALTRAN Station.'

I can navigate from my last location for you based on my internal maps and your average stride length, Jinji said. *There will be a margin of error.*

'Help me.'

One hundred and twelve paces ahead. Then stop.

A hand tugs Lucasinho's, hauls him to a halt mid-stride.

'I can't find Luna.'

In the dark and noise and fear, Lucasinho can't understand what the young voice one pace behind him is saying. How can Luna not find Luna? Then Lucasinho remembers: Luna was also the name of her familiar. Grandmother Adriana always pursed her lips and tutted at the conceit, and that her granddaughter had chosen a blue Luna moth – an animal – to skin her familiar.

'The network's down, anjinho. Stay with me. Don't let go of my hand. I'm going to get us somewhere bright and safe.'

One hundred and twelve paces, then stop. Lucasinho steps into the dark. *One step two step three step four.* The tunnel seems emptier now – the collisions fewer, the voices more widely spread – but every time Lucasinho brushes against another body he stops in place, silently repeating his last pace count. On the fifth halt, Luna interrupts.

'Why do we keep stopping?'

The step count flees like carnival butterflies. Lucasinho battles the urge to scream his frustration at his cousin.

'Luna? I'm counting steps and it's really important you don't interrupt me.' But the numbers are gone. Lucasinho's skin crawls in fear. Lost in the dark.

Eighty-five, Jinji says.

'Luna, do you want to help?' Lucasinho says. He feels Luna nod her head through the minute play of muscles in her arm. 'We're going to make this a game. Count with me. Eighty-six, eighty-seven . . .'

Lucasinho knows he has arrived at the intersection by the movement of air on his face. Sounds move in new paths. He smells mould, water, leaf-rot; the sweat of Twé. The air from deep inside the dark city chills. The heating is down. Lucasinho doesn't want to think too long about that.

Turn right, ninety degrees, Jinji advises.

'Don't let go now,' Lucasinho says and Luna's hand tightens on his but there is peril here. Jinji can easily measure steps but turning is a more subtle action. Miss the angle and he could lose the calculated path. Lucasinho pivots his right foot and presses heel to instep. His feet feel at right angles to each other. He turns left foot parallel to right. Breathes deeply.

'Okay Jinji.'

Two hundred and eight steps, take the second corridor.

Two corridors.

'We're going to move in to the wall,' Lucasinho says and side-shuffles until his outstretched fingers touch smooth sinter. 'You feel that? Reach out your little arm. Got it?'

A silence, then Luna says, 'I nodded my head there, but uh huh.'

'Count with me. One, two three . . .'

At one hundred and five Luna stops dead and shouts, 'Lights!'

Lucasinho's fingertips are so electric-raw he can hardly bear to hold them to the polished wall. They are as sensitive, as tuned, as nipples. He peers into the bottomless dark.

'What can you see, Luna?'

'Can't see,' Luna said. 'I can smell lights.'

Now Lucasinho catches a hint of the grassy, mouldy smell of biolights and understands.

'They're dead, Luna.'

'They might just need water.'

Lucasinho feels Luna's hand tug and slip from his grasp. He follows into the uncounted dark. *Take twelve steps to your left and resume your course,* Jinji orders. Lucasinho hears a rustle of fabric, feels a downward tug on his hand and, knowing that Luna is squatting down, crouches beside her. He can see nothing. Not a photon.

'I can make these work,' Luna declares. 'Don't look.'

Lucasinho hears fabric rustle, a thick trickle, smells the warm perfume of piss. A warm green glow spreads from the revived bio-lights. The light is barely enough to discern shapes, but it grows by the second as the bacteria feed from Luna's urine. A street shrine to Yemanja; a tiny 3-D printed icon ringed by a halo of biolights stuck to the floor and wall. The light is now strong enough for Lucasinho to see the two junctions Jinji described, and a body lying against the wall between them. He would have fallen over that, sprawling and lost in the dark.

'Here.' Luna peels off handfuls of biolights and presents them to Lucasinho. They are wet and warm in his hands. He almost drops them in disgust. Luna purses her lips in displeasure. 'Like this.' She sticks the little disc-shaped lights to her forehead, shoulders and wrists.

'This is a Malihini shirt,' Lucasinho protests.

'Designer today, deprinter tomorrow,' Luna declares.

'Who taught you that?'

'Madrinha Elis.'

Hand in hand, they take the long route around the body, then down the indicated corridor. The tunnel shakes to noises overhead, heavy things moving slowly, up on the surface. The trickster winds of Twé carry snatches of voices, clashing metal, cries, a deep rhythmic booming. Left here, up this ramp, around this curving peripheral road. A right turn takes them into the path of a mob of people milling in the dark corridor. Luna spins around.

'They can see our lights!' she hisses. Lucasinho turns, hides his glow.

'They're between us and the BALTRAN.'

'Back to 25th, up the steps and there's an old tunnel to the BALTRAN,' Luna says. 'You're big but you should be able to fit all right.'

'How do you know that?'

'I know all the sneaky ways,' Luna says.

In daylight Lucasinho would have slipped around and between and under the jutting machinery and old raw rock of Luna's sneaky way without a thought, but with his own body the only source of light, not knowing how far this tunnel goes or what surprise it might present to him, how much bigger or smaller it grew, panic grips

250

him. The terror of being trapped in the dark, his biolights ebbing, flickering, dying: unable to see, unable to move. Megatons of rock above him, the distant heart of the moon beneath him.

He feels sinter press against his bent back, his shoulders, and freezes. He is wedged. Unable to go forward, unable to move backwards. Future generations might find him, something mummified and desiccated. In a Malihini shirt. He must get out, he must get free. But if he lunges, lurches, body-panics, he will only jam himself tighter. He must turn, slide one shoulder through like this, then the other, then his hips and legs.

'Come on,' Luna calls. Her biolights dance before him; soft green stars. Lucasinho dips his left shoulder. Fabric catches and tears. In João de Deus, he will treat himself to a new shirt. A hero's shirt. Two steps and he's through. Twenty steps and he emerges from a crevice on 2nd Street he has never noticed before. Hand in hand, Luna and Lucasinho lope down the corridor to the BALTRAN. The BALTRAN station maintains a separate power supply. Twé, feeder of the moon, is well equipped with BALTRAN launchers. They step from the lock out on to a cargo bay wide enough to handle loading trucks.

'Jinji,' Lucasinho says. BALTRAN capsules hang before him in ranks and columns, a hundred metres high, far up into the heights of the launch silo.

The local network is available, Jinji says.

' João de Deus BALTRAN station,' Lucasinho says.

Jinji brings down a personnel capsule down and racks it in the access chamber. Now it asks for a destination.

I have a routing laid in, Jinji says. *The BALTRAN network is in use so it's not direct.*

'How many jumps?' Lucasinho asks.

Eight, Jinji says. *I'm sending you round the far side of the moon.*

'What's happening?' Luna asks as the BALTRAN capsule opens before them. She looks at the padded interior, the straps and crash webbing, the oxygen masks, with apprehension.

'It's going to take us eight jumps to get to João de Deus,' Lucasinho says. 'But it'll be all right. It'll just take a little longer, that's all. We have to go now. Come on.'

Luna hangs back. Lucasinho reaches out a hand. Luna takes it. He steps into the capsule.

'You've still got your lights on,' Luna says. Lucasinho peels them from him. The adhesive pads leave grubby, sticky rings on his Malihini shirt. He leaves the little glowing discs on the floor of the capsule. They were good and faithful and he is superstitiously loyal to things. Jinji shows him how to strap Luna in. He seals his own straps and feels the memory foam soften, learn and reform to his body.

'Good to go, Jinji.'

Pre launch sequence, the familiar says. *Once we have launched I will be in offline mode until we arrive at João de Deus.*

The door closes. Lucasinho feels pressure locks seal. The air con hums. The capsule is lit soft gold, a comforting, warm, peaceful hue. It looks like sickness to Lucasinho Corta.

'Hold my hand,' Lucasinho says, wiggling his fingers free from the webbing. Luna easily slips her hand free and into his. The capsule lurches and drops.

'Whoa!' says Lucasinho Corta.

The capsule is in the launch tunnel, Jinji says.

'Are you getting this?' Lucasinho shouts over the humming and rattling that now fills the capsule.

Luna nods. 'It's fun!'

It is not fun. Lucasinho closes his eyes and fights down the fear as the capsule shuttles out along maglev rails to the launcher. Jolts as Lucasinho and Luna are loaded into the launch chamber.

Prepare for high acceleration, the pod AI warn.

'Like a ride!' Lucasinho says without conviction and then the launcher grabs the capsule, accelerates it and every drop of blood and bile and cum in him rushes to his feet and groin. His eyes ache, pushed deep in their sockets, his balls are spheres of lead. He can feel every bone in his body pushing through his skin. The suspension harness is a web of titanium wires, cutting him into quivering chunks and he can't even scream.

And it stops.

And he has no weight and no direction, no up or down. His stomach heaves. Were there anything in it more than morning tea it would be all floating free in a constellation of bile. His face feels swollen and puffy, his hands unwieldy and bulbous; fat wiggling fingers gripped around Luna's hand. He can hear the blood rushing around his brain. Some of Abena's friends rode the BALTRAN for free-fall sex. He can't imagine anyone having sex in this. He can't see any kind of fun in this. And he has to do it seven more times.

'Luna, you okay?'

'I think so. Are you?'

She looks like Luna always looks; small, self-contained yet insatiably curious about whatever world she is encountering, cosmological, personal. Lucasinho wonders if she realises she is packed into a padded, pressurised can, flying high above the moon, aimed at the distant mitt of a receiving station, unable to change course, trusting absolutely in the accuracy of machines and the precision of ballistics.

Stand by for deceleration, the pod says. So soon? Hardly time to get to pre-foreplay, let alone the free-fall cum all the boys described with such detail and enthusiasm.

'We're going in,' Lucasinho says.

Without warning, something grabs Lucasinho's head and feet and tries to make him ten centimetres shorter. Deceleration is harsher but briefer than acceleration: red dots dance in Lucasinho's eyes, then he is hanging upside down in his crash web, gasping. Gasp turns into bark, into laugh. He cannot stop laughing. Heaving, wrenching laughter that tears at every strained muscle and drawn sinew. He could laugh up a lung. Luna catches his laugh. Upside down, they whoop and giggle as the BALTRAN launcher draws them in and turns them upright for the next jump. They arrived. They survived.

'Ready to do that again?' Lucasinho asks.

Luna nods.

The pod door opens. The pod door should not open. Lucasinho and Luna should remain sealed in for the entire sequence of jumps.

Please exit the capsule, Jinji says.

Cold air, heavy with dust, flows into the capsule.

Please exit the capsule, Jinji says again. Lucasinho unclips the crash webbing and steps on to metal mesh. He feels the chill of the mesh through the soles of his loafers. He feels this place was brought to life moments ago. Air-conditioning fans roar but the lights are dim.

'Where are we?' Luna asks a split second before Lucasinho.

Lubbock BALTRAN relay, their familiars whisper. Jinji shows Lucasinho a map location. They are on the western shore of the Sea of Fecundity, four hundred kilometres from João de Deus.

'Jinji, lay in a course for João de Deus,' Lucasinho commands.

I'm sorry, I am unable to comply, Lucasinho, his familiar replies.

'Why?' Lucasinho asks.

I am unable to launch capsules due to energy constraints. The power plant at Gutenberg is offline.

The lurch and drop of acceleration to free fall, free fall to electromagnetic braking, is nothing to the sick vacuum that opens in Lucasinho's belly.

They're trapped deep in the badlands.

'How long before power is restored?'

I am unable to answer that, Lucasinho. Access to the network has been compromised. I'm running on the local architecture.

'Is something wrong?' Luna says.

'The system is updating itself,' Lucasinho lies, numb and not knowing what to do. Luna is scared, and any answers he gets from

Jinji will only scare her more. 'We might be here for a little while, so why don't you go see if you can find us anything to eat or drink?'

Luna looks around her, hugs herself tight against the cold. Lubbock is not Twé with its multiple launchers and loading docks. This is a remote relay, an uncrewed node. It houses a service crew twice a lunar year for a day or two. Lucasinho can view most of it from the platform and sees nowhere to store food or water.

'This place is scary,' Luna declares.

'It's all right anjinho, we're the only people here.'

'I'm not scared of people,' Luna says but she trots away to explore her small new world.

'How long have we got?' Lucasinho whispers.

The relay is operating on reserve power. If main power is not restored within three days you will experience significant environmental degradation.

'Significant?'

Heating and atmosphere failure, chiefly.

'Get a call out.'

I have been broadcasting a distress call on the emergency channel since our arrival. I have not yet received an acknowledgement. Communications seems to be down all across Nearside.

'How can that be?'

We are under attack.

Luna returns with a can of water.

'No food,' she says. 'Sorry. Can you make it warmer? I'm really really cold.'

'I don't know how to, anjinho.'

He lies. Jinji could do it in a breath. Lucasinho has finally acknowledged that he will never be an intellectual, but even he can run the numbers: a degree in temperature is an hour less breathing. He takes off his Malihini and slides Luna's arms into the sleeves. It hangs from her like a cape, like dressing-up day.

'What else did you find?'

'There's a suit. A shell-suit, like the old one at Boa Vista.'

Lucasinho's joy is a chemical rush. A suit. Simple. Just walk out of here.

'Show me.'

Luna takes him to the outlock. It's small, designed for one person at a time. In the lock, a hard-shell survival suit, adjustable to a wide range of body shapes, bright orange. Like the one in which he had walked from Boa Vista to João de Deus. Just a short walk across the surface. *One* suit. Luna had said: a suit. He hadn't listened. He needs to listen. He needs every sense and nerve to be sharp, he needs not to rush to assumptions, or wishful thinking. Could-be's would kill them out here.

The will-be is that in three days the air will run out, and you have one moon suit.

'Luna, we may need to sleep here. Could you go and see if you can find anything we can cover ourselves with?'

She nods. Lucasinho does not know how convinced Luna is by his diversions but he prefers her gone when he asks Jinji the hard questions.

'Jinji, where is the nearest settlement?'

The nearest settlement is Messier, one hundred and fifty kilometres east.

'Shit.' Well beyond the range of a shell-suit. Walking to find help is dead at his feet.

'Are there any other surface-capable devices in this station?' He had heard Carlinhos use that phrase once. Surface-capable. It sounds strong and in-charge. Mão de Ferro.

The emergency shell-suit is the only surface-capable device, Jinji says.

'Fuck!' Lucasinho slams his fist into the wall. The explosion of pain almost drops him. He sucks on his bleeding knuckles.

'Are you all right?' Luna has returned with a thermal foil blanket. 'I'm sorry it was all I could find.'

'We're in trouble, Luna.'

'I know. The relay's not updating itself.'

'No. The power is out. I don't know when it will come back on.'

Luna is quick to understand and asks no questions. Lucasinho has no answers. He has three days of air, one suit and the nearest haven is one hundred and fifty kilometres away. A rover could cover one hundred and fifty kilometres in an hour.

There could be a rover parked right outside and he would never see it.

'Jinji, can you access the log?'

This is very simple.

'I want every rover movement over the last...' He makes up a reasonable number. 'Three lunes.'

Jinji throws an overlay of maintenance visits, prospectors, glass crews up on Lucasinho's lens. Lucasinho may not read or number well, but he is superlative at interpreting visual information. His skill at picking one person, one object, one narrative thread from a mob of people, a terrain of moving data, always amazed numerate, literate Abena.

An anomaly, a tangent to the orbits and loops of the service rovers.

'Enhance this one please.' Jinji isolates the track, a small rover, coming from the badlands, curving off north into the fastnesses of the Taruntius craterlands. 'Show me this one please.' Footage now: the rover skims the edge of the external camera's range, tracking in from the Gutenberg, heading into the badlands. Destination nowhere. There is not a settlement that way for a thousand kilometres. Lucasinho estimates it's moving at thirty, maybe forty kilometres per hour. 'Specs please.' Jinji complies. Once again Lucasinho's visual sense picks the information he needs from the blur of technical data. Range at optimum speed is three hundred kilometres, plus en-route solar recharging. From the footage, Lucasinho estimates the rover was a touch under its top speed.

The nearest settlement it could have started from, based on its course, is Gutenberg. Lucasinho tries to calculate range. The numbers clang like metal. 'Jinji, do the math.' Lucasinho's familiar has the answer on Lucasinho's lens before the last syllable of the question is spoken. On Lucasinho's lens is an arc of possible locations for the rover, based on its range, speed and direction. The minimum distance is ten kilometres. The maximum is twenty-five. 'Enhance please.' The little rover carries the linked-MH colophon of Bryce Mackenzie. A figure in a sasuit sits astride the rover. The sun is high, the time code reads ten days.

A rover. A sasuit. Lucasinho has one final question for Lubbock BALTRAN relay. One last chance for all to fall apart in his fingers.

'How long have I got, Jinji?'

This time the numbers are not displays or clever graphics. They are numbers, cold, unrelenting and impersonal. There is no time for hoping, waiting, pondering decisions, weighing up possibilities. If they are to walk out of Lubbock BALTRAN relay, he must go now. Every second of prevarication is watts of power, sips of air and water. Wait and hope or act and hope.

It is no decision. The numbers make it no decision.

'Jinji.'

Lucasinho.

'Power up the suit.'

The inlock window perfectly frames Luna. She waves. Lucasinho raises a titanium hand. He is a monster, an abandoner. A thief. He has filled his suit with Luna's air and water and power. What if he fails? What if he doesn't come back? He imagines Luna shivering on the steel mesh, growing colder, thirstier, hoping he will come back, hoping the power will restore.

He can't think that. He can't think of anything except what he needs to do, clearly and precisely.

'Okay Jinji, I'm ready to go out.'

Lucasinho touches the icon of Lady Luna by the outlock. Luck, and defiance. He beat Lady Luna once, in nothing but his skin.

But everyone knows the Dona never forgives a slight. The rush of depressurisation dwindles to silence. The outlock opens. Lucasinho steps out on to the regolith. Jinji guides him to the tracks of the Mackenzie rover. From there he can easily follow the trail north. He won't know for how far, how long, but he will know where he is going. Muscle memory never forgets and Lucasinho drops into the rhythm of walking in a shell-suit. It's easy to over-move. The haptics are sensitive, even on this old, cheap VTO model. Let the suit do the work.

Soon all other tracks diverge and only the twin tyre tracks of the Mackenzie rover lead Lucasinho. The sun is high, the surface is bright, Earth is a wan sliver of blue. Lucasinho sings to himself to keep his mind from drifting. The suit is equipped with games, music, old telenovella seasons, but entertainment systems take power. His songs fall into the rhythm of his steps, rattle round and round in his head like hallucinations. He finds he is singing his own lyrics to the tunes.

Lucasinho, time to call in, Jinji says.

'Ola Luna!'

The link is audio only, for power conservation reasons.

'Ola Luca!'

Luna's voice, divorced from her body, her presence, her image, sounds strange to Lucasinho. He is listening to a human being but something higher, rarer, wilder and wiser. Anjinho, he calls her, the old family endearment. Little angel. So she sounds to Lucasinho.

'How are you? Have you had your water?' Lucasinho left instructions for Luna to take a drink every twenty minutes. It diverts her from realising that she hadn't eaten since breakfast in the apartment.

'I've had my water. When are you coming back? I'm bored.'

'As soon as I can, anjinho. I know you're bored, but don't touch anything.'

'I'm not stupid,' Luna says.

'I know you're not. I'll call again in an hour.'

Lucasinho trudges on into the badlands of Taruntius. A single marching tune has lodged in his head and it is driving him crazy. He could ask Jinji how far he has walked, how long he might have to continue, but the answer could be dismal. The tracks lead ever onward. In his red and gold shell, Lucasinho tramps ever onward.

Something. The sole advantage of Lucasinho's boring moonwalk is that he has become acute to the landscape of the Taruntius and any variation in its monotony.

'Jinji, enhance.'

The visor shows him the aerial and masts of a rover reaching up above the close horizon. Over a handful of minutes the rover appears and suddenly Lucasinho is beside it. The sasuited figure he saw on the relay's cameras is still upright in the saddle. For an instant he is seized by the fear that the figure will lunge at him and smash a rock through his faceplate. Impossible. No one can survive that long in a sasuit. Certainly not, as he sees as he walks around the rover, a sasuit with a twenty centimetre gash running from right nipple to hip. That's a problem. Another problem. He will deal with that later.

'Where's the hard point?' Lucasinho asks. Jinji highlights the port and Lucasinho unreels his network cable and plugs it in. As he thought, the rover is as dead as its passenger. He grits his teeth as he runs the power cable from his suit to the rover, feels the transfer of charge from his batteries to the rover's like supernatural healing leaving him. He needs the rover's AI awake, even if he cannot spare the power to drive it back to the relay. Data spills across his lens, and he dives deep for what he needs. The brakes are off. The steering is unlocked. There is the tow-cable release. Lucasinho unreels the tow cable, throws it around his shoulder and clips it into a harness.

'Luna? I'm coming back.' Lucasinho leans into the harness. The rover resists him for a moment, then the haptic rig feeds power to the motors and overcomes the inertia. Lucasinho tows the rover back along the line of its own tracks.

Tracks stay forever on the moon. The surface is a palimpsest of journeys.

It is never as long coming back as going out.

Lucasinho rolls the rover to a halt. Jinji shows him the relay's charge point. Recharging the rover's batteries will drain almost all of the relay's power but he was committed to this course the moment he stepped out of the airlock on to the surface. The coupling connects, the rover wakes in a dozen tiny operating lights and beacons.

Next the sasuit. That's the way to think of it: a life-saving device that needs some work to make it operable. Don't think of the dead human being inside. Lucasinho tries to work out the best way to unhook the corpse from the saddle. She has frozen solid. He unclips the suitpack from the dead woman and opens the outlock.

'I'm sending something through to you,' he says to Luna.

'I can work a lock,' Luna says. 'And I've had my water.'

Lucasinho rocks the corpse gently on to her back and lifts her, legs bent at the knees, one arm at her side, the other resting on the control panel. He carries her to the lock. They must cycle through together. He can't ask Luna to haul a frozen corpse out of the airlock. It would still be burn-cold, it would be too heavy. It's a corpse. Lucasinho backs into the lock until the rear of his suit hits the inlock door. He drags the frozen body into the lock, hissing through his teeth in frustration as he tries to manoeuvre it around him, fitting his head and torso into the geometry of limbs and torso. Lucasinho is on his back, the body on top of him, its knees on his shoulders, his helmet between its knees, its head at the groin plates of his suit. Sixty-nining an ice-corpse. Lucasinho barks out a dark, fearful, private laugh at that. No one else will ever know that joke.

'Luna, I'm coming in. Stay away from the airlock. Just do what I say.'

Jinji cycles the lock. Lucasinho listens to the rising scream of air and it is the sweetest sound he has ever heard. He pushes himself out of the lock on his back, arms wrapped around the corpse. Lucasinho drags the corpse to the vacant BALTRAN pod and shuts it in. He doesn't want to think about the mess he will find after the body has thawed, but it's out of Luna's sight and there are other pods racked up, when the power – if the power – ever resumes.

He staggers out of the shell-suit. All strength has left him. He has never been so tired: mind, muscle, bones, heart. It's not over yet. It's not even completely begun. There is so much to do and only he can do it and all he wants is to lie against the wall and turn his back to all those things that must be done and beg a little sleep from them.

'Luna, can I have some of your water?'

He does not know where she appears from but she gives him her flask and he tries not to gulp it all at once to wash the taste of the suit out of his mouth. Suit water always knows it was recently piss.

'Luna, can I snuggle up with you?'

She nods and nuzzles up against him. She is wearing the rest of his clothes, a baggy 80s-style waif. Lucasinho folds his arms around her and tries to find comfort on the steel mesh. He fears he is too tired to sleep. He shivers. The cold has reached deep. You've so much to do, an insane amount to do and a thousand things could kill you yet but the start is made.

'Jinji, don't let me oversleep,' he whispers. 'Wake me when she's defrosted.'

'What?' Luna murmurs. She is a small nugget of warmth, coiled against his belly.

'Nothing,' Lucasinho says. 'Nothing at all.'

Lucasinho wakes, tries to move. Pain stabs through his ribs, his back, his shoulder and neck. The metal mesh is embossed on his cheek. His head is thick and stupid; his arm is dead and numb where Luna has fallen asleep on it. He slides the arm free without waking her. Luna sleeps like a stone. Lucasinho needs to piss. On the way to the head he has a wiser idea.

'What are you doing?' Luna is awake now, watching him empty the scanty contents of his bladder into the shell-suit.

'The suit will recycle it. You'll need the water.' Lucasinho's piss is dark and cloudy. Piss should not look like that.

'Okay then,' she says.

'Is there anything to eat?' Lucasinho asks.

'Some bars.'

'Eat all of it,' Lucasinho orders.

'What about you?'

'I'm fine,' Lucasinho lies in the face of the chasm in his belly. He has never known hunger before. So this is how poor people feel. Hungry and thirsty and short of breath. The short breath will come. 'I'm going to get us another suit and then we drive right out of here.'

'Is that the dead woman in the capsule?'

'Yes. Did you look?'

'I looked.'

He dreads this next part of his plan. Shards of panic at what he would have to do to get the sasuit woke him again and again from the drop into exhausted sleep. Do it fast, do it smart, give yourself no time to think. Lucasinho opens the BALTRAN capsule door, seizes the dead suited woman by the arm and drags her to the deck. She comes awkward, stiff-limbed. Lucasinho feels through the suit that she is not totally thawed. Lucasinho turns her face down. First he unlatches the helmet. He almost gags at the reek. Everyone stinks in a sasuit but this is something he has never experienced before. He fights down retch after retch. Stomach heaving, Lucasinho sets the helmet aside and peels back the webbing. Hands shaking, he opens the seal. Another gale of stench, which he realises is death. Lucasinho has seen death, but he has never smelled it. Zabbaleen take away the dead, in their soft-tyred jitneys, no mess, no dirt, no odour.

Lucasinho holds his breath as he peels the suit away from the flesh. Her skin is so white. He almost touches it, stops as he feels the cold deep within. Tricky now. He must pull an arm from a sleeve. The second should come more easily after he frees the first. The gloves suck at the fingers and the elbow fights him. Cursing, he sits on the deck, turns her face away from him and, one foot braced against the dead woman's shoulder, tugs the obstinate sleeve free from the body. In fast to pull free the other arm. Now he must roll the body over to work the suit down the torso and release the legs one at a time.

He stands over the dead woman and hauls at the suit. The body jerks. He pulls the suit down over her breasts and belly, smearing blood from the terrible knife wound down over the small convexity of the woman's stomach. Again, wiggling down over her buttocks. She has a flower tattooed on her left buttock. Lucasinho crumples into a sobbing, howling ball. The tattoo breaks him.

'I'm sorry I'm so sorry,' he whispers.

He takes a foot in two hands. The left, then the right leg pull free. The sasuit lies in his hands like a flayed skin. The blood-smeared woman lies on her back staring at the lights.

Now he must wear the suit. He peels off the shell-suit liner. In the deprinter it goes. Legs into legs, quick-smart, a wiggle and the sasuit is up to his chest. Don't think about the wetness on your skin. One arm, both arms. Lucasinho reaches for the lanyard to pull up the seal. He tightens the tensioning straps. The suit is too short for him. That tension in his shoulders, toes, fingers will become an ache. The plumbing is female. He'll endure that too. By the time he scoops up the helmet the printer has pinged out a new suit-liner, fresh, pink, Luna-sized. It's heavy on scant resources, but Luna needs a liner to interact with the shell-suit.

'Anjinho, I need a hand with this.'

Luna takes the roll of pressure tape from the airlock, seals the rent in the sasuit and walks around Lucasinho, wrapping him three layers deep.

'Don't use too much of that, we may need it,' Lucasinho chides. 'Now, you put on the liner and I'll charge our suits.'

'What'll I do with the clothes?'

Lucasinho almost tells Luna just to leave them, then realises that he would be throwing away valuable material, organics that might be the difference between life and death out in Pyrenaeus.

'Throw them in the deprinter and reprint them as pressure tape.'

'Okay.'

Lucasinho does not think more than a second about that other stash of valuable organic material, lying face up in the capsule dock.

Luna returns in the pink suit liner with a small roll of pressure tape. She peers into the open shell-suit and grimaces. 'It smells of piss.' She steps in, the suit reads her smaller body and adjusts the internal haptic skeleton to support her. 'Oh!' she says as the suit seals around her.

'Are you all right?' Lucasinho asks. Luna has never been in a suit before.

'It's like the refuge they took me out of Boa Vista in, but smaller. But better because I can move.'

Luna clanks along the decking.

'I take two steps and then it catches up with me.'

'It's really easy, the suit does all the work,' Lucasinho says.

Power air and water at full charge, the familiars announce. Every breath, every sip, every step is budgeted now.

'I'll go through the lock first,' Lucasinho says. 'I'll wait for you on the other side.'

It feels an age to Lucasinho, standing on the steps waiting for the lock to cycle, trusting and yet failing to trust in the pressure tape wrapped around the tear in his stolen sasuit, imagining the sudden evacuation of air as the tape gives way. It won't give way. It's been designed that way. Yet he can't quite believe it, and already his fingers and toes are cramped from the too-small suit. Lights flash, the lock opens, Luna steps out.

Lucasinho uncoils a data cable from his pack and plugs it into the highlighted socket on Luna's armour. 'Can you hear me?'

Silence, then a giggle.

'Sorry, I nodded.'

'We use less power if we're plugged together.'

Lucasinho is proud of the next bit. He thought it out as he was hauling the rover back to Lubbock. One rover, one seat. He positions Luna in her shell-suit on the saddle, then arranges himself in her lap. The shell-suit is slick and his seat is insecure. To come off at speed is to die. He hadn't foreseen this problem. In the same instant, he has the solution. Lucasinho tears off lengths of pressure tape and binds himself to Luna, calves, thighs, torso. He hears her giggle on the comms link.

'Good, anjinho?'

'Good, Lucasinho.'

'Then let's drive.'

Jinji is already interfaced with the rover AI. A thought and Luna and Lucasinho, taped and wired together, race away from the upraised horns of the Lubbock relay across the stony regolith of Mare Fecunditatis.

It is ten years since Duncan Mackenzie last set foot on the surface but he refuses the shell-suit. Once a jackaroo, always a jackaroo. The sasuit is new, printed to the body profile of a middle-aged man with fitness issues, but the rituals of locking the seals, tightening the binding straps, are as familiar as faith. The pre-surface checks are little prayers.

He strides up the ramp. Behind him the great ziggurat of Hadley is a physical pressure, dark and looming. His first few footfalls kick up dust like an amateur but by the time he reaches the firing range he has fallen back into the old jackaroo lope. He missed this. Five suits greet him. The shooting party has set up on one of the service lanes between the ranks of mirrors.

'Show me.'

A jackaroo in a shell-suit customised with a space-orc paint job slips a long device from her back. She levels and aims at the target.

Duncan Mackenzie zooms in to make out the object far down the lane.

'If she takes out one of my mirrors . . .' he jokes.

'She won't,' Yuri Mackenzie says. The shooter fires. The target explodes. The rifle ejects a heat sink pellet. The shooter turns to Duncan Mackenzie, awaiting instructions.

'It's essentially the same gauss rifle we used in the Mare Anguis war, but we've increased the acceleration. You can shoot it line of sight or engage the AI assist and fire over the horizon.'

'I'm not happy with the shell-suit,' Duncan Mackenzie says.

'The recoil from the more powerful accelerator is pretty savage,' Yuri says. 'The shell-suit has more stability. And it offers some protection, should the worst happen.'

'You've got twenty seconds rather than ten seconds,' Vassos Palaeologos says. Duncan Mackenzie rounds on him.

'No Mackenzie ever ran from a fight.'

'Boss, he has a point,' Yuri says. 'This is not our fight. The Asamoahs have never been our allies.'

'And we thought the Vorontsovs were,' Duncan Mackenzie says.

'With respect,' Yuri presses, 'we are uniquely vulnerable. VTO is taking out power plants all over the eastern quartersphere. Hadley could not sustain an orbital strike. Even an attack on the mirror array would effectively put us out of business. I can show you simulations.'

'Print up fifty,' Duncan Mackenzie orders on the common channel. 'Contract any Jo Moonbeam ex-military. And I'll need shell-suits. Not with that shit on them.' He flicks a gloved finger at the shooter's fangs, flames and skulls design. 'Something that will tell everyone who we are and what we stand for.'

He turns and strides back down the corridor between the brilliant mirrors to the dark slot of the outlook. Above him the pinnacle of Hadley blazes with the light of ten thousand suns.

*

'Cake,' says Lucasinho Corta, 'is the perfect gift for anyone who has everything.'

Coelhinho is one hour out from Lubbock, reaching down the gentle slope of Messier E's north-western wall. Luna gave the rover its name. Rovers, she insisted, should have names. To make the kilometres pass, Lucasinho argued that names were silly. Machines were machines. *Familiars have names,* Luna argued. And the rover remained Coelhinho. So Lucasinho suggested they sing shared songs and after that Lucasinho tried to remember a bedtime story Madrinha Flavia had told him, which Luna knew better. They told riddles, but Luna was better at those as well. Now Lucasinho is delivering a discourse on cake.

'Stuff is easy. If you want something, if you've got the carbon allowance, you print it out. *Things* aren't really so special at all. Why give someone something they could print themselves? The only special thing about gifts is the thought you put into them. The real gift is the idea behind the object. To be special, it has to be rare, expensive, or have a lot of you invested in it. Pai once gave Vo Adriana some coffee, because she hadn't had coffee in fifty years. That was rare and expensive, so that's two out of three – rare and expensive – but it's not as good as cake.

'To make cake you take raw, unprinted materials like bird eggs and fat and wheat flour, and you put your time and heart into them. You plan every cake – is it going to be a sponge or a kilo-cake, is it going to be layers or lots of little cakes, is it a personal cake or an occasion cake? Is it orange or bergamot or chai or even coffee; is it going to be frosted or meringue? Is it going to be in a box or tied up with ribbons, are you going to fly it in by bot, does it have a surprise in the middle, will it light up or sing? Should you be serious or joky, are there allergies or intolerances or cultural or faith issues? Who else will be there when they cut it? Who's going to get a piece and who isn't? Is it even for sharing at all, or is it private, passionate cake?

'Cake is subtle. Just one cupcake in the right place, at the right time, can say, *There is no one but you in the whole universe right now, and I give you this moment of sweetness, texture, flavour, sensation.* And then there are times when only something huge and stupid will do, like something I'd jump out of in full make-up, with icing butterflies and birds and little bots singing soap-opera songs, and it heals hearts and finishes feuds.

'Cakes have a language. Lemon drizzle says, *This relationship tastes sour to me.* Orange is the same, but hopeful. Kilo-cake says that all is well with the world, everything is good and centred, the Four Elementals are in harmony. Vanilla says: careful, boredom; lavender is hoping or regretting. Sometimes both. Candied rose petals say, *I think you're cheating,* but rose frosting says, *Let's make a contract here.* Blue fruits are for blue days, when you really feel the vacuum over you and you need friends or just a friendly body. Red and pink fruits are sex. Everyone knows that. Cream can never be eaten alone. That's the rule. Cinnamon is expecting, ginger is memory, cloves are for hurt; real or in the heart. Rosemary is regret, basil is being right. *See, I told you so*: that's basil. Mint is a horror. Mint is bad cake. Coffee is the hardest and it says, *I would move the Earth in the sky to make you happy.*

'That's social cake. Then there's the science of cake. Did you know cake tastes better on the moon? If you went to Earth and had cake you'd be so disappointed. It'd be flat and heavy and solid. It's to do with pore size and crumb structure, and crumb structure is so much better on the moon. Every cake you make is three kinds of science: chemistry, physics and architecture. The physics is about heat, gas expansion and gravity. Your raising agents push up against gravity. The less gravity, the higher it raises. You might think, so, if lower gravity makes for better crumb structure, wouldn't the perfect cake be one you made in zero gee? Actually, no. It would expand in all directions and you'd end up with a big ball of fizzing cake mix. When you came to bake it, it would be very difficult to get heat to the centre of the cake. You would end up with a soggy heart.

'Then there is the chemistry. We have our Four Elementals, and cake has them too. For us it's air, water, data, carbon. With cake it's flour, sugar, fat, eggs or some other kind of liquid. Take two-fifty grams flour, two-fifty grams sugar, two-fifty grams butter, two-fifty grams eggs, which is about five. That's your basic kilo-cake. You cream the sugar and butter. I do it by hand. It makes it personal. The fat encases the air bubbles and creates a foam. Now you beat the eggs in. Eggs have proteins that wrap around your air bubbles and stop them exploding and collapsing when they're heated. Then you fold in the flour. You fold it in because if you beat flour too hard you'll stretch the gluten.

'Gluten is a protein in wheat, and it's elastic. Without it, everything you bake would be flat. Stretch it too much and you end up with bread. Bread and cake are totally opposite ways wheat can go. I use special soft self-raising flours from wheat with low protein content. That means they have an agent built in that reacts and creates gas that blows up the gluten bubbles. That's why my cakes are sweet and short and crumbly.

'Baking is like building a city: it's all about trapping and holding on to air. The gluten forms pillars and cells that support the weight of the sugar and the fat. It has to stand up, it has to stay up and it has to keep everything inside safe, aired and watered. You have to create a shell that keeps the cake moist and light. The sugar does that; it allows the crust to colour and set at a lower temperature than the inside of the cake. It's all to do with caramelising. It's like the gas seal that keeps our air from escaping through the rock.

'Now, after all that, the baking. Baking is a three-part process: rising, setting and browning. As the temperature of the cake rises, all the air you've beaten in expands and stretches the gluten. Then at about sixty Celsius your leavening agents kick in and release CO_2 and water vapour from your eggs and whoosh, your cakes rises to its final height. At about eighty Celsius the egg proteins come together and gluten loses its stretch. Finally, the Maillard reaction takes over

– that's the browning I told you about – and seals the surface. It locks the moisture in – if you've done it right.

'Now comes the most difficult bit – deciding if it's ready to come out of the oven. It's dependent on many tiny things – humidity, draughts, air-pressure, ambient temperature. This is the art. When you think it's ready, take it out, let it stand for about ten minutes to come loose from the baking tin, turn it on to a rack and let it cool. Try not to have a piece as soon as it comes out of the oven.

'Then we get into the economics of cake. Take it out of the oven. We don't have ovens. Most of us don't have kitchens: we eat out from the hot-shop. Hot-shop ovens are totally different from the kind you use to bake cakes. You have to get one customer built and there are maybe twenty people on the entire moon know how to build an eye-level cake oven.

'So: the Four Elementals: flour, sugar, butter, eggs. Flour is the ground-up seeds of the wheat plant. It's a kind of grass. Down on Earth it's one of the big carb sources but up here in the moon we don't use it very much because it doesn't give very much energy for the space and resources it uses. It takes fifteen hundred litres of water to grow one hundred grams of wheat. We get our carbs from potatoes and yams and maize because they're much more efficient at turning water into food. So to make flour, we have to grow wheat specially, then harvest the seeds and grind them into fine dust. Grinding flour is even harder than building a cake oven – there are maybe five people in the whole world know how to build a flour mill.

'Butter is a solid fat derived from milk. I only use butter from cow milk. We have cows, mostly for people who like to eat meat. And if you thought growing wheat drank up water, for one kilo of dairy produce, it takes a hundred times that.

'Eggs. They're not so hard; eggs are a big part of our diet. But our eggs are smaller than eggs on Earth because we've bred smaller birds, so you have to experiment to get the number right.

'Sugar is easy – we can grow it or manufacture it, but a cake-baker

271

uses many kinds of sugar. There's unrefined, pure cane, general sugar, confectioner's sugar, caster sugar, icing sugar – sometimes you need all of these for just one cake. So, you see, even to make a simple kilo-cake, you're using things and skills that are rarer and more precious than jewels. When you taste cake, you're tasting all of our lives.

'And that's why, when anyone can print anything; cake is the perfect gift.'

'Luca,' Luna says.

'What is it, anjinho?'

'Are we there yet?'

'Not this crater, but the next one,' Lucasinho says.

'Promise?'

'Promise.'

Coelhinho climbs the low wall of Messier A crater.

'Okay,' Luna declares. 'But enough cake.'

Cake, and talk of it, is keeping Lucasinho Corta awake and alert against the cold creeping from the patched gash in the sasuit. He can seal the suit for atmosphere but there is nothing he could do about damaged heating elements. Lucasinho knows from his Moonrun training that human bodies radiate little heat in vacuum, but he feels the persistent chill draw the heat from his blood and heart. Cold creeps up on you, makes you comfortable and numb and dis-connected. It had taken all Lucasinho's strength to keep his teeth from chattering as he talked cake.

Coelhinho tips over the outer rim of Messier A double crater and a big six-seat rover flies up over the inner rim, bounces twice, races across the crater floor and slides to a stop in front of Lucasinho. He hits the brakes and prays Ogun he doesn't roll the top-heavy rover.

One rover, three crew. Safety bars lift, the crew drops down from their seats. Each carries the logo of Mackenzie Helium on their sasuit, each lifts a device from the equipment rack; a thing Lucasinho knows but has never seen before. A gun.

A jackaroo approaches Lucasinho and Luna, gun cradled, walks all the way around Coelhinho, steps in close to Lucasinho. Faceplate to faceplate.

'What's happening?' Luna says.

'It'll be all right,' Lucasinho says, then jumps in his skin as the Mackenzie jackaroo jams their faceplate against Lucasinho's.

'Turn your comms on, you fucking galah.' The voice is a muffled yell, conducted by physical contact.

Jinji opens the common channel.

'Sorry, I'm short on power,' Lucasinho says in Globo.

'It's not just power you're short on,' says the jackaroo. Now that comms are up each jackaroo's identifier appears above their shoulder: Malcolm Hutchinson, Charlene Owens-Clarke, Efron Batmanglij.

'We need power, water and food. I'm very very cold.'

'Couple of small questions first.' Malcolm swings his gun to point at Lucasinho. It is a long, hastily-engineered device, all struts and stabilisers, magazines and electromagnetic cartridge racks, quickly printed out and assembled. 'We live in the most gender-fluid society in human history so it's possible that Nadia has reassigned, but I've never heard of a reassignment that made you ten centimetres taller.'

As soon as comms went up, the suit would have flashed up the identifier of its owner, Lucasinho realises. The other two guns swivel on to him.

'Lucasinho, I'm scared,' Luna says on the private link.

'It's all right, anjinho. I'll get us out.'

'Nadia's suit, Nadia's rover. Judging by the amount of tape on that suit, something hit her a killing blow.'

'If I wanted to take her suit, do you think I would have done that much damage to it?' Lucasinho says.

'Are you sure that's the kind of answer you want to give me?'

Bars hover on the edge of the red on all vital read-outs on Lucasinho's helmet display.

'I didn't kill her, I swear. We were trapped at Lubbock BALTRAN.

I tracked her and brought the rover and the suit back and patched them up.'

'What the fuck were you doing at Lubbock BALTRAN?'

'We were trying to get out of Twé.'

'By BALTRAN.' Lucasinho hates that way that this Malcolm Hutchinson turns Lucasinho's every answer into the most stupid thing he has ever heard. 'Mate, the BALTRAN is dead. The whole eastern quartersphere is dead. Gods know what's going on at Twé. The Vorontsovs have shut down the railroads and they're blasting every power plant they see into a hole in the regolith. I've had half my squad wiped out by fucking nightmares with fucking knives for fucking hands so you'll understand if I'm a bit twitchy. So, where are you going and who the fuck are you?'

Lucasinho's belly is painfully empty but he could heave acid into his helmet.

'Let me talk,' Luna says.

'Luna, shut up. Let me handle this.'

'Don't tell me to shut up. Let me tell him. Please.'

The Mackenzie jackaroos are edgy. Lucasinho is about to talk himself into a bullet. A child's voice might talk down the guns.

'Okay.'

Luna's familiar opens the common channel.

'We're trying to get to João de Deus,' Luna says. The Mackenzie jackaroos flinch in their sasuits.

'You've got a kid in that thing,' Malcolm says.

'There was only one shell-suit at Lubbock,' Lucasinho says. 'I tracked down the rover and, yes, I stole the suit.' He remembers the name. 'Nadia's suit. I didn't kill her.'

'You're taking a kid across Fecunditatis in a shell-suit.'

'I didn't know what else to do. We had to get out of Lubbock.'

'You're a long way from João de Deus,' says the jackaroo with the Charlene identifier.

'Right now we need to get to Messier,' Lucasinho says.

'We've just come from Messier,' says the third jackaroo, Efron. 'We left three dead back there. The bots will cut you to pieces.'

'Hey Efron, kid present,' Charlene says.

'No point hiding the truth,' Efron says.

'We need air and water,' Lucasinho says. 'The rover is about out of power and we haven't eaten since I don't know when.'

'I'm really hungry,' Luna says.

Lucasinho hears Malcolm swear under his breath.

'There's an old Corta Hélio bivvie at Secchi. It's the nearest re-supply point now. We'll get you there.'

'That's halfway back to Taruntius,' Lucasinho says.

'Okay then, starve or suffocate,' Malcolm says. 'Or, in your case, freeze. Efron.' Efron detaches a small packet from his suitpack and tosses it to Lucasinho. It's a heat pack: slow-release exothermic gel in a glass container. 'That'll keep you warm. There's only one problem.' He prods Lucasinho's p-taped torso with the muzzle of his gun. 'It has to go inside your suit.'

'What?'

'How long can you hold your breath, mate?'

Lucasinho's head is reeling. Hunger, exhaustion, cold. Now he has to bare his skin to the cold surface of Lady Luna again.

'I've got a Moonrun pin,' he stammers.

'Well fuck-a-dee-fuck for you, rich boy. Moonrun is ten, fifteen seconds. We have to get the old tape off, get the pack in and tape you up again. Forty, maybe sixty seconds?'

That could kill him. The cold will kill him. Could, will. Again, Lady Luna makes the decisions for him.

'I can do that,' Lucasinho says.

'Good boy. Hyperventilate for one minute and then dee-pee the helmet. I'll need to link to your suit AI.'

'I have tape,' Luna says as Lucasinho peels himself from her shell-suit.

'Good girl. Charlene, Efron.'

Jinji switches the suit supply over to pure O2. It hits Lucasinho like an axe. He wavers, hands move to hold him up. He breathes deep, deeper, supercharging brain and blood with oxygen. He's done the Moonrun. He's run fifteen metres across the surface in only his skin. This is easy. Easy. But on the Moonrun he was brought down to micro-pressure over an hour. This will be instantaneous. *The human skin is a robust pressure containment surface*... Sasuit lesson one. All you need is something tight to maintain that pressure, hold water and retain warmth.

De-pressuring the suit in five...

Lucasinho empties his lungs. In vacuum you breathe out to stop your lungs rupturing.

... Two, one...

'Stand by,' Malcolm commands.

Evacuating. Air shrieks to silence as Jinji empties the suit. Lucasinho screams silently at the sudden pain stabbing through each ear. Charlene moves in with her blade, carefully cutting the tape and peeling it back.

'Keep still kid, hold him still.'

'Clear.'

Then burning heat as Malcolm tucks the pack inside the tight weave. Lucasinho has to breathe. He has to breathe. His brain is winking out cell by cell. He thrashes. A woman's voice, faint and high as a saint, shouts, *Hold him still.* Lucasinho opens his mouth. Nothing there. Expands his lungs. Nothing there. This is how you die in vacuum, everything closing down, narrowing in, throbbing. The tiny, distant voices, the iron hands holding him, everything burning.

Tiny distant voices...

And he's back. Lucasinho lunges forward. Safety bars hold him in. He's safe in a seat on the Mackenzie rover. Air. Air is wonderful. Air is magic. He takes ten deep breaths, in fast, out slow; in slow, out fast. Mouth, nose; nose, mouth. Nose. Mouth. Glorious breathing. Warm. Heat. He feels pain beneath his bottom left rib: the heat pack, tightly compressed by the sasuit and the p-tape. He'll bruise there, but Lucasinho appreciates the ache. It means he doesn't have frostbite.

'Luna?' he croaks.

'You're back then,' Malcolm says on the common channel.

'Over here,' Luna says. 'Are you all right?'

'If he's talking, he's all right,' Malcolm says. Lucasinho looks around him, at the cables and tubes plugging him into the rover. He thinks *water* and is rewarded with cold, pure refreshment from the nipple. Lucasinho's gasp of pleasure over the common channel makes the jackaroos laugh. 'It's still recycled piss, but at least it's someone else's piss,' Malcolm says. 'There's even some nutrient shit. I reckon you're starving enough to eat it.' Efron tethers Lucasinho's appropriated single-seater behind the big rover and swings up into his seat.

'So if you haven't any objections, Lucasinho Corta,' Malcolm says, 'we're going to Secchi.'

There is something in front of his face. Lucasinho wakes with a cry of claustrophobic panic. He's in the suit, the same fucking suit. Sleep-drool has dried on his cheek to a crystalline crust. He can smell his own face inside the helmet.

'You're awake.' Malcolm's voice. 'Good. We have a problem.'

Jinji resolves a map: the convoy and the Corta Hélio cache are obvious, as is the line of contacts between rovers and safety.

'Those are...'

'I know what they are, kid.'

'Can you circle round?'

'I can, but the moment they catch sight of us, they'll run us down. We're big and we're heavy and I've seen those fuckers move.'

'What do we do?'

'We're going to drop you and the girl. You take the other rover – there's enough charge to make it – and run straight for the bivvie. We'll try and draw the bots off.'

'But you said you couldn't outrun them.'

'Where's your fucking faith, kid? Without you, we might lose them. We might even take a few of them. These guns are pretty good at taking out the fuckers. What I know for certain is that if we stick together, we die together.'

Suitpacks are loaded with water and air, power cells charged. Luna positions herself in the saddle, Lucasinho carefully tapes her to the rover; then himself to her. Lucasinho has explained their danger simply and honestly and she knows what to do without question or instruction. The single-seater rover powers up at Jinji's touch. Malcolm touches forefinger to helmet: a salute before battle. He guns the big rover, circles and in moments he is over the horizon. Lucasinho waits for his dust plume to settle before opening up the single-seater.

No comms, Malcolm said. *See you at Secchi; or in the next one.*

You know who we are, Lucasinho said on a private channel. *Why are you helping us?*

Whatever comes out of this, it'll never be the same old moon again, Malcolm said.

'Luna,' Lucasinho says. They are plugged together again, for radio quiet and intimacy.

'What?'

'Have you had some water?'

'I've had my water.'

'We'll be there soon.'

Analiese Mackenzie waits at the inlock. The doors take forever to open, but here they come; dust-darkened despite the airblades, helmets and suitpacks hooked in their hands. Their boots are stone, their suits lead. Cold exhaustion in every sinew. The fighters shuffle past her, eyes downcast. They fought a battle at the gates of Hypatia. Demolition charges had destroyed the three bots that had survived AKA's arrow storm, but at the price of seven blackstars.

Suicide missions. And the rumours say that reinforcements are already dropping over Eastern Tranquillity, braking thrusters stuttering in the sky.

Reinforcements. How does she know a word like that?

He comes shuffling.

'Wagner.'

He turns to the sound of his name. He knows her. He cannot forget her, not in his dark aspect, the only Wagner Corta she has ever known. That doubt, that reticence that hesitates over the first step towards her isn't from fear of misrecognition but from guilt. He ran to Meridian. She told him not to come back to their home in Theophilus, but he knows he left her to face her own family alone. The Mackenzies have never forgiven traitors. She paid a price. He survived when her family destroyed his. He kept his head down and lived. He looks like death now. He looks defeated.

He looks at his crew. A handsome, strong-featured woman nods to him. *I'll take it from here, laoda.*

'Analiese.'

He can't understand what he's seeing. Theophilus is her home, what is she doing in Hypatia?

'Come on, little wolf.'

The bed fills the cubicle. Wagner fills the bed, spread and sprawled, somewhere deeper than sleep. Analiese was lucky to get even this tiny capsule. When the rail network went down, Hypatia, as the quartersphere's busiest interchange, became a refugee camp of street sleepers and hot-bunkers, stranded passengers lying in the warmth from the heat exchange ducts.

She leans against the corridor wall and watches the wolf. He is a mess. His skin is bruised and seamed from the creases of a too-long-worn sasuit. The soft brown she loved to touch is grey and dull with fatigue. He was never mass and muscle but he's bones and wire now. He can't have eaten for two, three days. He's terribly dehydrated. He reeks.

She traces back the path from bed to first sight; a touch of eyes at the University of Farside's 15th Paralogics Symposium workshop on doxastic and other belief logics. He glanced away first. She leaned to her colleague Nang Aein, still hung-over from first-night drinking, and asked, *Who is that?* Her familiar could have given her the name in a thought from the attendee list but this was conspiracy, she wanted him to see her ask about him.

'That's Wagner Corta,' Nang Aein said.

'Corta? As in?'

'The Cortas.'

'He has eyelashes to die for.'

'He's strange. Even for a Corta.'

'I like strange.'

'How are you with scary?'

'I'm not scared of Cortas.'

'Are you scared of wolves?'

Then the session broke up and everyone headed for tea and she kept her eyes on the scary Corta so she wouldn't miss whatever moment he chose to look back at her. Which he did, at the double doors of the colloquium hall. He had the darkest, saddest eyes she had ever seen. Dark ice from the birth of the world, held in the permanent shadow. As a child she had wounded all her toys, the better to nurse and heal them. She found him at the point of gravitational stability between three conversation clusters, tea-glass between fingers.

'I've never liked it either.' She had always been astute at the tiny observations that cued social openings. His tea was untouched. 'It's not a proper drink.'

'So what do you call a proper drink?'

'I could show you.'

On the third moccatini he told her about the wolf.

On the fifth she said, *All right.*

*

The little wolf sleeps for a night and a day and a night and wakes instantly, every sense glowing. His first words: *My crew.*

They're all right, Analiese says but he won't take her word for it, not until he's called through to Taiyang's Hypatia office. Zehra took care of the debrief and put Glass Crew Lucky Eight Ball on furlough. Taiyang can provide him with a basic access familiar but the full restore back-ups of Dr Luz and Sombra are at Meridian and communications across Nearside are still down. The sight of Wagner, familiar-less, digitally naked, arouses Analiese Mackenzie.

A night and a day and a night is an age in war. Where information fails, rumours thrive. Twé remains besieged, buried, silenced, while its agraria die in the gloaming, light-starved. Queen of the South has five days of food left, Meridian three. Hot-shops have been attacked; 3D-printers hacked. Taiyang coders have successfully reverse-hacked some of the possessed graders but any attempt to marshal them into siege-busting squadrons draws fire from orbit. Ice. VTO is firing ice from its mass driver. The Vorontsovs have a cometary head moored up there; enough ammunition to stage a new Late Heavy Bombardment. And the trains sit idle in the stations and the BALTRAN is down and any rover venturing up on to surface draws bots with blades on their feet. There's an entire Equatorial express stranded on the rails in the middle of the Mare Smythii. They ran out of water a day ago. They're drinking their own piss. Their air supply has failed. They're eating each other.

Rumours and whispers. Duncan Mackenzie has sent twenty fifty a hundred five hundred shooters – Jo Moonbeam soldiers one and all – to break the siege of Twé. Supported by AKA archers, they're going to assault Twé's outlocks and liberate the city. The Asamoah-Mackenzie army has been cut to pieces, their body parts scattered across the Sea of Tranquillity. Meridian is under siege. Meridian's power has failed and the entire city is in darkness. Meridian has been occupied. Meridian has already surrendered.

I have to get to Meridian, Wagner says.

You need to heal, Lobinho.

She hires a private cabin in a banya. Three hours should do it. There is a steam cell and a slab and a small plunge pool. Wagner lies prone on the sintered stone slab, glossy with sweat. With a curved strigil Analiese scrapes dirt and dust and caked perspiration from his skin.

'You were waiting for me,' Wagner says, cheek pressed on the smooth warm stone, head turned to one side.

'I was coming back from a concert in Twé,' Analiese says. 'I got stuck when the trains went down.'

'You helped me escape and I abandoned you.'

Analiese straddles Wagner's back and slowly scrapes the per-spiration-glued dirt from his neck.

'Don't talk,' Analiese says. 'Give me your arm.' It hurts still, a sudden tearing of a scab she thought long grown-over. Fresh blood.

'I'm sorry,' Wagner says.

Analiese slaps his lean little ass.

'Come here.'

She slips his cleansed, glowing skin into the hot water of the plunge pool. Wagner gasps, skin tingling. Analiese slips in beside him. They lean against each other. Analiese scoops wet hair away from her face. Wagner sweeps her hair behind her ear and runs his finger down the edge of her ear to the line of pale scar tissue that is all that remains of her left lobe.

'What happened?' he asks.

'An accident,' she lies.

'I have to get to Meridian.'

'You're safe here.'

'There's a boy. He's thirteen. Robson.'

Analiese knows the name.

'You're still not strong enough, Lobinho.'

She can't persuade him. She never could. She contends against forces beyond human strength: the light and the dark, Wagner's two natures, the pack. Family. Neck deep in warm, healing water, in the middle of a war, she shivers.

Secchi is a survival-scrape, a sinter tube no wider than the airlock at each end, bermed over with regolith. Lucasinho and Luna fit into it like twins in a womb. Lucasinho can't imagine the jackaroos in here as well. But there is air and water, food and regolith overhead, a place for Luna to slip out of the shell-suit. Lucasinho is swathed in so much p-tape the only way to remove his sasuit is to cut it off. The heat pack is a rectangle of dull, warm pain hard under his low left rib. The only comfortable way to lie is on his right side facing the wall. He lies on the pad that still smells print-fresh, drained in every joint and muscle but unable to relax for the drop into sleep. He lies in his dusty, too-small sasuit staring at the curving sinter wall, imaging the depth of dirt smeared over, the vacuum beyond, the tick of radiation through space, soil, sinter, Lucasinho Corta: listening for the sound of the lock cycle that mean Malcolm's jackaroos have returned, or the bots – which he has never seen but has imagined in every bladed, spiked, stabbing detail – cycling through to kill them in their cots.

'Luca. Are you asleep?'

'No. Can't you sleep?'

'No.'

'Me neither.'

'Can I come in with you?'

'I'm real dusty, anjinho. And stinky.'

'Can I come in?'

'Come on.'

Lucasinho feels the small, tight heat of Luna's body curl in around the curve of his back.

'Hey.'

'Hey.'

'This is all right, isn't it?'

'That meal was good, wasn't it?'

The bivvie's cached meals come in two varieties: tomato-based or soy-based. *Tomato*, Luna decided. She was a bit soy-intolerant. Lucasinho did not want any digestive irregularity in a six by two metre shelter. They prepared the self-heating meals one at a time, because the container popping open when the contents were heated was so more-ish. Lucasinho's saliva glands ached at the odour of tomato sauce on potato gnocchi.

'No it wasn't,' Luna says in her cousin's ear. 'It tasted of dust.' Then she laughs, a small private giggle that feeds on its privacy until she can't hold it in and Lucasinho catches it and together on the cot they laugh like they laughed after their first BALTRAN jump, until their breaths are short and their muscles ache and tears run down their faces.

Lucasinho.

Lucasinho, wake up.

You have to wake up.

He surges awake, bangs his head on the low ceiling. The bivvie. He's in the bivvie. He's been asleep two hours. Two hours. That's Luna beside him. She's already awake. Both familiars have woken them. That's bad news.

Multiple contacts are approaching.

'Shit. How many?'

Fifteen.

Not the Mackenzie Metals jackaroos, then.

'Can you identify them?'

They're maintaining communications silence.

'How long until they get here?'

At their current rate, ten minutes.

Get suited up, get Luna suited up, get out, get the rover running. Gods.

'Luna, you need to get into your suit.'

She's thick and dazed from broken sleep. He scoops her up and slots her into the shell-suit. She fully wakes as the infraskeleton closes around her.

'Luca, what's happening?'

'Luna, Luna, we need to get out of here.'

They need to get out quick and dirty. There's a trick; he saw it in a telenovella and had Jinji look it up to check if it was possible. It is. It'll buy them the precious minute it takes the lock to cycle. A minute is life.

Helmets lock, suit checks cycle and light green.

'Luna, hang on to me.'

Her suit-arms are long enough to wrap around Lucasinho's skinny frame. Gloves click on to the frame of his suitpack.

'In three, two, one...'

Jinji blows the lock. The shelter explosively decompresses. Lucasinho and Luna are blown from Secchi in a jet of bedding, soya and tomato meals, chopsticks, toiletries, ice-crystals. They hit. Impact drives the air from Lucasinho's lungs. Things crack. The heat pack is a steel fist. That never happened in the telenovella. They roll. Luna slams into the parked rover, Lucasinho into Luna.

'Okay?' he gasps.

'Okay.'

'Let's go.'

Lucasinho gasps in pain as he tapes himself and Luna to Coelhinho. He's damaged. What has he done to the suit?

'Hold tight.'

Luna's gloves lock into the rover's frame. Lucasinho kicks in maximum acceleration. The front wheels lift. If they go head-over-ass here, they're dead. Luna instinctively leans forward. Lucasinho gasps again as ribs and muscles grate. Coelhinho blasts away from Secchi. Its dust plume will be visible over most of West Fecundity. As long as Lucasinho can stay ahead of the bots. What had Malcolm called them? The fuckers. Fuckers they are. As long as the fuckers run out of power before him. He's had hours charging. The fuckers won't have had that. He assumes. Their batteries will be low. He assumes. Their battery capacity will be about the same as a Mackenzie Metals single-seat rover. He assumes. So many assumes. Fuckers.

'Jinji, are they there?'

They're there, Lucasinho.

'Are they close?'

They're closing.

'Shit,' Lucasinho swears under his breath. 'How fast?'

At our current speed, our courses will intersect in fifty-three minutes.

Courses will intersect. Familiar-talk for blades and blood.

'Jinji, if we shut down the sensors, external comms, beacons and tags, how much extra battery life will that give us?'

At our current speed, thirty-eight minutes.

'How far will that take us?'

Jinji rezzes a map, the rover's final resting place a flag twenty kilometres short of João de Deus.

'And if we match their speed?'

The destination flag shifts ten kilometres closer to the southern edge of the equatorial solar strip. Too far to walk. The decision is made.

'Take us as close as you can to João de Deus.'

Coelhinho speeds over the regolith and Lucasinho tries not to imagine blades at the back of his neck. He's tired of being afraid, so very very tired.

The line of black across the edge of the world is so total, so abrupt that Lucasinho almost stops the rover. Part of the world is missing. The black grows by the second, the metre, swallowing the world.

'It's Glassland,' Luna says. They have come to the border of the equatorial solar farm, the belt of black which the Suns are wrapping around the world. Perspective shifts with Lucasinho's understanding: the black is much closer than he thought. Will it take his speed? Will he crack it, will it shatter under him and collapse? Fuck it. There are fifteen killer bots behind him.

'Yay!' he shouts, and Luna echoes him and they roar full speed on to the glass.

When Lucasinho looks over his shoulder he can no longer see Coelhinho. Not even the tip of its aerial. There has been no report of the pursuing bots for twenty minutes now. Lucasinho and Luna are alone on the glass, the lithe white sasuit, the lumbering red and gold shell-suit. Glass: smooth, featureless, perfect black in every direction. Black above, black beneath; the heavens reflected in the dark mirror. You could grow crazy looking down at your own patiently marching image. You could walk in circles forever. Jinji steers them by offline mapping. A ghostly shape inside the glass is João De Deus, down beyond the horizon, never seeming to grow closer. Horizon: it is impossible to tell where sky ends and earth begins.

Lucasinho imagines he feels the warmth of the energy stored in the glass through the soles of his boots. He imagines he feels the tic-tic of fine pointed bot feet through the reflecting glass. Paces pass into kilometres, moments into hours.

'The first thing I'm going to do, when I get to João de Deus, is make a special cake, and we'll eat it all just ourselves,' Lucasinho says.

'No no, the first thing you're going to do is have a bath,' Luna says. 'I smelled you at Secchi.'

'Right then, a bath.' Lucasinho pictures himself sliding into bubbling warm water, chin-deep. Water. Warm. 'What are you going to do?'

'I'm going to have guava juice from the Café Coelho,' Luna says. 'Madrinha Elis used to take me and it's the best.'

'Can I have one with you?'

'Of course,' Luna says. 'Very cold.' And a dozen alarms light up red inside Lucasinho's helmet.

Luna has a suit breach, Jinji says in its ever-calm, ever reasonable voice.

'Luca!'

'I'm coming, I'm coming.' But he can see the water vapour jet in sparkling ice crystals from the shell-suit's left knee joint. The corrugated jointing has failed under the constant rub of dust. The suit is open to vacuum.

'Hold your breath!' Lucasinho shouts. The tape. The tape. The extra roll of tape he insisted Luna print out and bring with them. The one they might need: did need. Where is it where is it where is it? He closes his eyes, visualises it in Luna's hand. Where do her hands go? To the shell-suit's left thigh pocket. 'I'm coming, I'm coming.'

Luna's air supply is at three per cent, Jinji says.

'Shut the fuck up, Jinji!' Lucasinho roars. He snaps the roll of tape from the pocket and tears free the end, wraps it around the leg joint. Dust flies from his fingers: treacherous, abrading lunar dust. He wraps until the tape runs out. 'How much has she got, Jinji.'

I thought you wanted me to shut the fuck up, Jinji says.

'Tell me, then shut the fuck up.'

Internal pressure is stabilised. However, Luna has insufficient oxygen to reach João de Deus.

'Show me how to transfer air over,' Lucasinho shouts. Graphics light up all over Luna's suit. 'Are you all right?' Lucasinho asks as he locks the supply hose from his suitpack to Luna's. 'Talk to me.'

Silence.

'Luna?'

'Lucasinho, will you hold my hand?' The voice is small and afraid but it's a voice, rich on oxygen.

'Sure.' He slips his gloved hand into the shell-suit's gauntlet. 'Jinji, has she enough?'

Lucasinho, I have bad news. There is insufficient oxygen for you both to make it to João de Deus.

'Good to go, Luna?' A slight tremor in the shell-suit. 'Did you nod your head again?'

'Yes.'

'Let's go then. It's not far.' Hand in hand they walk across the black glass, treading on stars.

Did you hear what I said, Lucasinho?

'I heard what you said,' Lucasinho says. The shell-suit's stride is half a metre longer than his. He half-runs across the glasslands. His muscles ache; there is no strength left in his legs. He wants more than anything to lie down on the black glass and pull the stars over him. 'We're going because we have to go. What are my options?'

You don't have any options, Lucasinho. I have solved the equations and you will run out of oxygen a minimum of ten minutes before the lock.

'Dial me down.'

That is with me dialling you down.

'Do it.'

I did it two minutes ago. You could reclaim some of Luna's O2...

'Absolutely not.' Already the words are like lead in his lungs. Every step burns. 'Don't tell Luna.'

I won't.

'She has to go on. She has to get to João de Deus. You have to do that for me.'

Her familiar is preparing a script for that.

'You never know, though,' says Lucasinho Corta. 'Something will come up.'

I assure you it will not, Jinji says. *I really cannot understand this optimism in the face of sure and certain facts. And I am bound to advise you not to literally waste what little breath you have by contradicting me.*

'Whose breath is it anyway?' Lucasinho says.

You are going to die, Lucasinho Corta.

The certainty hits him, darts around his every obfuscation and denial and plunges its blade into his heart. This is where Lucasinho Alves Mão de Ferro Arena de Corta dies. In this too-small, patched-up, dusty sasuit. Mackenzies couldn't kill him, bots couldn't kill him.

Lady Luna has saved him for her most intimate death: the kiss that draws the last breath from the lungs. That red and gold suit, the stars and glass full of their reflections, that blue crescent Earth, these too-small gloves –these are his last sensations, his last sights; the hiss of the respirator and the half-felt thud of his heart the last sounds.

And it's not so bad, now it is close and inescapable. It always was. That's the lesson of Our Lady of the Thousand Deaths. The only important thing now is how he meets it, walking towards it, with will and dignity. His lungs strain. He can't catch enough air. Walk on. His legs are stone. He can't put one in front of the other. His helmet read-outs are all red. His vision is narrowing. He can see Luna's helmet, his hand in her hand. The circle tightens. He can't breathe. He has to get out. There is no dignity at the end. He tears free from Luna's hand, wrestles with his helmet, his suit, trying to get out of it. His brain is on fire. Red fades into white. An all-consuming whine fills his ears. He can't see, can't hear, can't breathe. Can't live. Lucasinho Corta falls into the white embrace of Lady Luna.

9: LEO – VIRGO 2105

The family carried Caio in an improvised litter – a kitchen chair gaffer-taped between two bamboos – up eight flights of stairs. Like the Pope. Like an invalid brought to a faith-cure. They helped him to the edge of the rooftop spa pool and set him on the rim, his feet in the water. Then they left the roof to Caio and to Alexia.

She had the tripod, she had the screen, she had the ice-cream. Caju. Not Alexia's favourite flavour but you had to go with what you could get and this was about Caio anyway. She sat beside him, feet in the cool, fizzing spa pool and they fed each other spoonfuls of caju ice-cream. Alexia sucked the little bits of nut from between her teeth. Then the moon came up and threw silvers across the sea and she pulled it down out of the sky on to her screen.

'The dark bits are called seas, and the bright bits are the highlands,' she said, zooming in on the Sea of Tranquillity. In days she had become the tower's expert on the moon. 'That's because people used to think they had water in them. What they really are are a different kind of rock, the kind you get from volcanoes, and that does flow a bit like water, so seas is probably a good thing to call them. That's the Sea of Tranquillity. There's the Sea of Fecundity and the Sea of Nectar and the Sea of Serenity and the Sea of Showers. There's even an ocean, out in the west of the moon...' She scanned the screen

– the magnification was pretty impressive for a budget model. 'The Ocean of Storms.'

'But they don't have storms on the moon,' Caio said.

'They don't have any weather on the moon,' Alexia said.

'Can I see the big dick now?'

'Certainly not.' King Dong was legendary; a hundred-kilometre long cock and balls marked out in rover tyre tracks on the Mare Imbrium by bored surface workers. Time and industry had blurred it but it was still the defining image of human activity on the moon. 'I want to show you the rabbit.' Alexia zoomed-out the screen to frame the whole moon. She traced the ears of Mare Nectaris and Mare Fecunditatis, the head of Mare Tranquilitatis; drew in the outline of the great Moon Hare.

'It's not very good,' Caio said.

'Well, people are always seeing faces in things. In China they believe that the Jade Rabbit stole the formula for immortality and took it away to the moon, and he's grinding out the herbs.' Alexia sketches in the pestle of Mare Nubium. She twisted her fingers on the screen and turned the image upside down. 'In the norte they see a face – the Man in the Moon? See it?'

Caio shook his head and frowned.

'I see it now! It's not very good either.'

'And sometimes they saw an old woman with a bundle of sticks on her back but I've never been able to see that,' Alexia said. 'On the moon, they see a mitten. From a surface-activity suit.'

'How can they see that if they're on the moon?'

'They've got maps.'

'Oh yes. Of course they do.'

Alexia traced the mitt: Mare Fecunditatis the fingers, Mare Nectaris the thumb, Mare Tranquilitatis the palm.

'That's pretty boring,' Caio said. Alexia had to agree that it was. 'Even the rabbit is better than that.' The tripod tracked the moon as it rose. The light on the rooftop garden was immense; the streets were dark again tonight, whole sectors browned out. *We light the lights,* that had been the boast of Corta Hélio.

'Caio, I've been offered a job,' Alexia said. 'A fantastic job. Crazy money. Money to get us all out of here, enough money to make sure we're never afraid again. The thing is, Caio, it's up on the moon.'

'On the moon?'

'It's not so crazy. Our Great-Aunt Adriana went. She went from this exact same apartment, all the way up there.'

'Her family all got killed.'

'Not all of them. People go to the moon, Caio. Milton went to the moon.'

'Milton got killed.'

Alexia swung her feet in the cool water, kicked spray at Caio but he was not to be toyed with.

'You've made your mind up, haven't you?'

'I'm going, Caio. But I promise, I promise, that I will get the best people to look after you. I will get you doctors and physiotherapists and your own tutors. I will look after you. When have I never kept a promise?' She regretted the words the instant they left her tongue.

'There's not much I can do, is there?'

'I wanted to show you what it was like, so you've an idea.'

'Are we not enough, Lê?'

Her heart cracked.

'Of course you are. You are everything; you and Mãe and Marisa. Tia Iara and Tia Malika and Tio Farina. But this place isn't. I want more, Caio. We deserve more. We were a great family back in Great-Aunt Adriana's time. There's a way out of Barra, and I've got one chance at it. I have to take it.'

Caio's cheek twitched. He looked at his feet in the now-still water.

'I will come back,' Alexia said. 'Two years; that's the time limit. Two years isn't so long, is it?'

Caio kicked water, splashed the screen. Alexia had no right to tell him off.

'Is there any more of that ice-cream?'

'All gone. Sorry.'

'Then can I see the big dick?'

Plastic carry cases and storage boxes blocked the corridor. Men in orange coveralls with three letter acronyms on their backs manoeuvred trolleys. Alexia, in Michael Kors and Carmen Steffens heels, squeezed between bulky pieces of white medical architecture and piles of cardboard boxes. The suite opened to her thumb. The interior was a grander confusion; coverall men packing and stacking, hotel staff standing by with helpless expressions.

'What's going on here?' Alexia demanded.

'Surprising, the amount of sheer physical material I have accumulated in three months,' Lucas Corta said. He navigated his wheelchair through shuffling feet and shifting boxes. Alexia kissed him twice. 'I rather enjoyed having things. It's such a novel experience. On the moon we dump and reprint. No one really owns anything. The carbon you use for this sheaf of papers is carbon you can't use for anything else. Locked up. Dead carbon. We are a planet of renters. I think I may have become a little avaricious in my amassing of the physical. Now it all has to go and I find I'm experiencing a sense of loss. I'll miss this shit.'

'No,' Alexia says. 'What is going on here?'

'I'm packing, Alexia. I'm going back to the moon.'

'Wait,' Alexia says. 'Shouldn't your Personal Assistant have been informed about this? As some kind of priority?'

'It's on my orders,' Dr Volikova says. Always Dr Volikova. Alexia knows better than to expect the doctor to update her on Lucas's health. She's known from their first meeting that the doctor does not like her, that she thinks Alexia is a grubby little opportunist. A malandra from Barra. Alexia has made sure that Dr Volikova knows the dislike is mutual. Give as you get: the iron rule of Barra. Alexia also knows that the doctor will not tell her the reason for this order unless she asks.

'I'm to be informed of anything that impacts on Lucas's work.'

The shifters and packers in orange freeze. A look from Lucas sends them on their business.

'At least a dozen medical AIs in five continents are monitoring my health,' Lucas said. 'Four of them reached a consensus that I need to leave Earth within the next four weeks to have a better than fifty per cent chance of surviving the flight to orbit.'

'Senhor Corta's physiology has deteriorated in the past two weeks,' Dr Volikova said.

'Earth is a harsh mistress,' Lucas said.

'Can we speak in private?' Alexia said to Lucas. He wheeled to his bedroom. Alexia closed the door. The familiar scanners and monitors, the breathing equipment, were folded away and pushed back. The waterbed stood alone, exposed, isolated.

'Lucas, am I your personal assistant?'

'You are.'

'Then don't treat me like your fucking niece. I'm not someone you've hired to stand around in a short skirt and high heels and make the place look pretty. You made me look stupid in front of those removal men. And who hired them anyway? That's my job. Let me do my fucking job, Lucas.'

'I made a mistake. I'm sorry. It's not easy for me to delegate authority.'

'I understand that, but when you're back on the moon, if I understand what you're going to do, you won't have many friends. I will stand with you but you must trust that if I say I will do something, I can do it.'

'Very well. I need you to leave Earth with me.'

You're trying to throw me, Alexia thought. You're watching my eyes, my throat, my hands, my mouth, my nostrils for any tell that I'm shocked. You engineered this whole show to see how I would react. You want to see if I'm the right stuff. Watch my eyes. They do not look away.

'I'm leaving for Manaus tonight for pre-flight training. It's the minimum necessary. I can confer online with my backers but there is work which must be finished up here in Rio.'

'What do I need to do?'

'I need to sign off on the bot design. I won't be able to do that. You need to see them physically, what they are capable of doing. Press them for delivery. VTO Manaus is standing by for shipping to orbit but they will need twenty-one days' notice.'

'I'll do this, Lucas.'

'I'll need you in Manaus five days before launch. The medical and physical examinations are quite rigorous. Your ticket is booked.'

Fuck him. He got her. Alexia stifled a smile.

'One more thing.' Lucas reached into his Boglioli jacket. Alexia admired Lucas Corta's suits. She had never seen him wear the same one twice. Always a flower in his buttonhole, always pink, always fresh. Always dewed, even on days when the heat on the Avenida Atlantica beat like a hammer on an anvil. A silver charm swung gently on from his grasp. 'Please.' Alexia crouched, bent forward as Lucas fastened the clasp around her neck. This was not a gift, this was not a jewel. This was a medieval knight receiving a grace. 'This is a code,' Lucas said. 'It's been in my family for generations. My mother gave it to me. I give it to you. If anything happens to me, if I'm unable to ask you for it, or consent to its operation in any way, use it.'

'How... when...'

'You'll know.'

Alexia lifted the charm, a two-bladed axe.

'The axe of Xango,' Alexia said.

'Lord of justice,' Lucas Corta said. 'My mother reverenced the orixas. She didn't believe, but she did honour them.'

'I think I understand that,' Alexia said. 'What does it do?'

'It summons the lightning,' Lucas said.

Alexia let the charm fall against her skin.

'How could you be unable to ask me for it?'

'You know what I mean.'

Alexia wheels Lucas back to the suite. The packers and shifters had marshalled the papers into boxes and the boxes into piles and the piles into ranks.

'One question.'

'Ask.'

'All this stuff, where the hell did you keep it?'

'Oh, I rented the suite next door as well,' Lucas Corta said.

'Come on,' Alexia said and lowered the tail-gate of the pick-up. Cushions, a cool-box of Antarctica, insect repellent plugged into the auxiliary socket. Norton's grin widened when he saw the foam mattress. Alexia pulled it across the back of the truck bed, hopped up and patted it. Norton turned the radio to a soft, late night burble and joined her. They pulled the cushions around them and sat side by side, legs hanging over the tail-gate, bottles in hands, looking down over the great glowing blade of lights that was Recreio dos Bandeirantes and Barra da Tijuca.

Alexia had discovered the hidden place under the eaves of the forest almost by accident, a smart turn on her way to a client that took her nowhere but this wide-spot on a service track into the Pedra Branca wildlife refuge. Pedra Branca was the last scrap of old growth coastal rain forest, battered and bleached by the environment changes, clinging to the hills above Recreio dos Bandeirantes. She got out of the pick-up; listened, breathed, looked far. She felt the shaded cool and the slow respiration of the trees. She saw a toucan flit across the high branches with a predated fledgling in its bill. She heard insects, far surf, wind. The endless traffic was muted to a low bass grumble.

Alexia loved her secret place, but she kept the taser to hand. Boys went feral here: on the run from the police, the gangs, the military, their families. The last time Alexia came up to Pedra Branca, the toe of her shoe had caught on a human tibia, dragged from deep forest by some scavenging animal.

She had thought long before bringing Norton here.

He was quiet tonight. She hoped the beauty had taken his breath and words. She hoped this was a different quiet from the five days he had not seen her spoken to her answered her calls answered his door, when she told him about the moon.

Alexia held up her beer bottle. Norton clinked it.

'Do they drink beer on the moon?'

'Liquor. They can't grow barley there. And they don't eat much meat either. And no coffee.'

'You're not going to survive long.'

'I'm trying to wean myself off it before I go.'

She could barely see Norton's face but she knew he had rolled his eyes again. She felt him settle back into the cushions.

'This is beautiful,' he said. 'Thank you.'

This is a gift for you, Alexia thought. *My special place.* She wondered who he would bring up here first, on the back of his scrambler. The meanness of the thought startled her.

'Norton.'

'I thought there would be something.'

'I've got a launch window.'

'When?'

She gave him the date. He was quiet again for a long time.

'I'm scared, Norton.'

He was a silent, shadowed, unmoving mass.

'At least put your arms around me or something.'

One arm. Alexia leaned into his body.

'It's only two years.' Movement in the underbrush: the pick-up flicks up its lights. Small feet scurry, startled by the light.

'Have you made your mind up about the business?'

This, again. Norton believed that he was the natural heir to Corta

298

Aqua. Alexia had been creative in hinting – without telling him directly – that he would drain the business dry in a month.

'I'm leaving it to Seu Osvaldo.'

She felt Norton stiffen with shock and anger.

'Seu Osvaldo runs a gay gym. He is not a water engineer.'

'He runs a successful business.'

'He's a fucking gangster, Lê.'

And what are you? Alexia thought.

'He's known and respected in the community.'

'He's killed people.'

'*He* never killed anyone.'

'That's a fine point, Lê.'

'He knows what to do and how to do it, Norton. You...' She bit the words off at the head.

'Don't. That's what you're saying, isn't it? Norton de Freitas isn't capable of running your business.'

'It has to be over, Norton.' The break must be clean. No ropes, no handles, nothing tying her to Earth.

'It's only two years. That's what you tell me.'

'Norton, don't do this.'

'You go, and it's one year, two years, three years and then you can't come back at all. I know how it works, Lê. The moon eats away at you until you're trapped there, no matter how much you want to come home.'

No promises, no placations, no offerings could help here.

'I'm going to the moon. The fucking moon, Norton. They will put me in a rocket and shoot me into space and I am so scared.'

They sat side by side in the back of the pick-up, looking through the gap in the trees down on to the lights of the marvellous city. They did not touch, they did not speak. Alexia opened another bottle but the beer tasted sick and dusty. She flung it far into the dark.

'Fuck it, Norton.'

'Let me train you.'

'What?'

'I've looked at this. You need to be physically trained up to go into space. Let me train you.'

Norton's offer was so incongruous, so silly, so sincere that Alexia felt a tiny bud blossom in her heart. Take forgiveness when you find it.

'What kind of training?'

'Core strength. Endurance. Weights and resistance training. Some running.'

'No running. I'm a stupid runner. Things flap about. I walk. With great poise and dignity.'

She felt Norton laugh, a bass rumble through the frame of the pick-up.

'We haven't much time but I can certainly get you fit to get launch-fit. You'll be toned, Lê. Pumped.'

Alexia loved the image those words conjured. She let her finger stray under her top to her belly. It was small, it was lean but it was skinny-belly. In a family of block-built aunts and uncles – Caio was a solid bollard of a kid, even Marisa was big-framed – she was the flagpole. The bean. Skinny-girl. Muscles down there. Abs.

'That would be the greatest leaving present you could give me.' Leaving. She emphasised the word. She did not want Norton to entertain any false hopes.

'It will be hard work.'

'This is me, Norton.'

'I'll pick you up tomorrow. Have you got proper footwear?'

'I've got work boots.'

'Shopping first, then.'

'That is my kind of pre-flight training.'

Norton lay back on to the mattress, swathed in citronella from the bug-repeller. He linked fingers behind his head and looked up into the leaf canopy.

'Do you know what's good exercise?'

*

It was the same room. Lucas wished now he had left some marks, some subtle scratches that would positively identify this as the quarantine suite in which he had been housed when he first fell to Earth. The water tanks, the solar panels, the comms dishes, the mean wedge of yellow concrete, blue sky, dusty brown trees. There had been smoke in the sky these past fourteen days. He could taste it even filtered and purged by the air purifiers.

Earth was suites of rooms, opening into each other. Air conditioned, pastel-hued, lighting-controlled, dust-free and serviced, smelling of cleaning products, over-trodden carpet and memories of room service meals. Earth was a series of petty glimpses, framed views, held at a distance behind an aircraft window, glass, a car windshield. Constrained and insulated.

One time he escaped the suite, broke the window, when Alexia took him to Barra da Tijuca to see the apartment in which his mother had been born. Raw sky, long vistas. Sand in his shoes – he had panicked, and that embarrassed him now. Traffic, the open sky. Smell of the sea, of sun burned into sand; vehicle tyres and vehicle batteries, cooking, piss, semen, death.

Lucas Corta eased himself out of his wheelchair and staggered to the window to look out at the tiny slot of Brasil.

He saw his face in the window, a ghost reflection on the ghost of Brasil. It wasn't the face of an old man, or a young man made old. It was a thing more horrific, the face of a man of middle-age dragged down by gravity. Every fold, every feature, every wrinkle and pore, the fullness of his lips, the upturn of his nose, his long, sensual earlobes, the hair of his beard, the folds of his neck, his chin, his cheeks, dragged down, weighed down, borne down, drawn down and out and attenuated. Bleached of all life, all vigour by gravity. Every piece of life and juice and fire in him leached out by the endless, unrelenting gravity.

He could not wait to go home to the moon. He could no longer imagine what it was like.

Earth was hell.

The trainer was different from the one who had made him Brasil-ready; a sullen young woman who willed death at Lucas each time she saw him in his vileness, but the sessions were as dispiriting as before, and so much more difficult. He would endure up to four Earth gravities at launch. Twenty-four lunar gravities.

There will be a crash team standing by in the cycler, Dr Volikova said.

Twenty-four gravities. No training could prepare for such abuses of the human body and Lucas looked at those minutes of burn with equanimity. The odds were tilted toward him living. That was enough.

He did not sleep the night before the launch. Calls to make, conferences to meet, details to scan and check. His allies were treacherous, this he understood the first day the careful agents of the terrestrial powers appeared in his virtual conference space. They had seen the wealth and power of the moon. They wanted it. They needed a face the moon would recognise, who knew that world, its laws and politics, its way and affairs. When he had served out his usefulness, when they had learned enough, they would turn on him. For now he needed to survive twenty-four gravities.

The rest of the night before launch he curated a playlist of João Gilberto to sing him to orbit. The whispered guitar chords, the murmured vocals, easy as prayers, were counterpoint to the thundering energies of space flight.

Adriana had adored João Gilberto.

He didn't eat the morning of the launch. He drank water and swam. The same solemn young man in the bad suit who had wheeled him off the shuttle on to Earth wheeled him back, along the corridors with their frustrating glimpses of the worn-out world, into the boarding tube.

'Abi Oliviera-Uemura,' Lucas said. 'I never forget a name.'

He left his walking cane, silver tipped, where the boarding tube met the lock.

Dr Volikova and Alexia were already strapped in. The flight was full: in addition to Lucas's immediate staff, Lucas's political partners were sending up diplomats and fixers.

'Good morning,' Lucas greeted Alexia. She forced a tight smile. Her terror was absolute. 'Space travel is a routine affair, now.'

He tapped up João Gilberto.

He did not grip the armrests when the spaceplane detached from the boarding tube and pushed back. He did not look in small fear at Dr Volikova on his left and Alexia Corta on his right when the craft rolled out on to the taxiway. He did not brace himself when it turned at the end of the runway and opened up the turbojets. He did not gasp when the SSTO made its launch run and acceleration dropped an office building on his chest. He did not cry out when it lifted, and turned its nose up and up and up until he felt he was looking up the barrel of some space gun and then the big motors kicked in.

The SSTO climbed high over the Amazon. At fifteen kilometres the main engine lit. The rockets kicked the SSTO skyward. A planet fell on Lucas Corta. He gave a small gasping cry as the air was forced from his lungs. He could not take a breath. He tried to look at Dr Volikova, give her some small non-verbal plea for help, but he could not move his head and there was nothing she could do, pressed into her seat by multiple gees, skin peeled back from his eyes and mouth.

Help me, Lucas Corta mouthed. His heart was crushed in a fist of glowing iron, tightening with every beat. He could not breathe. He tried to focus on the music, identify the chord changes, lose himself as he did when jazz took him through the agony of training, down to Earth. Gravity crushed him. His bones were shattering. His eyeballs must collapse, his skull was failing. His heart was dying, piece by piece pinched off and blackening. In a centre seat of a VTO Manaus SSTO, Lucas Corta was imploding. The pain was beyond anything

303

he had ever known, beyond even pain. It was annihilation. And it went on forever.

He saw Alexia's head turned to him, her features smeared and blurred by acceleration, outlined in fuzzy black, shutting his sight into a slot, a pane, a glimpse: the little double-axe of Xango. She was shouting.

Medic! Medic!

Chega de Saudade whispered in Lucas Corta's ears. The SSTO *Domingos Jorge Velho* climbed on pillars of fire. A column of smoke blew away on the wind over the rags of the Amazon rain forest.

Jorge-Maria brought beer and Orbison brought ice. Tia Ilia brought doces and Tia Malika brought skewers. Tio Mateo set up a barbecue on the balcony and made a great show of assessing wind strength and direction and coaxing flame from the least amount of kindling he could use. Wuxu from the 12th floor brought the music he kept playing that shook the building, the music nobody wanted to hear because what they wanted Wuxu for was his ability to flick streaming on to every screen in the apartment. He played his music anyway.

The ice went in the shower tray, the beer in the ice, the skewers went on the barbecue and the doces on plates that Marisa handed round the guests. The guests went on the sofas and Wuxu's streaming went on the big screens and the small screens. The noise in the apartment was extraordinary. Relatives, friends and neighbours from four floors down to the top of the tower piled in to watch the Queen of Pipes depart Earth.

Shut up shut up shut up, this is it.

The launches were so routine now that they had been relegated to a minority interest channel interrupted by advertising every fifteen minutes. The apartment fell silent. Wuxu's music thumped from the next room. Essen from two down snatched up a kitchen knife and went in to see him. The volume diminished but the music did not stop because no one could stop the music. The spaceplane rolled out on to the strip. The camera followed it until it dissolved into the heat-haze at the end of the runway. Nothing happened for so long someone asked Wuxu to check if the feed had frozen. Then a black dart appeared out of the silver heat shimmer, the heat haze. It hurtled towards the camera, then lifted clear. The whole apartment cheered. Up it went on a plume of fire. Then the feed cut to ads and the whole apartment jeered.

Alexia's mother wept inconsolably.

Wuxu took his music and all the kids back down to the 12th floor where they danced until the evening brown-out.

The shuttle came around the limb of the Earth into morning and kindled into light, a needle of sunlit silver. The shuttle raced at twenty-eight thousand kilometres per hour into the dawn. The Earth was blue and bounteous, cloud-curdled; the OTV minuscule against the vast curve of the planet, a sliver of technology. A thousand kilometres aft, the tip of the tether wheeled down from higher orbit, hidden in the sun dazzle. The shuttle passed into full sun. Short-lived shadows cast through the windows and ports, moved swiftly across the flight deck, dwindling toward the zenith, growing toward evening in forty-five minutes. Sudden evening. The SSTO crossed the Sahara, twilit duns and russet. Solar farms five hundred kilometres below winked at the setting sun and went dark. Ahead the Egyptian night burned along the Nile, a serpent of two hundred million lights. Nothing could declare more clearly that Egypt was the Nile. Darkness fell over the Caspian Sea; webs of light reached out across Central Asia: cities and highways, industry and powerlines.

One hundred kilometres from transfer. The SSTO unlatched the transfer module. The shuttle burned thrusters in flickers of silent plasma, matching vectors with the tether. The crane arm lifted the module free from the shuttle bay. Light flickered red, the crane made small, final alignments as the tether descended. At transfer their relative velocities would, for a few moments, be zero. Red lights to green. The tip of the tether engaged with the magnetic lock as the crane unlatched. With ever-growing speed the spinning tether swung the transfer module up from SSTO, now glowing with blue thrusters as it made its distancing burn.

At the top of its cycle the tether released the transfer module. It flew out high and free across the face of Earth into a rising sun. In the heart of the sunrise, a black speck: the VTO cycler *Saints Peter and Paul*. The tether spun onward around the blue planet. The transfer shuttle's only means of propulsion were clusters of docking thrusters. If the tether had thrown too hard it would miss the cycler and fly out, helpless, into space. Too soft and it would fall and burn across the morning sky in re-entry fire.

From twenty kilometres the cycler assumed a shape; a central spindle, rings stacked around it, environment tanks and manoeuvring engines at one end; the other a blossom of solar wings. A delicate moon-flower. Acceleration would snap the panels and spars like stems. Five kilometres. The tether threw true. It has never once failed in sixty years wheeling around Earth.

Vernier thrusters flickered again, turning the transfer module to mate with the cycle's lock. The two spacecraft, like reluctant dancers at a wedding, flew out of the night into a new dawn. Sunrise burnished the VTO logos on the transfer pod's belly to brilliant gold. Station keeping: the two craft held their chaste distance while final checks were made. Thrusters popped again. The relative velocity between the two craft was ten centimetres per second. Over the Sea of Japan the two craft met and docked. Clamps locked, seals pressurised. In the cycler lock, the VTO medical team stood by.

This could not be rushed.

The hatch opened.

The medics poured into the spaceplane.

Three days after the VTO cycler *Saints Peter and Paul* swung around the back of the Earth and out to the moon, Corta Aqua sent notices to all its customers. With the change of management it would be necessary to hire contract engineers to maintain the high quality of purity and supply. Regrettably, this meant that prices would rise. Just a little.

The spinning stars spun her dizzy.

The observation bubble was a toughened glass dome at the end of *Saints Peter and Paul's* spin axis, large enough to allow two to look out at space. Two young VTO women in bright tight flight-suits had brought her up to the hub and told her to wait. *Wait,* Alexia had called back, but they were already swimming along the central hand-line, kicking forward on soft flippers. *Should I hold place with the ship or should I turn with the stars?* If she braced herself against the observation bubble's rail the stars whipped by so quickly her head reeled. If she let go of the rail, spread-eagled and pushed herself into a spin, she still could not match the rotation speed of the stars and the apparent turning of the ship around her left her dazed, unable to focus and a choke away from vomiting.

Free fall and Alexia Corta were not a happy marriage. The muscles that Norton had painstakingly built around her core armoured her against the cruelties of liftoff but either over-operated or cramped when she tried to move in zero gee. Her feet, her hands and, most hideously, her face were bloated and tight. Her skin felt stretched and unclean, the lower air pressure in the cycler left her itchy. She could not control her hair, it went in her eyes, she inhaled it, was blinded by it, until a spacer gave her a net. When she tried to get around, her hands and feet moved like a small dog swimming.

She grabbed the handrail and pushed up into the dome. Alexia Corta gave a small gasp. She was floating in space. Swirling stars crowned her. If she looked down she could see the solar panels arrayed around her like the petals of a moon-flower. Beneath them were the nested habitat rings and if she pushed herself to the edge of the dome she could catch the edge of the comms and manoeuvring modules. She wheeled through space on a glass throne.

'There's a look, I suppose.'

The view had been so captivating that Alexia had not seen the figure approach. It hovered a metre from the guide-line, anchored by tethers and carabiners.

'What?'

'A Corta look. And a Corta impudence.'

'Gospodin Vorontsov.'

The man shrugged and grimaced. A man, she thought; the figure was so warped, so attenuated and extended, so stretched out in tubes and tethers that gender is the last identification. Were those colostomy bags?

'I am Alexia Corta.'

The man grimaced again, dismissed her outreached hand. He had subtly changed orientation to match her. Free-fall etiquette. Alexia remembered that.

'You were a water engineer. That's an admirable profession. Primal. Everything comes from water and ends with water.'

'Thank you, sir.'

'I hear he'll live.'

'He was clinically dead for seven minutes, sir. Your crash team got to him just in time. A severe myocardial infarction.'

'I told him Earth would crush his heart. So you're the last Corta.'

'Lucas is in recovery, sir.'

'You know what I mean. I was flying this ship when Adriana Corta went to the moon. Fifty years is a long time to wait for a Corta.'

'Fifty years is a long time to spend in space, sir.'

Valery Vorontsov's eyes flashed.

'Weird and sick. Inbred idiots, riddled with radiation. DNA rotting inside. Not like us. Not like us at all.'

'No, sir...'

'That's what they think. They've always looked down on us. The Asamoahs think we're barbarians. The Mackenzies think we're drunken clowns. The Suns think we aren't even human. Pity. I would have liked to have told Lucas to his face. I'll tell you instead.'

'Sir, I'm only . . .'

'The last Corta. You've got your gun.' Valery Vorontsov laboriously hauled himself around on the hand-line. His colostomy and piss bags bobbed after him.

'Sir!'

Valery Vorontsov stopped.

'Lucas gave me something. A code.'

'I am far too old for l'esprit de l'escalier,' Valery Vorontsov said. 'I simply cannot bear the sudden turns. Tell me what you have to tell me.'

'It's a command code. I don't know what it does.'

'What did Lucas say?'

'It summons the lightning.'

'You have your answer.'

'He said if he was unable to ask me for it, or consent to its operation in any way, I was to use it.'

Valery Vorontsov sighed heavily and completed his manoeuvre. He pulled himself along the line, soaring glides metres long. From the elevator lock he called back, 'Do you think the two worlds need a little lightning?'

The stars wheeling around her head, Alexia Corta lifted the axe of Xango the Just to her lips and kissed it.

You must trust that if I say I will do something, I can do it, she had said. Mão de ferro.

Alexia whispered the word of power Lucas taught her.

'Ironfall.'

10: SCORPIO 2105

Two hundred and forty. So many numbers in Luna Corta's head. Eight. One. Twenty-five. Eight. Thirty. Three. More than any of those small numbers, two hundred and forty.

Two hundred and forty. The number of seconds a human brain can survive without oxygen.

Eight. Per cent battery power remaining in Luna Corta's shell-suit.

One. Degree Celsius. The temperature to which Jinji dropped Lucasinho Corta's sasuit environment control as his air reserves ran out.

Twenty-five. Degrees Celsius. The temperature at which both the human diving reflex and hypothermia kick in, substantially buffering the brain against the effects of hypoxia.

Eight. The distance in kilometres to the nearest outlook of João De Deus.

Thirty: the maximum safe run-speed of a Mark 12 VTO shell-suit.

'Luna: Lucasinho gave me air, how do I give it back to him?' Luna asks her familiar.

You don't have enough air to get both of you to João de Deus, other Luna says.

'I'm not going to João de Deus,' Luna Corta says.

Three. The final number on Luna Corta's helmet HUD. The distance in kilometres to the outlook of Boa Vista.

You don't have enough air to get both of you to Boa Vista, Luna says.

Two hundred and forty. The number of seconds a human brain can survive without oxygen. Three divided by thirty. Luna can't do that math but it is how long it will take her at full run to get to Boa Vista, and it must be less than two hundred and forty seconds. But she has only eight per cent power, and there will be the extra mass, and will the suit let a nine-year-old girl run it at full speed?

Leave the numbers to me, Luna.

Luna commands her suit to kneel. The shell-suit hands are big and clumsy, Luna is inexperienced in the haptics and she has never picked up an object as precious as the one she tries to lift now.

'Come on,' she whispers, terribly afraid of breaking something as she slides the mitts under Lucasinho's body. 'Oh please, come on.'

She straightens her legs and scoops Lucasinho up in her arms.

'Okay suit,' she commands. 'Run.'

The acceleration almost knocks her backwards. Luna cries in pain as she feels her joints jerk and rip. Her legs are tearing from their sockets. They can't move this fast, nothing can move this fast. The suit gyros steady her, snap her back to balance. She almost drops Lucasinho. In her red and gold shell-suit, Luna Corta races across Mare Fecunditatis. She runs from black to grey, hurdling the line between Glassland and raw dirt. Regolith flies from her feet; a trail of slow-settling dust.

One hundred and ninety. That's a new number Luna her familiar has flashed up on her helmet. The number of seconds it will take her to reach Boa Vista's main lock. But then she has to get from the lock to the refuge. The lock has to open. The lock has to recognise her. How many seconds will that add to one hundred and ninety?

'Luna,' she says, and sings a song she has known all her life; one her paizinho sang over her bed when he came into the madrinhas' nursery every night. *Listen to my song, anjinho. Sing it back to me.* The song activates Boa Vista's emergency protocols.

What if the machines are broken? What if the power is out? What if a hundred different fails means the lock won't open? What if Boa Vista won't listen to her song?

In her shell-suit, legs screaming with cramp and joint pain, Luna Corta holds her breath.

I have acknowledgement from Boa Vista, Luna says.

Now she sees the beacons come alive; rotating red lights on pylons, guiding the lost and the moonwrecked home. Her cousin in her arms, Luna runs up the vee of guiding lights. Ahead is the sintered slope to the main lock, and a slot of darkness opening before her.

It hurts it hurts it hurts. Nothing has ever hurt so much. All across her helmet HUD numbers turn white. White for out. White for death. Centimetre by centimetre the line of darkness expands into a rectangle.

'Luna, show me the refuge.'

A yellow map overlays the grey and black: a schematic of Boa Vista. The refuge is a green cube ten metres beyond the lock. Luna focuses on it and her familiar fills the graphic with numbers. What Luna reads from them is some air, some water, some medical help. Some shelter, for a time.

She races under the still-rising guillotine of the outlock gate into the dark.

I don't have power for the helmet lights, Luna apologises, but the suit steers true, navigating by memory. There, the green in the dark, the soft green emergency light through the porthole. Kind, lovely green.

Two hundred and ten seconds.

'Guava juice, Luca,' Luna says. 'Guava juice from Café Coelho. Very cold.'

Helmet lights play across the bore of the tunnel, sweeping down the smooth walls, across the sintered guide-way, bobbing in rhythm with the bodies. Running figures, running as fast as they dare in this dangerous place; swooping, soaring strides covering metres in a step: Geni, Mo, Jamal, Thor and Calyx. Their sasuits are carnivals of colour and pattern: yellow and white chevrons; patches and stickers of sports teams; cartoon figures hand-drawn in red marker. The impassive, comically-beatific face of Vishnu. Luminous spots: this one moves in a disconcerting, alien dance through the dark tunnel. Terse instructions flicker from helmet to helmet. Debris here. Roof-fall. Live cable. Abandoned tram car. They quickly mark each obstacle with AI tags and bound on. This is a race.

Ten metres.

Got the tag.

Here.

The figure in the Vishnu-suit slips a power-jack from its shoulder and wedges it into the crack between the lock doors. Last time they came here they were assiduous in leaving no trace, defiling no memory, resealing every gate and portal. But this is a race. As soon as the crack is wide enough to admit a body, they slip through one by one, Geni, Mo, Jamal, Calyx. Thor wedges the lock open with a fallen strut and slings the power jack across his back. The Urbanistes pour through the inlock, down the steps into the grand desolation of Boa Vista.

Gods alone know what's out there.

The tag went off.

Those things could be on their way here.

Mo, the tag went off.

The tag went off. After months of silence. After the team's interest had migrated to industrial archaeology and the intriguing, almost sculptural wrecks of the helium-3 extractors destroyed in the opening BALTRAN bombardment of the Mackenzie-Corta war. After Lucasinho Corta's spitting rage in the bar drove a spike through the heart of their trust in their love of urbanisme. A tag went off. They had agreed not to go back to Boa Vista: the scale of the devastation was oppressive, the destruction too recent, the faces of the orixas too judging, the guilt of violation too strong. No ghosts on the moon, but

314

stone has a memory. Before they left they sowed the dead palace with motion sensor tags. Assuming pillagers, historians, other Urbanistes. Profaning feet. Or the memories of stone, walking.

Something had moved in the mausoleum of Boa Vista. The tag blinked and sent a notification to Geni.

What if it's a bot?

Geni sent the images to her team-mate's familiar. The tag's power was low, the resolution grainy and the image fleeting, but sufficient. A figure in a shell-suit. A burden in its arms.

That's not a bot.

Sasuit helmet lights lack the range to illuminate a grand ecosystem like Boa Vista and the interior of the old lava tube is perilous with fallen stonework, strewn debris and ice. Geni, Mo, Jamal, Thor and Calyx steer a course between the collapsed pavilions over the treacherous stones of the flash-frozen river, guided by their net of tags and AR overlays on their lenses but mostly by the pale green glow at the northern end of the habitat, by the main outlook.

Take a rover out to here, then straight down through the lock. Piece of piss.

Uh uh. Those bots you were so worried about, remember?

Fuck.

We go the old way. Through the tram tunnel.

The green glow is the emergency lighting of a refuge, low on power and resources. The Urbanistes race across the dead gardens of Boa Vista, dodging, sprinting, hurdling. Geni, Mo, Jamal, Thor and Calyx push in around the green-glowing porthole in the refuge lock door. Through the condensation streaks they can barely make out the figure in the shell-suit sitting on the floor, back to the door. The helmet is off. A kid. It's a fucking kid in that thing.

'Calyx.'

The neutro connects er suitpack to the auxiliary atmosphere supply port and feeds air.

There is another figure in a white sasuit, laid out on the floor.

315

Geni plugs her comms cable into the socket.

'Hey, hey. Can you hear me? This is Geni, Mo, Jamal, Thor and Calyx. We'll have you out of there right soon.'

They come swooping down through the rigging of the world, leaping, tumbling, soaring, turning somersaults. Electric colours, slogan T-shirts, headbands and wristbands, blue stripes on their cheekbones and bones and lips. A cascade of bodies, running railings, vaulting ducts and conduits, flying from struts, diving between cable runs. Moves and tricks Robson Corta can't match, only envy. He will, with practice. Endless practice. He unpicks their signature moves like magic tricks. Every move is built from a simple vocabulary. Learn that, you learn the magic. He never saw a trick that he did not try to take apart and appropriate.

They've come far, the Meridian traceurs, from each of the city's three quadras, cutting trails through the architecture of the city's roof; running for kilometres through the high places, cutting brief silhouettes against the burn of the sunline.

Golden circle.

Network down, trains not running, BALTRAN out, Twé under siege, bots and graders and things dropping from the sky and rumours walking the world on clicking titanium feet but there is a Golden Circle over in Antares Quadra, up in the roof of Tereshkova Prospekt.

The Golden Circle is a contest, a challenge that calls all traceurs to the high places.

The Meridian équipe drop around Robson Corta. They're older, bigger, stronger. Cooler. They know him. He's the kid who fell from the sky. The thirteen-year-old who fucked up his first run. Who's put out a Golden Circle. It stands above him, on the flank of the 112th duct junction in fluorescent tape.

No one speaks. Every eye is fixed on Robson.

'Have you got anything to eat?' Robson stammers.

A boy in purple tights throws him an energy bar. Robson crams it down without decorum or shame. It's been two days since he ran from Denny Mackenzie up into the high city. He hasn't eaten, has drunk only the condensation he can lick from the water tanks. He can fall three kilometres and walk but he's shit at running away. It was then he realised that he couldn't hide out at the top of the city waiting for the Meridian traceurs to turn up and rescue him. They must be summoned.

'You put up a Golden Circle,' says a woman in grey marl tights and a blue crop-top that matches her face make-up. Every traceur wears a differed pattern of blue. A Meridian thing. He will have to learn how to do it right. There will be rules about it.

'I know. I probably shouldn't . . .' He had fretted and fussed for half a day before finding the courage to steal the luminous tape he needed for his Golden Circle.

'No, you shouldn't,' the man in purple says.

'Why have you brought us here, Robson Corta?' blue woman says.

'I need your help,' Robson says. 'I've nowhere to go.'

'You've got money, Robson Corta,' purple tights man says. 'You're a Corta.'

'I ran,' Robson says, as he slowly congeals inside with the realisation that this may not go the way he wants. 'Denny Mackenzie . . .'

Purple tights man cuts in.

'No fucking way, Hahana.'

'Your équipe, Robson Corta,' blue woman, Hahana, says. 'The Queen of the South traceurs. The ones who taught you how to run. Do you ever keep up with them?'

'I've tried, but I can't reach them . . .'

'Do you know why you can't reach them, Robson Corta? Because they're dead, Robson Corta.'

Robson's breath catches. His heart reels. He is very high up and the fall is endless. His mouth makes noises he can't explain or control.

'Do you know how they died, Robson Corta? Mackenzie blades took them to Lansberg. They put them out the airlock. All of them.'

Robson shakes his head and tries to say no no no no no but there is no air in his lungs.

'You're toxic, Robson Corta. And you say, Denny Mackenzie? Denny Mackenzie? We can't help you. Even this may be too much. We can't help you.'

Hahana nods and the traceurs explode away from Robson in vaults and runs, somersaults and straddles, a dozen different motions, a dozen different traces up into the high city.

Baptiste who taught him the shapes and names of the moves. Netsanet who drilled him until those moves became part of him. Rashmi who showed him the feats his body could perform. Lifen who gave him new ways to perceive the physical world. Zaky who made him a traceur.

Dead.

Robert Mackenzie had promised that he would not touch Robson's équipe. But Robert Mackenzie was dead and the world which had been so certain, guided along rails, was melted, shattered, thrown to vacuum.

He killed them. Baptiste and Netsanet and Rashmi and Lifen and Zaky.

He is utterly alone.

On the second day Zehra joins Wagner in the repair bay. The damage to the rover is extensive but easily repairable. Pull a module, replace it with another. The work is steady and repetitive and falls into its own pace and rhythm. Wagner and Zehra work without words, without the need for words. Wagner's focus is intense. Analiese comes to see him in the workshop. Maybe he might want lunch. Maybe a break. She sees the familiar dark concentration, that can focus on one thing for hours on end. She wonders what the light Wagner is like. Would she even know him? The wolf and his shadow. She leaves the workshop without Wagner knowing she was there.

Hypatia is too small for a three-shift calendar and keeps Meridianal Normalised Time. At midnight on the third day the repairs are complete and Wagner and Zehra rest from their labours. The rover gleams under the floods. To the inexpert eye it is the same beaten six-wheeler towed into Hypatia main lock and pushed by its exhausted crew into the repair bay. That eye can't see the beauty of the new modules and motors; the fresh wiring and routing; the parts custom-designed by Wagner, bespoke-printed, hand-fitted by Zehra.

'When are you leaving?' Zehra says.

'Soon as the batteries are recharged and I've completed checks.' Wagner walks around the rover. His right eye flickers with diagnostics. The replacement lens is adequate but with every moment he resents more and more the dull, flavourless personality of the default familiar. It's one thing; stubbornly, indivisible.

'I'm coming with you.'

'You're not. Gods know what's out there.'

'You won't get out the lock without me,' Zehra says.

'I'm laoda...'

'And I slipped a line of code into the command chain.'

From the beginning Wagner has understood that his relationship with his junshi depends not on management but respect. When he met her, as junshi of the first glass crew he took out of Meridian Main lock, she sat back, perched on the rover step while older, dirtier hands tried to scare, intimidate, faze, bully the pretty Corta boy. When their ammunition was spent, she swung up into her seat on the opposite side of the rover. Not a word. Crews had been killed by enmity between laoda and junshi. As the machine drove slowly up the ramp into the outlock, Zehra said on the private channel, *You don't know what you don't know, Corta boy. But I'm with you.*

The batteries are full. The rover checks twenty different flavours of clean. Its crew is suited and booted, suit packs full. Wagner files a

319

departure plan. As the seat descends and the bar lifts, Zehra touches his arm.

'You've got a ten-minute window. Go and say goodbye to her.'

Wagner does not need his cheap and nasty little familiar to tell him that Analiese is in the pod. From the end of the catwalk he hears the buzzing, resonant harmony and seething drone of the setar. She's improvising: his dark self runs along the notes, finding his own progressions and sequences. He has no appreciation of music, he never has, but he understands and fears its power to enchant and direct the mind, its mastery of time and rhythm. Lucas used to lose himself in the subtle complexities of bossa nova, a chord for every note. Wagner saw in his brother's rapture something of the ekata of the pack, but it was singular, atomised joy. A private communion.

The music ends mid beat. Her familiar has told her he is at her door.

He loves the way she carefully places the setar in its case before anything else.

'You fill that suit well, jackaroo.'

'Better than when I came here.'

'Much better.'

When they disembrace, she slips a package into his gloved hand.

'I printed out your meds.'

Analiese's hand arrests Wagner as he tries to slip the bubble pack into a suit pocket.

'I can see it, Lobinho. Take some now.'

They hit so hard, so precisely that Wagner almost reels. He had confused a depressive state with combat fatigue and the intense focus of his need to reach Robson in Meridian. He has not made that mistake in years. Out on the surface it could kill him and Zehra.

'Thank you. No, that's, that's inadequate.'

'Come back. When it's over – whatever happens.'

'I'll try.'

Walking down to the vehicle bay, he hears again the sparkling of the setar. He has three minutes remaining in his departure window.

'I'll need that code,' he says to Zehra, back to back with her in the junshi seat.

'What code?'

Zehra shuts herself in with her music for the first twenty kilometres and Wagner is glad to be left alone with the experience of drop-back into full medication. It's a ride through an interior war zone. The physical world zooms in and out of focus. Attention flies to one subject, then veers to another fascination. He visualises Analiese's mutilated ear. It was not an accident. Accidents are never so neat. She paid for her betrayal. The hand behind the knife was kind. The customary Mackenzie price for betrayal is a finger. That would have silenced the bright joy of the setar forever.

How long has Zehra been talking to him?

'I'm sorry.'

'I said, I would have liked you to ask me.'

It's an easy run to Meridian, along the line of Equatorial One, on the glass. The rover's radar mast is up. Wagner's helmet shows no hostiles between him and the cache at Silberschlag. Comms with Hypatia are good, Taiyang engineers are restoring the network by rags and patches. The rail network is operating: at least one line, one train: from St Olga to Meridian. The war is over, the war is lost, the war is won, the war continues, the war has changed to something different; Wagner and Zehra drive through uncertainties and rumours. You can be in the middle of a war and not know it, Wagner thinks. And again his focus strays and again he must apologise.

'Ask you what?'

'You're going to Meridian for Robson. Did you think to ask me why I want to go with you?'

Wagner has assumed that Zehra journeys with him out of personal loyalty and, realising that, discovers he knows nothing about his junshi.

'No, I didn't. That was wrong.'

'I have someone back there.'

He never knew. He never thought.

'My mother,' Zehra says. 'She's old, she's alone and the moon is falling down around her.'

'Oh,' says Wagner Corta.

'Yes,' says Zehra Aslan.

They drive out along the pure and perfect glass.

Wagner opens the throttle and runs the rover at full speed. The solar belt is his terrain: smooth, safe, sane and boring boring boring.

Boring is good. Boring is no shocks and no surprises. Boring gets you back to the people you love.

Boring is the landscape of talk. In one hundred and fifty kilometres Wagner learns more about his junshi than he has in ten contracts. Zehra carries a third name: Altair. Aslan is her biological name, her contract name. Altair is her family name, her true family. Noma-themba, a Jo Moonbeam from Johannesburg, is her true mother. The Altairs are a nurture stream. No one has ever been born into the Altairs. All its members enter by adoption, fostering or partnership. Nomathemba adopted Zehra at the age of three months. She has three siblings and two co-mothers. Nomathemba has been dying slowly of silicosis for a year now, her lungs hardening, turning to moon rock. Zehra is in the process of adopting a little boy from Farside: Adam Karl Jesperson. It's scaring the living shit out of her, but the Altairs are strong. Zehra needs to complete the process and present Nomathemba with the latest bubble in the stream before her breath turns to stone.

Alarms flash all over Wagner's HUD. He skids the rover to a halt. Zehra is in his ear immediately. He stops. An hour west of Hypatia. He flicks the anomaly on to her visor. Together they climb up on to the top of the rover, each gripping the comms mast, to eyeball the shock and surprise. There is a concavity in the smooth black horizon.

322

'Something hit,' Wagner says.

'Hard,' Zehra agrees.

They edge toward the impact though the radar indicates no activity. For three kilometres Wagner nudges the rover through a debris field of black-glass teardrops. The teardrops shatter between his wheels and the black solar array. The final dozen metres are up a low ridge of shattered glass shards. Wagner thinks he see pieces of machinery among the glass. Machinery and other fragments. From the top of the ridge the rover looks down over the moon's freshest crater. Wagner and Zehra walk down the few metres to the crater lip. The suit visors give them the dimension: two hundred metres across, twenty deep. Not on the most recent satellite map of Flammarion.

'I'm getting a big heat signature off this,' Zehra says. 'Seismology says the place is still ringing like a temple gong.'

'It must have been something significant for VTO to risk a strike so close to Equatorial One,' Wagner says. 'Any chance?'

'No chance at all,' Zehra says.

'Mackenzies, Asamoahs?' Wagner asks.

'People with contracts and debts.'

They died, their elements fused with the molten silicon still radiating in the infra-red, but what affronts Wagner most, the offence that touches him, is the hole in the pure and perfect glass.

They meet the first overturned grader fifty kilometres westward. The moon is profligate with junk; obsolete and damaged equipment has always been abandoned in place. The helium fields of Fecunditatis and Crisium, the mines of Procellarum where the regolith has been stripped two hundred metres deep, are littered with extractors and sinterers, solar plants and graders. Metal is ubiquitous, metal is cheap. It's the elements of life that are precious. It is not unexpected to find a discarded grader. The surprise is to find one so comprehensively trashed. It looks as if it has been dropped from orbit. It lies on its side, panels stoved in, innards strewn in pieces around the corpse, suspension snapped, wheels at crazy angles. The dozer blade is snapped in two.

Five kilometres further on Wagner and Zehra come across two more graders; dead, smashed, one overturned, the other with its blade deeply embedded in the first grader's flank.

'Anything we can salvage?' Wagner asks.

'Yes, but I'm not going near that,' Zehra says.

'There are a lot of tracks,' Wagner says.

'All heading to Meridian,' Zehra says.

Over the horizon they enter the carnage; a wrecking yard, the graveyard of graders. Metal hulks capsized, upended, embedded in each other like monstrous machines fucking. Thirty-five graders. Wagner imagines the divine judgement of some heavy metal deity. The dead machines are powerfully sculptural and pathetic.

'They're not all dead,' Zehra warns. A grader, blade wedged deep in the engines of its rival, strains and heaves to dislodge itself. Its wheels spin on the black glass.

The grader comes out from behind a pile of scrap so tangled, so smashed Wagner can't recognise it as once-working machinery. It stops dead in front of Lucky Eight Ball and lowers its blade.

'Zehra,' Wagner shouts. She's already opening up the engines, reversing as fast as she can. But the same traitor glass that frustrated the dying grader betrays Glass Crew Lucky Eight Ball. Wheels spin, the rover crabs sideways. The live grader charges.

Zehra slews the rover; it waltzes across slick glass. The blade misses by a scant metre. The rover power-slides. Zehra fights for control. A jarring impact as Lucky Eight Ball side-swipes a dead grader.

'It's coming round again,' Wagner cries.

'I know that!' Zehra shouts. 'I fucking know that!'

The grader lines up. Attacks. Dies. Wagner sees the warning lights go dark on its steel skeleton. Power out. But it has momentum: an unguided, unthinking, unstoppable hulk. It bears down on Glass Crew Lucky Eight Ball. Zehra threads the rover through the narrow gap between blade and wreckage. And they are clear of the machine graveyard, out on clear and perfect glass.

'The Suns must have counter-hacked some of them,' Wagner says. 'Grader civil war. It must have been a hell of a spectacle.'

'You go ahead and sell court-side seats,' Zehra says. 'Tell you what though, those Suns may have saved Meridian.'

'I'm getting a rough ride here on the right,' Wagner says.

'I've got a dead wheel and motor rear right,' Zehra says. 'We must have wrecked it when we slid into the wreckage.'

'Will that affect us?'

'Not unless we run into more of that. I'll take it offline anyway. Let it free-run.'

After the battlefield, the run into Meridian is clear, quick and untroubled. Wagner raises Meridian control on his cheap and nasty little generic familiar.

'This is Taiyang Glass Crew Lucky Eight Ball, Lucky Eight Ball, tag TTC1128, requesting immediate ingress to Orion Quadra main lock.'

'Lucky Eight Ball, hold your position.'

'Meridian, we are damaged and low on air and water.'

Nice lying, laoda, Zehra says on the private channel.

Just an amplification of the facts, Wagner says. But he is angry. A thousand kilometres, through massacre, siege, war; attack and retreat, victory and flight, death and terror and he must wait for Meridian traffic control. You're keeping me from my pack, my loves, my boy.

'Line her up,' he orders Zehra. She takes the rover between the beacons to the lip of the ramp, facing the massive grey lock door.

'Glass Crew Lucky Eight Ball, clear the ramp area,' Meridian control orders.

'Requesting emergency ingress. I repeat, we are low on O2.'

'Your emergency ingress request is denied, Lucky Eight Ball. Clear the ramp area.'

'Laoda,' Zehra says and the same instant Wagner feels the shadow fall across him. He looks up into the belly lights of a VTO moonship hovering fifty metres above Lucky Eight Ball. Around it, station-keeping, seven more moonships hover on their thrusters. 'I'm moving.'

The rover scuttles away, the moonship settles on to the ramp. Wagner notes a personnel pod. Hatches open, steps unfold. Figures in shell-suits step down and walk down to the lock gate. The moonship lifts, another darts in, lands, disembarks armoured personnel. Each of the ships in turn follows.

'That's the entire moonship fleet,' Zehra says.

'That's seven hundred people,' Wagner says. The lock gate lifts, the hard-shell figures walk into the darkness. The gate descends.

'Glass Crew Lucky Eight Ball, clear to ramp,' Meridian control says.

'What happened there?' Zehra asks.

'I think that while we were out there, we lost the war,' Wagner says.

First come the drones. A swarm of them, a biblical plague, storming up from Meridian hub in a fizzing black plume. At first Marina thinks it is smoke – that great fear of the moon-dwellers: smoke: fire! Then she sees the plume divide into smaller streams, each aimed at a level. She freezes; her classmates, just released from the returnees group, freeze; Meridian freezes.

What are these things?

The streams form into smaller clouds, each following one of the quadra levels. The cloud engulfs Marina and her returnees. She finds herself eye to lens with a tiny, insect-sized drone. It hovers on invisible wings; she sees a prickle of laser light in her right eye. Her familiar has been interrogated. Then it zips away, with all its swarm, rolling up 27th.

Are you all right? The returnees ask each other. *Are you all right. Are* you *all right?*

The drone clouds bowl into the quadra hub, wheeling like a flock to take a new prospekt.

The returnee group has been confused, nervous. Its article of faith – that they will all go back to Earth – has been cracked by the inexplicable news breaking on their news feeds and Gupshup channels. Rogue graders. Killer bots. Twé besieged. Foods shortages no food shortages, food rationing no food rationing. Food riots, food protests. On her way to the meeting, Marina skirted a small, well-behaved protest beneath the old LDC chambers. Protesting about something that hasn't happened, to something that doesn't exist. The trains are shut down, the BALTRAN is shut down. The Moonloop is shut down. Luna is closed to the universe. Some of the previous intake are stranded, panicking that they have overstayed their physiological visas. A day or two won't make any difference, Preeda the facilitator says. What if that day or two becomes a week or two, a month or two? And what about the backlog? The Moonloop has only so many capsules. The cyclers are on fixed orbits.

The bone clocks keep ticking.

After the drones come the bots. Marina sees the pulse of movement sweep towards her down 26th East even as the word sweeps the network. Citizens trying to get off the streets. Diving into shops and bars, dashing for home, finding any cranny or sheltering crevice, taking a staircase or an elevator away from the rumours. *They're in the city. They're on the streets. You'll be all right if you're indoors. Get indoors they're knifing anyone on the streets.* Children swept up and carried in arms, frantic parents trying to contact teenagers, apartments closing street doors, shuttering windows.

I'm going back, Aurelia says.

I can make it home from here, Marina says. Home is in the opposite direction to the flow of the people. She takes the 25th Street ladeira at a trot. Marina runs straight into the bot at the bottom of the staircase, picking a slow, intricate minuet along 24th right. It's a jagged tripod of switchblade legs and flick-knife arms. Every part of it is edged and sharp. Every part of it can transform into a blade. Its many eyes register. Its head snaps to contemplate her.

There exist shocks so profound that the body's only response is paralysis. Not fear, though fear is right: this is the shock of the uncanny. The thing before her is so alien, so unsightly, so different from anything Marina has ever seen before that she cannot understand what she sees. The shock of the strange stuns her. Every part of it offends human sensibilities. She cannot move or think or act. But it moves, thinks, acts. Marina sees intelligence and intention in the eyes that scan her head to toe, then its attention snaps away. It dances on its three clicking stiletto feet. Now the fear comes. Marina sits shaking on the bottom step of the 24th Street ladeira. The God of Death looked at her and passed by. The new gossip wafts through the network: *It's all right, they won't touch you.*

Then what were they made for? Marina thinks.

The last wave is the suits.

Ariel and Abena, with most of the population of Orion Hub, are on their balconies or at the street handrail. Marina finds them. One detachment of suits comes up from the train station. They wear shell-suit armour decorated with Heavy Metal motifs: flaming skulls, fangs, demons, large-breasted women, big-cocked men, demons and angels and chains. Vorontsovs. Another detachment advances up Gargarin Prospekt from the outlock. They are dressed in black impact armour and carry small, black, projectile weapons. They advance in line and step. In the stunned silence of Orion Quadra their boots sound loud and intimidating.

'They're marching,' Marina says.

'They're terrestrial,' Ariel says.

'Are those guns?' Abena says.

'They're in for a big surprise when they try and shoot those things,' Marina says.

'Forgive me if recoil isn't at the top of my list of concerns,' Ariel says.

A third detachment emerges from offices and print-shops; not armoured, not armed and drilled, just people – moon folk – in everyday clothes and orange vests. They gather into groups of three and move up and out to every prospekt and street in Orion Quadra. Marina orders Hetty to zoom in on the vests: each carries a logo of the moon overflown by a bird carrying a twig in its beak. Marina is unfamiliar with the symbolism. Above are the words 'Lunar Mandate Authority'.

'Peace, Productivity, Prosperity,' Marina says, reading the motto beneath the world and bird motif. 'We've been invaded by middle management.'

Two boxes of guava juice and an empanada. They swing in Robson Corta's waist bag as he climbs up through the high fifties to the West Antares power conduit. He lost the bot ten levels ago – they have restricted battery life and can't climb. All they can do is try and follow him up by staircase and street and tag him for a writ. Good luck serving that, up above Bairro Alto. The danger is the human attention they attract, and the little machines are everywhere now, guarding every crumb and cup.

Robson's thieved from hot-shops in every quadra – it's always night somewhere in Meridian – but never Eleventh Gate. Thieving from your own hot-shop is shitting on your doorstep.

Two boxes of guava juice and an empanada – tilapia, he hates tilapia – is poor reward for a daring, dark-time descent of the West Antares conduit. Robson spent days navigating a safe path between the high voltage cables and the relays, marking it with luminous tape he filched from an off-shift duster's pack at a busy tea-stand. His ascent follows a trail of shining arrows and dashes. An arrow: a gap jump in the direction of the arrow. A greater-than sign: wall pass. A less-than sign, precision jump to a narrow location. An equals sign: cat jump. A vertical equals: wall run. A cross: dash vault or lash vault, depending on the orientation of the long axis of the vault. Downward slash right: under bar. Downward slash left: reverse under bar. An X: Do not touch. An asterisk: Danger of death.

Robson drinks the first juice on the level seventy traverse. He tucks the empty carton into his pilfer bag. Trash can fall, trash can get into the machinery, trash can be a treachery waiting at the far end of a jump. He saves the empanada for the nest. Robson searched for days across the high places before he found a sleeping place that was warm, protected, had access to water without damp and condensation, was secure so he would not roll over in his sleep and fall to his death. He lined it with filched packing and went down to the bars where the surface workers drank to steal thermal sheeting.

Every magician is a thief. Time, attention, belief; thermal sheeting.

Robson burrows into his nest of impact foam and bubble wrap and eats his empanada. He will save the last juice for later. He has learned to ration his treats. It will be a thing to look forward to. Boredom is the dark enemy of the refugee. Wanking is an enemy in a different mask; the mask of a friend.

Robson likes to believe that his high nest gives him a philosophical eyrie over the world. High above every other human, he can look down and contemplate. If food is guarded, it must have a value beyond the everyday. On his thieving missions he hears tea-shop talk. The trains are out, the BALTRAN too. The Vorontsovs are in charge of those: why would they shut them down? Twé has been buried in regolith. That would cut back on the growing season. The crops would dwindle, they might fail. The Asamoahs could be weird – every one he's ever known is – but they would never do that to their own capital. But if no one knows when there will be another harvest, that would explain bots guarding every empanada and bento box.

Then there are the most intriguing stories of all, the ones that make him linger a moment too long, his fingers a moment too slow on the object he means to steal. There are things out on the seas, in the highlands. Whole squads have been lost – killing things, with blades for fingers and swords for feet. Killer bots. Who would make a thing like that? The Suns could, but why would they? Why would anyone build a thing with no other purpose than to frighten, to intimidate, to threaten and control?

No one on this world, Robson decides. Huddled in his nest, warmed by the hum of a heat exchanger, his stolen blanket pulled around him, Robson concludes that, without any notice or declaration, without anyone actually knowing, the moon has been invaded. By Earth. By high blue Earth. But they couldn't do that on their own; they would need someone to transport their machines, their people. The only ones with the capacity to do that are the Vorontsovs. The Vorontsovs are in league with Earth to take control of the moon.

'Whoa,' says Robson Corta.

And he hears a click. A tap, a click-click tap. A leg, elegant and precise as a surgical tool, appears around the corner of the heat exchanger. The steel hoof draws a click from the catwalk. Robson freezes. An arm like a blossom of blades comes around the corner of Robson's nest, then a head. Robson thinks it's a head. It has six eyes and is articulated like no limb he has ever seen but he's sure it's a head by the way it snaps from side to side to study him.

Click. Another step, another leg. Another arm.

He pushes slowly away from it.

The bot is interested now. Click click click. It steps after him. Robson is on his feet. The bot lunges forward. Gods it's fast. Click click snap.

The bot freezes, looks down. One of its delicate hoofs is trapped in the wider mesh of Robson's nest. Its head flicks side to side as it studies the trapped hoof. In a second it will work out what to do. That second is all Robson needs. Only a practitioner of sleight of hand has the speed and skill. Only a traceur, a city-runner who fell from the top of Queen of the South to the bottom has the daring.

Robson snatches up his thermal blanket and throws a loop under the body of the bot. As it turns he steps past it, ducking under the bladed arms. He throws the ends of the blanket over the rail, heaves. Unbalanced, the bot totters. Robson ducks low, puts shoulder where legs meet body and heaves. Levers do the rest. The bot topples as it works its foot free; legs and arms wave, unfold into an atrocity of blades. Its weight and speed carry it over the low rail. It falls, blades snapping at air, impacts a crosswalk five levels down and comes apart. Junk rains down on Tereshkova Prospekt far below.

Robson slams back into the security of his nest. The blanket is wrapped around him and the heat exchanger is blood warm but Robson shivers. He can't believe what he did, what he dared. Would the bot have hurt him? It might have left him alone, but he couldn't risk that. He did what he had to do. He got away with it. He might not have got away with it. He can't think about that. He is shaking now. He feel sick. That empanada must have been bad. Tilapia: poisonous stuff. Liquid. He needs liquid. He's crying. He shouldn't be crying. Robson hugs his blanket more closely around him and sucks at the box of guava juice.

Luna arranges more tiny lights around the bed. Guardian lights at the cardinal points become a defending circle which she filled in with smaller circles. Circles of circles around the medical bed. She has a new idea about wiggling lines radiating from the big circle. Like sun rays or something. Luna likes symmetry, so she begins by laying out six sun-ray wiggles, each sixty degrees apart. She does not have enough to complete her pattern; she hisses in frustration. She will have to forage more lights. The Sisterhouse is generous with biolights.

Now it is time to water them. Squatting, Luna waddles around the ring of biolights with her little jug. A drop and a drop. The green glow brightens.

The noise is Mãe-de-Santo Odunlade entering the room. She thinks she's as quiet and mysterious as a miracle but to Luna her heavy feet and heavy breath and the small mutters that she doesn't know she makes are as noisy as a tunnel digger.

'Luna, we do have to get in to tend him,' says Mãe-de-Santo Odunlade Abosede Adekola. She is a round, old Yoruba woman in the whites of the Sisterhood of the Lords of Now. She clicks and rattles with beads and charms and saints. She smells a bit.

'You can step over them,' Luna says defiantly. The Mãe-de-Santo lifts the hem of her robes and steps into the circles of protecting light. She does not disturb a single lamp. Her feet are bare. Luna has never seen the Holy Mother's feet before.

'We've contacted your mother,' Mãe-de-Santo Odunlade says.

'Maame!' Luna cries, standing up and knocking over her jug of water. She summons her familiar, though the Sisters don't approve of them in the Sisterhouse. 'Luna, get my Maame!'

'Oh, not so fast not so fast,' the Holy Mother says. 'The network is still coming and going. We have our own channels. Your mother knows you're here in João de Deus, and that you're well, and she sends her love and says as soon as she can she will come and bring you home.'

Luna's mouth is an 'o' of deflated excitement. Luna the familiar unravels in sprays of pixels.

'What about Lucasinho?' she asks.

'It will take time,' Mãe-de-Santo Odunlade says. 'He is very badly hurt. A very sick young man.'

She leans over the body on the bed. So many tubes going in and out of it. Tubes to his wrists, his arms, his side. A big tube in his throat. Luna can only look at that one for the glance it takes to make sure he still breathes. A small thin tube coming out of his pee-hole. That makes her squirm. Wires and needles. Bags and sensor arms. He's naked, uncovered, palms turned up like a Catholic saint. He's in a place deeper than sleep. *Medically induced coma*, the Sisters say. He doesn't move, he doesn't dream, he doesn't wake. He is a long way away, journeying through the borderlands of death.

If the Sisterhood hadn't such good medical facilities. If the Urbanistes hadn't been so curious. If she had been thirty seconds slower opening the lock to the Boa Vista refuge.

If if if-ity if.

Luna is still not sure that Mother Odunlade's smell might not in fact be her smell. Suit-stink gets deep into the skin like a tattoo.

Different parts of Lucasinho's body gently rise and fall as the bed inflates and deflates to prevent pressure sores. He breathes, but that's the machine. Stubble is growing on his face, his stomach and his groin. He has a fine line of dark hair from his belly-button to his balls.

'Will you shave him?' Luna asks. He is fascinating and horrible.

'We'll care for him to the very best of our ability,' Mother Odunlade says.

'Do you think maame could come and we could all stay here with you?'

'Your maame is a very important and busy woman, my love. She has a lot to do.'

'I want him to wake up.'

'We all want him to wake up.'

The Sisters have said that it could be days before Lucasinho wakes up, or it could be weeks. It could be years. That's a thing from Madrinha Elis's berçário stories. The cute prince cursed to sleep forever in a deep secret cave. A kiss usually wakes them. She tries that every day, when the Sisters are all gone. Some day it will work.

Mãe-de-Santo Odunlade's lips move silently as she reads the screens around Lucasinho's head. Sometimes a word slips out and Luna realises that they are not numbers but prayers.

'Oh! I almost forgot,' says Mãe-de-Santo Odunlade and rummages inside her white gowns, a thing Luna's quite sure she should not see. She produces a wooden box, a big, flat wooden box, carved with flower patterns so fine and detailed they strain even Luna's eyesight.

'What is it?' Luna is ever-open to the possibility of presents.

'Open it.'

The box is lined with silky, shiny fabric. Luna loves the feel of it under her fingers. The Sisterhouse does not have a very good printer, but it is enough to print out lovely frocks. *Goodbye!* she shouted at the hated hated hated suit liner as she stuffed it into the deprinter. She never wants to wear anything clingy ever again.

Then she notices the knives. Two, nuzzled against each other like twins. Dark and hard and gleaming. Edges so sharp they cut the sight that beholds them. Luna touches fingertip to blade. It is as smooth and silky as the lining in which the knives rest.

'They are made of lunar steel,' Mother Odunlade says. 'Forged from billion-year-old meteoric iron mined deep beneath Langrenus crater.'

'They feel beautiful and scary at the same time,' Luna says.

'These are the battle knives of the Cortas. They belonged to your uncle Carlinhos. With these he killed Hadley Mackenzie in the Court of Clavius. With these Denny Mackenzie killed Carlinhos when João de Deus fell. They passed into our safekeeping. We aren't comfortable having them in this special place – there is too much blood on them – but for the love and respect we bear for your grandmother, we have protected them. Until a Corta comes who is bold, greathearted, without avarice or cowardice, who will fight for the family and defend it bravely. A Corta who is worthy of these blades.'

'Lucasinho should have them,' Luna declares.

'No, my love,' Mãe-de-Santo Odunlade says. 'These are for you.'

11: SCORPIO 2105

The scrunched-up ball of panty-hose hits Marina on the cheek.

'Field some fucking calls for me!' Ariel shouts.

The apartment is a crisis suite. Ariel is in her room, Abena in the kitchen area, talking talking talking on their familiars. Marina sits in the living area, looking out through the open door at the sun running on Orion Quadra. Head full of nothing but the words *tell her tell her tell her.*

'Abena's doing that.'

'Abena's talking to her aunt. I've got Sun Zhiyuan on hold.'

'What can I do?'

Tell her tell her tell her.

'Tell him a joke. Enquire about his grandmother's health. Ask him to explain quantum computing. That should fill half an hour.'

She couldn't do it when the Eagle deposed the LDC. She couldn't do it when the trains were shut down and the sky was closed. She couldn't do it when Twé was buried in regolith and besieged in the dark. She couldn't do it when an Asamoah-Mackenzie combat team was annihilated at Flammarion. She couldn't do it when there was a big space gun aimed at Meridian. The time was too full of history. The time was never right.

'Well, what are you doing?'

'I am trying to talk to Jonathon Kayode.'

'Haven't you got a private channel with him?'

'And he is not answering it, genius. Just field this call for me, Marina. Gods, I wish I still drank.'

Hetty takes the call.

'Zhiyuan géxià? Good evening. I am Marina Calzaghe, Ariel Corta's personal assistant. I understand you've been unable to contact the Eagle of the Moon's office for guidance on the current regime change. Ariel is trying to establish contact with the Eagle...'

And now regime has changed, the cities of the moon are occupied and the Soft War is over. The trains are running, the Moonloop is lifting cargo and passengers to orbit and VTO has confirmed her booking and scheduled her departure. Her ascent is scheduled and the time is still too full of history. The time is still not right to tell Ariel she is leaving her.

Adrian.

He's been waiting five years for this voice in the night. Adrian Mackenzie is awake, out of bed.

They're here.

Jonathon snores. He is a monster to waken. He must wake. Adrian shakes him ungently.

'Jon.'

He gulps air, big mouth-breathing Earthman. He has to wake.

They have accessed the lobby. Eyrie security is sealing the doors.

Adrian's second shake is timed with an alarm from Jonathon's own Eagle familiar. He wakes.

'What time is it?'

'We're under attack. Get dressed.'

Calliope opens camera windows on Adrian's lens. Three groups. One at the front, one coming through the vehicle exit, one descending from the upper terrace. They know where to go, what to hit and how to hit it. Shaped charges blow doors like paper in a depressurisation. The Eagle of the Moon freezes at the distant, flat cracks.

'My security...'

'They are your security.' That's how they know about the upper terrace exit. It had been Adrian's planned escape route. He has a Plan B.

Jonathon Kayode is pulling on shoes, shorts, trying to find a way into a shirt.

'Leave it!' Adrian shouts. 'Use the garden service ladder. They don't have anything coming up from below.' Now he relays long-rehearsed words to Calliope. Panels slide out of the walls. Racked inside, bathed in brilliant white light, body armour. Jonathon Kayode boggles.

'What?'

'You don't know everything about this place.' The chest and back plates are tight. He's grown fat. Fat and slack. No time for the greaves, the vambraces. He places the helmet on his head. 'Calliope has called a moto to the Level Fifty service door. It will take you to Mackenzie Metals' Meridian office. Jackaroos will meet you and protect you. Go!'

Last of all, Adrian Mackenzie draws the crossed knives from their magnetic field. Adrian lets the light catch their tungsten inlay, the intricate damasking of the blades. They are sublime. He snaps them into the sheaths at his waist.

'Go!'

Calliope shows Adrian three groups of armed and armoured men converging on the bedroom. They've hacked the Eyrie's security.

'I'll buy you as much time as I can.'

'Adrian...'

'No Mackenzie ever ran from a fight, Jon.'

A kiss, brief as a rain shower. Adrian Mackenzie flicks down his helmet visor.

At the wedding, in the midst of the celebrations, his father had taken him apart on to a high balcony overlooking Antares Hub. *For you.* Adrian opened the box. Inside, resting on pillows of titanium wool, were matched knives. Adrian grew up among blades, he knew knives, and these were unlike any he had ever seen before. Unlike any ever made in the history of Mackenzie Metals. *Try one,* Duncan Mackenzie said. The blade sat in Adrian's hand like a thing extruded from his bones. So well balanced, so secure. He cut and feinted, slashed. The dancing blade made a keening hum. *That's air bleeding,* Duncan said. *I couldn't be happier for you, son, but the day will come when you need a knife. Keep these for that day.*

Feet. Voices. The door blasts in.

Adrian Mackenzie's blades sing from their sheaths.

The Eagle of the Moon is a big man, an out-of-condition man, a man whose Jo Moonbeam muscle has slackened to flab. The blades catch him, wheezing, at the top rung of the ladder down to Level Fifty, in shorts and bedroom slippers. They haul him up, squealing and shrieking. Hands seize him, hands lift him. A slipper is kicked off, then the other. Hands transport him. Hands tear at him. Now he is naked, gibbering in fear. Hands, more hands. The blades carry him down between the precisely pruned bergamots. The Eagle of the Moon sees where he is being taken and thrashes, screaming. The hands hold him sure and steady. They carry him to the little pavilion that overlooks Antares Hub. The five prospekts of Antares Quadra are vaults of lights.

In perfect synchrony, the blades raise Jonathon Kayode and throw him far out into the twinkling air.

Atmospheric pressure in a lunar habitat is 1060 kilopascals.

He tumbles as he falls. This Eagle cannot fly and doesn't know how to fall.

Acceleration under gravity on the surface of moon is 1.625 metres per second squared.

He screams as he falls, arms and legs flailing as if he could climb empty air like a rope, until he hits the rail of the Thirty-third level bridge. An arm shatters, flaps at an unnatural angle. No more screaming.

Terminal velocity for a falling object in atmosphere is sixty kilometres per hour.

It will take the Eagle of the Moon a minute to fall from his Eyrie to the park at the centre of Antares Hub.

There is a physical property called kinetic energy. Its formula is $\frac{1}{2}mv^2$. Call it *impact. Impactability.* A large thing, moving slowly, can have low impact, low kinetic energy. A small thing, at high velocity, has high kinetic energy. Like an ice slug fired from a space-based mass-driver that can punch a hole through the rock cap of a lunar habitat.

And the other way around.

A thirteen-year-old boy, for instance, wire thin, falling from a kilometre, has a low kinetic energy.

A fifty-year-old man, big, overweight and out of condition, has a higher kinetic energy.

A minute is time enough to calculate that a thirteen-year-old boy, wire thin, might survive impacting Antares Hub at sixty kilometres per hour. And that a fifty-year-old man, big, overweight and out of condition, will not.

Hetty wakes her.

Marina, it's leaving day.

She set an alarm. As if she could forget to wake. As if she could sleep on the night she leaves the moon.

Of her few possessions, Marina hesitates over the Long Run tassels; the green bands and cords of São Jorge. They are a few grams, she has a mass allowance of a handful of kilograms. She sets them on the bed. They haunt the corner of her eye as she dresses, quickly, quietly, for this is a crowded house. They are small accusations: all leavings should be clean.

Clean, but not sterile.

Marina has dithered for days over what note she should leave. There must be a note: no question. It must be immediate and personal and there must be no possibility of Ariel stopping her.

A note, written by hand, left where no one can overlook it. Direct, personalised: a parting gift.

Abena grunts and opens her eyes as Marina takes the sheet of paper from the printer. She has been a permanent resident since the occupation.

'What you doing?'

'Long Run,' Marina lies. It's the only story that will infallibly excuse her leaving the apartment at four in the morning. Now she will have to dress for her alibi. Marina will depart the moon in running shoes, bra top and stupidly short shorts.

'Have fun,' Abena grunts and rolls over in her hammock. Ariel snores in her room. Marina crouches on her bed, knees pulled up, trying to write. The letters are painful and ill-formed. The words are excruciating. She goes to the refrigerator in hope of a steadying gin. Idiot. There hasn't been any gin, any vodka, any spirit since the fall of the moon. But she leaves the note sticking out of the door.

Last of all Marina ties the green bands around her wrists, her biceps, her knees and thighs. The decision about the tassels has been made for her. Abena wakes again as Marina opens the apartment door.

'Are you not cold in that?'

There are goose bumps on Marina's pale skin but not from the cold.

'Get some sleep. You've got a world to save in the morning.'

Stealthy dressing, hushed note-leaving, the silent sneaking and muffled closing of the door.

Marina, you have two hours to departure.

Marina stifles a choke as she walks to the 25th Street ladeira. The street is almost empty, the few faces who nod in greeting – she nods back – share the communal pleasurable guilt of those about their business before the light. A woman practises yoga in front of her

342

apartment; two men lean on the rail, talking quietly; a gaggle of kids reel home from a club or party: in the exchanged nod do they sense a special purpose, a particular emotional charge to her? A dim indigo light at the end of the quadra touches the walls and balconies. The sunline powers up for another day.

A bot and two VTO guards in heavy-metal armour wait at the top of the ladeira. Marina's heart clutches tight: afraid that if she makes eye contact they will recognise her, afraid that if she doesn't they will pull her in for suspicious behaviour. *You're Marina Calzaghe, you work for Ariel Corta. We need to ask you some questions. You're Marina Calzaghe, you abandoned Ariel Corta. Where do you think you're going?*

She turns a glance, a flick of the head. The VTO guards aren't even looking and one of the teens, out of his head, studies the bot with a kid's intensity, daring himself to get as close as possible to the barely sheathed blades.

A war was fought, a war was won and lost and nothing has changed. Kids get stoned and make out. Guys chat, women practise yoga. Long Runners head to their meet-points. A woman walks a ferret on a harness. The chib in Marina's right eye records the prices of the Four Elementals and the state of her account. A change of management, that's all. But that makes the deaths meaningless. The fighters who went down beneath the blades that the kid now touches weren't fighting for shareholder value. They weren't fighting out of personal loyalty to rich, remote Dragons. No one could fight for such things. They fought for their world, their life, their culture, their right not to be told what to do by aliens.

Marina rides the ladeira down. There are guards on every level. She makes a little recreational mental calculation: number of levels times number of ladeira on each side of the prospekt times number of quadras. That's a lot of bots and even more Vorontsovs.

On the 3rd Street ladeira a woman glances over from the up escalator. A young woman, in running gear, small and revealing: yellow braids banding her biceps, yellow bangles at her wrists; a green cord around her left knee, brilliant against her dark skin. A Long Runner. She nods to Marina: Sisters of the Run. Doubt fells Marina. She turns, almost runs back up the down escalator to follow her. Her heart will burst, surely burst. She wants to go with this runner. She wants to go back, to the apartment, to Ariel. She wants it more than anything.

The escalators carry them away from each other and tear the moment apart.

Down in Orion Hub she finds a bench under the canopy of the tall trees. Shadows deepen. She draws them round her. Only lovers and her in the park this morning. The indigo lightens to deep blue, turning the grove to a palisade of tree-trunks. Marina sits until the wrenching sobs in her breast ebb into something bearable, something that will pass, something that will allow her to look at a face without breaking down.

It was not Ariel but her brother, Rafa, who said that the only beautiful thing on the moon was the people. Beautiful and terrible. Like passionate, volatile, weak Rafa. Like vain, committed, lonely Ariel. Like beautiful, doomed, raging Carlinhos. Like dark, intense, loyal Lucas. *You work for us now,* he said. If she hadn't accepted the offer, if he hadn't offered it. If she had been an instant slower in intercepting the drone-fly. If she hadn't taken the wait-staff job at Lucasinho Corta's Moonrun party.

She would still be under this tree, taking this walk, riding the Moonloop elevator home.

This is a terrible world.

High in Meridian Hub, where the main boulevards of the three quadras meet in a vault three kilometres high, early fliers swoop and turn, wrapping helices of air around each other. Their wings flash as they catch the ten thousand lights of dawn. They spread nano-carbon feathers and catch the rising air, spiralling up until they are flecks of dazzle lost in deep blue.

She never got to fly. At the party before she went to flight training, she stood on the bar and promised everyone that was the one thing she would do. *They fly there.* She never got to fly on the moon; she never got to snowboard that semester when her friends went up to Snoqualmie while she finished the paper. The Girl Who Missed the Snow. The Girl Who Never Flew.

The Moonloop station is in the south-west buttress of Meridian Hub. It is discreet and unflashy but it is the pillar around which Meridian stands. The elevator was here, at the moon's closest point to the Earth, long before the first shafts were sunk far beneath the Sinus Medii. Marina passed through these doors only two years ago and nothing about them is familiar. A new world, new gravity, new ways of moving feeling breathing, the new chib in her eye charging her for every breath she takes.

The station never closes. The Moonloop never stops turning, wheeling around the world. The staff have been expecting her. There is a final medical test, some paperwork. Not very much. In a small white room, on a tall white chair, Marina is asked to stare at a black spot on the wall. A flash, a moment of blindness, blinking purple afterimages that seem to buzz on her retina and when she can see again the little numbers in the bottom right corner of her eye are gone.

Marina is off-chib.

She breathes non-regulated air.

She takes a deep lungful and almost falls off the stool, overdosed on oxygen. The woman in white who takes her from the small white room smiles.

'Everyone does that.'

After the shock, the doubt. What if she's wrong? What if something hasn't been explained? What if she has no right to the oxygen in her bloodstream? Marina begins to shallow breathe, sipping air, holding it like a precious child.

'Everyone does that too,' the woman says as she shows her into the departure lounge. 'Breathe easy.' The old lunar blessing. 'Your ticket covers everything from now until you step out of the OTV.'

That's the part she hasn't thought through. She's worked through the departure, over and over, in every detail and permutation, every motion and timing. She cannot imagine the arrival. It will be raining. That's all. She can't see past the curtains of warm grey rain to the planet beyond.

Five passengers wait in the lounge. There is tea, there is alcohol, but no one drinks anything but water. The sushi stands unconsidered on the cool plate, gathering bacteria.

As she expected, Amado, Hatem and Aurelia from the repatriation class are there. No words now, nothing more than a nod. No one casts a second glance at her running gear. No one dares eye contact. Everyone sits as far apart as possible. *And everyone does that,* Marina supposes the staffer would say. Marina has Hetty flick through her music but everything is either too trivial for the occasion or something she doesn't want tainted by attachment to an event as final as this.

'One more to come,' the staffer advises before closing the lounge door.

'Excuse me,' Marina asks. 'Have I time?' She nods to the bathroom. She could be worlds away before she gets to piss in comfort again.

Like a yawn, her piss-need communicates wordlessly and infallibly. Behind her the line is out the door.

Now comes the last ascender. It's not who Marina was expecting. Oksana had been the last in the current group in Marina's cohort. She is a short, narrow-eyed, frowning Ukrainian. This is a tall Nigerian man. Oksana must have changed her mind. Made her peace after the last group meeting. Re-opened her door and gone back into her house. Looped around the Vorontsov guards at the bottom of a ladeira section and headed back up. Turned her heel at the Moonloop station door. Chosen the moon. And Marina is swallowed in hideous doubt. Even now she could do it. Get up from this white couch, walk out of the door and go back.

To Ariel.

She can't move. Between leave and remain, she is paralysed.

Then a door opens at the other end of the lounge, another receptionist says, 'We're ready to board,' and Marina finds herself standing with the others and walking with the others out of the door through the pressure lock into the Moonloop capsule. She takes one of the seats that circle the central core. The restraints fold down around her and take away all doubt. The hatch seals. The countdown is perfunctory. Capsules like these arrive and depart hundreds of times each day. Yet she is afraid, in her sports top and running shorts and ribbons. Departs as she arrived: afraid.

The first stage of the ascent is a thrill-ride straight up the interior of Meridian Hub. In seconds she is half a kilometre high. The Moonloop capsule is a pressure body, built without windows, but external cameras feed images to Hetty. Marina sees Meridian Hub as a huge empty shaft, filled with the lights of ten thousand windows, lilac now in the dawn. Now she is above even the ascending fliers – there they are, sliding off the top of the thermal and circling down through the dusty gloaming.

She is leaving the moon in the morning, in the swelling light.

She glimpses the vents and fans, the power conduits and heat exchangers of the high city, then the camera cuts off as the capsule enters the airlock. The capsule jolts, she feels machinery move, locks seal, hears the shriek of depressurisation dwindle to a whisper to silence. Above her is the ascent tower. The Moonloop wheels around the moon, reaching down to snatch her from the top of the tower into space.

It will hurt, Preeda at the returnee group said. *It will hurt more than anything.*

'Ariel.'

All motos are strictly speed limited but when you are in the only one on the prospekt, in the lilac gloaming of Orion Quadra waking, speeding through the tall dark trees of Gargarin Park, you feel like you are travelling at the speed of love.

'Ariel, there's no point.'

Abena stirred again in her shallow hammock-sleep to the click of the closing door and the whir of the deprinter. Put them together. She saw the note trapped in the refrigerator door. Knew what had just happened. She read the note. Before she had finished it she was in Ariel's room.

'Marina's gone back to Earth.'

The moto was at the door by the time she had helped Ariel into the shift dress. *Do something with my face,* Ariel said in a voice of ice while Beijaflor tried to locate and call Hetty. Abena knelt on the seat and carefully applied two-tone eye shadow. The moto whirred unchallenged through each of the occupation force checkpoints.

I can't reach her, was all Ariel said. *I can't reach her.*

'I still can't reach her,' Ariel says.

'Ariel, listen to me.'

She left the note on the kitchen floor. Abena can still see every word, as if written by a white-hot needle on her retina.

I have to leave the moon. I have to go.

'Ariel, her capsule left fifteen minutes ago.'

The moto arrives in Meridian Hub and unfolds.

'Ariel, she's gone.'

Ariel snaps her head and Abena quails under the pale heat of her gaze. 'I know. I know. But I need to see it.'

The return capsule descends the wall of Meridian Hub, coming in from space. One dropped as one is picked up. Up and down, the endless carousel.

'I want you to go,' Ariel says.

'Ariel, I can help...'

'Shut up!' Ariel screams. 'Shut up you stupid, silly little bitch; shut up with all your fucking well-intentioned, cheerful, senseless, insensitive, ignorant, glib little homilies. I don't want your help, I don't want your charm, I don't want your therapy. I want you to go. Just go. Go.'

Sobbing, Abena reels from the cab. She runs to a stone bench by a wall of hibiscus. The lilac morning ebbs to gold, there are fliers tumbling through the shining air and it is hideous to Abena. Hateful woman. Vile woman. Ungrateful woman. But she can't help looking up through her hair, through the shivering sobs, to the helpless woman in the moto. The doors lie open around her like petals. Now her head is bowed forward. Now her head is thrown back. Abena tries to understand what she is seeing. She recalls how she felt when Lucasinho played around with other girls and boys. Anger, betrayal, a need to hurt as indiscriminately as she had been hurt. A desire to strike at the person who hurt her, and to see him struck. This is something else. This is a life tearing down the middle. This is total, eviscerating loss.

Her familiar whispers in her ear. *Ariel.*

'Abena. I'm sorry. I'm all right now.'

Abena does not know if she can face Ariel. She's seen a nakedness deeper than skin. She's seen vulnerability rip open a woman for whom composure is everything. Abena stands up, smoothes down her thrown-on clothes, breathes deep until the breaths no longer shudder.

'I'm coming.'

Then the motos and bikes pull in around Ariel's cab.

Armed and armoured figures step from the opening motos and slide from the bikes: Vorontsovs in umlaut-heavy stab-proof kevlar, mercenaries in whatever protection the printer delivers cheap, clumsy Terrestrial fighters in black battlesuits. They surround Ariel's moto.

Abena freezes.

Ariel needs her.

'Leave her alone!' she shouts.

One figure turns: a short woman, chestnut-skinned, in an incongruous Miuccia Prada dress and four-inch Sergio Rossi heels.

'You are?'

'I am Abena Maanu Asamoah,' Abena says.

Ariel's voice comes from the centre of the ring of armed males.

'Let her through,' Ariel says. 'She works with me.'

The woman in Prada nods and the fighters part.

'I'm sorry you had to see that,' Ariel whispers. 'You should not have seen that.'

Abena has a hundred responses but they are all well-intentioned, cheerful, senseless, insensitive, ignorant, glib. Banal, naive and jejune, Ariel had called her when they met at the Lunarian Society. All she has, Abena understands, all she has ever had are responses.

'We've come for Ariel Corta,' the woman in Miuccia Prada says. Abena can't place her accent but there is a baffling familiarity to her face, her eyes, her cheekbones. Network search returns nothing and the woman's familiar is a pewter sphere traced with damask filigree. *So why do I feel I've met you before?* 'The Eagle of the Moon requests a meeting,' the young woman says. Globo is not her first language.

'The Eagle's requests aren't usually delivered by armed idiots,' Ariel says and Abena wants to cheer.

'There has been a change of leadership,' the young woman says.

Now Ariel looks at the eyes, the cheekbones, the set of the mouth. Recognition – impossible recognition – dawns. And Abena realises where she has seen them before; on the face of the woman beside her.

'Who the hell are you?' Ariel asks in Portuguese. The young woman answers in the same tongue.

'I am Alexia Corta.'

The repair bots have been diligent, but Ariel's courtroom eye notices the smudges of smoke around the door frames, the dusty boot-prints on the polished sinter floors. Grains of broken glass glitter, caught where walls and floors meet. In a side room two bots diligently clean a large stain from the carpet.

Details are good. Details are disciplines. This is a court, she goes to a trial. Everything may be tried here, including her life.

The escort were ordered to remain in the vehicle dock. Alexia Corta's heels click with military rhythm on the hard floor. Ariel Corta reads the discipline and control in her every step. Jo Moonbeams overstep, overuse their over-powered legs. The new arrival fresh off the Moonloop bounding and soaring down Gargarin Prospekt is a joke sliding into stereotype. This young woman never puts a foot wrong. In Sergio Rossi heels too.

Another detail. A little bright coin tossed tinkling and twinkling into a pit.

Has Marina's capsule docked or is it still flying out, falling free, toward that far brilliant star? She could work it out with a few flight details from Beijaflor.

Ariel pulls her concentration back. Focus it here, focus it on useful information. Alexia Corta calls herself the Iron Hand, Adriana's old title. She models herself on Adriana. She has ambition and a high opinion of her ruthlessness.

'Please wait here,' Alexia Corta says to Abena.

'Do not offer to push me,' Ariel says.

'Of course, Senhora Corta.'

From the moment Alexia spoke her name, Ariel has known *who* she will find on the other side of the double doors, behind the stupidly ornate, pointless desk. *What* she finds erases all thoughts of Marina and pushes the present, pervading hurt down to persistent, dull and, in the end, bearable ache.

'You look like fucking death, Lucas.' Ariel speaks in Portuguese, the language of intimacy and rivalry, family and enemies.

He laughs. Ariel can't bear it. His laugh is the sound of precision mechanisms jammed by shattered glass.

'I have been dead. For seven minutes, I'm told. It was disappointing.

No looking down on things on top of the closet. No white light and spa-music. No ancestors calling me up the glowing tunnel.' He moves a bottle of gin to the centre of the big empty desk. 'My old bespoke recipe. The network never forgets.'

'I won't, thank you.'

She would love to. She would love more than anything to take the bottle away to a hidden place and drink it until everything went smooth and blurred and painless.

'Really?'

'Special occasions only.'

'A family reunited isn't a special occasion?'

'Don't let me stop you.'

'Alas, my medical team has put me in the same position as you regarding alcohol.'

This hollow, bleached, cracked shell is a puppet of her brother. His once beautiful skin is grey. Grey streaks his hair, his beard. His eyes are sunken, his skin patched with moles and liver spots from direct sunlight. His bones sag. Even under lunar gravity his muscles barely hold him upright behind the desk. Ariel notes the crutches leaning against the desk. It is as if, by some reverse relativity, thirty years have passed down in Earth's gravity.

'We can't go to Earth. Mother Earth will kill you. All that. I went, Ariel. She tried. I had a massive heart-attack on the transfer up. But she didn't kill me.'

Ariel catches Alexia's eye.

'Leave us.'

Lucas nods. 'Please, Alexia.'

Ariel waits for the door to close, though Alexia would be a fool if she were not monitoring every word spoken in the Eagle's Eyrie.

'And her?'

'She's clever, she's hungry, she's refreshingly ambitious. She may be the most ruthless person I have ever met. Including you, irmã. She ran a little business empire down there, producing and selling clean, reliable water to her community. They called her the Queen of Pipes. Yet when I offered her the moon, she came. She is the Iron Hand. She has the blood of Adriana Corta.'

'She will kill you, Lucas,' Ariel says. 'The instant your influence and position waver.'

'Family first, family always, Ariel. Lucasinho is at João de Deus. He's in a bad way. The Sisterhood of the Lords of Now are caring for him. I always thought my mother's attachment to them was a symptom of her decline, but they seem to be the focus of resistance to Bryce Mackenzie's occupation of my city. I'll deal with that in time. Lucasinho took Luna four hundred kilometres across the Mare Fecunditatis. Did you know that? He gave the last breath in his lungs to get his cousin to Boa Vista. On the Moonrun, he went back to help an Asamoah boy. He's brave and he's kind and I want him to be well and I want so much to see him again. Family first, family always.'

The rebuke is old but accurate and never fails to wound. It goes deep today, into already bruised flesh. Ariel has always chosen, will always choose, world over family. Like every facile truth, there is a deeper truth at the core of it, molten and spinning. The world chooses Ariel Corta. The world has always pushed itself on her; laid its insistent, needy hands all over her. Few people have character and talents enough to satisfy a world. It needs, she feeds it. It never stops asking, she never stops giving, thought it insulated her against anything or anyone else that might ask something of her.

'I won't be swept up into your happy little dynasty, Lucas.'

'You may not have a choice about that. How safe do you think any Corta will be when they learn who commands the Eagle's Eyrie?'

'I seem to have made a career out of saying "fuck you" to Eagles of the Moon,' Ariel says but she sees the traps Lucas lays around her.

'You were my predecessor's legal counsel,' Lucas says. 'I'd like you to continue in that position. See it as a change of management.'

'Your predecessor died at the bottom of Antares Hub.' Beijaflor filled in the political revolutions that unfolded while Marina Calzaghe left her. Defenestration. It makes Ariel shiver that there is such a term for such a murder; so precise, so perfumed and polite.

'I had nothing to do with that,' Lucas says. 'Jonathon wasn't a threat. He was finished, Ariel. He would have seen out his days with some sinecure lectureship at the University of Farside. I bore no ill-will to Jonathon Kayode.'

'Yet you sit at his desk, with his title and seals and authorisations, offering me your designer gin from his printer.'

'I didn't ask for this job.'

'You insult me, Lucas.'

He lifts his hands in supplication.

'The Lunar Mandate Authority needed someone who knew the moon.'

'This is not swapping one three-letter acronym for another. Board reshuffles don't come armed with orbital rail-guns.'

'Is it not?' Lucas leans forward and Ariel sees in his sunken eyes a light she had forgotten. It does not illuminate; it casts shadows. 'Really? You take the elevator up into the high levels and ask them if they know what the LDC did, if they can name even a single board member, if they even know who the Eagle of the Moon was. What they care about is the air in their lungs, the water on their tongues, the food in their bellies, who's fucking who on Gupshup and where their next contract is coming from. We're not a nation state, we're not a democracy robbed of the oxygen of freedom. We're a commercial entity. We're an industrial outpost. We turn a profit. All that's happened is a change of management. And the new management needs to get the money flowing again.'

'Representatives of the governments of Russia, India, Brazil, the USA, Korea, South Africa. The People's Republic of China sit in the LDC council chamber. You expect the Palace of Eternal Light to take orders from Beijing?'

'The Lunar Mandate Association is a multi-agency body. It includes corporate representatives from Earth and the moon.'

'VTO.'

'Yes.'

'What did you offer them, Lucas?'

'Security on Earth, empire in space and respect on the moon.'

'This is an invasion, Lucas.'

'Of course it is. But it's also sound business.'

'Did you destroy Crucible?'

'No,' Lucas says. Ariel does not reply. Her silence requires more from him. 'I did not destroy Crucible.'

'The command that hacked the mirrors was old Corta code. It had been in there, wrapped around the control systems for thirty years. Code just doesn't spontaneously activate. Someone had to wake it up. Someone had to send the instruction. Was that you, Lucas?'

'I did not give the command.'

'One hundred and eighty-eight deaths, Lucas.'

'I did not order the destruction of Crucible.'

'I'll have one of your gins now, Lucas.'

He pours unsteadily into a Martini glass, adds homoeopathic drops of vermouth, slides it across the Eagle's great desk. So many drinks Ariel has lifted, savoured, enjoyed purely and absolutely. Sharp, adult, personal sex in a glass. She leaves it untouched.

'You asked me to represent you, Lucas.'

'I did. You didn't give me an answer.'

And the gin is cold and beaded with moisture and is always dependable, always sure. Family or world. That had always been her dilemma. Lucas has cleaved through it with one stroke. Family and world. Accept his offer and have both. Ariel looks long at the glass standing on the desk of the Eagle of the Moon and it is easy. The simplest thing. It always was.

'I didn't, did I?' Ariel says. 'No. No, I won't. No.'

*

After an hour Lady Sun's patience breaks. She sighs and raises her stick in the direction of Alexia Corta.

'You.'

'Lady Sun.'

Lady Sun has studied carefully this young woman behind the small desk by the doors to the Eagle's office. Every muscle betrays her terrestrial birth. A Brazilian. Family. The legend is that Adriana found none of the Corta worthy of joining her on the moon. The girl has ambition, and discipline to reach it. She does not occupy her time with visible trivialities or distractions. She sits well, she has good stillness. So few younger people understand how to be still. Lady Sun summons her in part to break her infuriating self-possession, in part to see if she misses a move and sends herself soaring across the room. She moves well, if with obvious concentration.

'We have been kept waiting,' Lady Sun says. The board of Taiyang strike variations of boredom around the Eyrie's comfortable ante-chamber.

'The Eagle will see you when he is ready,' Alexia Corta says.

'We do not wait. We are not contractees.'

'The Eagle is very busy.'

'Not too busy to see Yevgeny Vorontsov.' The old drunken fool trooped in thirty minutes ago with his entourage of armoured dolts. Not even the decency to look embarrassed. Lady Sun had no doubt that his bodyguard was the junta of a younger, harder generation rumoured to be in control of VTO Moon. There was a consistent look. Muscled and disciplined. The design of their armour offends the eye. Garish and childish. Darius is a fan of the music from which they draw their iconography. Lady Sun finds a particular humiliation in being policed by figures from a boys' video game.

Policed. That such a notion should come to the moon.

'Senhor Vorontsov is a member of the LMA,' Alexia Corta says and on that the double doors open and Yevgeny Vorontsov, that great bear of a man, rolls out. The hard-faced young women and men in harder suits shoulder around him. They almost push him out of the room.

'The Eagle will see you now,' Alexia Corta announces. The Suns untangle themselves from long, bored waiting.

Alexia Corta steps in front of Lady Sun.

'You are not a board member, Senhora.'

Sun Zhiyuan freezes. The Sun delegation stops dead. Lady Sun enters first. That is the rule, the custom, the place of honour. Alexia Corta will not move.

'There has been an error,' Lady Sun says.

'You sit with the board of Taiyang, but you are not a board member.'

'You keep my grandmother waiting, then tell her she is not welcome,' Sun Zhiyuan says in a voice of low, intimate violence. 'Either my grandmother goes in, or none of us.'

Alexia Corta lifts two fingers to her ear, the gesture of a new arrival who has not yet learned the unconscious intimacies of familiars.

'The Eagle would be delighted to see Lady Sun,' she says. Wayfarer glasses hide her eyes and Lady Sun reads no embarrassment or education in the set of her facial muscles. This is a confident, arrogant young woman.

Sun Zhiyuan moves to allow Lady Sun to head the party.

'You are an insolent young woman,' Lady Sun hisses as she passes. She has never been so humiliated. Rage is a delight, a hot, feverish consuming sickness, a thing she never expected to feel so strongly at her age.

'And you are withered old scorpion who will die soon,' Alexia Corta whispers in Portuguese. The doors close behind Lady Sun and the board of Taiyang.

Jaime Hernandez-Mackenzie stops at the penthouse door, one hand on the door frame, gasping. His lungs rattle with a thousand stone needles. Old dust is killing him. Old jackaroos should not be woken before the dawn by a summons to a meeting.

Old jackaroos know an emergency when they hear one.

The only light comes from the window, where Bryce stands, a dark mass against the pointillist night-glow of Kondakova Prospekt. Jaime blinks in the gloom. His familiar tells him who is here and shows their locations.

'The Suns called in the loan,' says Alfonso Pereztrejo, Head of Finance.

'Fuck,' Jaime Hernandez-Mackenzie says reverently.

'The repayment plan is generous, but they want it back,' Rowan Solveig-Mackenzie says. 'Fecunditatis and Crisium are still only at forty per cent output and we have no reserves.'

'Lucas Corta has requested a meeting,' Alfonso Pereztrejo says.

'I will not kiss the fucking ring,' Bryce says, turning from the window. 'I will not surrender this to Lucas Corta.'

'VTO can embargo us,' Rowan says.

'Then Earth goes dark,' Bryce says. 'I know what he's doing. He'll let Duncan drive us into the wilderness while we keep the lights burning. A territory here, a territory there: the new board, LMA or whatever they call themselves, all they care about is that the helium ships.'

'It seems to me we need an agreement with the Lunar Mandate Authority,' Jaime wheezes.

'Lucas Corta is the gatekeeper,' Rowan says.

'I know what Lucas Corta wants,' Bryce spits. 'He wants his city back. I will depressurise his fucking city and every soul in it before I let him take it.'

'I've a less bloodthirsty option,' Jaime says. 'You've heard of the Sisterhood of the Lords of Now?'

'I've heard of it,' Bryce says. 'Some drum-banging rabble-rousing Brazilian cult.'

'People respect them,' Jaime says. 'And you might, a little more, when I tell you that I've heard that they are sheltering Lucasinho and Luna Corta.'

Bryce Mackenzie's back straightens, swells visibly against the street shine.

'Are they now?'

He travels alone, in a chartered railcar to the citadel of his enemy. On his arrival he is guided to its heart as only the correct doors open to him.

Lucas Corta's crutches click along the polished stone of Hadley.

Inevitable that Duncan would build a garden. Robert Mackenzie's Fern Gully had been a wonder of the moon. Robert Mackenzie created in fern and frond, wing and water. Duncan Mackenzie builds in stone and sand, wind and whisper. The environment is a hundred metres across, the ceiling agoraphobically high for tight-pressing Hadley. Lucas had felt the weight of its rock on his shoulders and now he is released. The air is dry and very pure and carries a sting of fine sand. A flagstone path meanders between gardens of raked sand. Shafts of light fall from high windows on to austere geometries of stone and sand.

Click, tap.

Duncan Mackenzie waits in the stone circle, Esperance shimmering over his shoulder. The upright rocks represent every type found on the moon and many from beyond. There are menhirs from the birth of the solar system; pieces of Earth and Mars blasted loose in titanic asteroid strikes and launched across space; the metal cores of meteor impacts buried a billion years ago.

Lucas does not fail to notice that every rock is shorter than Duncan Mackenzie.

'I could have gutted you a dozen times over,' Duncan Mackenzie says.

Lucas leans into his crutches.

'You'd be a hole in the regolith.'

'Mass drivers make good neighbours.'

'I have no quarrel with you, Duncan.'

'I was in Crucible. I ran with the rest of them when the mirrors turned on us. I heard the hands hammering on the escape-pod doors. I saw people burn, and I laid my father's familiar in the tabernacle in Kingscourt.'

'The history of violence is no help to us here,' Lucas says. 'Bryce has João de Deus. That's mine. You can have his helium business.'

'I want nothing from you.'

'I'm not gifting it to you. You continue your range-war with Bryce and the LMA will turn a blind eye.'

'And when I take back the fusion business, you take it from me. Corta Hélio reborn.'

'There's nothing I can say to convince you that I have no interest in helium. But I do want João de Deus.'

'Mackenzie Metals has no strategic interest in João de Deus.'

Lucas Corta contains a smile. He has the deal.

'We understand each other. I'll take up no more of your time.'

Halfway down the serpentine flagstone path, Lucas turns on his crutches.

'I forgot to say. In case you decide on a reconciliation with your brother, as you pointed out, I still have a mass driver.'

'The Vorontsovs have a mass-driver,' Duncan Mackenzie calls.

Duncan Mackenzie watches Lucas Corta click his way between the spirals and circles of combed sand.

Fucking Corta. Fucking Corta.

You have a big gun, but you've forgotten that the way to be safe from a big gun is to put something between it and you.

He waits until the doors have closed before calling Denny Mackenzie.

'Bring me Robson Corta.'

Fucking Corta.

*

Above eighty-five the elevators and ladeiras do not go. By staircase and steps, ladders and rungs, Wagner Corta climbs to the top of the city. Up into Bairro Alto, its overhang and ledges, its crawlspaces and wire-walks, its dispossessed and contract-less; up and out into the places where air soughs from vents, sighs around pipe runs and comms dishes and the narrow mesh catwalks beneath him tremble to the pulse of machinery so that, if that beat ever changes, Wagner grabs the handrail and forces himself to look straight ahead. To glance down through the grid is to court vertigo. The drop is two kilometres sheer to Tereshkova Prospekt.

Above one hundred even the handrails give out. Wagner edges along weld seams, around cold-dewed water tanks. He sits for five minutes, back to the warm flank of a heat-exchange stack, trying to summon the nerve to step over a three-metre gap between two humidity control units. In the end he grabs two fistfuls of sagging cable and swings himself to the farther ledge. Death by electrocution is quicker than death by falling. Yet here are signs of human habitation: water bottles, protein and carb bar wrappers, blown into crevices and crannies by the perpetual artificial winds of highest Meridian. Not even the Zabbaleen, legendary in their zeal to recycle every molecule of carbon, dare climb this high. Only the sunline is higher, and Wagner feels it as a constant, blinding oppression. The roof of the world burns. Yet fluorescent symbols, the ideograms of the free runners, point to still higher paths.

He has crossed seas and highlands, he has battled monsters and horrors, witnessed courage and despair, approached energies that could punch a hole through a city and empty it to vacuum. He has suffered exhaustion and starvation, dehydration and hypothermia, robots and radiation. This final half-kilometre of his journey to find Robson and bring him to safety is worse than all of those. Set a thousand kilometres of glass before him, drop him in the slashing riot of a robot war, bombard him with hyper-accelerated ice slugs: he will fight a way through them. Put a three-metre gap before him and two kilometres of howling air beneath him and he is paralysed. Wagner is afraid of heights.

Heart hammering, breath a succession of shallow sips, he pushes himself as deeply as he can into the crevice between two gas-exchange silos. The air is appreciably thinner at the top of the world. Wagner breathes deep, supercharging his body with oxygen.

'Robson Corta!'

Wagner calls three times, then collapses, panting. His head throbs. If only the fucking kid had his familiar switched on. But that's Rule One of disappearing; disconnect from the network. Wagner had only tracked Robson to the roof of Antares Quadra by sophisticated pattern recognition and passive trace analyses.

'Robson! It's me. Wagner.' He recharges his lungs and adds, 'I'm on my own Robson. Just me. I swear.'

His voice echoes around the titanic metal-scapes of high Antares. Wagner has always had a horror of loud voices, yelling, making noise. Drawing unwanted attention to himself. Loud people. He is the wolf that never howls.

He is the wolf that is shit-scared, hiding from the abyss in a steel cranny.

'Robson!' Again his voice rings out three times among the reverberating metal planes. He hates hearing himself.

'Wagner.'

The voice is so close that Wagner twitches in shock. He pushes himself back from the drop into his alcove.

Wagner's heart tightens in terror. Robson stands on a ten-centimetre flange, no handholds, no grips. The toes of his climbing shoes curl over the lip. Beneath them is two kilometres of clear air. Between Wagner and Robson is a five-metre gap. For all that Wagner can cross it it might be the void between moon and Earth.

'Are you all right?'

The boy is a mess. His shorts are stained and holed. One sleeve has been torn from his over-sized T-shirt and hangs free. His hair is a matted shock, half-way to dreads, his skin is filthy and mottled with bruises and healing abrasions. He was never a solid kid but he is famine thin. Wagner sees collar-bones at the wide neck of the T-shirt. His eyes are brilliant and feral.

'Are you?'

'Yes. No. Robson, I need to tell you, it's all right.'

'I fought a bot,' Robson says. 'I think it was just checking but it had blades. I flipped it. It didn't see what I was doing. It was like a trick. It hit the hundred and fifteen catwalk down there and came apart. Bits scattered from twentieth to fortieth. There was a debris warning so no one got hurt.'

'Robson, I've come to take you home.'

'I'm not going back there.'

'I know. Amal said. Né does love you, it's just, well, our love is different. Né got hurt bad, Robson. Né was trying to protect you.'

'Is Né all right?'

'Né'll recover.' A ruptured spleen, severe abdominal trauma. *They had an Iron Fist*, né told Wagner when he visited ner in the med centre. 'Né was trying to protect you.'

'I know. But I can't be like you, Wagner.'

'I know that now. We won't go back to the Packhouse. I promise.'

'What will you do?'

'I will be with you.'

'You need the pack. You're not you without them.'

Up on the catwalk, wedged into a crevice barely wide enough for his bony ass, knees pulled up and arms wrapped around them so they block out as much of the fearful awesome vista before him as he can, Wagner Corta's heart tears a little.

'I will have you.'

Robson says, 'You were out there, weren't you?'

'I saw things I couldn't believe. I saw things no one has ever seen before, I saw things no one ever should. I saw things I will never tell.'

Again, a long silence.

'Robson, I have to tell you, all those things I saw, I was scared, but not like I am now. I'm terrified, Robson. I can't be here. I feel like I'm dying, I don't know if I can move. Will you help me down?'

Wagner sees no physical effort, no tensing of muscles or preparation, but Robson soars over the void, reaches up a hand and catches a stanchion. He swings across the face of the gas-exchange silo, flies across the gap in which Wagner huddles, grabs a second stanchion and tumbles to land sure and poised on the access gantry.

Wagner crawled on his hands and knees across that gantry. Robson extends a hand.

'Take it. Don't look at anything but my eyes.'

Wagner inches forward. His leg muscles are numb, his ankles untrustworthy.

'Take my hand.'

He reaches out. For an instant he is falling forward and the gulf opens before him. Then Robson's hand has his and Wagner realises he has never touched this hand, embraced this body. There is strength here, softness and warmth. Stubborn resistance. Wagner staggers to his feet.

'Look at me.'

And he is around the second gas-exchanger, on to the access way.

'You all right?'

'I might hurl.'

'Don't do it over empty air.'

Wagner leans on the railing, panting, pale and sweating. Three times he feels nausea push up inside him, then he stands, panting.

'Let's go. First stop, a banya. You reek, irmão.'

Robson's smile could still stop worlds in their orbits.

'You're not too fresh yourself, Lobinho.'

Wagner lies a long time in the dim warmth of the hot room. Smooth stone beneath his back, a pleasing prickle of perspiration, beading and running, drawing deep fatigue from his muscles. Stars above him, inlaid in unmoving constellations on the dome. A full Earth in blue and white mosaic.

It's waxing. He can feel it, even deep in the caverns of the moon. He knows it's the medication, it always has been the medication, and his own physiological and psychological rhythms, but he senses without seeing that a blue crescent Earth stands over Meridian. He feels it tugging him to the unity of the pack. He can't go. He has a child. Lying on the slab folded in warmth, Wagner is seized by panic. Not just this Earthrise, but every Earthrise, he will be separated from the pack. He doesn't know how he can bear it. He will bear it. He must. He has a child.

Sombra chimes.

Hey, I'm out.

Robson perches on a stool at the banya's tea-bar. He's printed up an off-the-shoulder grey marl top, belly-cut, cuffs rolled up and three-stripe track pants. His hair is a glorious auburn puff ball.

'Smell better?' Robson says. He shines.

'Eucalyptus, menthol. Juniper. Bergamot, some sandalwood.' A final sniff. 'And a trace of frankincense.'

'How do you know that?'

'I know a lot of things in the dark.'

'I want to show you a trick,' Robson declares and takes his half-deck of cards from the pocket of his track pants. He picks a card and flicks it at Wagner. Presto: the card is gone.

'He holds it inside his hand,' a voice says. 'Between his thumb and palm. You can't see it from where you're sitting. I can.'

Magic is the art of misdirection. The hand diverts the attention *here*, and so it does not see the card being worked. Or Mackenzie Metals' First Blade arrive.

Denny Mackenzie leans on the tea-bar. He sees Wagner check the lobby for blades.

'I'm alone. Nicely done, finding the boy.'

'My name is Robson,' Robson flares. 'Not the boy, not Robbo. Robson.'

'Yes it is,' Denny Mackenzie says. 'Apologies for that. And you...' – this to the chai-seller – 'don't. I can take every one of your security, but there will be no trouble here.'

'What do you want?' Wagner asks.

'I heard you came all the way from Twé. We lost a lot of jackaroos there.'

'I did. What do you want?'

'I wanted to be at Twé, but I'm First Blade and that keeps me cooped up in Hadley. Barring occasions when Duncan needs me to run an errand for him. He wants Robson.'

Wagner steps between Robson and Denny Mackenzie.

'Wagner, this is commendable but you're really not a fighter,' Denny says. 'Duncan wants a nice warm body to put between him and your brother. Your mouth's open, Wagner. You're staring. You really didn't know? Where were you? Oh yes, of course. Your brother is Eagle of the Moon. Lucas Corta.'

'Lucas is...' Wagner begins.

'I think you'll find he very much is not dead, Wagner. Duncan wants a hostage. What Lucas wants is Bryce's head. Duncan is too much Mackenzie to realise that Lucas is not his enemy. He would be a fool to antagonise the Eagle of the Moon and whatever the LDC calls itself now. I'm no politician but even I can see that. There's a way out of this, Wagner Corta.'

'You owe me, Denny Mackenzie, and I make my third and final claim.'

'And I shall honour that claim, Wagner Corta.' Denny Mackenzie pulls his knife from the sheath inside his Armani jacket and kisses the blade. 'The debt is paid in full.' He re-sheathes the knife. 'Go somewhere far from here, Wagner Corta. Go right away.'

'Thank you,' Wagner says. He holds out a hand.

'I'm not shaking a fucking Corta hand,' Denny Mackenzie says.

From the door he calls, 'Robson. If you can trick with a card, you can trick with a blade. Bear it in mind.'

'Tio Lucas is the Eagle of the Moon?' Robson asks.

'I don't understand,' Wagner says. 'But I will.' *Go somewhere far from here,* Denny Mackenzie had said. Far from the blades of Duncan Mackenzie, far from the machinations of Lucas Corta. Far from the love and warmth and fellowship of the pack. Somewhere far, where another kind of love waits. 'Come on, Littlest Wolf.'

Denny thinks the sand garden a ridiculous affectation. The sort of thing that the Suns would waste resources on and then think themselves civilised and superior. Soft and sickly. The old Fern Gully made his skin crawl. Damp and green and living things. His skin felt infested every time he entered it. It had been Jade Sun's idea. That was when old Bob began to lose it. Mackenzies dig, Mackenzies smelt. Our work is our garden.

'I asked you to bring me a thirteen-year-old boy,' Duncan says.

'I repaid a debt.'

'We needed something over Lucas Corta.'

'I repaid a debt.'

'To a fucking Corta.'

'I repaid a debt.'

'You failed your fucking family.'

Denny Mackenzie holds up his left hand. The smallest finger is missing. The amputation was short and sharp but bearable. His seconds moved quickly to sterilise and cauterise the wound. He forswore analgesia. The pain is bearable. The chief irritation is the loss of sensation where nerves have been severed.

'You think that's enough?' Duncan says. 'Some stupid debt of honour and everything is all right? All privileges and accesses are revoked. Rights and permissions are nullified. You're cut off. You are no longer a Mackenzie. You have no name. You have no home. You have no father.'

The corner of Denny Mackenzie's mouth twitches.

'So be it.'

His heels sound on the flagstones as he walks away. He could trudge through the meticulous circles and waves of sculpted sand. Zen shit. That would be petty. He abides by the path. The golden figures on his chib fade to green. He breathes, for now. All he needs is breath enough to take him away from Hadley.

The jackaroos line the corridor outside the stone garden. Sasuits, work wear, sports gear, classic leggings and hoodies. Not a thread of 1980s retro. These are workers. Denny Mackenzie does not look as he walks between the lines of blades. As he passes knuckles touch brows in salute. Behind him a wave of applause grows, carrying him forward.

He clenches his left fist tight.

He gives the barest nod as he turns in the elevator and the door closes.

A ticket waits at the station. First class. His chib is still green. He knows who has paid for these. He takes his seat in the observation car. When the train emerges from the tunnel he turns to face Hadley. He watches the great pyramid until only the peak, brilliant with the light of ten thousands suns, is visible. Then it too is lost beneath the horizon.

There is still no feeling in the wound on his left hand.

A sliver, a paring, the least needle-scratch of Earth-light, shines beyond the train window. Robson is curled up in the seat, mouth open, drooling a little, deeply unconscious. Sleep is the great vehicle of healing, crossing great distances of renewal and regeneration. Wagner can't sleep, but it's not the wolf-light that keeps him awake. He has turned the last shreds of his dark-self concentration on the news – lunar and terrestrial – the commentators, the opinion pieces, the political forums and histories. He begins to understand what happened while he and Zehra made their hegira across the Sea of

Tranquillity, what his brother was working over those eighteen lunes since Corta Hélio fell, Boa Vista was destroyed, Wagner went into exile and two worlds believed Lucas Corta was dead.

He can see that the wars that swept the Cortas and Vorontsovs to power are skirmishes to battles that will shake the moon to its cold heart. Battles of philosophy and politics, family and privilege, power and dynasty, law and freedom, pasts and futures.

The wise wolf goes to ground.

Thirty minutes to Hypatia Junction, change for the local shuttle to Theophilus, and Annaliese.

Robson turns in his sleep. He gives a small cry, leans against Wagner. Wagner folds his arms around the boy. He is so thin and sharp, no softness or roundness to him. Robson burrows deeper into the warmth of Wagner's body and Wagner reclines his seat and settles back and looks out at the slender, traitor Earth. He rests his cheek on Robson's hair. Eucalyptus, menthol. Juniper. Bergamot, sandalwood, frankincense. And Wagner Corta finds that sleep is not so hard to find after all.

The clamps click around the moto. Lady Sun grasps a safety handle and in an instant she and Darius are tens of metres high, fast-climbing the flank of the tower. The forested floor of Queen of the South drops away, and in a further breath they are hundreds of metres up. Climbing. Darius looks through the transparent bubble at the hundreds of towers on Queen of the South, connecting floor to roof. After the strict horizontals of Crucible and the chiaroscuro labyrinth of the Palace of Eternal Light, a vertical world is thrilling. He presses his hands to the bubble. A kilometre high now, a kilometre and a half. The elevator slows and releases the moto on the hundredth level. The little cab self-drives around the peripheral ledge. There is no railing.

'Here?' The moto has parked in front of an unprepossessing roller door, industrial and bare of any identifying tag, physical or virtual. Who puts a warehouse on the hundredth level of Jain Mao Tower?

'Here,' Lady Sun says and waits for Darius to offer her a hand out of the car. Which he does, promptly and unbidden. A small, olive-skinned man with a neatly groomed beard steps out of a smaller access door inside the larger shutter. Darius notes his dress. Careful, classic, cut beautifully. He only needs three steps to reach his visitors but those steps are as considered, poised and economical as a dancer's.

'Lady Sun.' He kisses the old woman's hand.

'Mariano.' The dapper man bows. Darius takes the offered hand, feeling out the man's grip and muscle tone. He smiles.

'Wary, this one.'

'An admirable trait in a Mackenzie,' Lady Sun says. 'So much for you to work with and shape.'

'What is going on here?' Darius asks. He is one hundred levels up on an unguarded roadway. His options for flight are limited. 'Who is this man?'

'What is going on, my dear, is the slow and deliberate business of spite,' Lady Sun says. 'The Cortas have humiliated me. I cannot abide that. Humiliation in return is not an adequate revenge. I need a weapon that will cut the living heart out of them, cauterise them, take away their hope and their succession and erase them from history. I want them to watch as their children die and their line ends. I want you to be my weapon, Darius. It will take time, maybe longer than my time, but I take comfort in the knowledge that after my death, my revenge will be visited upon them. Some people find that word hard to say: revenge. They think it sounds theatrical, camp. Melodramatic. Not at all. Their tongues are too soft for it. Own the word. Taste it.'

The elegant man dips his head to Lady Sun.

'My name is Mariano Gabriel Demaria and I am the director of this establishment. I will be personally responsible for your education, training and deportment, Darius. We make weapons here. Welcome to the School of Seven Bells.'

*

No one wants to be the first to talk, but someone must talk, in a situation as strange as five strangers locked together in a pressurised capsule, flying free from the end of a momentum transfer tether.

Giggles first. Survivor guilt. *We made it!* (though everyone arrived by the same process, though dozens of people ride the Moonloop every day). Then the questions. *You okay? I'm okay, how about you? Everyone okay? Yeah that was a ride. What about Oksana? Okay?*

Marina? Marina?

'I'm okay,' she whispers. She's not, never will be. Nothing ever will be again. She has lost the only person she has ever loved and who, she knows with the firmament's certainty as the capsule orbits out to rendezvous with the huge Vorontsov cycler, has ever loved her.

The squad advances down the grade from the main outlock. Helmet lights cast long, weaving beams and strike jagged, expressionistic shadows from the debris. The limited reach of the beams only amplifies the greater darkness beyond.

The figure in the yellow shell-suit raises a hand. The squad halts: five dusters in sasuits, another figure in hard moon-armour.

'Light her up,' Lucas Corta says.

Bots scurry down the ramp into the big black. Light: the capsized roof of a pavilion, pillars shattered, leafless trees, frozen to their strong hearts. Moments later, another light wakes: the full, sensual lips of Iansa, a glint of ice. And another: the rocky channel of a dead river, a flash-frozen lawn. Within a minute the whole lava tunnel is illuminated. The faces of the orixas, dramatically underlit, look down on the ruins of Boa Vista.

Lucas Corta hears Alexia gasp on the common channel.

'You lived here?'

'This was my mother's palace,' Lucas says.

She manages the shell-suit well, Lucas thinks, for a Jo Moonbeam. Another of her conspicuous competencies. Lucas's excuse is that the inner skeleton supports his wreckage of a musculature. It's his first walk in vacuum since he was a kid. Since his mother took him to look at the light of distant Earth. Not quite, he realises. Five metres across the Mare Fecunditatis, from his rover to the Moonloop station. No suit, no oxygen, no pressurisation. His private Moonrun.

He walks down the ramp past the refuges. Luna brought Lucasinho there and somehow saved his life. Lucasinho walked Luna out of Twé. Foolish and brilliant. Kids.

Off the end of the ramp on to the desiccated lawn. His boots crunch the frosted grass to powder. The destruction is more than he imagined: Lucas realises that he has never envisioned dead Boa Vista, he has never let his mind stray to what happened that day Mackenzie blades blew the emergency lock and emptied the palace to vacuum. The devastation, the dark, frozen death is more than he imagined but less than he feared.

He never loved Boa Vista, not the way Rafa and Lousika, Luna and Lucasinho, Adriana loved it. He preferred João de Deus, his distance from the demands and dramas of family, his apartment with its balcony over Kondakova Prospekt, the finest sound-room in two worlds. Now this dead hulk is his and he will have it. The whole world is his.

His squad draw up around him: handpicked escoltas, old Corta Hélio hands one and all.

'Senhor Corta?'

'How soon can we start?'

Glossary

Many languages are spoken on the moon and the vocabulary cheerfully borrows words from Chinese, Portuguese, Russian, Yoruba, Spanish, Arabic, Akan.

A: Common contraction for asexual.

Abusua: Group of people who share a common maternal ancestor. AKA maintains them and their marriage taboos to preserve genetic diversity.

Adinkra: Akan visual symbols that represent concepts or aphorisms. Widely used by the Asamoah family.

Amor: Lover/partner.

Amory: Polyamorys, one of the moon's many forms of partnering and marriage.

Anjinho: Little angel. Corta term of endearment.

Banya: Russian sauna and steam bath.

Blackstar: AKA surface worker (derived from the nickname of the Ghana national football team).

Chib: A small virtual pane in an interactive contact lens that shows the state of an individual's accounts for the Four Elementals.

Coracão: My heart. A term of endearment.

Ekata: The oneness, the group mind of a wolf pack.

Escolta: Bodyguard.

Four Elementals: Air, water, carbon and data. The basic commodities of lunar existence, paid for daily by the chib system.

Galah: Australian rose-breasted cockatoo, used as a slang term for a noisy idiot.

Globo: A simplified form of English, the lingua franca of the moon, with a codified pronunciation comprehensible by machines.

Gupshup: The main gossip channel on the lunar social network.

Irmã/irmão: Sister/brother.

Jackaroo: Mackenzie Metals slang for a surface worker, from an Australian word for a male apprentice sheep-station hand.

Jo/Joe Moonbeam: New arrival on the moon.

Junshi: Second in command of a Taiyang surface squad.

Keji-oko: Second spouse.

Kotoko: AKA council, of rotating memberships.

Kuozhao: dust-mask.

Ladeira: A staircase from one level of a quadra to another.

Laoda: Boss of a Taiyang surface squad.

Laowei: Mandarin Chinese slang term for non-Chinese.

Madrinha: surrogate mother. Literally 'Godmother'.

Mãe/Mamãe: Mother/Mum.

Malandragem: The art of the trickster, bad-assery.

Miudo: Child.

Moto: Three-wheel automated cab.

Nana: Ashanti term of respect to an elder.

Nikah: A marriage contract. The term comes from Arabic.

Oko: Spouse in marriage.

Omahene: CEO of AKA, on an eight-year cycle rotation.

Orixa: Deities and saints in the syncretistic Afro-Brazilian umbanda religion.

Santinhos: 'Little Saints'. Slang name for residents of João de Deus.

Sasuit: Surface Activity suit.

Saudade: Homesick melancholy. A sophisticated and essential element of bossa nova music.

Ser: Form of address used to a neutro.

Tia/tio: Aunt/uncle.

Zabbaleen: Freelance organics recyclers, who then sell on what they find to the LDC, which owns all organic material.

Zashitnik: A hired fighter in trial by combat: literally defender, advocate.

Dramatis Personae

CORTA

Ariel Corta: former lawyer in the Court of Clavius.

Marina Calzaghe: Personal Assistant and bodyguard to Ariel Corta.

Robson Corta: son of Rafa Corta and Rachel Mackenzie.

Luna Corta: daughter of Rafa Corta and Lousika Asamoah.

Lucas Corta: second son of Adriana. Jonmu of Corta Hélio.

Amanda Sun: former oko of Lucas Corta.

Lucasinho Corta: son of Lucas Corta and Amanda Sun.

Wagner 'Lobinho' Corta: fifth (disowned) son of Adriana Corta. Analyst and moon wolf.

Dr Carolina Macaraeg: personal physician to Adriana Corta.

MADRINHAS

Flavia: host mother to Carlinhos, Wagner and Lucasinho Corta.

Elis: host mother to Robson and Luna Corta.

MACKENZIE METALS

Robert Mackenzie: founder Mackenzie Metals; retired CEO.
Jade Sun-Mackenzie: second oko of Robert Mackenzie.
Alyssa Mackenzie: oko of Robert Mackenzie (d).
Duncan Mackenzie: oldest son of Robert and Alyssa Mackenzie, CEO of Mackenzie Metals.
Anastasia Vorontsova: oko of Duncan Mackenzie.
Apollonaire Vorontsova: keji-oko of Duncan Mackenzie.
Adrian Mackenzie: oldest son of Duncan and Apollonaire Vorontsova; oko to Jonathon Kayode, Eagle of the Moon.
Denny Mackenzie: youngest son of Duncan and Apollonaire Vorontsova. First Blade following the death of Hadley Mackenzie.

MACKENZIE HELIUM

Bryce Mackenzie: younger son of Robert Mackenzie, Head of Finance for Mackenzie Metals, father of numerous 'adoptees'.
Hoang Lam Hung: adoptee of Bryce Mackenzie and briefly oko to Robson Corta.
Analiese Mackenzie: dark-amor of Wagner Corta in his dark aspect.

ASAMOAH

Lousika Asamoah: Omahene of the Kotoko of AKA.
Abena Asamoah: political science student and sometime amor of Lucasinho Corta.
Kojo Asamoah: colloquium colleague of Lucasinho Corta and Moonrunner.

Adelaja Oladele: (briefly) amor of Lucasinho Corta.
Afi: colloquium colleague of Abena at Twé.

SUN

Lady Sun: the Dowager of Shackleton, grandmother of the CEO of Taiyang.
Sun Zhiyuan: CEO of Taiyang.
Sun Gian-yin: Yingyun of Taiyang (vice CEO) of Taiyang.
Sun Liwei: Head of Finance, Taiyang.
Jade Sun: oko to Robert Mackenzie.
Tamsin Sun: Head of Legal Services, Taiyang.
Darius Mackenzie-Sun: son of Jade and Robert Mackenzie.
Amanda Sun: former oko to Lucas Corta.

VTO

Valery Vorontsov: founder of VTO. CEO VTO Space.
Yevgeny Vorontsov: CEO of VTO Moon.
Valentina Vorontsova: Commander VTO cycler *Saints Peter and Paul.*
Dr Volikova: personal physician to Lucas Corta.
Grigori Vorontsov(a): former amor of Lucasinho Corta.

LUNAR DEVELOPMENT CORPORATION

Jonathon Kayode: Eagle of the Moon. President of the Lunar Development Corporation.
Vidhya Rao: economist and mathematician, White Hare and Lunarian Society member, independence campaigner.

SISTERHOOD OF THE LORDS OF NOW

Madrinha Flavia: joined the Sisterhood after her exile from Boa Vista.

Mãe-de-Santo Odunlade Abosede Adekola: Holy Mother of the Sisters of the Lords of Now.

Irma Loa: sister and former confessor of Adriana Corta.

MERIDIAN/QUEEN OF THE SOUTH

Mariano Gabriel Demaria: director of the School of Seven Bells, an assassins' college.

THE WOLVES

Amal: leader of the Meridian Blue Wolves pack.

Lunar Calendar

The Lunar Calendar is divided into twelve lunes named after the signs of the Zodiac: Aries, Taurus, Gemini, Cancer, Leo, Virgo, Libra, Scorpio, Sagittarius, Capricorn, Aquarius, Pisces, plus a New Year's Day at the start of Aries.

The days of each lune are derived from the Hawaiian system of naming each day after a different moon-phase. Thus the lune has thirty days and no weeks.

1: Hilo
2: Hoaka
3: Ku Kahi
4: Ku Lua
5: Ku Kolu
6: Ku Pau
7: Ole Ku Kahi.
8: Ole Ku Lua
9: Ole Ku Kolu
10: Ole Ku Pau
11: Huna
12: Mohalu
13: Hua

14: Akua
15: Hoku
16: Mahealani
17: Kulua
18: Lāʻau Kū Kahi
19: Lāʻau Kuū Lua
20: Lāʻau Pau
21: ʻOle Kū Kahi
22: ʻOle Kū Lua
23: ʻOle Pau
24: Kāloa Kū Kahi
25: Kāloa Kū Lua
26: Kāloa Pau
27: Kāne
28: Lono
29: Mauli
30: Muku

Additionally, the larger cities (with the exception of Queen of the South) operate a three-shift system: mañana, tarde, noche. Each shift eight hours apart. Noon in mañana is 8 pm in tarde and 4 am in noche.